Energy Dependence Day

by

Christian F. Burton

Published by C. Fischer B., LLC
P.O. Box 630215
Littleton, CO 80163

Printed by CreateSpace

ISBN 978-0-9912052-0-2

Library of Congress Control Number: 2013922158

Edited by Heidi B. Jason
B. Line Editing
http://www.heidibjason.com/

Acknowledgments

Special thanks to my wife Cheryl for helping me see this book through to a successful conclusion. Thanks also go out to Laurence MacNaughton for his in depth critique of my initial manuscript which was substantially longer. Ana Grigoriu of Kingwood Creations helped bring the cover to life. Heidi Jason acted as my editor extraordinaire and patiently pointed out my numerous and often repetitive grammatical errors. I hope John likes the jam.

Chapter 1: Ibtidaa

"Climb up, Husam," his father said.

Husam looked skeptically at his father. While he'd initially been intrigued by the large, colorful truck, he didn't know they'd be riding on top of it. Suddenly, all the ads and brightly colored images seemed less enticing. Climbing up the metal ladder that was screwed to the side of the truck, a large painted eye stared at him.

"Hurry up," Husam's mother implored.

They were leaving Kabul, Afghanistan. Husam wasn't quite sure why. As his father passed up their luggage, two burlap sacks filled with clothes, Husam looked down warily from his perch and watched his parents climb up. Once they were settled, his mother checked her handbag for the umpteenth time to ensure she had the water, then pulled her veil tightly against her face.

Their seat consisted of a large wooden box that was bolted to the top of the truck. It was like a big, deep sandbox without any sand. Sitting cross-legged, Husam shifted uncomfortably on the rough wooden floorboards. When the truck started moving, it swayed from side to side. Husam, afraid they'd topple over, reached his hand up and clung tightly to the side.

For a ten-year-old boy, it was a miserable trip. No matter how Husam sat, he couldn't get comfortable. Plus, when he was sitting, he was barely tall enough to see over the edge of their wooden compartment. Whenever he tried kneeling, his mother would make him sit back down. Not that it mattered though. The dust and smog created by the other vehicles made it difficult to see much of anything anyway. For much of the trip, Husam hugged his knees and stared at a knot in the floorboards.

Several hot and dusty hours later, the truck pulled up to a gas station in Tarkham. They all climbed down to stretch their legs and go to the bathroom. When he returned to the truck, Husam saw his father arguing with the truck's driver.

"*Paysee!*" the driver demanded.

"I already paid for passage all the way to Peshawar."

"No, no, no! You must pay for gas as well."

"That was not part of our arrangement."

Cautiously, Husam climbed up to his seat atop the truck. His mother was already there, but she looked concerned. Suddenly, a loud voice from below startled them both.

"Get down," the truck driver yelled. "Get down now!"

Peeking over the side, Husam saw the driver climbing up the ladder. Husam huddled close to his mother, but there was little she could do. Upon reaching the top, the driver grabbed their bags and threw them to the ground.

"No!" his mother wailed.

"Get out, you *spei*!" he spat.

After throwing down their luggage, the driver jumped to the ground. He pushed Husam's father aside and stomped toward the cab of the truck. Frantically, Husam and his mother struggled down the ladder while the driver revved the truck's engine.

"Liar! Thief!" Husam's father yelled, but the driver just ignored him.

Together, Husam and his parents watched helplessly as the truck peeled away from the gas station and disappeared down the highway. After gathering their belongings, Husam's father went to talk to the gas station attendant while Husam and his mother waited outside.

"It's about five kilometers to the border and then another five to Landi Kotal," his father said when he returned. "There's a trail about one kilometer down the road. If we take that, it's even shorter."

So, they gathered their belongings and started off. For a while, they walked along the highway. The rush of wind created by the large trucks zooming past almost knocked Husam over. He was glad when they turned off onto the trail, at least initially. However, the rough terrain and his father's quick pace soon soured Husam's mood.

"Pick up your feet," his father scolded.

Grudgingly, Husam trudged forward on the narrow mountain path. Purposely, he dragged his feet, kicking up a cloud of dust around him. His mother looked back and forth between her son and her husband with a pained expression.

"Slow down, *graan*," she said finally.

"If we don't get to Landi Kotal before nightfall, we'll be sleeping on the streets," his father said.

"Couldn't we have found someplace in Tarkham?" she asked.

"The Afghanistan I know is *merr*. We have to leave, start anew."

"But why now? We've been through tough times before."

"The Americans are leaving, and once they are gone, it'll be even more chaotic."

"And will life in Peshawar be any different?"

"It can't be any worse."

As his parents argued, Husam lagged farther and farther behind. Absentmindedly, he stooped down and picked up a rock. It was gray and flat. The edges were sharp. Angrily, he threw it at a scraggly camel thorn tree.

"So it's all the *Amrikaayi's* fault," Husam grumbled.

He tromped forward kicking stones as he went. Nothing made sense to him. No matter where Husam turned, it seemed like he didn't belong. He was from the wrong family or the wrong tribe. Soon, in addition to all that, he would be from the wrong country.

Looking forward, the path weaved alongside a steep, rocky ridge. Near the ridge-top, Husam could see several dark caves where he imagined exploring inside and finding buried treasure. Suddenly, he saw several men running out of one of the caves. They had rifles slung over their shoulders.

As Husam watched, the men broke into two groups. One group scrambled eastward, while the other ran to the west. They seemed to be in an awful hurry, but Husam couldn't figure out why. All of a sudden, the air above him screamed, and the cave disappeared in a cloud of fire, dust, and thunder.

"Mother!" Husam screamed, but he couldn't hear the sound of his own voice.

Up ahead, he saw his mother turn and hold out her hand, motioning Husam to stop. As a rumbling wave of rock shook the ground, Husam saw his father running to help her, but it was no use. Frozen, Husam watched as an avalanche of rock engulfed his parents.

"No!" Husam screamed. Falling to his knees, he was enveloped in a cloud of dust and grit. Coughing, Husam stood up and inched forward. He couldn't see anything. The entire landscape was cloaked in a brown cloud.

"Mom? Dad?" he called, but the only response was the noise of a small rock tumbling in front of him. Husam held his breath. Everything was still. Slowly, he continued to creep forward, but the trail they'd been following had disappeared under a blanket of jagged stones. Tentatively, Husam stepped forward. The rocks shifted unsteadily beneath his feet. He could go no farther.

"Where are you?" Husam wailed. As the dust settled, he wiped his eyes and searched longingly for his parents.

Suddenly, a man with a rifle appeared behind Husam. "They're dead," he said.

"No," Husam said, shaking his head.

"They're gone, son," the man's voice said firmly. "You'd better come with me."

"No!" Husam yelled. He paced anxiously at the spot where the trail disappeared.

"My name's Yaman Utbah," the man said while putting his hand on Husam's shoulder. "What's your name?"

"Get away from me!" Husam shrieked.

Angrily, he twisted out from the man's grip and navigated forward over the rocky debris. His feet slid out from under him and he fell. As Husam struggled to get up, he saw something. A hand—his mother's!—was sticking out from the rubble, covered with dust and bent awkwardly at the wrist. Shocked, Husam began shaking uncontrollably. He threw up and collapsed in a heap.

Cautiously, Yaman Utbah stepped forward to retrieve the boy. He picked Husam up in his arms and carried him off, another orphan of the drones.

#

At a hospital in Dhahran, Saudi Arabia, another ten-year-old boy sat alone on a bench. While looking at his reflection in the brightly polished linoleum floor, Abdul Hafiz Al-Faruq tried in vain to swallow back the tears. His mother was sick, and although no one would tell him anything, he knew it wasn't good.

Teary eyed, Al-Faruq looked down the hall to the nursing station where two doctors were talking. While he couldn't hear them, he knew from their expressions they were talking about him. His father had died years ago and now his mother was dying. What were they going to do with him? Every so often, they would pause their conversation and look in his direction. Summoning his courage, Al-Faruq got up and walked toward them.

"Can I see my mother?"

"Umm, she's sleeping right now, but I don't think that would be a problem," one of the doctors replied.

"Thank you," said Al-Faruq, as he turned and walked down the long hallway to his mother's room. His feet felt heavy. While he desperately wanted to see her, he was afraid. He didn't like seeing her this way. She looked so pale, and there were too many tubes sticking in and out of her. When he reached her room, Al-Faruq paused in front of the doorway.

Cautiously, he entered the room. There were four beds, but only one was occupied. The blinking lights emanating from the medical equipment did little to cheer the dimly lit hospital room. After taking a seat next to her bed, Al-Faruq reached out and took hold of his mother's hand. She stirred.

"Al-Faruq?" she asked weakly.

"I'm here."

"Have you gotten anything to eat?"

"Yes mother."

"If you need anything, don't be afraid to ask one of the nurses," she encouraged him.

"Mother?" Al-Faruq asked as tears welled up in his eyes. "What's going to happen to me?" Al-Faruq watched as his mother took a deep breath.

"Al-Faruq," she said, struggling with the weight of their conversation. "I've called your uncle, and he's agreed to take you in."

"No, I . . . I won't leave you!"

9

"It's already been decided," she said, squeezing his hand. "You'll get to live on a farm, and harvest dates. It'll be much nicer than living in the city."

"I don't want to go."

"You have to," said his mother, gently. "I'm sorry you have to grow up so quickly. But let my memory be a source of strength for you rather than a weakness."

"Why? Where are you going?"

"Al-Faruq, I know this is hard. But every sun must set. I can't pretend I'm not sick." Wearily, she turned to look at Al-Faruq. "You need to start this new chapter in your life."

"No! I won't leave you! Don't go!"

"It's not up to me!" she said, teary eyed. "You're a good boy— don't let life's hardships make you otherwise."

As a tear ran down her cheek, she pulled his hand closer and gave it a kiss. Exhausted, her hand dropped back down at her side. "Your uncle is coming to pick you up in the morning," she said finally. "I'm sorry. There's just no other way."

As his mother closed her eyes and went back to sleep, Al-Faruq buried his face in his hands and sobbed. It was the last time they would talk. His uncle came to retrieve him early the next morning.

His mother died a few days later.

Chapter 2: Military Patrol

As their squad trudged along the Saudi-Yemen border just outside of Jizan, Sergeant Al-Faruq was worried. He'd endured ten years in the service of his uncle, before leaving for the army. Now, after spending four years climbing up the ranks, this lieutenant was putting it all in jeopardy.

Where the heck does he think he's going? We're supposed to watch out for Houthi rebels. Not actively go out and engage them. If the lieutenant takes us much farther south, we'll be in Yemen. This royal prick doesn't have any clue what he's doing.

The lieutenant, who was a hundred-and-whatever in line for the Saudi throne, evidently thought that some kind of military commendation would move him up a few spots. Frankly, Sergeant Al-Faruq could do without babysitting his royal highness during his quest for personal development. As the squad paused, kneeling near the top of a ridge, the sergeant moved up alongside the lieutenant. "Don't you think we're getting a little too far south," he whispered.

"Who's leading this squad? Huh? You or me?" the lieutenant demanded.

"You are, sir," Sergeant Al-Faruq offered politely. "But this is well outside our normal patrol area."

"Well, if you're afraid we might bump into some rebels, why don't you just hang out in the back?" the lieutenant said, motioning to the rear of the squad.

Al-Faruq returned to his previous position, third, just behind the radio operator. The lieutenant motioned him farther back, but Al-Faruq stood his ground. His squad mates shifted their feet uncomfortably, but no one said anything. The lieutenant glared at Al-Faruq for several seconds before turning his attention back to the rocky landscape in front of them.

Afraid? Al-Faruq fumed. *The only thing I'm afraid of is this idiot's complete disregard for orders. We're given a designated patrol area for a reason. We're given specific rules of engagement for a reason. This unit isn't his personal toy. He's going to risk this entire unit for what? Career development?*

11

Slowly, the squad crested the ridge. Dense scrub and rocks limited their progress, and the lieutenant had few options as they picked their way down the other side. Nonetheless, the squad continued forward. Peering ahead, Al-Faruq saw the sunlight glint off a rock about twenty feet ahead. His eyes scanned the area. While none of the vegetation in this area looked particularly green, the brush up ahead looked extremely dry, dead. Al-Faruq held up his hand signaling everyone behind him to stop and get low.

Crouching, he slowly shuffled forward. "Lieutenant! Something's not right."

The lieutenant ignored him and continued forward.

Sergeant Al-Faruq saw the sunlight reflect off something up ahead. "Lieutenant! IED!" Al-Faruq shouted.

His face red, the lieutenant turned and glared at the sergeant, but when he opened his mouth to reprimand him, it happened. The explosion launched the lieutenant sideways and knocked Sergeant Al-Faruq on his back. Small arms fire erupted west of their position. His ears ringing from the force of the blast, Al-Faruq struggled to gain his bearings. The entire earth still seemed to be shaking. "Return fire! Return fire!" Al-Faruq screamed.

Taking cover behind a rock, Al-Faruq looked back to where the lieutenant had been standing. The lieutenant's body lay mangled on the ground, bent over backward, with his head touching his heels. The radio operator who had been positioned between them, lay motionless on the ground, bleeding from a large gash on his head.

Al-Faruq steadied himself and fired in the direction of the rebels, then crawled over the rock-strewn path to the radio operator. "Fall back! Fall back!" he yelled, grabbing the radio operator by the collar of his fatigues.

While the crest of the ridge was only a short distance away, it took forever to reach it. Firing indiscriminately over his shoulder, Al-Faruq struggled after the rest of the squad, dragging the radio operator behind him. As he neared their defensive position behind an outcrop of rocks, another squad member crawled forward to help him. Together they pulled the radio operator to the relative safety of their position and worked to get his pack off.

The enemy's small arms' fire tapered off and the sound of helicopter rotors filled the air. *Thank Allah. Someone must have heard the blast and radioed for backup.* "Let's get this wound bandaged," Al-Faruq barked. The rest of the squad exchanged shocked glances, but said nothing. Grabbing the radio operator's neck, Al-Faruq checked for a pulse. There was none.

Sergeant Al-Faruq sat stoned faced as the helicopter landed nearby. After scattering the rebels, his squad piled into the copter and headed back to base. Although he'd never been so physically tired, the notion of sleep seemed far off. The ringing in his ears made the helicopter's rotors sound muffled, and the sunlight that bathed the surrounding desert landscape seemed dim. Both the lieutenant and the radio operator were dead. There were certain to be questions. Would he have the right answers?

#

Sergeant Al-Faruq sat uncomfortably outside the brigade commander's office. It had been several weeks since the squad's run-in with the IED. While all of his surviving squad mates had returned to active duty, Al-Faruq was still medically red-flagged.

I occasionally got headaches before this happened. Why is it a problem now? Even when I'm headache-free, the doctors act like they don't believe me.

In the back of his mind, Al-Faruq knew that the lieutenant's death complicated matters. *They interviewed everyone else in the squad about the incident. Why not me? What had they said? Were they afraid to tell the truth given the lieutenant's family ties? I did everything I could to get him to turn around. What was I supposed to do? Shoot him in the foot? The dumb ass would still be alive. Of course, I'd be dead or in jail.*

Thankfully, the commander's aide interrupted his thoughts. "Sergeant Al-Faruq. The commander will see you now."

Al-Faruq rose, straightened out his fatigues, and entered the commander's office. As he entered, the commander threw a large file folder down on his desk and stood to greet him.

"Sergeant Al-Faruq. How are you feeling? Better, I hope."

"Yes sir," Al-Faruq replied stoutly while standing at attention.

"At ease, Sergeant. Have a seat," the commander said motioning Al-Faruq to a chair. Al-Faruq took a seat and the commander leaned against the corner of his desk scratching the back of his head. "As I'm sure you're aware, there's been an investigation into the events surrounding your unit's last patrol."

"Yes sir, but I'm confused as to why I haven't been interviewed. I . . . "

The commander raised his hand to interrupt. "Sergeant Al-Faruq, your performance record is stellar. Regardless of what that report says, I know you did not lead the squad into that IED."

"What! I was the one trying to keep us out of trouble!"

"Look, given the politics of the situation, my hands are pretty much tied."

"What does that mean?" Al-Faruq asked, his face turning red.

"Well, if you stay in the military, you'll be facing a demotion. Plus, your chances of future advancement would be severely limited."

"Sir, you can't be serious!"

"The lieutenant's family has been pushing for a court martial and, shall we say, a more permanent punishment," the commander replied emphatically. "Now, I've got a colleague who works in the Saudi Arabian Investigative Directorate. SAID has a recruiting program underway right now, and your military service would count toward your government service requirements for retirement. I really think that your skills would transition well to the *mubahith*."

Al-Faruq buried his head in his hands. *How could this be happening? Did the rest of the squad have no backbone? How could they hang me out to dry? The military is the only place I've ever felt in control of my own destiny. The only place where I could rise above my past, and now it's being taken from me.* Al-Faruq straightened up and tried to regain control of his emotions.

"Sergeant!" the commander barked. "Are you listening?"

"Yes . . . Yes sir," Al-Faruq replied quietly.

"Sergeant, I'm sorry, but at this point your military career is over. Now, unless you've got something else to fall back on, this program is your best bet. The captain will help you with all the necessary paperwork. I'll touch base with my SAID contacts and let them know your application is on the way."

Al-Faruq sat stoically at attention, his discipline restored.

"That's it soldier, buck up. You're only twenty-four years old. This isn't the end. It's a new beginning."

Chapter 3: Two Masters

The sun shone brightly as Professor Mahmud Ratib walked down the sidewalk to the bank entrance. The building's glass windows mirrored the bustling city streets of Dhahran, Saudi Arabia. A sidewalk *shawarma* vendor pushed his cart toward the business district in hopes of catching the lunch rush. Iridescent lamps warmed the spit of lamb that spun behind the glass enclosure, while outside the bank entrance, a woman clad all in black sat begging.

Dressed in a white *thobe* and red-and-white *ghutra*, the professor walked by her without a second glance and opened the door. Once inside, the air-conditioned chill felt refreshing, as a male receptionist escorted the professor to the loan manager's office. The polished marble floor sparkled, and Arabian orchids decorated the bank's interior creating a pleasant smell. After being handed a cup of tea, the professor stepped into the office.

His chest puffed out pridefully, Professor Ratib took a seat. He had just received tenure at the university and had come to refinance his mortgage. He had grand plans of putting an addition on his house. As he sipped his tea, the professor scowled impatiently while wondering what was keeping his loan officer. Finally, the door behind him opened.

"Mr. Ratib," the man said. "Sorry—"

"Professor Ratib," he corrected him. "I understand. You're very busy."

"Y . . . Yes, Professor Ratib. I'm sorry to keep you waiting," the man said. The loan officer sat down and flipped through the professor's paperwork. "I was surprised to get your call. You're only four years into your current loan."

"Well, I'm tenured now, and I'd like to build an addition onto my home," Professor Ratib said in a matter-of-fact tone.

"Okay, but we took your prospective tenure into account when we negotiated the existing loan. Plus, given where rates are right now, the additional income would simply be eaten up by interest."

"What?" the professor asked, dumbfounded.

"It's just not a good time to refinance. As far as home improvement loans go, your current income isn't adequate given all the other debt you're carrying. Plus, you've had several late payments."

"This is ridiculous! Do you even understand what tenure is?" Professor Ratib asked. "I'm a respected member of the university. I'll be the department head in a few short years."

"Well, if you paid off your credit card debt," the loan officer said while flipping through the professor's file. "The ratios would be much more favorable. But as of right now, I'm afraid I can't help you."

Professor Ratib glared angrily at the man and set his small ramekin of tea down with a loud clank. "Thank you for your time," he said icily. He got up and walked quickly out of the loan manager's office. His face beet red, the professor headed for the exit.

Once outside, the professor stared up and down the street while making a mental list of the other banks in the area. A woman's voice interrupted his train of thought.

"P . . . Professor Ratib? I think you dropped this."

The professor wheeled around to see the dirty beggar woman holding an envelope in her outstretched hand. "What?" he snapped.

"I believe this is yours," she said, keeping her head bowed. "You are Professor Ratib—"

"Shut your mouth. Don't talk to me!" the professor said snatching the letter from her hand. He looked at it suspiciously. It did indeed have his name on it. "Where did you get this?" he demanded.

"I found it here on the sidewalk," she said. "I thought you dropped it."

Professor Ratib scanned the area, convinced it must be some kind of scam. Nervously, he felt for his wallet. "You lie," he snarled, but the old beggar woman had already departed. As the professor watched the woman scurry away, he considered going after her. Then, he thought better of it and walked back to his car.

After reaching his car, the professor got in, locked the doors, and ripped open the envelope. Inside, he found a substantial amount of cash and business card that read, "Tom Rider's Arabian Exports." On the back of the card, there was a handwritten message. "Lunch at Al Sqaik, 12:30. $$$$."

Professor Ratib counted the money and then looked at his watch. It was twenty minutes past noon. Looking ahead, he saw an Al Sqaik's less than a half block up. It was Saudi Arabia's version of KFC. The professor rubbed his jaw thoughtfully and put the cash in the glove compartment. If nothing else, it was proving to be an interesting day. Promptly, he exited his vehicle, locked it, and walked down to the restaurant.

As he got closer, Professor Ratib eyed the restaurant's clientele. Several diners were seated at the outdoor café, but one in particular stood out. At a table by himself, sat an older, disheveled, foreign gentleman. The man's graying hair stuck up oddly, and his suit coat was worn and wrinkled. When he saw the professor coming, he waved heartily.

"Professor Ratib! Come and have a seat," he said.

The professor did not wave back, but he continued forward nonetheless. "Do I know you?" he asked, upon reaching the table.

"No," the man admitted, "but you went to school with a friend of mine back in the states. Do you remember Rick Rutledge?"

"Vaguely," the professor admitted, and it was true he'd been educated in the West.

"The name's Tom Rider," he said holding out his hand.

Professor Ratib shook his hand politely, and the two men sat down. Rider bent down and got out a velvet-covered portfolio that contained a variety of necklaces.

"Don't worry," Rider whispered. "It's just for appearances' sake."

Professor Ratib looked at him warily, but said nothing.

"Would you like to order something?"

"No thank you," the professor replied.

"Ha! You just want to get down to business, eh?"

"And what sort of business would that be?" Professor Ratib asked.

"The information business," Rider responded, while holding up a gold necklace with a diamond pendant on it.

"I'm a university professor. Just what kind of information are you after?"

"Well, we've found that universities can often be hotbeds of radical beliefs," Rider said as he picked up another necklace.

"Who's we?" the professor asked.

"A friend. Your country's ally. Surely, an educated man such as yourself sees what's going on. Liberal elements throughout the Middle East are pushing for reforms. Look at Iran, or even here in Saudi Arabia."

The professor nodded. "Doesn't America favor those liberal forces? You're always pushing our government to improve women's rights and human rights in general, not to mention freedom of religion."

"Politics isn't an American invention. Don't you have leaders who say one thing when they mean another?"

Professor Ratib smiled wryly. "I suppose that's true."

"You'd be protecting your own country and getting paid to do it. Think it over. You've got my card. If you're interested, just give me a call," he said with a wink. With that, Rider packed up his things and left.

#

Back at the university, Professor Ratib walked down the hallway mulling over all that had happened. *It couldn't have been a coincidence. First, I'm turned down for the loan. Then out of the blue, this Rider fellow shows up and offers me a job. Well, perhaps "job" isn't the best way to describe it.* Nonetheless, the professor couldn't think of it any other way. Lost in thought, Professor Ratib reached for his office door.

"Professor Ratib," a familiar voice called.

Professor Ratib turned and looked down the hall. It was Professor Hadi, the department head who was nearing retirement. He had two other men with him. "Professor Hadi. How can I help you?"

"These are my two dear friends, Yaman Utbah and Imam Abdul-Mu'izz Al-Hashim."

Professor Ratib greeted them with a warm handshake and a kiss on each cheek. "*As-salaamu `alaykum*," he said.

"Could we step into your office for a moment?" Professor Hadi asked.

"Certainly," Professor Ratib said. "It might be a tight fit though. My office isn't as big as yours."

"Ha! All in due time," Professor Hadi replied.

Professor Ratib opened the door to his office. Inside was a dark gray metal desk with a swivel chair sitting behind it. On either side of the desk rose two overflowing bookcases. In front of his desk, there were two chairs. Professor Ratib uncovered a third chair by relocating a stack of books.

"I wasn't prepared for visitors," Professor Ratib said. "Can I get you anything?" he asked.

"No, no, we've been socializing for quite some time already," Professor Hadi answered.

"Professor Hadi was just telling us that you'd be taking over as department head soon," Yaman said.

"Well, I don't know about soon," Professor Ratib said.

"Soon enough," Professor Hadi interjected as he closed the door.

"Over the years, Professor Hadi has acted as a conduit for us to connect with the younger generation," the Imam began. "We were hoping that you'd be able to do the same."

"Of course," Professor Ratib said naively. "I'll help in whatever way I can."

"Good, good," Yaman said. "The cause of Islam needs lions as well as lambs. The government foolishly relies on the West to fight our battles for us."

"Yes," Professor Hadi agreed. "However, they tend to expect much in the form of payment."

"Not monetarily mind you," the Imam said. "But, they want us to turn our backs on Islam. They want us to change our laws, our customs, and our way of life."

"Rest assured Professor Ratib, you'll be compensated for every recruit that you provide," Yaman cut in.

"Recruits?" Professor Ratib asked.

"Professor Hadi will show you the type of men we're looking for," Yaman continued, with Professor Hadi and the Imam nodding their agreement. "The next year or so can act as your apprenticeship. I'm generally looking for half-a-dozen new recruits each summer, strong willed young men who can act as guardians of the faith."

Professor Ratib nodded nervously.

"Now more than ever, we need to keep the current generation focused on the true tenets of Islam," the Imam added. "We cannot let their minds be poisoned by the West's propaganda. We need young men with sharp minds and steadfast character."

"Let's not overwhelm him," Professor Hadi interjected. "Life will show him what he does not know."

With that, Professor Hadi and his guests departed. Alone in his office, Professor Ratib contemplated the day's events. While he had not been able to refinance, Allah had provided him with not one, but two ways to make additional money.

Which of these blessings will I deny? Am I to choose, or should I embrace both?

Professor Ratib took out Rider's business card and flipped it back and forth between his fingers. It had been an interesting day indeed. Finally, he put the card in his desk drawer and began preparing for his next class.

Chapter 4: Shopping Trip

Professor Ratib detested rug shopping with his wife. To make matters worse, Iba had insisted on dragging along their petulant teenage daughter. The sullen eyes peering out from behind Azzah's *hijab* said it all. Once they were in the store, Azzah immediately distanced herself from them, pretending to be interested in the plethora of prayer rugs that hung against the wall. The smell of incense and tea wafted through the dark store as the shopkeeper led Professor Ratib and Iba up a small flight of stairs.

"I keep my best rugs up here," the shopkeeper said brightly. "I reserve my top quality merchandise for local customers. You will not be treated like a tourist here, Professor Ratib."

#

"Let's go," Iba implored Azzah.

"It's not like I can go anywhere," Azzah snapped back, glaring defiantly at her mother.

With pursed lips, her mother shook her head. "Stay out of trouble," Iba said finally before heading up the stairs.

Azzah rolled her eyes and sat down against the wall at the bottom of the stairs. After watching her mother waddle up the stairs, Azzah stared despondently at the floor in front of her. As far as Azzah was concerned, she was a prisoner in this screwed-up country.

In the U.S. and Europe, kids my age are getting their driver's licenses, going to rock concerts, and just plain hanging out. Meanwhile, I'm either stuck at home with my parents or locked up in a girls' school with a few hundred other future brides. Father is already preparing to marry me off to some bookworm at the university. I can't believe he actually brought that short, fat blob by the house to meet me. I'd rather die than marry that fat pig.

From her vantage point, Azzah could see the shopkeeper's son talking with two foreign customers. While their faces were obscured from view, they wore Western clothes. Their voices sounded strange. They spoke English, but it had a strange drawl to it, not anything like her father's English.

"I'm gonna check out the inside," she heard the one man say.

"Aw' right, don't touch anythin'," another deeper voice replied.

Azzah watched intently, as a short, wiry man in his early twenties browsed aimlessly. From her seat, Azzah admired his taught arms and angular face. She wasn't overly fond of his short spiky blond hair, but he looked intriguing. Cocking her head slightly to one side, she listened to her parents dickering with the salesman upstairs. Azzah focused her eyes on the young man. She could hear him whistling as he poked around the store. She smiled gently behind her *hijab* as the young man stopped and gazed around the room. Suddenly, his eyes focused on hers. Smiling, he walked over to her.

"Well, hi thar," he said sweetly, with his strange drawl.

"Shh," she said while putting her finger in front of veil.

As he crept forward with a quizzical look on his face, Azzah glanced up the stairs. All of a sudden, an impulsive idea took form in her brain. Maybe, a wedding wasn't a forgone conclusion after all. She glanced cautiously up the stairs. Impulsively, she uncovered her face and smiled sweetly at the young man.

He smiled back and wagged his finger playfully. "You're not supposed to do that, are you?"

Azzah motioned for him to come closer. Her heart was racing. This would be the ultimate humiliation for herself and her parents if she was caught, but she didn't care. This would put a stop to her father's meddling. Kneeling down on the floor, he was now close enough to touch. Azzah grabbed him around the neck, pulled him closer, and whispered in his ear.

"Have you ever kissed a desert rose before?" she asked.

"No," he replied with a shake of his head.

Her heart racing, Azzah leaned forward and pressed her lips against his. His chin felt rough and scratchy against her skin, and he smelled like an odd mix of mint and sweat. Nonetheless, his lips sent a spark of excitement coursing through her.

A loud gasp arose from the top of the steps. Azzah didn't even need to look. It was her mother.

Reflexively, Azzah shoved the young man in the chest knocking him on his backside. "Aghhhieee!" she screamed. Then, she ran crying hysterically up the stairs to her mother while frantically trying to fix her veil. Azzah's brief moment of exhilaration had now been replaced by doubt and fear. How long had her mother been watching? Did she see who had initiated the kiss?

"Mother! Mother! Help me!" Azzah cried.

"My sweet *habibati!* What happened?"

"I . . . I don't know? He . . . he dropped his wallet, but didn't notice."

"What?"

"So, I picked it up and tried to hand it back to him. He took it and said he wanted to thank me properly. I didn't understand what he meant. It happened so fast," Azzah stammered.

"What's going on?" her father asked angrily.

"Some strange man?" Iba said unsteadily.

"What?" Professor Ratib asked perturbed.

"He attacked Azzah."

"He what!" Professor Ratib said with alarm, eying them suspiciously.

"He . . . he tried to grab her," Iba said cautiously.

His face turning red, Professor Ratib rushed over. "Where is he?"

"He went out the front door," Azzah said nervously.

"Is there a problem?" the shopkeeper asked.

"Some man attacked my daughter," Professor Ratib said loudly.

"What did he look like?" the shopkeeper asked.

Fidgeting nervously, Azzah was unsure whether or not she should answer.

"Well?" her father demanded.

"Um . . . he was English, or a westerner, and he had blond hair."

Roughly, Professor Ratib grabbed Azzah by the arm and dragged her over to the upstairs window. "Do you see him?"

Apprehensively, Azzah scanned the crowded streets below.

"Do you see him?"

Below, Azzah saw a stockily built black man leading the young man she had kissed away from the store. The black man looked angry as they jostled forward through the crowded market streets.

"Well?" her father demanded impatiently.

"Th . . . there," she cried, pointing haphazardly.

"Where?"

"In front of the shoe store," Azzah replied as she saw the young man knock over a small display of shoes.

"The police are on their way," the shopkeeper interjected holding a cell phone in his hand, but Azzah's father wasn't listening.

Frightened, Azzah watched her father charge for the stairs. Azzah stayed by the window, secretly hoping the young man and his companion would escape. She didn't want her father hearing the young man's side of the story. It would only complicate things.

From above, Azzah watched as her father bounded out of the store and onto the sidewalk. Roughly, he pushed forward through the crowd, but it was no use. Even from her vantage point, she could no longer see the young man with the spiky blond hair. Silently, Azzah breathed a sigh of relief as her mother joined her by the window.

"When the police arrive," Iba said in hushed tones. "Let your father do all the talking. The young man attacked you, and when he tried to pull off your veil, you pushed him away and ran to get me."

Azzah nodded uncomfortably. In the pit of her stomach, she feared her mother knew the truth. It was something in her mother's eyes–she had seen more than she was letting on.

"Listen to me," Iba said sternly. "That young man followed us in here. Do you understand? I saw him on the street earlier. He followed you in here and pounced as soon as he had a chance."

"But, he dropped his wallet," Azzah said nervously.

Iba slapped Azzah sharply across the face. "The young man attacked you, and when he tried to pull off your veil, you pushed him away and ran to get me," she rasped. "Repeat it back to me."

Azzah stared blankly at her mother.

"Repeat it!"

"Um . . . he'd been following us. Wh . . . when you went upstairs, he attacked me. He tried to pull off my veil, but I pushed him away and ran to get you."

"The police probably won't even want to talk to you, but if they do," Iba's voice trailed off. Suddenly, she hugged Azzah tightly and started wailing.

"Mother!" Azzah protested trying to pull away, but then she saw why.

On the sidewalk below, a *mutawa* officer had arrived on the scene. As he was talking with the shopkeeper, he looked up coldly at Azzah and Iba. Self-consciously, Azzah checked to make sure her veil was pulled tightly against her face. She too started wailing along with her mother. Her insides were twisted, and she was afraid she might throw up.

Soon, Azzah saw her father return. Gesturing down the street, her father talked animatedly to the officer. The *mutawa* nodded grimly and took out his radio. With his hands on his hips, Azzah's father stood stoically next to the officer. Suddenly, he turned and looked up at them. The stern expression on his face sapped what little remained of Azzah's strength.

From that point on, everything around her seemed to move in slow motion. The officer talked on his radio while Azzah's father expressed varying degrees of frustration. At one point, two additional *mutawa* arrived on the scene. Azzah held her breath while they huddled together. Once they were finished conferencing, they talked at length with her father. Based on his expression, they hadn't caught her attacker. Azzah hid her emotions behind her veil.

Thankfully, none of the *mutawa* bothered to take her statement. For once, being a second-class citizen had its advantages. At this point, Azzah wasn't sure she could have handled it and feared she would have fainted on the spot. Still, she took some small measure of satisfaction in the fact that she'd gotten away with it. After all, it was only a kiss.

Chapter 5: The Raid

Al-Faruq's team crouched next to the high, mud-brick wall that surrounded Yaman Utbah's compound. It was almost midnight, but the moon's light shone brightly. Personally, Al-Faruq would have preferred some cloud cover. At times like these, he took comfort in the darkness.

This was it, the culmination of two years as an SAID investigator. In the monarchy's effort to crack down on terrorism, Detective Al-Faruq had excelled beyond all expectations. He'd caught lots of little fish. Tonight, he was trolling for a big one.

"Team 1 is in position," he barked over his mic. "Team 2?"

There was no response.

"Team 2. Are you in position?"

He was greeted by nothing but dead air.

"What the hell?" he cursed under his breath. "Team 2, are—"

Suddenly, sirens erupted. Startled, Al-Faruq looked up and watched as two local police vehicles descended on his team's position. In a matter of moments, he and his team were bathed in bright searchlights.

"I can't believe this is happening," Al-Faruq said incredulously. Exasperated, he told his team to stand down.

"This is the police," the young officer yelled. "D . . . drop your weapons. Put your hands up against the wall," he stammered.

"I'm Detective Al-Faruq of the Saudi Arabian Investigative Directorate," Al-Faruq said while holding up his badge. "We're here on official business."

A second officer stepped forward. "Shut up! Get your hands on that wall, or I'll shoot you where you stand."

Al-Faruq did as he was told and turned around. "Contact Captain Zahir. This has all been app—"

Whack! The police officer brought his nightstick down hard against Al-Faruq's back. "I said shut up!"

Wincing, Al-Faruq fell to his knees as another police car pulled up behind them. A heavy-set police officer got out and quickly called the officers off.

"What are you fools doing?" he said. "Do you know who these men are?"

While the local officers squabbled amongst themselves, Al-Faruq picked his badge up off the ground and stood back up. Turning around, he glared angrily at the local officers. They'd been duped, and someone had talked.

#

Dressed in a black *thobe* and white *ghutra*, an older man in his early fifties sat writing at his desk. Suddenly, a younger man ran in.

"Yaman!" the young man said. "The police have arrived. We need to get you out of here."

"No," Yaman Utbah said firmly. "You go, Husam. I'm the one they're after."

Husam rushed over to Yaman's side and grabbed him by the elbow. "Come on!"

"Have you learned nothing?" Yaman scolded him. "Things are not always what they seem," he whispered tersely. "Sometimes, you must let the enemy think they've won in order to determine who your true friends are. Lay low and watch your back. Once things calm down, get in touch with Imam Al-Hashim. I'll be fine."

"But?"

"We don't have time to argue. Go out the back. Now!"

Confused, Husam did as he was told. After rescuing him from the drone strike, Yaman had become like a father to Husam, and while he couldn't bear leaving him behind, he couldn't imagine disobeying him either. "Yes, *sidi*," he said, and he left Yaman in his office.

Out in the hallway, he ran into Jasim.

"Where's Yaman?"

"He's not coming."

"What? Then, we'll have to fight them off," Jasim said, brandishing his weapon.

"No, Jasim. Yaman has a plan. We need to leave, out the back."

As police sirens echoed in the background, the two men weaved their way through the building, which was part armory, part apartment complex. Upon entering a narrow hallway that led to the exit, they heard a muffled gunshot. Quickly, they took refuge in a nearby storage room. While the room would have normally been filled with boxes of ammunition, it was now empty.

Next, they heard shouting. "What do you think you're doing?" a voice called.

"Shut up," another voice answered. It was followed by two more gunshots.

"That sounded like Nu'man and Muhanned," Husam said.

Jasim peered out into the hallway. "Muhanned!" he called, but instead of an answer, there was another gunshot. Jasim fell back, his face bloodied. "Aghh!"

"Jasim!" Husam tore off his *ghutra* and applied it to the wound.

"Muhanned shot me!" Jasim exclaimed. "Mother fucker!"

Thankfully, it wasn't as bad as it initially appeared. "It just grazed you," Husam assured him. "You'll be all right. Keep pressure on it."

Husam leaned Jasim against the door, and glanced out into the hallway. It was empty. With his gun at the ready, Husam prepared to lead Jasim out. "Can you follow me?"

Jasim nodded. He held Husam's *ghutra* tightly against the right side of his face. There was blood dripping from his chin. "If you see Muhanned, shoot him."

They crept forward, staying low. When they reached the end of the hall, Husam saw an open doorway to his left. Looking inside, he saw Nu'man lying in a pool of blood on the floor. The feet of another man were visible, lying motionless behind an empty safe.

"Muhanned robbed us," he said in disgust.

"Figures," Jasim said. "Fucking mercenary."

"Let's go," Husam said motioning to Jasim with his hand.

In moments, they were at the back door.

"Stay clear," Husam warned. "I'll kick the door open and see what type of response we get."

"Wait," Jasim said. "Let me get down by the window. If I see anything, I can return fire."

He threw Husam's bloody *ghutra* down on the floor and sneaked over to the window. The right side of his face was swollen. Slowly, he cracked the window open with the nose of his gun.

"Ready?" Husam asked. Jasim nodded. Husam kicked open the door and crouched off to the side. Two shots whizzed through the doorway. Jasim returned fire. After another volley of gunfire, Husam shouted to Jasim. "Cover me!"

Husam leaped out the doorway, taking refuge behind an old pickup. He glanced back and motioned Jasim forward, letting several shots fly as Jasim scrambled out.

"What now?" Jasim asked when he reached Husam's side.

"They're covering the exit to the main road," Husam said, while securing a new clip in his handgun. "Let's make a run for the firing range. There are plenty of places to hide, and we can regroup."

Jasim grunted in agreement as he reloaded. "Ready? Go!"

While Jasim kept their adversaries busy, Husam sprinted for a palm tree that marked the path to the firing range. After taking cover behind it, he returned the favor for Jasim. Meticulously, the two men picked their way down the path, taking cover when it presented itself. After dispatching a couple of their pursuers, they encountered no more resistance.

"I guess they decided we're not worth the effort," Husam said.

"Or we killed them all," Jasim replied.

"I doubt that," Husam said. "But, either way, I'll take it."

#

By the time Al-Faruq's team breached the compound, there was little point continuing. Team 2, which was charged with covering the compound's rear exit, was thirty minutes late. They'd encountered delays similar to Al-Faruq's team. Any bad guys present when Al-Faruq's team first arrived simply walked out the back. Yaman, his wives, and his children were the only ones left in the compound. They found Yaman Utbah calmly sitting in his office.

"Hands up!" Al-Faruq ordered as he entered Yaman's office with his gun drawn.

"Oh, of course," Yaman said. "Whatever you say."

While another member of his team handcuffed Yaman, Al-Faruq went over to the row of file cabinets that lined the wall to his right. One after another, he pulled out the drawers. They were all empty.

"Looking for something officer?" Yaman asked.

"We already have enough evidence to arrest you," Al-Faruq said icily.

"Obviously," Yaman replied. "If you hadn't, you never would have gotten approval for this little raid in the first place."

"Take him away," Al-Faruq ordered.

With his hands on his hips, Al-Faruq watched as Yaman was escorted out. Then, he turned back toward the empty file cabinets. "Aghh!" he screamed. Angrily, he tipped over the file cabinet at the end of the row. It landed with a crash. As Al-Faruq walked away, he heard something clattering inside the cabinet. It almost sounded like a bunch of marbles being spilled.

"Click, clack, click, clack—click."

Al-Faruq looked quizzically at the cabinet as it lay motionless on the floor. Slowly, the sound trickled to a stop. Crouching down, Al-Faruq carefully opened the top drawer. Several flash drives spilled out on to the floor. He inspected the file cabinet more closely. A plastic bag, which had evidently contained the flash drives, was taped to the inside of the cabinet. When he tipped the cabinet over, the bag broke.

Al-Faruq smiled mischievously and depressed the button on his mic. "Sergeant! Meet me back in Yaman's office. I think I found something." When the sergeant arrived, Al-Faruq showed him where the flash drives had been hidden. Together, they searched through the other cabinets. Perhaps the raid would bear fruit after all.

Chapter 6: Cultivating Resistance

Imam Abdul-Mu'izz Al-Hashim paused momentarily and gazed across the throng of followers kneeling before him. Then he continued his *khutba,* or sermon. Although short of stature, the Imam's booming voice belied his outward appearance. His graying hair and beard gave him a grandfatherly appearance, but his sermons were more reminiscent of a stern father lecturing his children than that of a loving grandfather. His dark brown eyes hawkishly surveyed the crowd of worshipers as he used his piercing glare to back up the tenacity of his words. Even the most pious Muslim could be brought to serious self-reflection after one of his fiery sermons.

"Let's say, a stray dog wanders into your yard one evening, but unlike many of the strays you've encountered before, which are dirty and scraggly, this dog is the most beautiful animal you've ever seen. The dog rubs up against your leg, playfully nuzzles your hand, and then begs for some food. Well, normally you wouldn't feed a stray, but this dog is so beautiful and well-mannered that you make an exception. You feed the dog some scraps and pat it on the head. Then, as you turn to go back inside, the dog bites you and runs off! You're incredulous. How could a dog, that was so outwardly beautiful and docile, bite you? The next evening the dog returns again wagging its tail like nothing happened. Are you going to feed it again? How many times have you fed the American dog, only to be bitten?" he asked.

"While few Muslims would ever profess to love America and its imperialistic, anti-Islamic policies, many Muslims continue to immerse themselves in its popular culture. They do so at their own peril. As you go about your daily life, remember to praise Allah with your actions as well as your heart. Ultimately, they are one and the same."

#

Professor Ratib knelt reverently as Imam Al-Hashim's resounding voice called out. Inside he was conflicted and twisted with guilt. *The truth is . . . my life is a sham. In the classroom, I talk about how America is more concerned with stabilizing oil prices than they are with democratization. I talk about how their primary goal is to open up new marketplaces for their greedy corporations. Yet, my own home is an altar to the West. It's filled with Western products.*

There were few, if any, people who Professor Ratib felt were intellectually superior to himself, but Imam Al-Hashim was one of them. So, when the Imam had asked for his advice, he was floored. *Why did Imam Al-Hashim ask me to evaluate terrorism's impact on U.S. policy? Was it some kind of test? Is he concerned about my loyalty? Does he really want to know what types of targets I'd recommend?*

While Professor Ratib's meetings with Imam Al-Hashim were normally very routine, tonight he prayed for guidance. *May Allah guide my tongue. May my words impress Your holy messenger and grant me favor with him.*

Once the final prayer was finished, the professor knelt patiently as the mosque emptied out. Several minutes passed. When only a handful of worshipers remained, Professor Ratib made his way to the Imam's office, located at the end of a narrow hallway behind the podium. Two large, dark mahogany doors marked the entrance to the Imam's enclave. The doors were already ajar as Professor Ratib knocked apprehensively.

"Come in," the Imam's voice answered.

Slowly, Professor Ratib pushed the door open. No matter how many times he visited with the Imam, he still felt nervous. The sparsely furnished room looked more like a library than an office. The walls of the room were lined with bookcases that were filled floor to ceiling. Imam Al-Hashim sat cross-legged on the floor in front of a large, silk rug that covered practically the entire floor. With several books open around him, he sat scribbling in a small notebook. He motioned the professor forward.

"Nice to see you Professor Ratib. Please, come in. Close the door if you don't mind," Imam Al-Hashim said with a smile. "Do you have another donation?"

"Yes." Professor Ratib bowed reverently and presented the Imam with a large manila envelope. "It's not as much as I had hoped. However, I do have a meeting scheduled with one of our primary supporters."

"No need to apologize. I question whether we've been giving our supporters their money's worth anyway." Imam Al-Hashim grimaced. "Perhaps it's my age or simply due to years of perseverance, but lately, I'm less optimistic about our ability to overcome our adversaries."

This statement surprised the professor. Yet, as he looked upon Imam Al-Hashim, he noticed a haggard appearance he'd never seen before. "Are you feeling all right?"

"Yes, yes. Just tired." As he spoke, some brightness returned to the Imam's expression. "Professor Ratib, we've talked at length about Islam's struggle to overcome tyranny many times. While you've always been candid, I've often sensed that you're holding something back. Have you thought about what I asked you during our last meeting?"

"It's not really my place to judge. I'm . . . I'm just a small player in a much bigger picture," the professor stuttered. Usually, the Imam took ample time for pleasantries. He was surprised at how quickly he had delved into business.

"You're a highly educated man. Plus, you've lived in enemy lands, so to speak. I'm interested in your opinion."

"I don't have the background to evaluate this properly or to make these types of decisions," Professor Ratib asserted.

"When the Americans invaded Iraq and tried to turn it into their puppet, we talked about the resistance forces' methods. While you don't strike me as squeamish, I sensed that you disapproved of the beheadings. Why?"

Somewhat taken aback, Professor Ratib searched for words. "Well . . . "

"Go on," Imam Al-Hashim urged.

Professor Ratib took a deep breath, then continued. "When images of a bombing or a beheading flash across the average American's television screen, they don't see any justification for it.

They feel victimized, and they simply want their government to protect them."

"No justification? Are you serious?" Imam Al-Hashim exclaimed. "Are they blind?"

"You need to understand that most Americans' world view is very limited. The U.S. government exerts significant control over the media. Therefore, the average American doesn't see the true face of Israel, or the Zionists' efforts to crush Islam. They are systematically repressed. The Holocaust is given great emphasis in their primary and secondary education. In addition, few are aware of the carnage that U.S. companies beget upon third world nations, so they feel little if any responsibility for it. Therefore, to honestly answer your question . . . yes, they are blind in some respects."

"Then, what can we do to open their eyes?"

"We have to assume a more nonviolent stance. Our efforts to condemn U.S. policy hold little weight when bloody bodies are our calling card. In fact, they undercut our ability to court liberal elements within America. We need to show the corporate-controlled American government for what it really is—a capitalist bully that wants nothing less than to strip this region of its natural resources."

"We've targeted oil refineries before, with little success," Imam Al-Hashim pointed out.

"We need to pick softer, less protected targets and not be so concerned with a 9/11-type of impact. By harnessing more moderate elements within our society, perhaps we could hit hundreds of smaller targets rather than concentrating all our resources on one large one. If we concentrate on disruption rather than total destruction, we could expand our army. Many followers share our beliefs but are unwilling to give the ultimate sacrifice."

"Hmmm . . . death by a thousand cuts," the Imam mused. "But how will that facilitate change any better than our current methods?"

"If Americans don't like what's on the news, they simply change the channel. However, they all drive cars and many use heating oil to warm their homes. Our primary goal should be to raise the price of oil. Review the entire supply chain and attack it at its weakest points. Every time the price of oil increases, we'll gain a bigger audience. No American would be able to tune us out. The American economy is weak. The more we can destabilize it, the better. The American giant will be crushed under the weight of its own debt."

"What about the response here at home? Some of our best financial supporters are in the oil business."

"Ultimately, OPEC as a whole will simply pass on any extra expense to the consumer. Our supporters' pocketbooks would feel little if any pain. Here at home, we need to expose the monarchy for what it truly is, a corrupt and decadent puppet of the West. We both know that the monarchy is often ambivalent toward the laws of Islam. They drink and indulge in all kinds of excess. We must capture them in the act and put it on display for the whole country to see."

As Imam Al-Hashim studied him intently, Professor Ratib wondered if he had gone too far. The Imam was a difficult man to read. Tonight, there seemed to be a sense of urgency in the Imam's eyes.

Imam Al-Hashim looked down momentarily as if to gather his thoughts. Then, he looked up with an insistent expression and confided in the professor. "In some respects, it seems that the political climate has turned against us. Many of our brothers-in-arms spend more time in hiding than they do fighting for the cause. The time has come to bring new soldiers into the fold. While you've always been a valuable contributor, I need to tap into your insight as well."

"I am your humble servant."

"What you have told me, this is just what we need to get back on track. These are the types of ideas that will energize our organization."

"Thank you," Professor Ratib replied. His head was spinning.

"In order to flesh out some of your ideas, I want to start meeting with you once a week. I will be introducing you to other members of our team. When you spoke of tapping into more moderate elements of our society, did you have specific people in mind?"

"I still keep in contact with many of my former students. Certainly, some of them would be willing to take on a greater role in support of our struggle," the professor stated confidently. "Many of them have positions in industry that we could leverage. Others have key skills that could be better used to serve Allah."

"Good, good . . . " Imam Al-Hashim said. "Come up with a mental list of names. Twenty candidates would be a good starting point. As you think of potential prospects, keep in mind that loyalty is our utmost concern. It's often helpful when the men share common bonds, whether it be family or village ties, classmates, belong to the same mosque, etc."

"I understand."

"I need you to take on this challenge," the Imam encouraged him.

"If it is Allah's will, then I will do it!"

Chapter 7: Changing of the Guard

Once Professor Ratib departed, Imam Al-Hashim opened the envelope that the professor had delivered. Turning to the bookcase, he climbed atop a small step stool and reached for a large book on the top shelf. Checking to ensure that the door to his office was still closed, the Imam took half of the money that Professor Ratib had gathered and stuffed it inside the hollowed out book. There was so much money inside that the Imam had trouble closing it. After returning the book to the shelf, the Imam resumed his position and called for Afaz.

Seeing his assistant poke his head around the edge of the door, Imam Al-Hashim said, "You can show Muhanned in now."

"Yes sir," Afaz acknowledged, then disappeared to retrieve the Imam's guest.

While the Imam had always given freely to Al-Qaeda, it seemed more like a protection racket of late. Muhanned was nothing but a thug. The Imam's attempts to engage him in theological discussions were met with blank stares. Unlike his predecessor, Yaman Utbah, he provided the Imam with few details about resistance efforts or how his financial support was being used. Frankly, he was disappointed that Muhanned hadn't blown himself up by now. The Imam had never met a more likely candidate for a suicide mission.

Muhanned was standing impatiently just down the hall. While the length of his beard and *thobe* might signal highly conservative Islamic beliefs, it was nothing more than a uniform and belied his true religious nature, or lack thereof. Put simply, he was not there to elicit spiritual guidance from the Imam. On the contrary, he was there to collect.

Nonetheless, the Imam greeted Muhanned warmly when Afaz escorted him in.

"Muhanned. Please come in. Can I get you anything?" The Imam asked.

Muhanned shook his head quietly.

"That'll be all, Afaz," Imam Al-Hashim stated as he waived off his assistant. Afaz bowed and retreated quietly from the room. The Imam returned his attention back to his guest. "How can I . . ."

"You know why I'm here," Muhanned interrupted angrily as he closed in on the Imam.

"Very well," the Imam countered with annoyance as he threw the money-laden envelope at Muhanned's feet.

Muhanned retrieved the envelope from the floor. He eyed it suspiciously while weighing it in his hand.

Sensing his distrust, the Imam replied. "I'm sorry if it's a little bit less than usual, but we're still waiting to hear back from one of our more generous supporters."

Muhanned nodded. His jaw was clenched as if pondering whether to believe the Imam or not. "Your support is always appreciated," he offered, but his delivery was less than convincing.

As Muhanned abruptly turned to leave, the Imam saw a shadow move across the bottom of the doorway. "I did have one quick question," the Imam interjected as he stood up. "Is Husam Asad still in the area?"

"What's it to you?" Muhanned asked.

"He used to do odd jobs for me when he wasn't working for Yaman. If he's not engaged with other responsibilities, I have some errands that I need taken care of."

Muhanned scratched his beard thoughtfully. "He's not doing anything for me. I think he's working on a construction crew, building houses or something like that. I'll let him know you have some work for him."

"Thank you," the Imam said as he walked Muhanned to the door. "Should I contact you when I hear from our other donors?"

"That won't be necessary," Muhanned answered. "You can add it to next month's donation."

"Very well," the Imam answered. As Muhanned walked down the corridor, the Imam's eyes followed him coldly. *Muhanned has no respect for me or Allah. How did this thief take over after Yaman's arrest? My donations do nothing more than line his pockets. It's definitely time to start taking matters into my own hands. I can't just sit and watch the movement be corrupted.*

Husam wiped the sweat from his brow as the hot sun beat down on this new housing development just south of Dhahran. The beads of sweat that dripped from his forehead sizzled when they hit the clay roofing tiles that he was installing. Husam wore thick rawhide gloves to protect his rough hands. While the drudgery of his task put him in a sleep-like trance, the sight of a black Mercedes pulling into the parking area caught his attention. Upon recognizing the man that stepped out of the car, Husam cursed and focused on him with a deadly glare.

What the hell is he doing here? Husam spat over the roof's edge. *Come to finish me off himself?* Husam hammered another tile into place. *Just keep your eyes on him. Even he's not stupid enough to come after me in broad daylight.*

Husam had always been close to Yaman Utbah. It was Yaman who had taken him in when his parents were killed. But Yaman's arrest had left a power void in the organization; a void that Muhanned was all too happy to fill. To consolidate his power, Muhanned had made efforts to remove or discredit several of Yaman's closest allies, Husam included.

While he and Jasim had escaped the night of the raid, they'd been cast as traitors. Yaman had been right. Muhanned showed his true colors that night, and nothing had been the same since. After a couple of months on the run, things had finally settled down. Muhanned had kept his distance of late. Husam wondered what had changed.

Looking down from his rooftop perch, Husam watched intently as Muhanned walked over to the site supervisor's pickup. Thoroughly annoyed at having to leave his air-conditioned haven, Husam's supervisor, Lubaid, was less than inviting. "What do you want?" he asked gruffly. "This is a closed work site. Authorized personnel only," Lubaid griped.

"I'm looking for Husam Asad," Muhanned stated flatly.

"He's busy. Why don't you try him at home," Lubaid blustered as he turned back to his truck.

Muhanned blocked Lubaid's path. "Surely, he must have a break or something coming up. I'll only be a moment."

Feeling suddenly uncomfortable with the presence of this visitor, Lubaid looked warily at Muhanned. "His shift ends in twenty minutes."

"Great," exclaimed Muhanned as he leaned against the door to Lubaid's truck and lit a cigarette. "I'll wait here for him."

Lubaid glared at Muhanned. Then, he turned and looked up at the roof. "Husam," he yelled. "Husam!"

Seeing Lubaid huff toward him, Husam had to laugh. *Evidently, Muhanned convinced the fat prick that it was in his best interest to come get me. Hope he's not just here to jerk me around. With my luck, he'll screw up the only legit way I can make ends meet.*

"Husam!" Lubaid waved angrily. "I don't know who this friend of yours is . . . "

"What?" Husam held his hand to his ear pretending he couldn't hear.

"I said, I don't know who your friend is . . . "

"I can't hear you."

"Get down here," Lubaid yelled loud enough so that anyone within a block of the job site could hear. "Now!"

Husam walked over to the edge of the roof and climbed down the scaffolding while Lubaid fumed. "What's the problem?" Husam asked.

Lubaid spoke in hushed tones. "I don't know who this friend of yours is," he sputtered angrily, "but . . . "

"He's not my friend," Husam interrupted.

"I don't give a fuck who he is. You know damn well I don't allow visitors on the job site."

"Then tell him to leave," Husam said as he started climbing back up the scaffolding.

"He's your problem. Not mine. If you want to keep this job, get your butt over there and get rid of him."

With a sniff, Husam nodded and turned in Muhanned's direction. Walking slowly, he eyed Muhanned closely, took off his gloves, and stuffed them under the tie of his *thobe*. Meanwhile,

Lubaid stomped around and exhorted Husam's counterparts to keep working. As Husam approached him, Muhanned took one final drag from his cigarette.

"Well?" Husam asked when he was within earshot.

Muhanned smiled, threw his cigarette to the ground, and crushed it under his sandal. "Just hear me out. No harm in that is there?" he asked.

Husam shrugged. He was unconvinced.

"Husam, you have to realize," Muhanned said. "The night of the raid, I didn't know who to trust. I was concerned that you were compromised."

"So, what's changed?"

"Time," Muhanned answered. "It seems that my concerns were unfounded. Plus, I've had time to reflect on your contributions, and I realize now that you're a valuable asset."

Husam rolled his eyes and stifled a laugh, but Muhanned seemed not to notice.

"How well do you know Imam Al-Hashim?" Muhanned asked.

"He's always been a generous supporter," Husam answered, but the hair on the back of his neck stood on end.

"I met with the Imam the other day, and I'm concerned."

"Concerned?" Husam asked.

"Donations have been down significantly over the past several months. I'm concerned that the Imam has outgrown his usefulness. Given his advancing age, I think it's time to facilitate a change."

Husam nodded, and hid his emotions behind his weather-worn face. *If he thinks that I'm going kill Imam Al-Hashim for him, he's crazy.* Husam swallowed hard and measured his words. "I'm not sure that would be the best course of action."

"Then, you'd better get used to working construction," Muhanned said curtly. "I thought that you'd be the best man for the job, but if you don't have the stomach for it . . . "

Husam turned his eyes briefly to the ground. *This idiot has no clue what he's doing. Imam Al-Hashim's support is crucial to the cause. Plus, he's not the type of man you cross.*

"Donations are down," Husam said. "I get that, but what if it's not the Imam's fault? According to Yaman, the Imam's contacts are invaluable. Let me poke around the mosque, and see what I can find out. We shouldn't cut down the tree that provides us shade."

Muhanned scowled. "And if it is his fault?"

"Then, I'll take care it," Husam lied.

"All right," Muhanned acquiesced. "Perhaps I'm being impatient, but we can't keep operating like this. I'll give you one month to investigate. If you can't fix the problem, I'll initiate a changing of the guard myself."

As Muhanned return to his car, Husam breathed a sigh of relief. *I've bought the Imam some time, but not much. Muhanned has no sense of loyalty to anything or anyone. Ultimately, the only way to protect the Imam will be to dispose of the jackal.*

Chapter 8: First Steps

As he knelt on the rug in Imam Al-Hashim's office, Husam stared blankly into space. Having come straight over from the construction site, he was exhausted. His face was caked with dried sweat, his eyes tired but intense. He needed to convince the Imam that his life was in danger. When the Imam entered the room, Husam quickly got to his feet.

"Husam," the Imam said cordially. He hugged Husam and kissed him on each cheek. "Working hard I see."

"I apologize for my appearance," Husam said. "I've been working at a construction site on the outskirts of town."

"No need to apologize," the Imam assured him.

"Muhanned paid me a visit today."

"Ah, and did he tell you that I had some errands for you?"

"Not exactly," Husam replied.

The Imam laughed.

"Muhanned can't be trusted," Husam said hastily. "He wants you dead."

Imam Al-Hashim brought his finger up to his lips. "I know," he whispered knowingly, "but unfortunately he's not my only concern." The Imam nodded toward the door. "Afaz!" The Imam said loudly. After a moment, the Imam's assistant poked his head around the door.

"Yes," Afaz answered.

"Please get us some tea, and then go out front to welcome Professor Ratib. When he arrives, escort him to my office immediately."

"Of course," Afaz replied. Bowing slightly, he exited the room.

The Imam's eyes were fixed on his departing assistant. "There's room in the courtyard for another resident," the Imam said coldly.

Husam acknowledged the Imam's request with a nod as the corners of his lips broke into a smile.

"When you're done with that I'd like to introduce you to Professor Ratib. He has some ideas that I'd like to pursue."

"What about Muhanned?" Husam asked impatiently.

"As long as I keep filling his pockets he won't bother me. We can deal with him later. In the meantime, we can't let him destroy everything that Yaman believed in," the Imam said adamantly.

A knock on the door preceded Afaz's arrival with the tea. He placed the serving tray on a small, round mahogany table that was positioned just inside the entryway. Quickly, he readied two white ceramic teacups for Husam and the Imam.

"Thank you, Afaz," Imam Al-Hashim stated politely. "Please let me know when Professor Ratib has arrived."

"Of course," Afaz answered before disappearing quietly from the room.

#

"I wish I could hear what they're saying," Afaz mumbled, outside the Imam's office. *It's been months since Husam has been here, and he's never met with Professor Ratib before. This is just the kind of thing I need, to impress that new agent. Maybe, I could get him to increase my compensation.*

After waiting outside the mosque entrance for about five minutes, Afaz saw Professor Ratib approaching. With the wind increasing and the temperature dropping, he wondered if a sand storm was approaching. "It sure is cold tonight," Afaz said as the professor approached.

"Yes, yes it is," Professor Ratib agreed.

"Imam Al-Hashim is expecting you."

"Thank you," the professor answered.

"What brings you back so soon?" Afaz asked.

"Oh, I just have something to discuss with Imam Al-Hashim," Professor Ratib answered quietly.

Afaz decided not to probe further. *If I'm patient, I should be able to listen in on some of their conversation while I'm clearing the tea. Of course, the Imam's been after me to clean the rugs in his office. Perhaps, I can get an earful that way.*

After knocking softly on the Imam's office door, Afaz poked his head in. "Professor Ratib is here to see you."

"Come in, Professor. Come in," the Imam said. "Husam Asad, this is Professor Mahmud Ratib." Husam nodded politely.

"Imam Al-Hashim," Afaz interrupted, "would you like me to get to work on these carpets for you?"

"No, thank you," the Imam replied. "Actually, I need you to show Husam the broken window in the courtyard. He's going to come by early tomorrow morning and fix it."

"What time?" Afaz queried. "I could come in early and help him. In the meantime, I can get these rugs cleaned up for you."

"First, show Husam the broken window in the courtyard. Then you can work on the rugs," the Imam ordered.

"Yes sir," Afaz replied, trying to hide his agitation. As Afaz turned to leave, the Imam whispered something in Husam's ear. Husam nodded and followed Afaz out.

Leading Husam to the courtyard, Afaz was despondent. *What's there to show him? It's nighttime.*

A stone archway framed the entrance to the courtyard, which was part cemetery, part bank, and part armory. Upon reaching the entrance, Afaz suddenly found himself lurching headlong into one of the archway's pillars. Stunned by the pain, he could see nothing but explosions of color, dark purple, blue, and black. With his head throbbing intensely, Afaz's body was quickly jerked back. His neck fell into a vise like grip, and his chin was twisted back violently toward his shoulder. A moment later, his neck gave way, his body went limp, and his mind was overcome by darkness.

#

It had been nearly an hour since Husam and Afaz had left. Imam Al-Hashim looked energized as he talked with Professor Ratib about the individuals that the professor had selected for the new operations. While Professor Ratib had come up with over thirty names, the Imam had whittled the list down to twenty. After breaking the candidates up into groups of four, Husam returned looking even more hardened and weather worn than before.

"Husam, come and sit down," the Imam beckoned. Husam approached tiredly and sat down cross-legged on the floor with the professor and the Imam. "As I had started to say before," the Imam continued, "This is Professor Ratib, one of our most loyal and successful recruiters."

The two men shook hands. Professor Ratib almost jumped when Husam's cold rough hand tightly grasped his own. "Your hand is cold as ice," the professor remarked. "Here—have some tea."

"Thank you," Husam responded.

While Professor Ratib poured a cup of tea for Husam, the Imam continued. "Husam, I'm tired of watching Muhanned run Yaman's organization into the ground. Of late, our operations have had more to do with settling old scores than attacking the enemy. Muhanned is nothing but a thug. He lacks vision. Professor Ratib has contacts within industry that we can leverage to target our attacks where they'll hurt the most. Not mindless suicide missions, but precise hits against vital equipment. Professor Ratib's contacts have knowledge and access. You and your men have the operational expertise. Together, we can paralyze the West and strangle the corrupt monarchy."

Chapter 9: Class Reunion

The red sun was setting behind the dunes as I met with three of my closest friends. Dressed in traditional Islamic clothes, we huddled closely together around a small campfire. During the winter months, it gets surprisingly cold in the Saudi desert, especially once the sun goes down. Dema, Tahir, Siraj, and I attended the same *madrasah* when we were teenagers. Then we were classmates together at Arabian University in Dhahran.

At the time, given the U.S. occupation of Afghanistan and Iraq, anti-American sentiment was widespread on campus. While there was certainly no lack of forums on campus in which to express such sentiments, Professor Mahmud Ratib's class on Islam and the West was probably the most respected. Professor Ratib, who taught in the Islamic Studies department, challenged us to look beyond rants about jihads and helped provide a historical context to how Western imperialism affected the Islamic world as a whole.

"Why do you think Professor Ratib invited us out here?" I asked.

"Beats me, Raja," Tahir answered. "What did he always say during class?"

"You actually expect me to remember something from class," Siraj joked.

"He always told us to resist the urge to join the fight in Iraq," Dema remembered out loud. "There would come a time when we'd need soldiers here as well."

"Teachers pet," Siraj said slyly. Everyone laughed.

"So, you think he invited us out here to join some kind of revolution?" I asked incredulously.

"Raja! Didn't you read his invitation?" Dema asked. "Come join me in the struggle for Islam and Saudi Arabia. Plus, have you read any of his newsletters lately? His rhetoric has become a lot more incendiary."

"I guess, but that still seems like a bit of a stretch," I replied.

Siraj agreed. "He's probably just trying to organize a demonstration."

"You hardly ever showed up for class," Tahir joked. "Why would he expect you to show up for a demonstration?"

"Maybe he thought it would give me something to do."

While all of us finished college, Siraj Raahil had never found a full-time job. In Saudi Arabia, this was not unusual for people our age. Unemployment was high. Frankly, the rest of us were exceptions to the rule. I was an accountant by trade, but spent most of my free time scuba diving. Tahir Rafiq was a low level manager with the Persian Gulf Oil and Refining Company, known as the PGORC, and Dema Mundhir managed his father's small music store. Though unemployed, Siraj was an amateur photographer and video buff whose claim to fame was providing footage of a fire to a local television news outlet.

Suddenly, Professor Ratib appeared from out of the shadows. Though startled, we all stood up to greet him. He was carrying a small satchel. "I'm so sorry for keeping you waiting," he apologized.

"We figured you were paying us back for all the times we were late to class," Siraj said.

The professor smiled thinly while we laughed. "It was not intentional," he answered, motioning everyone to sit down. "I suppose you are all wondering why I invited you."

We all nodded. My gut told me it wouldn't be to reminisce about old times.

"As I've often said, the fight against Western imperialism will require the support of forces within industry and within the Saudi workforce to help combat societal corruption." As he spoke, I felt like we had been transported back in time, and we were all back in his classroom.

"While you may think you don't have the skills, the backgrounds, or the resources necessary to take on the establishment, I'm here to tell you that you're wrong. I'm here to tell you that nothing could be further from the truth. Allah values each of you, even if the monarchy doesn't," the professor said.

Professor Ratib then reached into his satchel and pulled out four sealed envelopes. He handed one to each of us. A gust of wind punctuated the tense silence. The fire flickered.

"What's this?" Tahir asked quizzically.

"Not a test I hope," I said, trying to lighten the mood. "I already have my diploma. You can't take it back now." Once again everyone laughed, except for Professor Ratib.

"No," Professor Ratib responded. "This is more serious than any test." Slowly, he looked at each of us. "Our nation stands on the precipice. Everywhere we turn, evil forces strive to undermine our Muslim society. Your time has come. It's time to stand up for what you believe in."

As we exchanged glances, I saw Dema roll his eyes.

"Inside these envelopes are instructions detailing how each of you can provide support. I'm not asking you to take up arms. I'm simply asking you to use your talents and positions to further our cause."

Dema looked uncomfortable. I could only imagine what he was thinking.

"Before opening the envelopes, you must decide whether or not you are prepared to take this next step, a step that moves us from talk to action. The letters are for your eyes only. Do not discuss the letters with anyone—not your families, not each other. If you are not prepared to take this step, if you want to walk away, do it now. I will leave while you decide. If you chose to go, leave the letter at your seat. You will not hear from me again."

With that, he rose. "Search your hearts. I know you'll make the right choice. You have thirty minutes to make your decision."

An initial hush fell over our group, and Professor Ratib disappeared into the night between the dunes. After a few moments of uncomfortable silence, Tahir finally interrupted the sound of the crackling fire. "Wow! The professor always talked about this, but I never really thought it would happen."

"So . . . what on earth do they need an accountant for anyway?" I wondered out loud.

"I don't know. Maybe they need help with their taxes," Siraj joked. "At least you have some kind of formal skill. What do they need me for?"

"Al-Qaeda's new camera man," quipped Tahir.

"I'm not moving to Afghanistan," Siraj said. Laughing, he pretended to throw the letter into the fire.

Everyone was laughing except for Dema, "How can you joke about something like this? He may not be asking us to pull the trigger ourselves, but we'll be working for people who will."

"What's this?" Tahir asked. "A few years ago, you were ready to rush off to Iraq to fight the Americans. Now listen to yourself."

"First of all, we're not in college anymore, and there's a difference between fighting the Americans and targeting our own countrymen or our own government," countered Dema.

"Professor Ratib didn't say anything about targeting our countrymen." Tahir stated. "In fact, he said the exact opposite. We'd be involved in non-violent resistance in support of Islam and our nation."

"Just because we're not pulling the trigger ourselves doesn't mean that people wouldn't be getting killed or that we wouldn't bear some responsibility for their deaths."

Tahir shook his head incredulously. "Professor Ratib's always been straight with us before. Why don't you trust him now?"

"I think that incident with his daughter changed him," Dema replied.

"You're kidding, right? This is Professor Ratib we're talking about," Siraj broke in. "I mean, he's not the type to do something like this on a whim."

"I'm sorry friends, I just am not comfortable with this," Dema concluded abruptly. "Please forgive me. Be careful. If you need me, you know where to find me," he said as he stood up to leave.

Although we were surprised by Dema's decision, we all rose to give him a parting embrace. I made a mental note to stop by his music store the next week. As he exited between the dunes, the rest of us stood fast. If this was a game of wills, only Dema had flinched. In a few moments, Dema's footsteps had all but disappeared in the sands.

"He sure has changed," Tahir observed.

"Well, given that he manages a music store, he's got to feel like Professor Ratib is against him," I said in Dema's defense.

"You know how the professor rants about the evils of importing American culture."

"On the other hand, if Dema doesn't stock Western music in his store, he's not going to make it. It's what sells," Tahir stated.

"Yeah, and he couldn't exactly tell his father that he didn't want to take over the family business," added Siraj. "So . . . are we gonna open these?"

"I think we're supposed to wait for Professor Ratib," Tahir said. Then, he glanced around at each of us. "Do we know what we're getting ourselves into?"

"Probably not," Siraj answered, "but I'm just an out-of-work slacker. I'm not an upstanding professional like you two."

"Hmpf . . . sometimes work just reinforces many of Professor Ratib's points," Tahir answered sourly. "We're all just small cogs in a big machine, easily replaceable unless you were born under a brighter star."

"Ha, ha," Siraj laughed. "You are quite the poet tonight. Even out here in the desert, you measure your words."

"Okay, how about this," countered Tahir. "My boss's idiot son could mistakenly load camel shit into our tankers, and he'd still make more money than me."

"Ahhh . . . better. Much better," cheered Siraj. "How about you Raja? You ready to help keep the books straight and do inventory for Al-Qaeda?"

"Ehh," I said with a shrug. I really didn't know what to say. "Accounting's accounting."

"Yeah, but there might be slightly higher penalties for arithmetic errors," Siraj interjected.

I had to laugh. "I understand your frustration, Tahir," I said. "No amount of hard work will ever change who our ancestors are. While you and I make a good living, it's nothing when compared to the royal family, and we're the lucky ones. Do you ever look at our Muslim brothers from Pakistan and Afghanistan? The ones that are on these work crews?" I asked.

Tahir and Siraj nodded their heads.

"It's embarrassing," Tahir agreed.

"They work incredible hours and get paid next to nothing building palaces, roads, or whatever for the monarchy," Siraj said.

"Exactly," I said. "They barely make enough money to survive. Meanwhile, you see members of the royal family who buy new Range Rovers every year. It's not because they work hard or are particularly smart. It's simply because of who they are. Their bloodlines."

Lost in thought, I poked at the glowing coals of the campfire with a stick. "It's almost like we're stuck in a caste system."

"Like India?" Siraj asked.

"Yeah! There's only so much we can do to improve our lot in life."

"That's all true," agreed Tahir, "but is the path that the professor's proposing going to change that?"

"I don't know, but it doesn't feel right to just give up." I answered. "We can't hide our heads in the sand our whole life."

Although it had seemed like hours, Professor Ratib returned exactly thirty minutes after he had left. "You all are very quiet," he commented upon his return.

"Well, Dema said some things before he left," Tahir replied. "I guess we're probably all wondering whether or not we're making the right decision."

"For years," started Professor Ratib, "I've stood on the sidelines and done nothing but talk. What good has it done? Look at your own lives, your parents' and grandparents' lives. Is this the Saudi Arabia that they embraced? Is this the Saudi Arabia that they dreamed of?"

As I looked at Tahir and Siraj, it was obvious that class was back in session.

"The monarchy has sold out to American interests. The scraps that trickle down to the Saudi public are nothing compared to the extravagances that the monarchy indulges in on a daily basis. They provide the U.S. with cheap oil and a marketplace for their goods. And now, when we try to rid our homeland of these infidel influences, they strike us down. Their support of the Islamic establishment is mere lip service. They only adhere to Islamic law when it serves their purposes."

We nodded in solemn agreement as Professor Ratib continued. "It's time for average Saudi citizens like us to stand up and be counted. Each one of us needs to use our individual skills to help liberate our nation."

"But what can we do," asked Siraj?

"Hundreds of things," Profess Ratib explained. "You have numerous skills, talents, and knowledge that can help further our cause. You don't need to know how to shoot a gun or build a bomb. The people I'm working with are trying to broaden their political base and be more inclusive."

For a moment, I lost track of what the professor was saying. *The people he's working with? Who exactly is that?*

"We want to create havoc, not destruction; chaos without calamity. If we can attack American interests without bloodshed, the U.S. will have no leg to stand on when they attempt to retaliate. The world will see that it's not about protecting the American people. Rather, it's about controlling resources and money. When the truth becomes self-evident, forces within their own nation will rise up and condemn them. Open your letters, and you'll see how you can each play a part."

After glancing cautiously at one another, we opened our letters. Siraj and Tahir each wore studious expressions as they concentrated on the details of their assignments. Meanwhile, I was having difficulty focusing. If Siraj or Tahir had any doubts about the actions they were being asked to undertake, they hid their feelings well.

Tahir finished first. He set down his letter in the sand and looked quizzically at the professor. "Professor Ratib," he began, but the professor quickly interrupted.

"I know that you all will have questions, but now is not the time," the professor said. "Remember, do not discuss the contents of the letters with anyone. Obviously, there is some risk involved in what you'll be asked to do, but the less you know about the overall operations the safer you'll be. Now, burn your letters in the campfire."

The three of us exchanged nervous glances. Then, one by one, we each threw our letters into the fire. As I watched the letters burn, I was filled with anxious excitement. Yet, I was apprehensive as well. What if Dema was the smart one?

Chapter 10: In the Shadows

Hidden by dusk's shadows, two men dressed in black *thobes* and *ghutras* lay prone on top of a high sand dune. While they were dressed similar to the local *mutawa*, this would have been a bit outside their normal jurisdiction. One of the figures had binoculars. He trained them on a small group of men sitting round a flickering campfire tucked between the dunes below. The other lay on his back taking a drag on a cigarette.

While Husam respected Imam Al-Hashim's decision to refocus their operations following Yaman's arrest, he was uncomfortable with Professor Ratib's expanding role. He didn't trust him. The professor had book smarts, but he was becoming increasingly involved in planning operations and recruiting people to assist in those operations. As he watched the professor's small gathering, Husam was very concerned about these new "recruits" the professor had assembled.

"They're liable to turn down the professor's offer, and we'll be tying up loose ends all night long," Husam whispered to Jasim while looking through the binoculars.

Although he had never been in the military, Husam had spent much of his life at one terrorist training camp or another. In fact, he'd met his scar-faced counterpart, Jasim, at one. While he often worked in construction, it was not his true profession.

"All right, the professor is leaving. Be ready to move," Husam cautioned.

Jasim tossed his cigarette aside, and rolled over on his stomach. "Guess now we'll find out whether we'll be working with these guys or burying them, eh?"

"Maybe both," Husam deadpanned. "They aren't running for their cars at any rate, but they haven't opened their letters yet.

"Come on," Jasim chided, "They'll be nothing but bit players. There's nothing in those letters that should scare them."

"It doesn't take much to scare these middle-class, college types," Husam countered. "Talk is one thing. Action is another."

"They'll be easier to control if they're a little scared," Jasim pointed out.

"I like operations to be nice and predictable. Fear can make people unpredictable," Husam said.

"I'd rather have them scared than cocky. The scared ones are more cautious. They've got something to lose. While they may not fully understand the consequences, they respect them."

"Hmmm . . ." Husam grunted. He paid little attention to Jasim's musings. "Evidently something's funny," Husam said. "One of them doesn't seem to get the joke though. Dema, I think."

"Should I take care of it?" Jasim asked.

"If you go, I'll just spend all night wondering whether or not you took care of it," Husam said dryly as he handed over the binoculars. "He's bolting. Stay here and watch the others. I'll take care of him."

"You don't want to wait until he's closer to home?"

"Nah, if he's leaving already maybe he doesn't care about the cause or his friends as much as Professor Ratib thought. Better deal with him now before he becomes a problem."

"All right. Don't stay out too late," Jasim said.

Leaving his perch, Husam slithered down the dune and hoofed it behind the ridge of sand to the parking area. He wanted to beat Dema back and make sure no other vehicles had shown up. He didn't need any uninvited guests.

When he reached the dunes edge, Husam felt for the small leaden club in his front pocket. While surveying the area, Husam pulled on a pair of tight fitting black gloves. No new vehicles had arrived.

With five SUVs parked side by side, Husam had no trouble finding cover from the retreating Dema. Removing the club from his pocket, he slunk behind Siraj's Jeep Cherokee, keeping his head below the roof line. Dema's Chevy Suburban was the next vehicle over. Peeking through the Jeep's windows, he saw Dema trudging, head down, between two dunes.

Husam shook his head in disgust and crouched down. *He must really trust the professor. Given the nature of the meeting, you'd think he'd be a bit more self-aware. He doesn't seem to realize he's in any danger. Relying on any of these guys to support operations is foolish.*

Husam watched for Dema's feet. When Dema reached his vehicle, Husam slid quietly around the rear of the Jeep and closed in quickly. As Dema opened the Suburban door, Husam brought the club down swiftly against the back of his victim's head. As Dema slumped to the ground, Husam caught him around the waist to slow his descent.

Grabbing some ace bandages from the leather pack that was tied to his waist, Husam bound Dema's hands and feet. Wrapped correctly, the ace bandages would bind his victim as tightly as rope without causing bruising or rope burns. He wrapped another bandage around Dema's head, covering his mouth, then grabbed Dema's keys and opened the rear hatch. Quickly, he collected Dema and placed him in the rear of the Suburban.

Next, he grabbed a bandanna from his pack. Husam tied off Dema's arm around the bicep. After slapping the inside of Dema's arm to bring out the veins, he produced a small syringe and administered a lethal mix of drugs into the arm. Dema's eyes opened wide as Husam closed the rear hatch. After sliding behind the wheel of the Suburban, Husam steered the vehicle down the makeshift dirt road that bordered the dunes, turning on the radio to drown out the kicking and grunting sounds coming from the back.

While Husam guided the Suburban over the rocky terrain adjacent to the dunes, a popular *nasheed* played. A verse from Ya Taiba would be the last thing that Dema would hear. Husam sang along, his voice raspy and cold.

A bullet would have been quicker, but then I'd have to spend more time disposing of the body. Plus, the sound of a gunshot might alert the professor and his crew to my presence. Making this look like a drug overdose will be easier in the long run. The stigma of drug use in Saudi Arabia would lend itself to a less than thorough investigation.

After skirting the dunes for a half-mile, Husam directed the vehicle between two dunes. As luck would have it, he saw the remnants of an abandoned campfire. Confident that this "parking spot" was off the beaten path enough, Husam backed the SUV up to the pile of charcoal sticks. The other recruits would not see

Dema's vehicle here. All was quiet in back as Husam turned off the engine.

Husam got out, strolled back, and opened the hatch. Dema's eyes were still open, but the bandage covering his mouth was bloody, probably from biting his own tongue. Husam grabbed Dema's neck to check for a pulse. There was none. Satisfied, he removed the bandages binding Dema's wrists, ankles, and face.

After propping up the body against the rear seat, he put a syringe in Dema's lifeless hand. He'd plant some additional drug paraphernalia at Dema's home later that night to complete the ruse. Finally, he returned the keys to Dema's pocket and began jogging back through the sand to where Jasim was watching the others.

With his *thobe* dragging along the sand, Husam weaved between the dunes. Sweat dripping from his forehead, he saw Jasim perched atop the sand dune above him. Jasim was looking through the binoculars as a cigarette dangled from his lips. Husam climbed up the wall of sand and resumed his post next to him.

"Has anyone else tried to leave the party?" Husam asked. Jasim shook his head and handed the binoculars to Husam.

"Professor Ratib came back. They read their orders, and now they're burning them in the campfire," Jasim whispered.

"Hmmm," Husam acknowledged. He smiled and looked skyward. "The Americans' satellites will do them no good here. Just a small campfire flickering in the desert. By the time they see the light, it'll be too late."

#

Detective Al-Faruq's car bounced along the makeshift road that skirted the sand dunes. He'd been called in by the local police to investigate a potential overdose. Since drugs were used by terrorist organizations to fund their activities, the SAID was often brought in to investigate drug-related deaths.

As Al-Faruq rounded the corner of a large dune that was drifting across the road, he saw a squad car parked next to a large white Suburban. Al-Faruq rolled down his window and waved as he approached. The young officer, dressed in a dark gray shirt and pants with a black beret, threw his cigarette to the ground and waved back.

"Detective Al-Faruq?" the young man asked as Al-Faruq's vehicle rolled slowly to a stop.

"Yes," Al-Faruq responded with his badge in hand. "Sorry it took me so long to get out here."

"That's all right. He's not going anywhere," the young man said.

"So, what are we looking at?" Al-Faruq asked after getting out of his car.

"I'm just guarding the vehicle. They didn't want me poking around."

"Did they say who the car was registered to?"

The young officer just shrugged.

Fair enough. Guess I'm on my own.

The young officer stayed behind as Al-Faruq walked over to the Suburban. The driver's seat was empty, but the rear hatch was open. Stepping cautiously toward the back of the vehicle, Al-Faruq could smell the body before he could see it.

Al-Faruq pulled his *ghutra* across his face and surveyed the scene. It could have been worse. In some respects, the dry desert environment helped preserve the body, but having the body open to the elements invited critters. First, the bugs would arrive, then the birds. If exposed long enough, the presence of the birds would attract larger scavengers and other predators.

By the looks of things, the body was fairly fresh. Al-Faruq put the time of death at about thirty-six to forty-eight hours ago. So far, the birds hadn't done too much damage to the corpse's face. The sleeve of the man's *thobe* had been pushed up to his bicep. Looking closer, Al-Faruq could see the spot where the man had shot up. A strange, dark green trail led from the needle mark, up the man's vein.

In the man's other hand was a syringe. Carefully, Al-Faruq pulled up the sleeve. No needle marks there. He continued to survey the man's body up and down. There was a spot of dried blood on the man's sock where his anklebone jutted out. Al-Faruq frowned and searched the man's body for any type of identification. Finally, he found the man's wallet. The driver's license said Dema Mundhir.

"What did you get yourself into, Dema?" Al-Faruq murmured.

Chapter 11: Financial Support

Professor Ratib met with resistance supporters almost every other weekend. Tonight marked the second of his quarterly meetings with Fakhir Ihsan, one of their most generous benefactors. Once every three months, Fakhir would pile up his entourage, his security personnel and the like, and drive out into the desert for the evening. While the professor generally dreaded these nomadic gatherings, it was the best way to meet with Fakhir while still maintaining some modicum of secrecy. Plus, Professor Ratib always left with a substantial wad of cash for the "university."

While the university did get some of the money, the rest was always passed on to Imam Al-Hashim. Well, almost always. There'd been a few times when he'd subtracted a small handling fee, but this time the money would be used to help create something new. An organization that would de-Americanize his country and would restore core Islamic values to the Kingdom of Saudi Arabia.

As the caravan of SUVs bounced slowly down the makeshift desert road, Professor Ratib worried incessantly. *Do I really have the confidence to lead a movement like this? My own wife and daughter treat me with disdain. I talk tough in the classroom about upholding Islamic values, but I don't command the respect of my own wife and daughter at home. It's that damn American soldier's fault. Even here in Saudi Arabia, I can't protect my own family from the West's hedonistic ways. Only with Imam Al-Hashim's help can I regain my self-respect and show my family that certain ideals are worth risk and sacrifice.*

With their final destination in sight, Professor Ratib tried to refocus on the task at hand. The caravan slowed as an island of dunes rose out of the rock-strewn desert landscape. Fakhir's entourage would soon go to work unloading the SUVs, putting up the tents, and preparing the food. For all the trappings of home that Fakhir dragged with him on these gatherings, the professor was amazed at the speed with which Fakhir's staff put everything together.

In less than an hour, before the sun disappeared over the horizon, his staff set up three large tents. One tent housed the women and children. Another tent was for Fakhir's wait staff. The largest of the three tents allowed the men to relax with a hearty meal and to engage in an informal *majlis*. The meeting enabled Fakhir to conduct business, discuss problems, and address grievances with his invited guests. During the *majlis*, Professor Ratib would speak with Fakhir about the university's "funding needs."

Aside from the staff tent, which was configured for food preparation, the tents were furnished with large silk rugs and wall-to-wall pillows. In the summer, the tent walls were rolled up to let in the desert air and provide Fakhir's guests with views of the night sky. On cooler nights, they were tied down to keep in the warmth of the communal fire and portable propane heaters. While Professor Ratib had to admit that the food and accommodations were spectacular, all the trappings of wealth and comfort ruined the desert's natural beauty. Given the sheer size of Fakhir's entourage, it was nearly impossible to appreciate the desert's simple wonders.

With everyone piling out of the SUVs, the chatter of mindless small talk broke the desert's serene silence and gnawed at the back of Professor Ratib's head. "So, Professor, what are the kids learning at college these days?" asked one of Fakhir's guests.

"Well, we have a rather broad curriculum at the university. Everything from mathematics and engineering to Islamic phil–"

"Good, good . . ." the portly man interrupted, "It's important to keep the kids' minds occupied. Keeps them out of trouble. Eh?"

His jaw clenched, Professor Ratib just smiled and nodded. *Fool! Easy money from oil has seriously stunted the intellectual and spiritual growth of the nation.*

Meanwhile, the conversation moved on. The portly man started blabbering on about his new high-def, 3-D television. The professor wondered if he was selling them.

"It's Sony's largest 3-D television yet," he gushed. "Sixty inches across, and the picture is crystal clear."

"How much did it cost?" Asked another one of Fakhir's guests.

"If you have to ask, you probably can't afford it," the portly man joked. The group erupted with laughter.

Professor Ratib quietly slipped away from the group and directed his eyes up to the darkening night sky. The stars were just beginning to shine through. *So much greed. It's a disease, a disease that has infected my wife and daughter too. It doesn't matter how much money I make. It'll never be enough for them. I can see that now. I've been so stupid. I've sold my soul for the sake of money. I can only hope, that through my service to Imam Al-Hashim, Allah will forgive me.*

Lost in thought, Professor Ratib did not hear his host approaching. "Professor Ratib," Fakhir said jovially.

The professor jumped.

"I didn't mean to startle you, but I must ask. What are you doing over here all by yourself?"

"I'm sorry, Fakhir. Sometimes, it's nice to get away from all the noise and chatter. There were times, not too long ago, when life was a lot simpler," Professor Ratib said glancing wistfully at the stars.

"I know what you mean. Change does not always equal progress. Am I right? Someday, we'll be able to balance progress with our core values. There are some things that shouldn't change."

"Very well put," the professor agreed.

"In any event," Fakhir said. "Dinner is ready, so come, let's eat." Fakhir guided Professor Ratib back to the party. As they came upon small clusters of party-goers, Fakhir politely herded them to the main tent. "Come, my friends! We can't let all this good food go to waste."

The smells emanating from the tent were mouthwatering. The feast included a variety of lamb dishes including *kouzi*, *markok*, and *arayess*. There was *hamour* and *shaour*. Plus, chicken *kebabs* and *sambusek*. Vegetable-oriented offerings such as *loubia*, *fattoush*, and *falafel* were also served, as were a variety of Arabic breads with *hummus* and *tahini*.

Large, ornate silver platters heaped with food were placed on a large silk area rug in the middle of the tent. The pattern on the rug displayed a large flowering tree with birds of every shape and color dispersed throughout the branches. The platters were carefully placed on the tree's flower blossoms.

Fakhir sat at the base of the tree, perhaps symbolizing the roots from whence tonight's feast originated. Throw pillows circled the large area rug, along with smaller throw rugs that provided Fakhir's guests a place to sit. Once everyone was seated, Fakhir's servants darted about, refilling spent platters and guests' glasses with quiet efficiency. All the while, a large *hookah* was passed around, and the revelry grew more bold and boastful, despite the lack of alcohol.

#

When the conversation around the tent had subsided and the feeding pace diminished, Fakhir motioned to the head servant. Soon dessert trays and tea replaced the heartier fare. *Baklava, kunafi,* and *ma'amul* were served. Fakhir receded to the far end of the tent where beaded curtains created a small sitting room. Here, Fakhir prepared to conduct the evening *majlis*.

Diya Nabil, a Bedouin tribal elder who attended at Fakhir's behest, was the first to be heard. Summoned by one of Fakhir's servants, the sturdy, compact old man walked purposefully toward the sitting room where Fakhir greeted him warmly with a handshake and a kiss on each cheek. Diya's nomadic tribe continued to inhabit areas where Fakhir's oil rich family conducted operations.

The two men sat down cross-legged on a round silk rug that acted as the focal point of the small room. "What can I do for you?" Fakhir asked as he poured a cup of tea for each of them.

"My tribesmen lost two goats and three camels after the animals drank water from the Barakah Oasis. The water looked shiny and tasted bitter," Diya stated.

"We haven't conducted operations in that area for some time," Fakhir answered with some skepticism.

"The Barakah Oasis is an essential stop on our trading route. My people will not drink from it. Can this poison be cleansed from the oasis?"

Given that maintaining a good relationship with Diya's tribe was well worth a handful of livestock, Fakhir acquiesced. "I will have the water tested at once. What livestock were lost?"

"Three goats and four camels," Diya embellished.

#

While Fakhir and Diya haggled over the appropriate compensation for the lost livestock, Professor Ratib sat lost in thought. While Diya was at least twenty years older than the men seated around the tent, he was in better health than most of them. Where Diya's thin frame was sinewy and well honed, the other men in attendance were fat and soft featured. Professor Ratib looked at them in disgust.

They're better fit for dressing up like Santa Claus at an American mall than for rising up against the monarchy. They've been lulled into complacency. They know and care little about their ancestry, and some of them are even wearing blue jeans under their *thobes*. It is no wonder many of their sons have lost respect for them. I see kids like that every day in my classes. Young men longing for a connection, a connection to something other than money or possessions.

The professor's thoughts were interrupted as one of Fakhir's servants bid for his attention. "Professor Ratib, Fakhir will see you now."

"Thank you," Professor Ratib said politely. Quickly, he got up and walked to the rear of the tent. Standing just outside the beaded partition, he heard Diya and Fakhir finishing up their discussion.

"I hope your people will find the compensation adequate," Fakhir offered.

"Yes. On behalf of my tribe, I thank you."

"Oh! Before you go," Fakhir continued. "Have you come across any outsiders recently? As always Diya, your people are my eyes and ears in the desert."

"No, we have not," Diya answered, shaking his head resolutely. "If my people see any strangers, I will send word immediately."

"May Allah bless you and your tribe," Fakhir said as he concluded their conversation. Diya nodded, turned, and stepped through the beaded partition. When Diya saw the professor standing there, he smiled politely and parted the curtain to let Professor Ratib enter.

"Professor Ratib," Fakhir said jovially as he rose to welcome his guest. "Did you get enough to eat?"

"Everything was wonderful. Thank you for inviting me."

"How's everything going?" Fakhir asked with what seemed like genuine concern. "There are more arrests every time I turn on the news. The monarchy seems to be in the West's back pocket these days. Yes?"

"The arrests are usually nothing more than window dressing," Professor Ratib replied confidently. "It actually makes recruiting easier whenever they crack down. In a sense, the veil has been lifted and the public can see the monarchy for what it truly is."

"Manipulative and controlling," Fakhir said with a laugh.

"As a matter of fact, yes," Professor Ratib agreed.

"I'd just hate to think that my support is simply falling back into the monarchy's hands."

"The monarchy always exaggerates the amount of money and weapons seized in order to appease their Western masters. Rest assured, your money is in good hands, supporting operations against the West and its allies."

"Good, good," Fakhir said.

"While the West spends billions of dollars trying to protect their citizens, our operations cost a fraction of that. Have they made things more difficult? Sure, but don't let the periodic lulls of inactivity fool you. The West's aggressive posture is unsustainable. With continued support from donors like you, we will bring the West to its knees."

"I understand completely," Fakhir said. "I didn't mean to imply . . . "

"No, no, you have every right to be concerned," Professor Ratib deferred. "Now more than ever, your support is essential."

"I know my money is in good hands. Hands guided by Allah's will," Fakhir said as he produced a large manila envelope and offered it to the professor.

"Thank you. May Allah bless you always," Professor Ratib nodded respectfully as he accepted the envelope.

"No thanks are necessary. There's more where that came from, eh?" Fakhir said with a chuckle. "I like to think we're sticking it to the West from both ends, you with your operations and me with mine. Oil is like a beautiful woman to them. They can't get enough of her, and now the Chinese have acquired an appetite for her too. Allah smiles on us."

"Yes, yes he does," Professor Ratib agreed. Then he added, "Don't let the news discourage you. We have some operations in the works that should broaden Allah's smile even further. Have faith. Allah will see us through."

Chapter 12: Pencils Down

Professor Ratib eyed the clock sternly. It was time for class to begin. Purposefully, he walked over to close the classroom door.

"No, no . . . Wait! I'm right here Professor Ratib," a voice called.

Professor Ratib peered crossly down the corridor.

"Professor Ratib! I have that data you wanted from Tahir," Jad said. In his outstretched hand, he was holding the flash drive that his cousin had given him. "Tahir was running late. You know the buses around here."

"Thank you Jad," Professor Ratib responded cautiously. "Now please take your seat."

Jad hurried into the classroom to the great amusement of several of his classmates.

"What's your excuse this time," Amal whispered as Jad sat down next to him.

"I was running an errand for the professor. It's all good."

Amal just shook his head and laughed. "You're a trip, Jad. You are a trip."

"All right. Let's get started," Professor Ratib barked. After placing the flash drive next to his laptop, he strode confidently up to his podium. "Get out your journals and give me two hundred words outlining the concept of *velayat-e faqih*. You have thirty minutes."

With his class sufficiently occupied, Professor Ratib plugged the flash drive into the USB port on his laptop. He selected the folder titled, "Energy," opened the largest file, and quickly scanned the document. It listed the key drivers of U.S. gasoline prices, outlined petroleum area defense districts, and detailed the Americans' major utility providers. In addition, it highlighted several key flashpoints where environmentalists and the utilities were clashing. The report was part document/part website, and included a number of imbedded links to internet sources.

Reading intently, Professor Ratib dug into Tahir's report. Upon finishing, he nodded with satisfaction. *This is definitely Tahir's best work. He never wrote anything this detailed in class.*

Perhaps he is maturing. The Imam will be pleased. This should go a long way toward helping us focus our efforts.

Professor Ratib looked at his watch. *If I let class out a little early, I can drop this by the mosque before noonday prayer.* He'd been surprised by the Imam's sense of urgency with regard to his ideas. It made him feel important. *Maybe Allah has plans for me yet. I won't fail him this time. I can't fail him. To hell with Iba and Azzah. Their never-ending demands corrupted me, my faith in Allah, and my faith in myself.*

Professor Ratib shook off his thoughts of inadequacy. Then, he closed Tahir's research and disconnected the flash drive. "Five more minutes," he said, his voice booming. He grabbed his newspaper, flipping the pages noisily as his students wrote feverishly.

"Time's up," he said loudly. "We're going to finish up a little early today," he continued, to the surprise of the class. "Continue with the readings, as outlined in the syllabus. If you found this little exercise difficult, maybe you need to go back and review. On your way out, stack your journals here on the table. You're dismissed."

Focusing on his laptop, Professor Ratib checked his e-mail while the class filed out. The professor didn't want to make eye contact. He didn't have time for questions. When one student lingered after handing in his journal, the professor snapped at him. "If you don't take advantage of it, I won't bother letting you go early in the future." After that, the remaining students exited hastily.

Once they were gone, Professor Ratib packed up his things and headed for the door. If he wanted to see the Imam prior to noonday prayers, he'd have to hurry. After locking the classroom door, the professor walked quickly down the corridor and out to the parking lot.

His mind wandering, Professor Ratib tried to keep his nerves in check. The Imam's assistant, Afaz, had disappeared. Husam, on the other hand, was now constantly by the Imam's side.

The professor tried to make sense of it all. *Husam's no cleric, that's for sure. Bodyguard would be a more apt description. I wonder how they ever met? Husam and the Imam are cut from different cloth. Still, I guess you can't spread revolution with academics only. You need soldiers.*

Professor Ratib's drive to the mosque was uneventful. When he arrived, throngs of worshipers were gathering for noonday prayer. Quickly, he ran from his car, hoping to catch the Imam before prayers began. However, when he knocked on the Imam's office door, it was Husam who answered.

"Professor?" Husam asked warily. He stared icily down the hallway.

"Is Imam Al-Hashim in?" asked Professor Ratib. "I have the research that he—"

Husam held up his hand to quiet him. Then, he roughly pulled the professor inside the Imam's office and closed the door. "Professor! You do realize that we're moving past academics into actual operations."

"Well, yes . . . of course."

"Real world operations can go south in a hurry if security is compromised."

"Yes, I understand, but—"

"No, I don't think you do. The Imam is being watched. If you start showing up more often or at unusual times, it will attract attention. I don't think you're ready to deal with the kind of attention it may attract."

Frustrated, Professor Ratib held up the flash drive in front of Husam's face. "Please have him review the file titled, 'Energy.'"

Husam curled his fingers tightly around the professor's wrist and grabbed the flash drive with his free hand. "I will make sure he gets it. However, in the future, do not deviate from your normal worship schedule. It's for your own safety and the Imam's as well." Husam released the professor and stared at him icily.

Professor Ratib nodded sullenly while rubbing his wrist. Inside he was seething, but he knew better than to cross Husam. It wouldn't be good for his health.

#

Husam eyed Professor Ratib as he slunk off to *Jumu'ah. He'll get over it. I needed to teach him a lesson. We're headed into uncharted territory with these guys. They're not fighters. They don't have the necessary training. If I let them be sloppy, they'll either end up dead, or worse, they'll compromise everything.*

With the flash drive in hand, Husam walked over to one of the bookshelves that lined the Imam's office. After studying the books that lined the shelf, he selected one, opened it up and hid the flash drive inside, then returned the book to the shelf. He'd sit down with the Imam and review the information later.

With the *adhan,* or prayer call, echoing loudly, Husam left the Imam's office. After locking the door behind him, Husam turned to his left and entered the minaret staircase. He climbed the twisting steps two at a time, entering a small room at the top. An old speaker dangled precariously from the wall just inside the doorway. The dusty room was empty except for an old wooden chair, on which rested a pair of binoculars. Husam picked them up and sat down. From there, he spied down from the minaret's spade-shaped windows.

Imam Al-Hashim's voice crackled over the old speaker as he delivered the *khutba.* Meanwhile, Husam trained his gaze toward the parking lot. *No sign of Muhanned. The Imam's playing a dangerous game. Muhanned's already suspicious. The Imam can only hold out on him for so long. I wish he would just let me get rid of Muhanned, once and for all.*

As if on cue, a black Mercedes pulled into the parking lot. Husam was actually relieved. He hadn't seen hide or hair of Muhanned since that day at the construction site, and he didn't have the resources to keep proper tabs on him. When Muhanned exited his vehicle, Husam set down the binoculars and headed downstairs.

At the bottom of the staircase, Husam cracked the door open and peered out into the hallway. Quietly, he watched Muhanned creep over to the Imam's office. After picking the lock, Muhanned pushed the door open.

"You sure picked a strange time to visit the Imam," Husam blurted out.

Muhanned wheeled around. "Husam," Muhanned said with a look of agitation. "I was actually looking for you."

"Really?"

"I sent you to keep an eye on the Imam, but I hadn't heard back from you. Is everything okay?"

"Why don't we step inside the Imam's office?" Husam offered. "It's open, isn't it?" he said, shooting Muhanned a cold stare.

"Well, have you found out anything?" Muhanned asked as Husam shut the door quietly behind them.

"About what?"

"About the reduced donations," Muhanned said.

Husam smiled wryly as he scratched his chin. "The Imam was having problems with his assistant, but it's been taken care of."

"Problems?"

"Afaz was stealing from him."

"Then, where's the money?" Muhanned interjected.

"He spent it. I guess," Husam answered nonchalantly.

"He spent it? Are you sure?" Muhanned asked, his voice rising. "Where is this Afaz? I'd like to ask him some questions."

"He's in the courtyard, but I don't think you'll be able to get much out of him," Husam answered.

Muhanned grimaced. "He's dead. Right?"

Husam nodded.

"Maybe next time, you could give me a heads-up beforehand. Think you could do that?" Muhanned asked. "Information is generally more important than retribution. More often than not, both can be obtained."

"I'll try to remember that," Husam answered coolly.

"Hopefully, you've stopped the bleeding. I'll be expecting an appropriate donation at month's end," Muhanned added.

"Well, it will take the Imam time to recover from his losses," Husam answered, "but I'll do my best."

"You do that." Muhanned sneered. As Husam opened the door, Muhanned pushed past him roughly. "I'll be in touch."

Husam watched Muhanned intently until he exited the mosque. "No, I'll be in touch," he said under his breath.

74

Chapter 13: Planning for Tomorrow

After finishing *Jumu'ah*, Imam Al-Hashim returned to his office. It was probably the best he felt all day. Prayer energized him. However one look at Husam, who was pacing back and forth in his office, tempered his mood. "What's wrong?" the Imam asked with concern.

"Muhanned stopped by."

"Ah, I see. And what did he want?"

"I caught him trying to break into your office."

"Wondering if he could find more precious donations, no doubt," the Imam said with a sigh.

"I implied that Afaz had been skimming from our donations. While I may have bought you some time, Muhanned will be expecting the usual amount next time," Husam answered.

"Aghh, you needn't have bothered," Al-Hashim replied. "It doesn't matter how much we give him. He'll only want more."

"You shouldn't underestimate him," Husam continued. "He's not like Yaman. It's a business to him, not a cause. If he thinks that you're holding out on him, he'll—"

"He is not my primary concern," the Imam said. He waved his hand as if he were brushing away a fly. "We have more important matters to discuss. Did Professor Ratib drop off the research I requested?"

"Yes, but—"

"Husam!" the Imam said sharply. "We cannot let Muhanned distract us from the task at hand. We cannot let his lack of faith infect us. If he is not willing to use the money and resources that Yaman developed, then we will."

"But he will kill you!" Husam implored.

"You cannot live trying to hide from death. If Allah wills it, death will find you. Don't focus on how we might fail. Focus on how we will succeed," the Imam lectured. "Now. Are the preparations in place for our efforts here at home?"

"Yes," Husam answered.

"Then bring the professor's research here."

Husam walked over to the bookshelf and retrieved the flash drive while Imam Al-Hashim booted up his laptop. Husam handed him the flash drive.

"Thank you," the Imam replied. "I have several blank flash drives over in the cabinet. Can you get them for me?" Al-Hashim asked, pointing. Obediently, Husam retrieved them.

Imam Al-Hashim inserted Professor Ratib's flash drive. As it activated, he asked, "What are we looking for?"

"The file name is 'Energy,'" Husam answered.

The Imam opened the file and began to review the document. "How many agents do we have in America?" he asked.

"A couple dozen," Husam answered, "but I don't know how reliable they are."

"Why do you question their loyalty?"

"I wasn't questioning their loyalty, but there is a big difference between gathering information and conducting operations. I've worked with many of these young men in Yaman's training camps. Many aren't ready to take the next step."

"A key part of Professor Ratib's plan is to target small, unprotected resources. We're not trying to take down the World Trade Center."

"I know, but I still question what kind of impact it will have."

"When combined with our attacks here at home, the attacks abroad will destabilize energy prices even further. Many of these infidel nations are crumbling under the weight of their own debt, and what does the monarchy do? It increases oil output to help prop up these corrupt regimes. It is time for us to wield the sword that Allah has put in our hands."

"I understand," Husam answered. "I'm just trying to be realistic. Some of these men will not follow through."

"When they see our success here, they will seize the opportunity. Those who don't will have Allah to answer to. Have faith Husam. Have faith!"

"Faith didn't bring down the World Trade Center," Husam grumbled. "Planning and execution did." He took a deep breath, exhaled slowly, and looked over the Imam's shoulder at the computer screen. Suddenly, the Imam's energy seemed to vanish from him. His hands trembled over the keyboard and his shoulder's sagged. "Are you all right?" Husam asked.

"Yes, yes I'm fine," Imam Al-Hashim said. "It's been a busy morning. I . . . I need to rest. Please review the information and prepare orders for our operatives." He got up and walked unsteadily to the small bedroom just off his study. The room contained a foldout cot and had a bathroom adjacent to it.

"Do you need any help?" Husam asked softly.

"No, I'm fine," Imam Al-Hashim answered. "Review the data. I'm counting on you," he said.

The Imam trudged slowly over to the medicine cabinet and pulled out several prescription bottles. *This new medicine doesn't make me feel any better than the old medicine. Erlotinib, bevacizumab . . . Aghh . . . What's the difference? It's all the same. I still feel terrible. I'm just delaying the inevitable.* The Imam downed his medicine, stepped over to the cot, and lay down.

#

Husam watched the Imam out of the corner of his eye. Imam Al-Hashim had always been thin, but not fragile like this. He'd aged several years in the last couple of months. As the Imam lay on his back with his eyes closed, it wasn't hard to imagine that the end was near, another casualty in the war of life. Husam shook the image from his head.

Focus! It's all the more reason to push forward. I need to help the Imam realize his dream—our dream—before it's too late. Perhaps the Imam's right. I lack his faith, his vision. My mind is too bound by this earth. I only see people's limitations, not their potential.

With a grim determination, Husam concentrated on the document. As he read, he pictured each of his Muslim brothers halfway across the world embedded with the *Amrikaayis*. They'd all passed through Yaman's training camps.

While they may not be soldiers, they each had their own set of strengths and weaknesses. Utilize their strengths. Aghh! In some cases that's easier said than done. That Palestinian kid, Nasim

Talib, is about the only one I'd trust with anything resembling a complex operation. Well, I guess Dakhil el-Dirar and Maaz Zakariya aren't that bad either, but the rest of them would hurt themselves making Molotov cocktails.

Husam furrowed his brow and continued reading. While the Imam seemed focused on oil-related targets, the report covered the American's entire energy mix, including nuclear, coal, natural gas, oil, and renewable energy. In his mind, Husam began to break it down. *It's a huge network. Impossible to defend. There are literally thousands of soft, unprotected targets.*

The more he read, the more confident he became that maybe the Imam was right. One graph showed how much the price of oil rose after previous terrorist attacks, and the targets weren't even oil related. Maybe, this was the way to finally make them pay.

We only need to affect a small percentage of the network. We want to spread fear and uncertainty, not shut off the spigot. Plus, geographically separated, simultaneous attacks would leave U.S. intelligence scrambling. It's all right here. Whether it's the gasoline for their cars or the electricity for their homes, it's all one big chain. Attack the links!

Slowly, Husam began to refine a general list of targets. He categorized the list into hard, medium, and soft targets. The list of hard targets included refineries, power plants, and drilling rigs. *While I can't rely on my overseas brothers to attack these types of targets, I can attack these targets locally with more seasoned operatives.*

The list of medium targets concentrated on transportation networks and intermediate points within the supply chain. *Our newer operatives can attack these targets both here and abroad. It's just a matter of determining whom to trust. As for the soft targets, I'll leave these for the less-skilled agents. Even if they aren't successful, their efforts will provide a welcome distraction.*

Husam had cased oil-related targets within the Persian Gulf before. Since several of their top contributors had ties to the oil industry, his superiors had been reluctant to pull the trigger. But now? Now, he was in charge, and he had reliable sources on the inside.

Over the next few hours, Husam refined his target lists with pen and paper. He jotted down who would be assigned to what targets, and sketched out the preferred method of attack. The sound of Imam Al-Hashim's voice, still groggy from sleep, interrupted his train of thought.

"How's it going?" The Imam asked as he struggled over.

"It's going well," Husam answered.

"You don't sound convinced."

"I need to talk more with the professor's recruits, especially those working within the oil industry, before I can determine the viability of our plans."

"I'll instruct Professor Ratib to make the necessary introductions," the Imam said.

"Also," Husam continued, "based on this report, I think we should broaden our horizons to other energy-related targets besides oil. This would give our overseas operatives more flexibility."

"Whatever you feel is best," the Imam said. "Remember, we have some new recruits headed abroad for college orientation. If you prepare the flash drives now, they can act as couriers. Our brothers overseas will not fail."

Husam nodded. "Would you like to go over what I've outlined?"

"No, no," Imam Al-Hashim said shaking his head tiredly. "The less I know, the better."

Chapter 14: Student Visa

Nasim Talib had been studying in the U.S. at the University of Texas for over three years. A Palestinian by birth, he'd grown up in Israel's West Bank. Although his parents were well educated, they had trouble holding down steady jobs due to the constant violence and border closures. Hence, money had always been tight. Only a scholarship from the Palestinian Education Foundation, the PEF, had made his education possible.

#

I'd always been a good student, but nothing exceptional. Still, my parents badgered me into applying for all kinds of collegiate scholarships. I knew that the chance of me actually getting one was practically nonexistent. When news of my PEF scholarship arrived, I couldn't believe it. With my mother and father in tears, I thought somebody had died. However, much to my surprise, I not only garnered a scholarship, but one that would send me to college in America.

It was only during my PEF orientation that I began to fully understand why I'd been chosen. While many scholarships have specific grade level requirements, my PEF scholarship was contingent on other "extracurricular" obligations. During my time in America, I'd report on American reactions to overseas attacks, case potential targets, and act as a courier.

I can't lie. I love living in the United States. Who wouldn't? When you've lived your entire life under warlike conditions, there is a sense of comfort that envelopes American life. While drugs, violence, and poverty root themselves in small pockets of America, it's nothing compared to life in the West Bank.

I've seen my brother's dead body being carried through the front door by neighborhood friends. I've seen my uncle's home bulldozed over to make room for Israeli settlers. I've endured curfews, snipers, bombings, and tanks rolling through my neighborhood. Until I came to America, I'd never known anything but violence and fear.

After a lackluster first semester in Austin, I finally realized the opportunity that I'd been given. I redoubled my efforts in the classroom in hopes of staying in America for as long as possible. With graduate school on the horizon and a solid part-time job that enables me to send money home, I want to ensure I'll be able to retain PEF backing.

It's strange how you can love something and hate it at the same time. While the U.S. form of democracy does a relatively good job of protecting the rights of its citizens, American capitalism is probably the biggest threat to human rights around the world. In order to obtain the natural resources required to maintain its economy and standard of living, the U.S. government consistently supports oppressive regimes.

The average American is generally well meaning but naïve. Maybe it stems from the notion that the "pursuit of happiness" is an inalienable right, but the majority of Americans are much too busy to be concerned with how their government's foreign policy decisions are impacting the rights of other people around the world. There's the occasional protest, to be sure, but their convictions pale in comparison to the sacrifices that my countrymen are willing to make.

While an Israeli incursion into my West Bank hometown will sometimes leave my parents housebound and without electricity for days, the action will garner only a thirty-second block on the nightly news. That's if you even watch the news. There are hundreds of other channels to watch. In my opinion, Americans are very sheltered and out of touch with the real world. You can debate as to whether it matters that the bullets that killed my brother came from an M-16 as opposed to an AK-47, but it matters to me.

#

Hence, as Nasim reviewed the latest correspondence from his PEF contact, there was no doubt in his mind that he would complete his mission. While the short note looked innocuous enough, it contained a hidden message.

11/25/13

Dear Nasim,

How are you doing? Good, I hope. Could you visit Target again for us and pick up some more of those Legos for your cousins? That store is local, right? The toys that you sent (transformers?) for Lubaid and Kaseem are great. They are fun to play with and keep them busy. They use up lots of batteries (real power hogs). I know. I shouldn't complain, but you know me. I'm never satisfied.

Oh, I tried to call you the other day, but the lines were down. More blackouts again. Not as many as last year. Yeah! Attacks have been down significantly. Don't forget your Dad's birthday on 5/30! We'll be taking a trip to visit your Aunt Z on her birthday. We're leaving the last week of June. We'll get back on 7/04. Well, I've gotta go. I'll write more later.

Love, Mom

"Target transformers and power lines. Attacks 5/30, 7/04," Nasim mumbled.

In the back of his mind, Nasim knew something like this was coming. In September, he received similar orders. Only then, it was a test to determine whether or not he'd follow through. So in October he had constructed a small explosive device using over-the-counter fireworks he'd collected. According to the newspapers, he knocked out power to more than 10,000 people. Since he'd used fireworks and set off the device on Halloween night, authorities focused their attention on local juvenile offenders.

This time however, he'd need to put together something more substantial. Nasim had no qualms about the choice of targets. He'd cased plenty of facilities like this, and they were, for all intents and purposes, unprotected. Nonetheless, his mind was filled with questions.

I'm only one person. How much of an impact can I really make? If I'm lucky, I'll be able to hit maybe three or four targets before the local police catch on. Even if I hit that many, the impact will still be relatively localized.

While getting caught is a distinct possibility, I don't want to be stupid about it. I'll have to review my list of regional targets and determine the best places to hit. If I trigger them remotely, I could set up several devices within, say, a hundred-mile radius and then skip town.

Mentally, Nasim went through a checklist of the things that he'd need. *Gasoline-fertilizer-based shrapnel devices would do the trick if properly placed. I can use cell phone triggers, a small amount of gunpowder or something similar to kick things off, and nails for shrapnel. It's not like I'm trying to take down the entire transformer—just fuck it up a little. The only last minute item I'll need is gasoline.*

Since arriving in America, Nasim had been collecting the required materials. Whenever he had breaks, he'd travel around Texas and the surrounding states in his old minivan. He'd pick up things here and there in small quantities and store them in one of several storage units. Over time, he pre-positioned everything, from fertilizer and nails, to model rocketry supplies. To throw off anyone conducting a cursory inspection, he'd throw in junk from garage sales.

I don't know why I bother though. As long as I pay the bill on time, they never hassle me. They may have their lists of prohibited items, but it's not like they ever check. My units are a veritable treasure trove of contraband. I've got model rocket engines and fireworks. I remember being so worried about inspections that I'd hide the stuff at the absolute bottom of the box underneath clothes or books. What a waste of time.

At least I'll have plenty of time to plan. The attacks aren't scheduled until summer. Finals should be over with, so I don't have to worry about that. I'll probably have to miss graduation though.

Nasim shook his head. His parents would be disappointed. While they wouldn't have been able to make it, he knew they'd want a picture of him receiving his diploma.

Well, it can't be helped. Sticking around wouldn't be smart. I'll send my diploma straight home just in case something goes wrong. Still, if I'm smart, maybe I'll be back for post-graduate classes after all.

Chapter 15: Test of Faith

While Tahir thought his report detailing the world's oil supply chain was a difficult assignment, fulfilling the professor's inquiries had only gotten harder. Once he'd been introduced to Husam Asad, the questions became increasingly more detailed. Tahir was beginning to regret his decision that night in the desert.

Husam was keenly interested in the Persian Gulf Oil and Refining Company where Tahir worked. He wanted to know if there were any single points of failure? What type of security was in place? He wanted detailed personnel information, phone numbers, addresses. The list of questions went on and on. But gathering information was easy compared to the task at hand.

All I have to do is place the explosive device in the trash bin behind the headquarters building. By the time it goes off, I'll be long gone. No one would suspect me. It's not going to hurt anyone. I'm worrying about nothing.

Tahir had been a PGORC manager at Port Control Headquarters in Dhahran for three years. The office where he worked remotely managed all the oil tankers entering Saudi Arabia's largest petroleum port, Ras Tanura. The port itself was located approximately forty miles north of Dhahran. As Tahir approached the headquarters entrance gate, he continued to reassure himself.

I've come in late like this a hundred times. The guards know me and they've got no reason to suspect anything. Heck, I've had to wake up the guards more than once just to get them to open up the gate, so there's nothing to worry about.

A barbed wire-topped fence surrounded the facility, and the electronic gate was controlled by a key card. Once you passed through the gate, an ID and bag check was notionally required. The entrance was protected by two guards who sat in a small metal and glass enclosure. Looking ahead, Tahir could see the guards playing *mancala*.

Whew, it's Haddad and Kareef. No problem.

"Working late again, Tahir?" asked Haddad.

"Yeah, I just have a little paperwork that I need to get a jump on," Tahir replied.

"They ought to give you a raise," joked Kareef.

"There's a thought. Who's winning tonight? You guys better not be gambling," Tahir said with a wink.

"No, no. Just a friendly game," said Haddad. "You don't need to sic the *mutawa* on us again."

"You know darn well that I had nothing to do with that." Tahir said with a laugh as he signed in.

"I'm not so sure. He showed up right after you left. You probably called him on your cell phone."

"Yeah, right. Have a good one," Tahir said.

Making his way along the access road to his office, Tahir ran through everything Husam had told him. He needed to place the device in one of the large trash bins on the southeast side of the headquarters building. It was just a test to review fire department response times, guard procedures, and so on.

However, Tahir knew there was another purpose for the "exercise." *Husam wants to see if I'll actually do it.*

Dusk was approaching as Tahir parked his car in the main lot. At this time of day, it was relatively deserted. Despite it being a twenty-four-hour facility, most of his co-workers had already headed home. It was a couple of hours before evening prayer when Tahir reached the facility. He decided to get a little work done before planting the device.

Device? Who am I trying to kid? It's a bomb. Regardless of how small it is, it's a bomb. Nonetheless, it would be a lot darker in an hour, so Tahir forced himself up to his office.

While he wasn't thrilled about placing the device so close to his office, Husam hadn't given him much choice. *What's so special about the trash bins on the southeast side of the building anyway?*

As Tahir walked along the sidewalk between two tall, mirrored-glass buildings, the headquarter offices were on his right. He could see the red sun glimmering off the glass as he swiped his key card and headed inside. He took the elevator to the second floor and tried desperately to concentrate on work.

I need to check the repair status on that French tanker. If it's not completed in forty-eight hours, I'll have a cranky tanker captain sitting in the Gulf twiddling his thumbs.

Upon exiting the elevator, Tahir looked around cautiously. The office looked empty as he weaved through the maze of cubicles. However, when he got to his desk, he realized the ridiculousness of it all. *Depending on how big a fire erupts from this small incendiary device, the repair status of the tanker would be a moot issue.*

Tahir booted up his computer and checked his e-mail for updates. After answering a few messages, he sat there staring at his bag. He couldn't concentrate, and his nerves were starting to get the best of him.

I sure hope that Husam doesn't decide to blow this thing early.

Tahir took a deep breath, and then exhaled slowly.

Get a hold of yourself. Don't screw this up. Focus on the big picture.

He tried to concentrate on what Professor Ratib had told him. This was the only way to rid the country of corrupt Western influence. Since the monarchy was not popularly elected, civil disobedience and terrorism were the only way to affect meaningful change. Still, that was a lot easier said than done.

I'm just another cog in the big wheel of corruption, and I've gotten used to it. It's always easier to let someone else pay the price.

Tahir's thoughts were interrupted by an annoying, yet regrettably familiar voice.

"Working late again?" asked Qutaiba Ihsan.

Tahir nearly jumped out of his seat.

"Whoa, didn't mean to scare you."

Qutaiba was the incompetent-boob son of their former director. He served no other purpose than to drink tea, eat donuts, and spy on the lower level managers for his father.

"Yeah . . . I was just coming in to review the repair status on the French tanker. If they can't finish by tomorrow night, we'll need to get another repair crew in there," Tahir replied.

"Huh . . . Oh, yeah. Right. Good thinking."

"What are you doing here this late?" Tahir asked.

"My father wanted me to pick up a copy of that briefing we had the other day. You know, the one that outlined our on-time departure percentages. Do you have a copy?"

"Yeah, just a second. I'll send it to printer one. Okay?"

"Printer one?"

"The printer that's right outside your office," Tahir said slowly while pinching the bridge of his nose.

"Oh . . . Thanks."

Tahir bit his tongue. *Please . . . please just pick up the report and leave. Who's he kidding anyway. He needs a copy of that briefing. Really? He's probably looking at porn on the internet. What a joke!*

"The little green light's blinking, but nothing's happening," whined Qutaiba.

"Just give it a minute."

"Okay, here it comes. Thanks."

Qutaiba collected the papers and headed to the door. "You need help with anything?" he called casually over his shoulder. He didn't wait for Tahir to answer.

Tahir looked up and saw the office door closing. "That'd just be my luck. Qutaiba stays late to help me with some work."

Tahir peered over the edge of his cubicle, then did a quick walk through to see if anyone else was still hanging around. Cautiously, he walked over to the water cooler while surveying the other cubicles. Finally satisfied, he returned to his desk.

He looked anxiously at his bag. *Should I open it part way now? I don't want to be struggling with the zipper as I'm trying to get the thing out. I need to be able to grab it easily and toss it in the dumpster.*

The device itself wasn't much to look at. Just a battery hooked up to what looked like an old beeper. From there, it had some wires going to a small wad of explosives encased in brown paper. It would fit easily in a shoe box.

Putting the bag on his lap, Tahir unzipped the bag part way and nervously practiced reaching in and grabbing the device. He heard a noise and stood up uneasily. The sudden whir of the air-conditioner allayed his fears. Shaking his head from side to side, he leaned against his desk.

Let's get this over with.

Tahir shut down his computer, grabbed his bag, and headed for the door. After scanning the office one more time, he headed out. This time, however, he took the back stairs. As he cracked open the rear exit, he was relieved to see that it had gotten much darker. Also, the wind had picked up a little. *Was that a good thing?* His eyes searched for signs of activity, but all was quiet, so Tahir exited the building and headed over to his target.

A few yards from the dumpster, he stopped and pretended to tie his shoe. Once again he checked for signs of activity. His heart felt like it was going to pound out of his chest.

There's no one here. Hurry the fuck up!

With a renewed sense of purpose, Tahir stood up and quickly covered the remaining distance. He reached in his bag, grabbed the device with his left hand, and dropped it in the dumpster. He could still hear it settling down amongst the garbage as he quickened his pace toward the parking lot.

"Crap," he grumbled audibly. "Where's my car?" Panicked, Tahir stood there, dumbfounded.

Get a hold of yourself. Okay, I just need to get my bearings. Since I came out the back, the car should be . . . there.

Tahir walked hurriedly to his car. He wanted to run, but that would look suspicious. However, if he didn't hurry, he'd miss his rendezvous with Husam. He looked nervously at his watch.

Damn, I've got to hurry. Why's it still so fucking hot?

The wind did little to alleviate the sweat that was now dripping off his forehead, and his legs felt like lead. After taking what seemed like an eternity to reach his car, Tahir drove nervously back to the entrance. As he approached the gate, he could see that the guards were still playing mancala. Tahir waved.

"Leaving already?" chided Haddad.

"I'm late for evening prayers," Tahir said as he signed out. "You guys have a good night."

Tahir breathed a sigh of relief as the gate faded in his rear view mirror. He promptly drove over to the mosque where Husam would be waiting.

I'll attend evening prayers just like always. Husam will kneel next to me. Since I planted the device successfully, I'll pass Husam a small scrap of paper with a plus sign written on it.

A minus sign would have indicated a problem. In that case, a subsequent meeting was scheduled for midnight at the King Khalid off-ramp. Tahir didn't want to attend that meeting.

"Come on, I can make it," he said glancing at the dashboard clock.

The mosque was a fifteen-minute drive from work. Tahir's heart pounded nervously as he pulled down a cross street to park. After grabbing his prayer rug from the back seat, Tahir scribbled a plus sign on a small scrap of paper. He unrolled the rug halfway, placed the scrap of paper inside, and rolled it back up tightly.

Walking up to the mosque, he could tell that it was going to be crowded. Looking around anxiously, Tahir scanned the throng of people. *How is Husam going to find me? Has he been following me this whole time, or is he just waiting by the mosque somewhere?*

The mosque wasn't overly extravagant, but it was relatively new. Built in the late 1980s, as the city grew in support of the burgeoning refineries, the white stucco building was adorned with two tall minarets at one end. The arched entryway was crowded. Upon reaching the door, Tahir felt a slight tug on his sleeve. Tahir looked over his shoulder and saw Husam.

Unlike Professor Ratib, who looked like he'd blow away in a strong wind, Husam Asad was tall and muscular, and his skin was worn and leathery from the elements. It was Husam's face and eyes that gave Tahir pause. Tahir had never seen a smile cross the man's lips. Husam always wore a stony expression that offered little insight into his true intentions.

After passing through the arched doorway, the crowd of worshipers entered the mosque and dispersed across the large white marble floor. Tahir turned left and started a new row purposefully rolling out his prayer rug close to the wall. Husam rolled out his prayer rug, if you could call it that, on Tahir's right.

The old rug was practically worn through and sand outlined the floor where Husam had placed it down. Having grabbed the small scrap of paper as he rolled out his rug, Tahir now placed it on the floor between himself and Husam. Kneeling down to pray, Husam grabbed the paper and stuck it in his shoe without even looking at it. Neither spoke as the Imam recited the evening prayer.

Husam left quickly following the end of the service, but Tahir stayed behind to reflect on the evening's events. While he'd initially been excited about the challenge that Professor Ratib had outlined for them that night in the desert, he was beginning to have second thoughts. In the back of his mind, he couldn't help but wonder if his friend Dema's overdose was truly an accident. While the two had grown apart over the years, he couldn't imagine Dema using drugs.

Had he really changed that much? They found drugs in his house too. Could someone like Husam have planted them? Did Professor Ratib truly understand what he had gotten them involved in?

As the questions continued to echo in his mind, Tahir prayed for Dema and for his family. They had been disgraced by the news. Then, resolutely, Tahir rolled up his prayer rug and walked back to his car.

You're just soft and weak. All talk and no action. Don't let self-doubt keep you from serving Allah.

Chapter 16: New Assignment

"A fire in a dumpster knocks out comms to port control. Seriously? What are the odds?" cursed Basim Dabir. He had firemen milling about, interviews with the port authority, incident reports, damage assessments—whenever something like this happened he was buried in paperwork for weeks.

"Some idiot throws a lit cigarette into a dumpster, and now I've got the SAID calling me," Basim grumbled as he dialed the phone. "Hello? This is Basim Dabir. Yes, I'm returning Chief Hamal's call."

"Just a moment please."

Several years ago a refinery fire would have been an internal PGORC matter. Now, the Ministry of the Interior saw a terrorist behind every sand dune. Basim imagined that the SAID chief had another stack of forms for him to fill out.

Finally, there was an answer. "Hello, Chief Hamal speaking."

"This is Basim Dabir from PGORC port control. I must say I was surprised to get your message. I mean, this was just a small fire. I can't imagine why the SAID would even be interested in this."

"Well, it did knock out your communications for four or five hours, and delayed the departure of several tons of crude oil. When something like that happens, more often than not we're going to get involved."

"I've already discussed this incident with the fire department, internal security, and the port authority. How many times do I have to keep answering the same questions?" argued Basim.

"I assure you that the detective I assign to this incident will review all that information prior to contacting you. Now, he may ask you to clarify certain details, but we will make every effort to ensure that we are not simply going over the same old ground."

"Wonderful," Basim answered.

"Once I check my detectives' workloads, I'll assign someone to conduct our investigation, and we'll be out of your hair. All right?" asked Chief Hamal.

"Fine," answered Basim, finally resigned to the fact that there was nothing he could do to change Chief Hamal's mind.

"Should I have my detective call you directly?"

"Sure."

"Okay, you'll hear from us no later than tomorrow," the chief concluded.

Exasperated, Basim slammed the phone down and stared helplessly at the pile of paperwork on his desk.

#

Actually, Chief Hamal didn't need to check the workload of his detectives, he already knew whom he would assign. Detective Al-Faruq was the man for the job. A former army sergeant, Al-Faruq had been discharged after his squad encountered an IED. While he'd been medically red flagged by the army, Al-Faruq had passed his SAID physical with flying colors.

If Basim thinks he's buried in paperwork now, wait until Al-Faruq digs into this. He's nothing if not thorough. Meticulous is a more apt way to describe him. If anyone can determine what caused that fire, it's Al-Faruq. Plus, it'll keep him out of my hair for a while.

Chief Hamal got up from his desk, stuck his head out his office door, and called for Detective Al-Faruq.

"Close the door please," Chief Hamal said as Al-Faruq entered. "I've got a new assignment for you. There was a fire over at PGORC headquarters. While the fire department feels it was an accident, the brass wants to make sure their investigators didn't miss anything."

"So the fire department's assessment is that the fire was an accident, but SAID headquarters feels that it's arson," Al-Faruq reiterated skeptically. "If they already know the answer, why do I need to bother investigating?"

"Al-Faruq, I know you're still upset about the Utbah raid, but you've got to let it go," Chief Hamal said, shaking his head.

"The raid was compromised. We have a leak. Doesn't that bother you?" Al-Faruq asked.

"Headquarters is taking the lead on that," the chief replied.

"What happened to all the evidence we recovered?" Al-Faruq asked pointedly.

"It's under review. Yaman Utbah's in jail. What more do you want? Yaman Utbah's a high-profile target. These things take time. Now, forget Yaman and get to work. You're my best investigator. Investigate the fires and compile your report."

"And then what?"

"As long as you haven't lost your objectivity, I'll submit it up the chain. I've talked with Chief Adnan from the Dhahran fire department, and he's assured me that his department will cooperate. Okay?"

Al-Faruq nodded.

"Your primary point of contact at the PGORC facility is Basim Dabir. His contact information is in the file," Chief Hamal said as he pushed the case file across his desk.

"Yes sir," Al-Faruq answered.

#

Al-Faruq took the case file and headed back to his desk. Despite Chief Hamal's assurances, he knew this was a shit assignment. The fire department certainly wouldn't want him to find anything contrary to their official assessment. Nonetheless, Al-Faruq opened the case file and started reading.

Unlike most of the desks around the office, which were cluttered with wrappers and debris from the local bakery, Al-Faruq's desk was immaculate. His desktop calendar clearly delineated any and all appointments, while a more detailed description of the current day's appointments was displayed on a printout hanging from his cubicle wall. On the right side of his desk, a file holder neatly separated his open case files. His pens and pencils were in two separate containers and were placed just above his desk calendar. When he wasn't carrying it, his sidearm was located in the top right drawer, while his ammunition was located in the bottom right drawer.

Despite the occasional jeers from co-workers, Al-Faruq saw no point in letting his workspace devolve into a pigsty. While his counterparts could easily waste thirty minutes filing through the mound of debris on their desks in search of a particular piece of information, Al-Faruq had no such problems. He needn't worry about misplaced notes or missed appointments. Everything he needed was right at his fingertips.

Upon completing a short cover sheet outlining his new assignment, Al-Faruq picked up the phone to call Chief Adnan at the fire department. "Might as well get this over with," he said as the dial tone buzzed in his ear. Punching in the number, Al-Faruq tried to clear the negative thoughts from his mind. "I've had worse assignments."

"Chief Adnan," grouched the voice on the other end of the line.

"Good morning, sir. This is Detective Al-Faruq over at—"

"So, you're my SAID-appointed guardian angel on this PGORC fire, eh?" Chief Adnan interrupted.

"Yes, sir," Al-Faruq answered, rolling his eyes.

"If you ask me, this was just a case of bad luck. The dumpster that caught fire was located right beneath the conduit where their primary comms were routed. Nothing sinister."

"Hmmm, okay. Look, Chief Adnan," Al-Faruq said while rubbing his temple with his free hand. "I know you're busy, so if someone in your department could just fax over the incident report, I'll get out of your hair."

"Oh? Sure, we'll get that right over to you."

"I'll look over the report, talk with the PGORC officials, and then go over everything with someone from your office . . . say, tomorrow afternoon?"

"Ahhh . . . All right."

"How does two p.m. tomorrow sound," Al-Faruq asked, pushing for a specific time.

"Fine," Chief Adnan replied irritably.

"That sounds great. Thank you very much for your—" Chief Adnan had already hung up. Al-Faruq stared up at the ceiling. "Never a dull moment."

Chapter 17: The Investigation

As Detective Al-Faruq parked in front of the PGORC facility the next morning, he was still less than thrilled about his assignment. *When will the SAID brass learn to leave well enough alone? They're always sticking their noses in where they shouldn't.*

After dropping a few coins in a beggar woman's cup, Al-Faruq crossed the street toward the security gate. The woman eyed him curiously.

In front of the gate, a stout man with a finely trimmed mustache and beard was pacing back and forth. "Basim Dabir?" Al-Faruq asked, smiling when he reached the other side.

"Yes," Basim replied before shaking Al-Faruq's hand. "Let's head over to my office for some tea."

"Fair enough," Al-Faruq consented reluctantly. While Detective Al-Faruq would have much rather gotten started, he realized the formality of tea and small talk was probably unavoidable. Sometimes, he conceded, it actually proved insightful. As they passed through security on their way to Basim's office, however, he couldn't help but start in on business.

"How long do you keep copies of the sign-in log on file?" he asked the guard as Basim signed him in.

"Uh . . . six months," answered Haddad warily. He moved from his slouched position and sat up straight.

"Hmmm . . . " Al-Faruq acknowledged as his eyes scanned the guard office.

"There'll be time for that later," Basim stated while motioning Detective Al-Faruq to the door. Once outside, Basim pointed at a small, white, Nissan pickup. "We'll take this over to the headquarters building. Hop in," he encouraged. "It's a ways out there. We don't want to hoof it at this time of day."

As they drove down the access road to the port control buildings, Basim engaged in the usual small talk that Al-Faruq disdained. "So, how long have you been a detective?"

"I've been on the force for two years," Al-Faruq answered.

"What did you do before that?"

"I was in the military."

"Oh? For how long?"

"Four years."

"Wow, what made you decide to give it up?"

"Well, after I had a run-in with an IED, the military didn't need me anymore."

"Didn't need you anymore, eh? There's got to be more to the story than that."

"Not really," Al-Faruq answered quietly.

"I guess that happens sometimes," Basim said.

"So, are dumpster fires a common occurrence around here," Al-Faruq asked, attempting to change the subject.

"I wouldn't say common, but they happen from time to time," Basim answered.

"Do your security personnel conduct patrols out here?" Al-Faruq asked as he pulled out a small notebook.

"Well, sure," Basim answered, "but given the amount of heavy equipment in use, we try to limit patrols to off-hours. It takes quite a few people to keep everything moving, and it's not safe having extraneous personnel milling about. Plus, the constant presence of security personnel would unnerve many of the TCNs."

Detective Al-Faruq nodded as he jotted down the details in his notebook. "So, you employ a lot of third-country nationals. Have you had any labor problems?"

"Nothing out of the ordinary."

"Well, what's ordinary?"

"We had a couple of people on report last month due to tardiness. One of the crane operators was reprimanded for not wearing his hard hat. Little stuff like that. Nobody's been fired recently or had their pay docked."

"Hmmm. Okay. I'll need copies of the sign-in logs for the week prior to the fire. Also, I'd like to look at the vacation schedules, a list of anyone who'd been sick or injured prior to the fire, and a list of the individuals who'd been reprimanded in close proximity to when the fire occurred."

"Whoa, hold on. Let's get up to my office first, so I can write this all down," said Basim as he parked.

As they walked along the sidewalk next to Port Control Headquarters, Al-Faruq surveyed his surroundings. While they had passed a number of more industrial looking structures on their way there, the port control office building would look at home in downtown Riyadh. The mirrored windows reflected the green, well-kept grounds. Rounding the corner of the building, Al-Faruq saw a portion of the wall that was stained with soot. It reached eight to ten feet above the top of the dumpster.

"This is where the fire occurred," Basim said as they went by. "Not much damage, but the conduit just above the dumpster houses our comms. I guess the heat from the fire melted the fiber optic cables. Caused havoc with the tanker schedule."

"So, you replaced the dumpster?" Al-Faruq asked looking at the brightly colored dumpster in front of him.

"Yeah. The other one was pretty burnt up, so our trash contractor swapped it out for a new one," Basim answered. Detective Al-Faruq shook his head.

Up a little farther, Basim led the detective up a small set of stairs to the rear entrance. "We'll go through here and take the elevator up to the main office," Basim said as he swiped his key card.

Al-Faruq noticed a security camera above the rear entrance. "How long do they keep the footage for the security cameras?" Al-Faruq asked, pointing at the camera.

"I'm not sure," Basim answered, realizing this was going to take a lot longer than he'd anticipated.

They took the elevator up to Basim's office in silence. Once the doors opened, Detective Al-Faruq followed Basim through a maze of cubicles. Al-Faruq shivered slightly as they entered the supercooled, air-conditioned office.

"It's cold in here."

"We're using computers for practically everything nowadays, so we have to keep the office clean and cool," Basim said as he opened the door to his office. "Have a seat. I'll go get us some tea."

Al-Faruq took a seat in a black swivel chair. He watched Basim through the clear glass office door. On his way to get tea, Basim stopped to talk to one of his co-workers.

"Why does that guy look familiar?" Al-Faruq mumbled.

A young man in his mid to late twenties was talking insistently to Basim. Then, after listening to Basim's response, he nodded his head and returned hurriedly to his desk.

Agghh, where have I seen that guy before? It's going to bother me the rest of the day if I can't remember.

When Basim disappeared from view, Al-Faruq turned his attention to Basim's office. While not very large, the office had personality. The lightly stained sandalwood desk looked somewhat out of place given that gray cubicle walls and black plastic desks dominated the rest of the office. The desk was cluttered, but not totally devoid of organization. The sticky notes that clung to the sides of the computer monitor contained what Al-Faruq assumed were often used phone numbers. The beige walls were covered with family pictures: a trip to the dunes, sandcastles at the beach, and such.

The slight creak of the door signaled Basim's return, as he backed through the door with a small tea set in his hands. "Sorry to keep you waiting."

"Well, it looked like work intervened for a moment there," Al-Faruq answered.

"Yeah, Tahir cornered me. I guess an equipment malfunction delayed the departure of one of our tankers, so it backed up the schedule. Nothing we can't handle," Basim said as he set down the tea on his desk and poured a small cup for the detective and himself. "Here you go."

"Thank you," Al-Faruq responded politely. While he'd grown more patient as an adult, the pace of Saudi culture still grated on him. Nonetheless, he'd give it a shot. "Those your kids?" Al-Faruq said, gesturing at the pictures on the wall.

"Yeah, two kids. Adiba and Zakiy. They're twelve and ten. We went out to the dunes a few weeks ago to try out our new ATV. The kids had a blast. The beach pictures are from our vacation in Egypt. The Mediterranean is just beautiful. How about you? Do you have any children?"

"No," Al-Faruq replied. After taking another sip of tea, he got down to business and opened his notebook. "What kind of waste is disposed of in that back dumpster we looked at?"

"Just stuff from the office, I guess," Basim answered struggling to hide his dismay. "We have a janitorial service that comes through every night and cleans up. Actually, one of their crew members reported the fire."

"How often are the dumpsters emptied?" Al-Faruq continued.

"Twice a week, every Monday and Thursday morning."

"Is pretty much anything and everything thrown into these bins, or do you have special arrangements for hazardous materials?"

"We obviously have materials that require special handling for disposal."

"I'll need a list of those materials."

"Okay, I can run off a copy for you," Basim answered while searching his desk for a pen.

"Do you have any internal documentation related to the fire?"

"Yes, of course."

"I'll need copies of that as well."

"Ah . . . okay," stammered Basim, somewhat taken aback by Al-Faruq's rapid-fire questioning.

"No threats of any kind precipitated the fires. Correct?"

"That's correct."

"And you said there have been no recent labor problems or disputes?"

"That's right."

"And, no one's been fired, reprimanded, or had their pay docked recently?"

"Well, none of our core or skilled workers have been let go, but we have a pretty high turnover in some of the unskilled positions."

"Do you conduct any kind of background checks prior to filling these, unskilled, positions?"

"Ah, no. Those positions are generally contracted out to a placement firm."

"Does the placement firm do background checks?

"I . . . I suppose so, but I don't know for sure."

"What placement firm do you use?"

"There are a couple of different ones. I'll get you their names along with contact information." The phone on his desk started ringing. "Just a second," Basim said. "Basim Dabir. What! You've got to be kidding. Well, I'm kind of in the middle of something. Can't it wait?" Basim rolled his eyes agitatedly as he fumbled through the papers on his desk. "Okay! Give me ten minutes and I'll be there. I said, I'll be there in ten minutes!" Basim reiterated with irritation. "I'm so sorry about this Detective Al-Faruq, but I'm afraid we're going to have to cut our meeting short."

"I'm sorry to hear that," Al-Faruq said, doing his best to hide his irritation.

"Give me a minute, and I'll get someone from our security staff to provide you with all the information that you've requested and escort you back to the gate."

"Thank you."

"One moment," Basim said as he dialed the phone. "Hey, Gamali. This is Basim. I have Detective Al-Faruq here in my office. He's investigating the fire. I've been called into a meeting, so I need you to escort him back to the security office and provide him copies of the information that he's requested." Basim paused. "Copies of the sign-in logs prior to the fires, copies of our incident reports, et cetera," Basim answered. "Look, I don't have time to discuss this," Basim said as he turned his chair away from Al-Faruq. "Just get over here now and take care of it. Do you understand me? Outside my office in five minutes."

Basim stood up and apologized. "Once again, I'm sorry about this Detective Al-Faruq. Gamali Kareef will escort you back and get you the information that you need. If you have any problems or have any additional questions, please don't hesitate to call me."

"I'll review what I have," Al-Faruq replied, "but we'll probably need to set up another time to go over everything."

"All right. How about Monday morning?" asked Basim as he looked at his calendar.

"Same time?" Al-Faruq asked.

"That'll work," Basim answered as he scribbled the appointment down on his calendar. "Let's head outside."

Once again, they weaved their way through the office cubicles to the exit. The two said little as they walked out to the parking lot. After several uncomfortable minutes during which Basim checked his watch every thirty seconds, Gamali finally arrived driving a small two-man electric car. He looked less than pleased. Basim introduced him to Al-Faruq.

"Detective Al-Faruq, this is Gamali Kareef. He'll take you back to the security office and get you what you need."

Al-Faruq nodded politely in Gamali's direction, but got no reaction.

"Thank you for coming," Basim said, shaking the detective's hand. "Now, I must be going. I'm already late for the crisis du jour."

Detective Al-Faruq climbed into the car with Gamali. He was a short, squat man with a bushy mustache and overall disheveled appearance. From the looks of his security guard uniform, Basim may have interrupted Gamali's nap. Unlike the drive out, the return trip was significantly quieter. While Al-Faruq could do without the small talk, it was never fun to be somewhere you're not wanted. He waited until they were close to the security office before outlining the information he needed. Gamali acknowledged his request with little more than a grunt.

Once inside the office, Gamali grudgingly started collecting the information. Al-Faruq could tell it was going to take a while, and looked out the window tiredly. *Where have I seen that young man before? I could swear it was down at the precinct sometime. Basim called him Tahir. I'll have to watch for that name on the roster and sign-in logs.*

Al-Faruq took out his notebook and reviewed his notes. Aside from knocking out their communications, the fire had caused little damage. Therefore, the fire chief saw little point in investigating the incident further. If he read the fire department's report correctly, it didn't look like they even tested for explosive residue. Al-Faruq tapped his pen against his lips.

I can't believe they already removed the dumpster. Maybe I could convince Chief Adnan to test the residue that's on the building. How hot would the fire have to be in order to melt the fiber optic cables?

It took Gamali over an hour to compile even half of what Al-Faruq had requested, and the squat guard grumbled practically nonstop the entire time. With midday prayers less than fifteen minutes away, Al-Faruq decided to wrap things up. Religious or not, he had the distinct feeling that neither Gamali nor any of the other security personnel would lift a finger to help him during prayer time.

I might as well gather up what he's got and head back to the precinct. It's not everything, but it's enough to get started.

"Thank you for very much for your help," Al-Faruq said. "Oh, I noticed a security camera on the rear entrance of the port control building. Would I be able to set up an appointment to go over the footage from the night of the fire?"

"I'll have to check with my supervisor, but he's on break," Gamali responded. "You're wasting your time if you ask me. We may not have the finest security force in the world, but we're not going to just let someone walk in here with a bomb."

Turning away, Detective Al-Faruq rolled his eyes. "Thank you for your time," he said as he headed out the door. *Not the finest, eh? No kidding. While I've been waiting, several people have walked through the Entry Control Point with bags, and the guards didn't search a single one of them. What a joke.*

Chapter 18: Morning Swim

The glow from the rising sun grew steadily brighter as it reflected off the blue waters of the Persian Gulf. A stately yacht dubbed the *Amirah*, or Princess, rocked rhythmically with the morning waves. On deck, two men dressed in white *thobes* with red-checkered *ghutras* sat topside, their hands greedily clutching steaming cups of hot tea in the brisk morning air. One chewed on a cigarette. While they had cast fishing lines over the port-side bow, they paid them little attention.

Fidgety and stiff, the duo seemed out of place amidst such elegant surroundings, and the pristine condition of the *Amirah* only made their rough edges more noticeable. Nonetheless, their appearance, albeit odd, was less than threatening. To discount this duo, however, would be a mistake. For their appearance belied what was happening under the waves that lapped against the *Amirah's* spotless hull.

#

While Raja Ubaydi usually enjoyed scuba diving, today he was a nervous wreck. The sunlight filtering down from the surface above did little to calm his fears as he prepared to activate the mines. Even though Raja was an experienced diver, he had never done anything like this, and he was not overly confident in his counterpart's expertise. Despite what the average person might think, explosives and water could be a dangerous mix. Diving could be unpredictable enough without having to deal with this crap. He breathed a sigh of relief after he activated each mine, thankful it hadn't blown up in his face.

It didn't help that during the trip here, Latif and Jasim had disposed of what looked to be a body. On the first night of their trip, Raja was awakened by the sound of footsteps out on the deck. As he had slipped out of bed and peered through the cabin blinds, he could see Latif and Jasim dragging something or someone along the deck. It was wrapped in a large rug, and the rug was tied down with diving weights. The two had trouble lifting the whole mess over the side. With the sound of the splash resonating in his ears, Raja had forced himself back to bed. Maybe now he knew why the one cabin door had been locked since his arrival.

The second night of the trip didn't afford him much sleep either, as he obsessed about everything Jasim had outlined for him earlier that day. "Certain aspects of the mines are rather ingenious," Jasim explained, with a cigarette dangling from his lips. "But the mines can't be activated until after they've been deployed, and they have to be powered up manually in a series."

Raja could read between the lines. *It's not that the mines can't be powered up before being deployed. Rather, they're afraid that the mines might blow up while they're deploying them. I guess that's where I come in.*

Jasim and Latif would deploy the mines just before sunrise and weigh anchor at a sandbar approximately 200 to 250 meters away from the drop-off point. Raja would follow a tether out to the mine cluster. Then, he'd secure the mine anchors, check their depth, and activate the mines.

"The reason for the complicated activation process is to ensure that we don't waste all ten mines on a single target," Jasim said. "Initially, only one of the ten mines will be armed while the rest will be in 'standby' mode. Once the primary mine is triggered, it will send a signal arming the next mine in the series and so on."

"Aren't the other nine mines going to go off when the initial one explodes?" Raja asked.

"No," Jasim explained. "The initial charge, which is triggered by a proximity fuse, simply propels a secondary charge upwards to the target. Instead of exploding on impact, the secondary charge attaches itself to the ship and detonates only when the ship has reached a specific depth. Regardless of whether the initial charge is triggered by a ship traveling to or from the port, the secondary charge shouldn't explode until the ship is well out to sea. This will make it very difficult for anyone investigating the incident to determine what caused the explosion, where it originated, or how to guard against future attacks."

As Raja completed his final checks, he flexed his fingers, which were growing stiff and weary in the cold water. *Couldn't this have waited until summer? Why now? Just concentrate–get this done and get out of here.*

Okay, the primary mine is armed and active. He kicked over to the next mine in the series. *All right, this one's active and in standby mode.* It took Raja another five minutes to complete his final checks, but it seemed like forever. *Okay. The communication link between the mines looks good, and they're all receiving a signal. I'm done.*

Raja was preparing to leave when something caught his eye. On one of the mines was a green, white, and red symbol. He squinted through his mask. *Geez, is that an Iranian flag?* He considered scratching it off with his diving knife but then thought better of it. *With my luck, the damn thing would probably blow up in my face. I've completed all my checks. It's time to get the hell out of here.* After checking his air gauge for what seemed like the hundredth time, Raja detached the tether from the mine cluster and followed it back to the boat.

The dive had taken him just under an hour. Although he was cold, he wasn't any worse for the wear. Nonetheless, Raja was still apprehensive. This trip was more than he had bargained for. With the sound of his breathing as his only companion, Raja had trouble staying positive. As he slowly followed the tether hand-over-hand, he couldn't help but wonder how it had come to this. While his disdain for the monarchy was high, was this the only way to attack their corruption? Had Professor Ratib told him and his friends the whole story?

Through his work as an accountant, he was quite familiar with how some members of the royal family ran their businesses. While a tight-fisted approach was the norm as far as payroll for laborers was concerned, lavish expenditures were customary for management. Given his knowledge of their finances, he found it increasingly difficult to rationalize their treatment of the laborers that worked for them. Driving to work each morning, he would often see dozens of laborers crammed in the back of pickup trucks on their way to a job site. It just wasn't right—but neither was this.

#

Raja surfaced near the yacht, cautiously approached the stern, and detached the tether. The gentle waves and the orange-pink clouds did little to slow the beating of his heart. While he half expected to be greeted by a harpoon or a gunshot, Latif greeted him with a hearty wave.

"Did you see any fish down there," Latif joked. "We haven't even gotten a nibble since you went down there. You're scaring all the fish away. Everything went okay, yes?"

"Yeah, everything went fine," Raja replied wearily.

"Good!" Latif nodded with satisfaction. "Need any help?"

Raja slipped off his tanks and handed them over to Latif. As Latif lifted the near empty tanks into the boat, Raja took off his fins and climbed up the ladder on to the deck.

"Were the mine anchors tangled up at all?" Latif queried.

"No, but they were huddled too close together. I had to spread them out. Luckily, the mines were a lot lighter than I expected."

"Yes, I thought so too. According to Jasim, they're not designed to sink the target, just fuck it up a little."

"Where is Jasim?" Raja asked worriedly as he pulled off his wetsuit.

"He's making sure no one's sneaking up on us. We don't want the Saudi Coast Guard hassling us about fishing here," Latif said with a wink. "We'll get going soon. Relax. Your work is done. I would've activated the mines myself, but I'm a lousy swimmer. Go wash up. Ihsan left us some steaks in the galley."

Sure enough, when Raja returned topside, he was greeted with a plate of food. He eyed the food suspiciously. Jasim flicked his cigarette overboard and chided him. "If I wanted you dead, I'd shoot you, and I sure wouldn't waste one of the steaks on you first. Besides we've probably got a few more fishing trips coming up before we're through." Both Latif and Jasim laughed heartily as Raja dug into his meal, smiling wryly.

"Wow!" Raja exclaimed. "This is really good. So, who's the chef?"

Jasim grunted and looked over at Latif.

"I'm on Ihsan's kitchen staff," Latif said. "If it wasn't for him, we would've had to bring you out here in a row boat."

"So you cook for Ihsan," Raja said, nodding in approval.

"Ha," scoffed Latif. "The head chef hardly lets me touch the food at all. Primarily, I just slice and dice, but I keep my eyes and ears open. Cooking's not as hard as that prick would have you believe."

Actually, picturing Latif as a chef wasn't that difficult. A pudgy man with soft features and a jovial attitude, Latif Ferran was less than imposing. Despite his worn clothes, he carried himself with a dignity beyond his social status, and he appeared confident and self-assured.

Jasim Saqr, on the other hand, exhibited a much rougher exterior in both personality and mannerisms. Jasim was tall by Arabian standards. With an athletic build and large hands, Jasim looked like a boxer. His facial features did little to discount that thought, with a flat nose and a long scar that ran across his right cheek. He moved around the boat with catlike quickness and stealth. He had startled Raja several times during the trip.

The three men greedily downed their breakfast while the sun began its ascent skyward. Raja was surprised they hadn't left the area immediately after planting the mines, but Jasim and Latif seemed in no hurry.

"The only incriminating evidence of our mission is underwater, eh?" Jasim grinned as he nodded his head toward the water. "Now, we can enjoy ourselves."

Raja looked around. Ihsan's boat was certainly the place to do it. The *Amirah* was over twenty meters long with room for eight guests in four well-furnished staterooms. Due to his anxiety over planting the mines, Raja hadn't really taken in the opulence of his surroundings. The *Amirah* was immaculate both inside and out.

As they finished up breakfast, Raja looked over the crystal white deck. No scuff marks, no rust stains, just a beautiful sheen on all the boat's surfaces. He couldn't imagine how they obtained permission to use it. Why would anyone living this type of lifestyle want to get mixed up in this sort of thing? Maybe it was the same not-so-subtle mix of guilt and coercion that had led him here.

Chapter 19: Agents, Contacts

Agent Steve Jamison didn't know much about his contact, but at least Socrates was punctual. Evidently, the guy was a professor at the local university. Socrates' real name was Mahmud Ratib, but the dossier that Jamison had on file was inadequate at best and alluded to his predecessor's general incompetence.

Nonetheless, as Agent Jamison inspected the man sitting only a couple of tables away at this small downtown café, it wasn't hard to picture the man staring down disapprovingly at his students. Something in the way he treated the waiters. Not quite haughty, but definitely superior. They were beneath him, at least in this man's mind.

I can't put my finger on it, but there's something different about Socrates today. He looks nervous and fidgety. Jamison took a sip of tea and scanned the café. He looked over the other café patrons as well as his contact. *His clothes look normal, he didn't bring any unusual items or packages with him, and the rest of the café floor is clear of any unattended items. He doesn't seem to be avoiding eye contact with anyone in particular.*

Next, Jamison turned his attention to the bustling city street. Although they were inside, the café itself was open to the street. A metal garage-like door enabled the proprietor to close the establishment after hours or during prayer time. In any event, it provided Jamison with a clear view. Outside, there was steady stream of people, but Jamison focused on anyone who was not moving, looking for stationary figures that might be tailing Socrates.

Jamison identified two possibilities. There was a man sitting in a parked car across the street. He had a scar on his face and was smoking a cigarette. Then there was another man looking at magazines in front of a local newsstand. Of the two, the man at the newsstand appeared to be Jamison's best bet. The man seemed particularly interested in something or someone in the café.

Wearing a white *thobe* and *ghutra*, the stocky, athletic man glanced over at the café periodically while sifting through the magazine rack. During the short time that Jamison had observed him, several people had bought papers and moved on while this man browsed. Most newsstand operators would have pushed the man to make a selection, but the stand's proprietor eyed the man warily and didn't engage him in discussion.

Jamison glanced at his watch. *It's about time for Socrates to leave. Does he realize he's being followed? If so, the proper protocol would be to abort the drop and dispose of his newspaper in the trashcan. Your move, Professor.*

Patiently, Jamison peered over his steaming cup of tea. After a couple of minutes, Socrates finished the small pastry he had ordered and paid his bill. Looking slightly unsure of himself, he grabbed his newspaper and headed for the door. Jamison looked on as Socrates dropped the newspaper in the trashcan. *All right, good job. Message received. Now, what's our man at the newsstand going to do?*

Upon seeing Socrates leave the café, the athletic man at the newsstand paid for the newspaper he had just picked up and proceeded in the same direction as Socrates, with the paper tucked under his arm. Jamison got up and paid his bill. *Okay, he's interested in the man, not the information. Let's see what happens next.*

Since he knew Socrates' route, Jamison wasn't in a particular hurry. He strolled slowly out of the café, looking briefly at some rugs displayed by the vendor next door. Jamison noted that the scar-faced man had picked up a passenger and left. After fending off the rug salesman, Jamison proceeded over to the lot where Socrates usually parked his vehicle.

The forty-eight year old agent looked the part of your average businessman. Slightly balding and softer than he liked around the middle, Jamison was nearing the end of his career. He had been assigned to Dhahran, Saudi Arabia, a little over one month ago, after his predecessor had been diagnosed with lung cancer.

The parking lot was several blocks away, and Jamison had little trouble making up the time he had lost on the two men. About seventy-five yards from the lot, he spotted the man from the newsstand. "I see you," Jamison muttered under his breath as he watched the man cross the street.

110

His quarry was leaning against a light post. After checking his watch, the man took the newspaper from under his arm and pretended to read. Socrates exited slowly in his Suburban. The man peered over the top of his newspaper as Socrates passed his position. After checking his watch again, the man walked toward a small silver sedan and got in.

Jamison meandered closer to the parking lot, dodging pedestrians leaving a nearby bus terminal as he went. Despite the crowds, he was able to get close enough to catch the license plate number of the vehicle. Jamison pulled out a small notebook from his pants pocket and copied down the car's tag.

Damn! Just when I'm about to get some real intel from Socrates, this happens. I'll have to get this tag number to my contact at the NIC. See what I'm dealing with. Scared informants aren't much better than dead ones.

Based on their protocols, Socrates was supposed to refrain from contacting Agent Jamison for two weeks. Then they would attempt the drop again at the fallback location. If nothing else, it would give Jamison time to check out this tail.

As the silver car disappeared from sight, Jamison turned to head back to his office. *What did my supervisor say? It's a quiet little outpost. Just my speed. Whatever. Cheer up! This is the most excitement I've had since I got here.*

Chapter 20: Desert Flowers

Azzah Ratib and Kalila Mawiyah had known one another since they were kids. However, over the past several years they had grown further and further apart. Now, both in their early twenties, their outlook on life had taken divergent paths. Azzah, who was twenty-one, viewed her Muslim responsibilities as chains, while the twenty-year-old Kalila considered adherence to established Islamic norms as her religious duty.

While Azzah's verbal jabs had initially seemed like playful commentary on Kalila's acceptance of traditional values, her barbs had become increasingly hurtful. If not for their mothers' friendship, Azzah and Kalila would have had little to do with each other. Yet, here they were, together again, as their mothers sat down for their weekly luncheon at Azzah's home.

"Why don't you two go into the other room and watch TV or something while we catch up," Kalila's mother, Abra, suggested.

"Okay," Kalila replied. Azzah rolled her eyes despondently. As the two slunk off, Abra and Iba began chattering incessantly about the week's events. In the living room, Kalila opened the book she had been reading and curled up on the floor with some throw pillows. "You can watch what you want. I'm going to read."

"Hmpf . . . Fine," replied Azzah as she grabbed the remote and started flipping channels. Azzah settled on an Arabic version of MTV and turned up the volume. As the western music videos with Arabic subtitles blared, Kalila cringed silently. In an effort to elicit a response, Azzah turned up the volume again . . . and again . . . and again.

"What is your problem?" Kalila finally protested.

"What?"

"Do you really need to have the TV that loud?"

"Why? Is it bothering you?"

"You know it is. You only have to see me once a week for a couple of hours. If you can't be nice, you could at least be less antagonistic."

"Wow, that's a big word. I'm sure your future husband will be impressed with your vocabulary," Azzah said.

At least he won't think I'm some whore wannabe. "Can you just please turn it down a little," Kalila pleaded. "I can't believe your mom lets you watch that crap anyway."

"You're such a prude."

"I'm a Muslim. That's not my culture or my heritage," Kalila countered, looking dismissively at the television.

"I'm just seeing what the rest of the world has to offer. The women in these videos are free to be whomever they want. They're not second-class citizens," Azzah argued defiantly.

"I think you're confusing freedom with exploitation. Would you seriously have more self-respect wearing a thong out in public as opposed to a *hijab*?"

"Western women are empowered. They're not subservient dolts."

Kalila looked up from her book. "If you want to talk about empowerment, then we could talk about the upcoming Kuwaiti elections where over 75 percent of eligible women have registered to vote, or the Iraqi parliament that has over forty female members. Not some trashy American video."

"Listen to you, oh Queen of Sheba. At best, you'll become a school teacher helping the monarchy brainwash young girls."

"Hmpf, and what's your life goal? Beheading for adultery?"

"I'll find a way out of this stupid country."

"How? You totally blew off what few educational opportunities you had here. Plus, after that incident between you and that foreign boy, you think your Dad's going to let you go to some college in the West?"

"I can handle my Dad. You'll see. You may be book smart, but you've got a lot to learn. I'll be gone before you even realize how trapped you really are."

The ringtone from Azzah's cell phone saved Kalila from having to continue the conversation. She turned her attention back to her book while Azzah left for the private confines of her room.

#

"Hey . . . Yeah, just a second," Azzah said as she closed her bedroom door. "Sorry, Cala. We've got company here."

"Anyone I know?" Cala asked.

"I doubt it. Just my mom's best friend and her brainwashed daughter, Kalila."

"Is she the one who'd like to wear her *hijab* indoors too?"

"Yeah," Azzah agreed. "She probably should. I swear makeup has never touched that girl's face."

"Would it really make a difference?" Cala asked.

"Ha," Azzah snickered. "You're probably right. What's up?"

"You have any plans for New Year's Eve?" Cala asked.

"Oh yeah, my parents always throw a huge bash," Azzah said sarcastically.

"Well, if you think you can get your butt over here that night, my cousin's invited us to a party at the Regency Hotel in Bahrain."

"Yeah right," Azzah said in disbelief. "How's he going to get us across the border?"

"Come on, this is Cala you're talking to. My cousin and I have royal blood. The border guards aren't going to hassle us. Not unless they want to be manning some post in the Empty Quarter."

"Ring in the new year in Bahrain? I'm so there!"

"You have anything cool to wear?" Cala asked skeptically.

"I can come up with something."

"I know you can come up with something, but I don't want you looking like some Bedouin princess," Cala teased.

"Don't worry. If my attire doesn't meet your royal approval," Azzah said haughtily, "I'll . . . just borrow some of your clothes."

"I don't think so," Cala replied.

"When do I need to be there?" Azzah asked.

"We'll probably leave here around ten or ten-thirty p.m., but you can come and hang out earlier if you'd like."

"All right. I'll let you know for sure next week. Is that cool?"

"Not a problem," Cala answered. "Oh, crap! It's my mom. I gotta go."

"Okay, talk to you later."

Azzah hung up the phone and flopped down on the bed. *New Year's Eve in Bahrain? I can't believe it. I'll never want to come back. Now, there's a thought.* Azzah smiled mischievously, but it faded quickly. Mindlessly, she walked over to her closet and picked through her clothes.

While her encounter with the American serviceman had squelched her father's plans to marry her off, she felt like a prisoner. Isolated and alone, Azzah struggled to be happy. As she pulled out a little black dress that was hidden at the back of her closet, she continued to daydream. *I wonder what it's like to be free. Free to dress how I want. Free to act how I want. It must be wonderful.*

#

"Uhgg," Kalila groaned. Azzah had left the TV blaring. "Why mother continues to drag me over here is beyond me."

Kalila decided that the bench seat by the foyer window would provide a quieter reading spot. Quietly, she tiptoed over to the window so as not to draw attention to herself. After re-arranging the bench seat pillows into a more comfortable position, she adjusted the blinds to provide a view of the street.

"Pretty quiet," she said glumly. There were a handful of parked cars, and a mother playing with her two young daughters in the driveway directly across the street. Covered in black from head to toe, the mother was wearing a traditional *habiya* while her girls wore pretty sundresses with floral prints. "Enjoy it while you can," Kalila said wistfully.

It's not that I don't understand Azzah's frustration. It's just that she takes everything to the extreme. Just because women in other cultures act or dress a certain way doesn't mean that they are role models. Some are, and some aren't. Not all forms of modernization are progress. The kind of women that Azzah idolizes are just plain slutty. You have to be smart enough to look beyond the hype, and Azzah just isn't. She's infatuated with the product, not the reality that such a lifestyle would bring. You can be a modern woman without totally turning your back on your faith.

When her father dropped them off, Kalila had noticed a young man sitting in his car.

Hmmm, is that guy still sitting in his car reading the paper? That's odd. But he was kind of cute. Oh, get real! What kind of guy sits in his car reading the newspaper for two hours? On the other hand, if he's still out there when I leave, maybe I should number him and find out.

In Saudi Arabia, numbering was a method of flirting. It entailed exchanging phone numbers by throwing wadded-up pieces of paper between vehicles.

Ugh, I'm just as bad as Azzah, wanting what I can't have. Besides, the guy could be some kind of freak. Anyway, with my father driving, it's not like I'd be able to really throw it at his car. At best, I could maybe drop it out the window. He probably wouldn't even notice, and then anybody could pick it up. Still, what harm would it be?

While sharia law effectively segregated men and women in the Kingdom of Saudi Arabia, the laws did offer a certain amount of protection in a situation like this, provided your father wasn't psycho.

All he'd have is a phone number. Geez, take a chance once in a while. I mean, how many times have you actually spoken to a guy other than your dad or brother?

Looking around nervously, Kalila crept over to the end table and grabbed a blank sheet of paper from the notepad by the phone. Returning to her perch, she bit her lip thoughtfully as she composed the note.

Too harsh?

Maybe, but if he didn't have a sense of humor about himself, she didn't want to talk to him anyway. As Kalila folded the sheet of paper tightly into a triangle, she peered out the window again at his car. He didn't look as young as she thought. Probably waiting for his wife.

Aghh, I'm already starting to lose my nerve.

"Kalila," her mother called. Kalila jumped at the sound. "Kalila?"

"Yes mother," she replied.

"Oh, there you are," her mother said upon finding her. "It's about time to go. I just called your father. He should be here in a few minutes."

"Okay."

"Where's Azzah?"

"She's in her room. She had a phone call."

"Oh, well make sure you say goodbye," her mother said pleasantly as she returned to the kitchen.

Yeah right. Whatever.

Leaving her spot atop the windowsill, Kalila returned to the living room to retrieve her *habiya*. Hearing her father at the door, she quickly donned the outfit over her clothes. With only her eyes peering out through the opening in the veil, Kalila walked out to the car with her mother, where they both sat in the backseat.

While her mother chattered at her father, Kalila cracked her window. The short note that she had penned was damp from being clutched in her sweaty palm. As her father backed out of the driveway, Kalila raised her hand to her cheek. Hiding the note behind her fingers, she rested her head on her hand. Nervously, she watched the rear view mirror for her father's prying eyes.

"Not too fast," her mother scolded. "There are a lot of kids in this neighborhood."

"Maybe you should drive," her father quipped, knowing all too well that women weren't allowed to drive.

"You just keep an eye out for the kids."

As their vehicle passed the man's car, Kalila slid her hand up and flicked her note out the window. Briefly, their eyes met. The young man had a quizzical look on his face. Kalila quickly looked away feeling like she'd been caught doing something wrong. Careful not to turn around, she watched the side view mirror to see if he'd get out of his car to pick up the note, but the young man's car quickly disappeared from view. Frowning beneath her veil, Kalila sat lost in thought as they continued home.

Chapter 21: Stake Out

Detective Al-Faruq was parked a couple of houses down from his quarry. Even with the air-conditioner going full blast, Al-Faruq's car felt like an oven. It had been a little over a month since his meeting with Basim. While the fire department had initially balked at testing residue from the trash bin fire, Al-Faruq eventually won out, and results of the testing indicated the presence of an incendiary agent.

However, since PGORC used several chemicals that would fit the bill, Chief Adnan argued that the presence of these chemicals indicated nothing more than improper material disposal. Case closed as far as the fire department was concerned. For Al-Faruq, it didn't quite add up. Based on his discussions with Basim, the chemicals in question were used in a different section of the complex, far removed from port control. The chances of those particular chemicals inadvertently finding their way into that dumpster were remote at best, so Al-Faruq continued to dig.

Interestingly enough, the young man that Al-Faruq recognized at Basim's office had been at the precinct just a few months earlier. His name was Tahir Rafiq. Al-Faruq interviewed him while investigating Dema Mundhir's death. At first, Al-Faruq considered it nothing more than a coincidence, but then he was assigned another missing persons case. In this new case, a young man named Rashim Fasil was missing. By the time Al-Faruq found him, he had succumbed to an apparent drug overdose as well.

Upon comparing the case files, Al-Faruq noted that a stack of newsletters had been found in Rashim's apartment. Coincidentally, a similar newsletter had been found in the glove compartment of Dema's vehicle. In both instances, the newsletter was traced back to a college professor named Mahmud Ratib. A quick review of university records showed that both Fasil and Dema had attended Arabian University at the same time and both had taken classes from Professor Ratib.

As Al-Faruq dug deeper, he found that more than a half-dozen of Professor Ratib's former students had recently died from drug overdoses. Hence, Al-Faruq decided to keep an eye on the professor. The way he figured it, the professor was dealing drugs to his students, and Tahir was helping him smuggle the drugs in via the refinery.

It wouldn't be difficult for Tahir to get a bag full of drugs past the security guards that I saw. But Tahir seemed pretty upset by Dema's death. Was he just naïve? Didn't he know that his friend was on the stuff? And what about the fire? Maybe, something spooked him, so he throws the drugs in the dumpster. Then, he starts the fire to dispose of the evidence. I should have had them test for drug residue as opposed to explosives.

"Aghh! I'm missing something," he grumbled. "One thing's for sure though—the professor sure can't afford to live in this neighborhood on his teaching salary alone."

Based on Al-Faruq's research, the professor's house was over 3,000 square feet. A beautiful adobe structure with a large front patio and an arched entryway, professional landscaping, and a three-car garage that housed a Suburban, an SUV, and a luxury sedan. His wife didn't come from money, and she had no job. He had a twenty-something daughter living in the house, but she provided no income either. Where was all the money coming from?

Unfortunately, Al-Faruq's surveillance had turned up nothing. Professor Ratib spent most of his time at the university. Outside of class, the professor spent little, if any, time with his students. Based on the university's mail room records, the professor had received no packages in over a month, and he had not met with Tahir during the time that Al-Faruq had been following him. A review of the professor's phone records turned up little as well.

If he's communicating with his former students, it's got to be through e-mail, but I can't get approval to tap into his e-mail on just a hunch.

Al-Faruq set down his newspaper and picked up the copy of the professor's newsletter he'd brought with him. He read through the newsletter for the umpteenth time.

Nothing particularly earth shattering. Fight the American devil by staying away from Western products. Hmpf. Doesn't exactly practice what he preaches. It's our responsibility to hold

119

the monarchy accountable for following Islam's true path. Okay?
What I really need is his mailing list. Who else besides Rashim and
Dema is on it, have others suffered a similar fate, and if so, why?

Al-Faruq set the newsletter aside. He hated having so many questions and so few answers.

Just then, a white sedan pulled into the driveway. The driver, a man in his late forties or early fifties got out and went to the front door of the professor's house. Al-Faruq recognized the car and looked down at his notes. It was Mr. Mawiyah. He was just there to pick up his wife and daughter. He must have dropped them off earlier. It looked like they visited Iba and Azzah every Wednesday.

As he watched, two women dressed in black exited the house. Al-Faruq chuckled at the sight of a pair of pink tennis shoes peeking out from underneath the young woman's *habiya*. The two women got into the back of the car, and Mr. Mawiyah took his position behind the wheel. As their vehicle approached his, Al-Faruq subconsciously checked the plate number against his notes.

When Al-Faruq looked up, he was surprised to see the young woman's eyes staring right at him. Her hand was resting along the top of her door and the window was cracked. She flipped something out of the window, then quickly averted her eyes as the car drove past.

Al-Faruq watched the triangular-shaped piece of paper fall to the ground and bounce on the pavement. After staring in disbelief as it settled next to his car, he switched his gaze to the rear view mirror. Once the car had disappeared from sight, Al-Faruq turned his attention back to the piece of paper. She obviously dropped it out of the window on purpose, but why? It was probably nothing, just a piece of trash. Nonetheless, sooner or later, his overactive sense of curiosity would require him to check.

Al-Faruq looked down the street and then checked his rear view mirror. In the blistering midday heat, the street was deserted. He couldn't resist seeing what it was, so he opened the car door and stepped out. After glancing again for traffic, Al-Faruq picked up the piece of paper and returned to his car.

After getting situated, Al-Faruq carefully unfolded the scrap of paper. "Did you get stood up or are you just a slow reader? Call or text me at 672-555-3407. K."

"You've got to be kidding me," he said. "Some detective I am. I must stick out like a sore thumb in this neighborhood." After staring up at the ceiling of the car for a moment, Al-Faruq turned his attention back to the professor's house, but he had trouble concentrating.

What would you say to her? Aside from the truth, there isn't much reason for me being out here. Regardless, it's not like there would be any future in it. My parents are dead, and my uncle has no use for me. Who would make the introduction? Given my resources, I couldn't even come up with an appropriate dowry. Her parents would never let me meet her.

For a moment, Al-Faruq just sat and stared at the note. He was stuck in a life with few options. No matter which way he turned, he was facing a dead end. Finally, motion on the street in front of him brought his mind back into focus. He tossed the note onto the car seat.

A white Chevy Suburban pulled into the professor's driveway. Al-Faruq checked the license plate against his notes. It was the professor's brother, taking his sister-in-law and niece out on yet another shopping trip. That would mean the house would be empty for the next three or four hours.

I'll have to get in there and see if I can turn up anything.

As the white Suburban idled in the driveway, Al-Faruq surveyed the neighborhood. All was quiet. Still, given the whole note thing, Al-Faruq decided to find a different parking spot before heading in. There could be some more nosy neighbors out there. Al-Faruq waited to see if Iba and Azzah were indeed headed out. Ten minutes later, the two women, clad in their traditional black *habiyas*, left the house and entered the Suburban. Al-Faruq watched the Suburban drive out of sight, then started his car and moved up the street a block and a half.

After making a quick U-turn and parking, Al-Faruq exited his car and strolled toward the professor's home. Nearing the house, Al-Faruq went over a plan of action in his head. It was a pretty big house, but the professor probably had a study. If he could find that, then maybe he could uncover the distribution list for the professor's newsletter.

Since the professor wasn't a member of the royal family, a search warrant wasn't really necessary. Al-Faruq walked up the front steps and turned the knob on the front door. It was open. Given that you could lose a hand or even your head, depending on the offense, crime was not much of a factor in neighborhoods like this, and few people bothered locking their doors.

Al-Faruq closed the front door and surveyed the home's layout. The interior was well furnished. A large silk rug covered the wood floor in the foyer. Dozens of large pillows framed the rug, which backed up to a gas fireplace. To his right, stairs led up to the second floor, while in front of him a couple of steps would take him down into the kitchen.

Al-Faruq stepped down into the kitchen. A spacious living room was on his right. It contained a large sectional couch and big screen television. Beyond the living room was a short hallway with two doors. Did one of those doors lead to a study? He tried the first door. It was a bathroom.

What's behind door number two? Jackpot!

The second room contained a large office desk and computer. Fully stocked bookcases lined two sides of the room. Al-Faruq moved around the desk and situated himself in front of the computer. It was on. Taking the mouse, he started poking around. Nothing looked promising in the documents folder, so Al-Faruq scanned the other folders.

"There you are," he whispered confidently.

He saw a folder titled, "NEWSLETTER." He clicked on it. Within the folder, sub-folders had been created for each year. Al-Faruq opened the current year folder and scanned the file names. There was a file for each month, but where were the recipients?

He opened up the November newsletter, and scanned the first page. He paged down to the second page. Then, he noticed from the document statistics that the newsletter was eight pages long. The newsletters he had in evidence were only two pages long. Al-

Faruq hit the page down key several more times, and there they were. The recipients' addresses were embedded in the file.

All right, that was easy. Just plug in the flash drive, click save, and I'll be good to go. Fishing the flash drive from his pocket, he dropped it on the floor. After kneeling down to retrieve it, he inserted the flash drive and waited for the computer to recognize it. Al-Faruq was copying the files over when he heard a sound. The garage door was opening.

Al-Faruq groaned. Frantically, he closed all the programs that he had opened. His eyes darted back and forth between the flashing green light on the flash drive and the door to the garage. There would be no time to eject the flash drive properly. Angrily, he yanked the drive from the USB port and scrambled to the back door. It was locked. He fumbled open the door and stumbled out into the backyard.

Al-Faruq crept cautiously toward the front of the house. Glancing inside the garage, he saw the professor's car. *What's the professor doing here? Figures, the day I decide to go inside and look around, he comes home for lunch.*

Al-Faruq was kicking himself all the way back to his car. *Please tell me I got something. Damn it! Who knows when I'll get another chance? The professor's liable to notice that someone was on his computer. He could delete the files or set up some kind of password protection. I'm no hacker. Why did he have to come home today?*

Al-Faruq squeezed the flash drive tightly in his hand. "You got it," he whispered. "Don't worry. You got it."

Chapter 22: Studying for Finals

Nasim Talib sat at his computer studying intently. However, instead of studying for the test that he had the next day, he was reviewing a report that a PEF recruit had dropped off during orientation. It shouldn't have taken Nasim by surprise, but it did. Nasim had known about the visit for months and had planned to show the recruit around campus, but he wasn't expecting the recruit to hand him a flash drive.

What had the kid said? Something like, I was told that this would help you finish your thesis. And I just give the poor guy a blank stare. Like, what the heck are you talking about? Duh, I can only imagine what he'll report back. Well, I guess I'll have to show them through my actions rather than words.

Nasim continued reading the report. Periodically, he'd consult the road atlas that was open on his lap. He'd have to hit a target and move quickly. By utilizing remote detonators, he'd be able to get some distance between himself and the targets, but his chances of getting caught would increase significantly as time and targets went by.

He studied the road atlas intently. He needed to stay flexible and not be a slave to some predetermined route. At each step along the way, he needed options, target options, and places where he could lay low. As he mentally plotted potential routes, he thought about some of the places he'd stayed during his U.S. travels.

Hotels were out. He'd be better off sleeping in the van at a KOA or a full service rest stop. Nasim traced his finger along one route. He noted its proximity to storage units where he had stationed supplies. He could fill up on gasoline pretty much anywhere, but he couldn't remember how many detonators he had.

A knock on the door startled him. "Just a minute," Nasim yelled. Quickly, he closed the PEF report and threw the road atlas down on the floor. Then, he stumbled over a couple of pizza boxes on his way to the door. "Dammit Nathan!" he cursed at his absent roommate. "Why doesn't he ever pick up his shit. I'm coming." Finally, he reached the door and opened it to reveal Nathan's on-again off-again girlfriend, Nicole Stacey.

"I'm so sorry, Nasim," Nicole said as she stepped inside. "Is Nathan here?"

"No, I thought he went to class for once," Nasim answered.

"Well, if he did, I sure didn't see him there," Nicole said. "He needs to pass that class in order to graduate. I swear it's almost like he's failing on purpose."

Nasim just shrugged and watched helplessly as Nicole plopped herself down on the couch, grabbed the remote, and turned on the TV. Nasim genuinely liked Nicole, but he couldn't figure her out. How could this smart, thoughtful, beautiful girl be with such a loser. It didn't make sense. Resigned to the fact that she wanted to talk or just hang out for a while, Nasim closed the door and slowly headed back over to the computer.

"Do you think he's an alcoholic?" Nicole asked.

"Who?" Nasim asked, pretending he didn't know.

"Nathan, you numbskull."

"Uh, I don't know," Nasim answered. He tried to search for the right words. "Probably," he continued when the silence grew awkward. "He definitely has been drinking a lot lately, but I don't know if that qualifies him as an alcoholic or just your average undergrad."

"Ha," Nicole laughed. "I suppose it seems like everyone drinks a lot compared to you."

"I have a beer now and then," Nasim retorted. "Just not for breakfast."

"Yeah right! I can't even remember the last time I saw you with a beer in your hand. Plus, isn't it against your religion?"

"Well you're a Christian, aren't you? You're not always on top of those Ten Commandments, either."

"Touché, Nasim, I guess you've got me there." After pausing for a moment, she smiled at Nasim and said, "I really know how to pick them."

"What do you mean?"

"Well, it just seems hard for me to find a nice guy. You know?"

"Umm, not really," Nasim responded.

"So, you don't have any problems meeting nice girls?"

"No . . . I mean, yes," he stammered. "It's just a lot different in my culture. Marriages are arranged. It's not about going out and finding someone. It's difficult to explain. It's just a lot different."

Nicole tossed the remote onto the cushion next to her and got up to see what Nasim was doing. She walked over to Nasim and put her hands on his shoulders. Then, she noticed the road atlas that was lying on the floor. "Oooo, you planning a trip?" she asked.

"Oh, I usually bum around during the summer, sightseeing."

"Like where?"

"I've been to the Alamo, the Grand Canyon, the Golden Gate Bridge. Tourist stuff. Places your parents probably dragged you to as a kid."

"Hmmm, sounds like fun. You need any company?" she asked.

"Ha, it's probably not what you'd consider a vacation. It's pretty low budget. I usually end up sleeping in the van."

"That doesn't sound all bad. I think it'd be nice to get away and travel," Nicole said softly as she slid her hands down from Nasim's shoulders to his chest. "Of course, it'd be more fun if I had a nice guy with me," she whispered in his ear.

Fear and excitement gripped Nasim. They'd kissed once. Nasim remembered it as he breathed in the smell of her hair. It was the night Osama bin Laden was killed. The whole campus had erupted into one big party. To Nasim, it seemed strange, given that few of the students had made any real sacrifices due to 9/11 or the wars in Iraq and Afghanistan. Nonetheless, the party raged on. Deciding it was best to lay low, Nasim stayed inside, but just after midnight, Nicole came in, carrying an obviously drunk Nathan. It wasn't the most pleasant of exchanges.

#

"Hey Nasim, the Marines got your boy Osama," Nathan said with a sneer.

"Nathan, get real. You are such an ass," Nicole retorted.

"It's okay," Nasim said to Nicole.

"Hey, that's just like Osama. I heard one of his bitches tried to protect him."

"Ughhh," Nicole rolled her eyes. "Nasim, can you please help me get him into bed?"

"Sure thing," Nasim nodded as he grabbed Nathan's other arm.

"Fuck off, you two, I don't need any goddamn help." Unsteadily, Nathan pushed Nicole and Nasim aside and stumbled forward. He tried to steady himself on the back of the couch, but his hand missed, and he tumbled to the floor. "Fuck! Goddamn it!" he growled as he tried to get up.

"You want to just leave him there?" Nicole suggested.

"Nah, I've got work to do," Nasim said. "Let's get him into bed. Let him sleep it off."

Nicole nodded in agreement and reached down to give Nathan a hand. "Come on Nathan. Let's get you to bed."

"Leave me alone," Nathan protested before he slipped again and banged his head on the floor. "Uhggg!"

Sensing that this would be their best opportunity, Nasim and Nicole each grabbed an arm and dragged Nathan into his bedroom. Despite his angry protests, they flopped him on his bed face down. "Go fuck yourselves," Nathan said tiredly as his eyes closed. "Fucking assholes."

"Whatever, Nathan," Nicole responded as she and Nasim left the room.

Once they were back in the living room, it happened.

"I'm sorry a . . . about what Nathan said," Nicole offered sincerely while rubbing Nasim on the back. "I know you're not a terrorist, but it's still got to be hard."

Then she leaned in and kissed him. It started out as just a soft kiss on the cheek, but then it grew. Gradually, each kiss became longer and stronger than the previous one. Until suddenly, they stopped, foreheads touching, breathing heavy. Abruptly, Nicole turned and ran out of the apartment.

#

While Nasim never talked with Nicole about that night, he'd never forgotten about it either. Now, here they were again, alone together, but this time as she kissed his neck it felt different. He didn't feel guilty, he didn't care if Nathan caught them, and he didn't want her to stop. Turning his head, Nasim's lips met hers.

Then, Nicole moved out from behind the chair and straddled Nasim's lap. He pushed the chair away from the computer desk to give her more room. Suddenly unafraid, Nasim moved his hands underneath her T-shirt, one hand along the side of her body and one hand in the small of her back. Her skin felt warm and soft against his hands.

"What are those hands doing? Hmmm?" she asked.

"Uh, just exploring," Nasim replied.

"Oh, you're an explorer, eh?" Slowly, Nicole reached down with both hands and pulled off her shirt. "See anything worth exploring?"

"Ummm, well . . . "

Nicole smiled, undid her bra, and dropped it on the floor. Nasim pulled her close not knowing what to think. *Why is she doing this? What could she possibly see in me? She's so beautiful, so sexy.*

Nasim felt scared, but not scared enough to stop. *Don't worry about it. It doesn't matter. Just let it happen. Be with her.*

"Should we adjourn to the bedroom?" Nicole asked. "Unless you'd rather study."

"I could probably use a break," Nasim answered grinning.

Nicole got off Nasim's lap. Taking him by the hand, she led him to the bedroom. "Oh, I'd better get my shirt and stuff, in case someone comes home. You got any protection?" Nicole asked.

"Um?" Nasim grimaced.

"Don't worry, I think I've got a condom in my purse," Nicole said. She kissed him and went to grab her things. Nasim watched her go. Naked from the waist up, her jeans curved nicely around her hips. He took off his shirt, and struggled to unzip his jeans.

"You in a hurry or something?" Nicole asked upon her return. She closed the door and slid her jeans and panties down to the floor. Then, she stepped out of them and walked toward Nasim. "I can help with those," she said quietly.

They kissed as she unzipped his jeans the rest of the way. She pushed them off his hips and held up the condom that she'd hidden in the palm of her hand. "Do you want the honors or should I?"

"Uh?"

"Never mind," she said as she ripped open the packaging and rolled the condom on.

"Are you sure?" Nasim started to ask, but Nicole put her hand to his mouth and guided him back to the bed. "I'm not sure that I'm very good at . . . "

"Just kiss me," she replied.

Nasim did as he was told. He kissed her as passionately as he knew how. His hands grabbed her tightly, not wanting her to disappear.

"I'm ready when you are," she whispered.

Nasim rolled on top of her. After sliding inside her, she wrapped her legs tightly around him. Rhythmically, she pulled his hips into her with her legs. With his heart beating wildly, Nasim did his best to match her. He didn't want it to end. He held on as long as he could before his body caved into an uncontrollable shiver. He continued to kiss her softly, hoping it was good enough to secure another chance. The fact that Nicole kissed him back filled Nasim with relief.

Chapter 23: Another Day in Paradise

Agent Steve Jamison looked wearily at the clock. Evidently, his business contact couldn't make it before prayer time. No matter how hard he tried, Jamison just couldn't get used to the pace of business in Saudi Arabia. No wonder his predecessor had let things slide. Between prayer time and tea, it was damn near impossible to get anything accomplished. Meetings took twice as long, if they happened at all. The Saudis always had a built-in excuse for postponing a decision. The harder he pushed, the slower they moved.

The storefront he operated as a cover was sparsely furnished but clean. The small adobe-walled outer room contained a small wooden counter. An old, worn-out, green swivel chair stood behind the counter and gave Jamison a clear view of the street. The unvarnished wood floor was covered with an area rug from one of the local merchants, and the walls were lined with shelves that contained samples of the merchandise Agent Jamison presumably purchased locally and exported to the U.S. The products included leather purses, wallets, jewelry, and a few other knickknacks. A golden-colored, beaded curtain separated this outer room from his backroom office.

Getting up from behind the counter, Jamison walked stiffly over to the entrance, locked the door, and pulled down the tattered shades. Then he headed back to his office. In the backroom sat a large oak desk cluttered with empty Styrofoam coffee cups, a laptop with docking station, a couple of plastic file trays overstuffed with papers, and a plastic cup filled with pens and pencils.

Jamison sat down and logged in to his secure e-mail. *I can't believe it. I've got more e-mails regarding rug and jewelry orders than I do regarding actual intelligence work. I guess with the rest of the Middle East blowing up, our focus is elsewhere. No one seems to remember that the majority of the 9/11 assailants were Saudi nationals.*

Nonetheless, he continued to file through his messages. *A response from the NIC. Let's see who was tailing Socrates. Hmmm*

. . . The car is registered to one Abdul Hafiz Al-Faruq. Oh great, that's Detective Abdul Hafiz Al-Faruq. What would a detective from the Saudi Arabian Investigative Directorate want with Socrates? I hope they're not pulling a Pakistan and trying to round up all our contacts. That's the last thing I need.

Then Jamison remembered something. He bent down and picked through the cluttered files in the safe that was hidden beneath his desk. *We've got a contact inside the SAID, don't we? Ah ha! Here it is.*

Quickly, he perused the documents in the folder. *Hmmm, Rider sure didn't utilize this guy much. Of course, who knows if this file is up-to-date. I'd better run it up the chain and see what they think.*

Jamison typed angrily as if the force with which he hit the keys would convey his mood. "Saudi Arabian agent tailing Socrates. Drop aborted. Unsure if contact compromised. All other scheduled drops have occurred without incident. Can attempt contact of our SAID contact, however asset has been dormant for over 6 months. Please advise. AJ." He sat back frowning, unhappy with the message, but unsure what else to say. He couldn't afford to lose another contact.

Prior to Agent Jamison's arrival, Rider had been grooming a young man with ties to a prominent local mosque.

I finally get him set up on a consistent schedule, and he disappears. Recruiting in this area was tough enough before the whole Pakistan thing. Now, it's damn near impossible. I guess I'm supposed to hand them cyanide pills along with their first payment. I swear sometimes headquarters acts like we're working with professional spies. I mean, come on, most of these people are basically right off the street. No training. No nothing. They simply live near someone that we're interested in. Period!

"I don't know," Agent Jamison grumbled as he dropped the file folder on the desk. *They're assets pure and simple. Nothing more. Nothing less. It just seemed that in the old days I was working with engineers, military officials, etc. They were educated. They knew what they were getting themselves into. Now, more than half of my contacts are poor and uneducated. What little money I give them seems more like charity than anything.*

His thoughts turned to BMO1 or Black Moving Object 1. It was a rather crass code name that had been given to one of his Saudi female contacts and alluded to the color of her *habiya*. *She's already treated like a number in Saudi culture, and we're doing the same damn thing.*

In his estimation, BMO1 was his most valuable asset. Based on her file, she had planted literally dozens of miniature video and sound recording devices for them. Once, while being beaten by an angry shopkeeper during a mission, she crawled under a table to evade him and still had the presence of mind to plant the listening device rather than abort. The fearless widow did all this for about ten dollars a week. Yet some of the information she helped them gather was literally priceless.

Priceless to us. Worthless to them.

When she wasn't running errands for the CIA, she could be found begging for alms outside one of the local mosques. Without a husband, she was considered practically rubbish in their culture. Somehow she persevered.

I don't know how she does it. She lives a hard life, but she's a survivor. Even without the measly stipend that we give her, she'd find a way to make ends meet.

Jamison continued to go through his e-mail. There were a couple of RFIs—Requests For Information—but nothing out of the ordinary.

"Assess strength of opposition to the Saudi monarchy," he read.

Really? And how exactly am I supposed to measure that? The Saudis are definitely worried. They can see what's happening around them, they've increased police presence throughout the country, and they've upped payments to all Saudi nationals. Still, I see no evidence of a formal, consolidated opposition. Then again, I thought I was looking for terrorist threats to the U.S., not the Saudi monarchy.

Jamison winced. He felt a headache coming on. Nonetheless, his mind kept churning.

132

The Saudi religious establishment certainly has no love for the United States, but they rely on the monarchy to help enforce sharia law. They're pushing the government to be more conservative while the opposition tends to stem from younger, more liberal elements of Saudi society. Right now, my sources are focused on potential terrorist threats, which generally come from the anti-American, Islamic, ultra-conservatives. I'd really have to start from scratch if I wanted to truly gauge the strength of the more liberal elements within Saudi society. Hell, they'd probably be better off paying some computer nerd to lurk on internet blogs and Twitter, than rely on me.

"We always end up supporting these damn totalitarian regimes too long," Jamison said. He got up from his desk to get a refill, but the coffee pot was empty. Agitated, he grabbed the coffee pot, walked over to the bathroom, and filled it up in the bathroom sink. After clumsily putting in a new filter and dumping in some coffee grounds, he got a new pot brewing.

With his cup still empty, he returned to his desk. He still needed to review the video footage that BMO1 had turned in. After pushing back his chair, Jamison bent down, reached underneath his desk and pawed through the safe again. As he nudged the thick safe door, it creaked loudly.

"My God, this thing is old," he commented. Then, he reached into the safe and pulled out a small video device. He hooked it up to his computer and began reviewing the video. "Who am I looking at here?" he asked himself as he clicked on the pause button.

He retrieved a well-worn map from the safe. *Let me see. This is footage from camera five. That's the one covering . . . uh, Husam Asad.*

He checked his notes. *Okay, Husam runs small ops for Al-Qaeda on occasion. More of a gun-for-hire than anything. This should be exciting. At least the camera is set up with a motion sensor, otherwise this would be totally mind-numbing.*

Agent Jamison clicked play and slogged through the video. The camera focused on the alleyway just outside Husam's apartment. The area was pretty run down. Aside from Husam's place, most of the surrounding apartments in the old adobe building were empty.

"He heads out, he comes back, he heads out, he comes back," Agent Jamison grumbled.

Upon hearing the coffee pot finish its brewing cycle, he paused the footage and trudged over to fill up his cup. He returned, chewing on the hot beverage greedily, and resumed his task.

"Finally, a visitor," Agent Jamison exclaimed as the video showed Husam arriving at his apartment along with another man who was smoking a cigarette. "Damn, he's a tall mother fucker. Nice scar too," Agent Jamison noted. "Right cheek."

He repositioned the video to a spot where he had the best view of the man's face. "Agent Rider didn't have a file on you. Ahh, you're probably just one of Husam's old high school buddies." Agent Jamison chuckled. Then, he captured the frame and submitted it to headquarters for facial recognition.

After transmitting the image, Jamison continued reviewing the footage. An hour and two cups of coffee later, another man caught his eye. "What do we have here? I don't think Husam's home," he commented as he watched the man knock on Husam's door. When no one answered, the man picked the lock and entered.

"Hmmm, something's familiar about this one, but I can't quite put my finger on it," Jamison murmured as he paused the footage. "What are you up to anyway? No good, no doubt." After about five minutes, the man emerged from the apartment, made sure the door was locked, and left.

Jamison continued watching the footage. When Husam returned home that evening, he stopped short in front of his doorway. Then, he scanned the alley suspiciously. "He's a smart one," Jamison commented as he watched. "Where are you going?"

Husam disappeared off screen, and once again Jamison was staring at the doorway to Husam's apartment. Jamison hit fast forward. A moment later, the doorway to the apartment opened from the inside. Husam peered out briefly before shutting the door. He obviously had another way of getting in. Jamison rewound the footage and watched the man enter Husam's apartment again.

134

Well, if he planted something it must have been small. Ditto if he took something. Husam is on to him though. Probably tearing his apartment apart right now. Agent Jamison chuckled. He played with the video until he found a clear image of the visitor's face. Then, as he did with the scar-faced man, he submitted the image to HQ for facial recognition.

Agent Jamison looked at the clock. *Evening prayer should just about be over. Guess I'll grab a shawarma on my way back to the hotel. Aghhh, what I'd give for a cold beer. A lukewarm soda'll have to do, I guess.*

He locked up his laptop and materials in the safe, reviewed his schedule for the next morning, and headed for the door. "Another day in paradise," he said sarcastically.

Chapter 24: Port Call

"First a dumpster fire knocks out our comms, and now this. Two tankers reporting hull damage. What are the odds?" Basim grumbled as he drove out to the Ras Tanura facilities. "The harbor pilots better have not been asleep at the wheel. We can't be running tankers into shoals left and right."

Whenever Basim was asked to come down to Ras Tanura, it was never a good sign. Last time something like this happened, he had to bring in an underwater welding crew to fix the problem. Not only did it block up a heavy slot for a week, but PGORC had to pay for the repairs.

"Basim Dabir," he said loudly as he handed his security badge to the gate guard.

"Come to join the party?" the guard asked.

"What?" Basim asked quizzically.

"Never mind. You're clear."

Basim sped angrily toward the docks. The highway that connected the employee compound to the port and refinery ran along a thin isthmus. The waters of the Persian Gulf shimmered under an endless blue sky as Basim made his way along the access road to the harbor office. As he looked over at the facility, the refinery's steel storage tanks grew out of the sand like iron dunes.

Although he had the AC on high, Basim was sweating profusely. "Is this damn thing even working?" he said while pounding on the dashboard.

Based on the e-mail, the harbor pilots had set up a meeting because they were troubled by the reports of tanker damage. While the harbor pilots weren't perfect, they weren't a skittish lot. When mistakes were made, they owned up to them. In this case however, he couldn't get a straight answer from anybody.

Then, to top it all off, the battery on his cell phone went dead on the drive out. "Now, I've got no idea what the hell I'm walking into," Basim grumbled.

As he pulled into the harbor office parking lot, Basim received another shock. A military Humvee filled with Saudi Army personnel was exiting the lot just as he was pulling in. "What the hell are they doing here? This can't be good," he murmured. With an oil tanker looming on his left and the harbor office warehouse on his right, Basim parked his car and headed into the office.

The north pier warehouse was beginning to block out the setting sun as Basim entered the building. PGORC prided itself on having some of the best harbor pilots in the world. They were true professionals and not prone to whining. Today, he could hear them grousing before he even opened the door.

"Goddammit! They're not tellin' us the whole story," Texas pilot Boone Reynolds shouted. "I've been working these waterways fer years. I know this here area," he said pounding on the table. "There's no way that there tanker ran aground during entry."

"Too right," Miles Johnson from Australia chimed in. "Why won't they let the wet welders in to start repairs if it's just a simple grounding?"

"That tanker did not run aground!" Boone reiterated.

"Calm down guys," Basim interrupted.

"Well, look who's finally here. All hell's breaking loose, and you can't answer your goddamn phone," Boone griped.

"What did the initial report say?" Basim asked while glaring at Boone.

"It's gone walkabout," Miles answered.

"What?" Basim asked quizzically.

"We don't know," Miles continued. "They confiscated it."

"Who did?" asked Basim.

"That fucking colonel took it," Boone replied.

Basim put his hands over his face and took a deep breath. "Let's back up. Start at the beginning. How did this all get started?"

"When the *Ocean Mary* was docking, the spotter saw something dragging underneath her belly, like it had snagged something, so the tanker captain sent one of his divers down to investigate. Next thing you know security's called in and then the military. The *Ocean Mary's* damn tanker captain won't tell us anything. Security's done got guards posted outside her, and they won't tell us shit," Boone answered.

"While you were takin' the trolly on your way out here, they've closed down everything. Nothing's going in or out," Miles added.

Basim tried his best to calm the group down. "All right, all right. I'll go talk with security and find out what's going on. In the meantime, there's no point getting your blood pressure up. Whatever is going on, it's going to take a while to sort out, so head back to your quarters or grab a deck of cards, but stop griping!"

"Hmpf. All right," Boone grunted.

"Right," Miles said with a nod. "She'll be apples, Boone, you'll see mate. It wasn't your fault. Something else is up."

"So, Gamali Kareef is leading the security response?" Basim asked to no one in particular.

The group nodded.

"Well, where is he?"

"He left with them military blokes," Miles answered.

"Aghh, can someone lend me their phone, my cell's dead," Basim asked.

Boone offered up his.

"Thanks," Basim said as he dialed Gamali's number.

"Hey, this is Basim. Where are you? We need to talk. Okay, stay there. I'll come to you."

He handed the phone back to Boone.

"Give me thirty minutes. I'll talk with Gamali and get to the bottom of this. Okay?" Everyone nodded.

On the phone, Gamali Kareef had said he was by the *Ocean Mary* facilitating the turnover between the PGORC security detail and the military guards. The tanker was berthed farther down the north pier. Basim could hear the waves lapping against the pier as he strode over to the *Ocean Mary*. He'd never been out on the pier when it was this quiet. *Nothing's going in or out? There's going to be hell to pay after this mess is cleaned up.* In his mind, he could picture tankers lining up in the gulf. A perfect example, if there ever was one, for the phrase, "time is money."

Up ahead, he could see Gamali talking with a member of his security detail. By the looks of things, they were going to have one military guard along with one member of the PGORC security force guarding the vessel.

Wonderful, a guard guarding a guard. Yet, something tells me this isn't where the true threat is. Basim waited about twenty feet away while Gamali finished up his conversation.

When Basim walked over, Gamali didn't seem particularly happy to see him. "Look! There's not much I can tell you," Gamali grumbled. "I'm under strict orders from the military."

"So, when the chairman asks me why we've shut down the entire port, I should just refer him to you?" Basim asked.

"And if something gets leaked to the press, I'll just refer the military to you," Gamali retorted.

"Look, I'm the least of your problems. We've already got six or seven tankers lined up out there right now," Basim said gesturing at the gulf. "What do you think those tanker captains are doing right now? Huh? Sitting on their hands? No, they're calling their superiors. They're saying hey, guess what. Ras Tanura's closed. Whatever the problem is, we need to get our shit together and communicate something," Basim argued.

His jaw clenched, Gamali stared at Basim. Moving closer, Gamali responded in a quiet rasp, "They found some kind of explosive device attached to the *Ocean Mary*. Military divers are currently inspecting the other tankers. They found a similar device attached to the *Coronado*. We're waiting to see if the devices can be deactivated and removed."

"Okay, but like I said, we need to tell the tanker captains out there something. Who do I coordinate our response with?" Basim asked.

"Ah . . . Colonel Malik Imad," Gamali answered. He scribbled down the colonel's contact information on a small piece of paper and handed it gruffly to Basim. "But remember, I didn't tell you anything."

Basim stared blankly at Gamali as he huffed away, then headed back to the harbor office. Upon entering the warehouse, all the harbor pilots looked up expectantly. Basim held up his hand.

"Give me a minute, guys," he said. "Can I borrow your phone again?"

Boone tossed him the phone. Basim caught it and ducked into a nearby office. After closing the door, he paced anxiously and dialed the Colonel's number.

"Hello, Colonel Imad speaking."

"Hello, this is Basim Dabir. I'm the chief PGORC scheduler. Can I talk to you for a moment?"

"I'm afraid I can't give you much in the way of details over the phone," the Colonel answered.

"Yes, I understand your security concerns. However, I have more than a dozen tankers currently in transit to the Ras Tanura facility. I need to understand what my options are. I could re-route some of the tankers to Dhahran or Jiddah, but several of the tankers are already anchored offshore. What do I tell them?"

"Just say that due to mechanical issues, berth access is temporarily unavailable," Colonel Imad said.

"Well sir, that might work with a couple of them, but it's not normal for our shipping to be totally shut down like this. I mean ships are always coming and going. The tanker captains are going to know something's up."

"You're just going to have to stall them the best you can until we know what we're dealing with," the Colonel answered.

"Okay, ah . . . " Basim stammered, "If you inspect a tanker, and it's clean, can they make way?"

"It's way too early to even think about that," the Colonel snapped.

"I understand. Is there anything you need from us? At port control, I have access to all the shipping manifest data. Our harbor pilots know this waterway like the back of their hands. Perhaps they can help in some way," Basim offered.

"Gather up everything you have on the *Ocean Mary* and the *Coronado*. I'll see what I can do to get you back up and running. As for now, that's the best I can offer," Colonel Imad responded. "Let me hand you off to my aide, so you can exchange contact information."

"Yes sir," Basim responded, but the Colonel was already gone. After talking with the Colonel's aide for a couple of minutes, Basim went out to face the harbor pilots.

"What's the word," Boone asked.

"Well, we've got two, uh, damaged tankers," Basim answered while measuring his words. "It's the *Ocean Mary* and the *Coronado*, but the damage is unrelated to anything you guys have control over."

"That's bull dust," Miles said.

"Come on guys, that's all I can tell you right now," Basim said. "Use your brains. The military's involved. If your shift is over, go home, but keep your mouth shut. If you're supposed to be clocked in, then stay here and hopefully this will be over sooner, rather than later."

"So, hurry up and wait," Boone said.

"Hurry up and wait," Basim echoed.

As Basim turned to leave, a loud rumbling noise cut through the chatter of the squabbling harbor pilots. Wide eyed, Basim stopped short his hand reaching for the door. Outside, they could here yelling and a siren sounded. Basim felt the blood drain from his face, and for once, the harbor pilots were speechless.

Chapter 25: The Puzzle

Detective Al-Faruq stared tensely at his computer screen. "Yes! The files copied over." He breathed a sigh of relief. "Now, let's see if they'll open," he whispered as he selected a file. The flash drive churned sluggishly, but finally the file opened.

"All right," he said under his breath. Quickly, he paged down to find the mailing list. "Wow! Let's see, there are forty-two addresses per page, times six pages, that's over two hundred and fifty recipients. This is going to take a while," he said. He looked up at the clock with a pained expression.

Al-Faruq printed out the address list and logged into the National Information Center. The NIC database housed a variety of information on all Saudi citizens. One by one, he input the names into the NIC database. He wanted to see if any of the individuals had criminal records.

"Damn, this thing's running slow today," Al-Faruq said, looking tiredly at the blinking cursor. He looked up at the clock again. "Guess I'm going to miss evening prayer again."

It had become a habit of late, a bad habit, but whenever he went to prayer time, he'd start thinking about his life. The same question kept circling round his head. *Is this the life Allah meant for me, or did I do something wrong? Aghh, snap out of it.*

Despite the slow response time, Al-Faruq kept plugging away. "Hmmm, another overdose," Al-Faruq noted. It doesn't look like being on this mailing list is good for your health. After finishing up the first full page of addressees, Al-Faruq counted up the number of individuals that were reported missing or dead.

Twelve out of forty-two. All within the last six months. He looked closer at his notes. Of those that were listed as deceased, five of six had overdosed on drugs. Al-Faruq tapped his pen against the end of his chin.

Why all of these overdoses in the last few months? If the professor is dealing, he's been doing it for a while based on his spending habits. Did he simply get a bad batch, or is there something else going on?

Detective Al-Faruq moved on to page two and typed another name into the database, then leaned back in his chair waiting for the system to respond. Suddenly, a voice startled him. It was Chief Hamal.

"Detective Al-Faruq?"

"Yes sir?"

"Good, you're still here. Do you have a moment?"

"Sure," Al-Faruq replied apprehensively.

"So, how's your investigation of the PGORC fire going?"

"Well, the fire department's report indicates the presence of an accelerant, but there are several chemicals which PGORC utilizes that could fit the bill. The question is, how did those chemicals find their way into that particular dumpster?"

"What do you mean?"

"Port control is geographically separated from the refinery facilities where the chemicals are used."

"Hmmm," Chief Hamal nodded. "If it were something more than an accident, do you have any suspects?"

"Security cameras show that a port control technician named Tahir Rafiq was the last individual to exit the facility the night of the fire."

"Motive?"

Al-Faruq outlined his theory about Tahir and the university professor to Chief Hamal, but the chief seemed distracted and kept looking back toward his office. Al-Faruq began to wonder if the chief was paying attention at all.

"Great work!" Chief Hamal said patting Al-Faruq on the back. "Let's focus on this port control technician. This professor, uh, Professor Ratib is outside the scope of our investigation."

"Yes sir," Al-Faruq answered while trying to ignore the tingle that just went up his spine.

"Keep me posted," Chief Hamal said as he turned and headed back to his office.

I never mentioned Professor Ratib's name. I know I didn't. Why is he outside the scope of this investigation? Who's pulling the strings here?

For a moment, Al-Faruq stared blankly at the computer screen. Then, he continued down the list of names in front of him. *The professor may be outside the scope of this investigation, but he is the key. Whatever is going on, the professor is the link between the names on these pages and the truth behind the fire. I'm sure of it.*

Al-Faruq piled through the names. It took him a few more hours, but finally he finished. All told, sixty men from the mailing list had died or been reported missing during the past several months. "That leaves one hundred and ninety two still alive," Al-Faruq murmured after scribbling down the math on a scrap of paper. "Including Tahir, about a dozen still live here in Dhahran."

Al-Faruq highlighted the twelve addresses. *I can't keep tabs on all of them, but maybe I can shake them up a little. If I investigate these deaths and ask them about their former classmates, maybe something will turn up. Someone will get scared. Then, I just need to see who they run to.*

Satisfied, Al-Faruq logged off his computer. The puzzle was starting to come together. *If Chief Hamal wants me to leave the professor alone, I can oblige him . . . for now. Just don't expect me to give up.*

Al-Faruq weaved slowly between the office cubicles and headed for the exit. His fellow detectives were long gone. To most of them, this was your average nine-to-five job. Of course, most of them had families. *I'd probably head home too, if there was someone worth going home to.* Suddenly, his thoughts turned to the note.

I could text K, or I could give her a call, for that matter.

Al-Faruq tried to shake the thought out of his head. He knew the idea was crazy. What if her father found out? He knew nothing about the guy. If her father was one of those ultra-conservative types, he might go after her, and there'd be nothing Al-Faruq could do to stop it. He'd seen it happen; honor killings, beatings.

I shouldn't have picked up the note in the first place. I've got to get her out of my head. It's just not in the cards for me. Given my background, I should be happy I've got a job and an apartment. I could be out on the streets, or worse.

As he exited the parking lot, Al-Faruq kept trying to convince himself that he was happy, that he had everything he needed, but it wasn't working. In the back of his mind, he kept wishing, he kept hoping that there was some way. He'd beaten the odds before. Perhaps, he could beat them again.

Don't lose hope. Mother wouldn't want you to lose hope.

Chapter 26: A Text or Two

Kalila dropped her cell phone on top of her dresser and got ready for bed. She'd given up hope that her flirtation with the young man outside of Azzah's house would bear any fruit. *He probably didn't even see the note, so it's not like he actually rejected you. It wouldn't have led to anything anyway.*

In the Kingdom of Saudi Arabia, most marriages were still arranged. Kalila's mother had gone to great lengths to educate Kalila about her responsibilities as a Muslim woman, future wife and mother. While Kalila knew her parents wouldn't simply offer her up to the suitor with the largest dowry, this did little to alleviate her apprehension.

Kalila knew they would have her best interests at heart, but she'd heard so many horror stories. Stories of rape and physical abuse, stories involving homosexuality, and stories about families that weren't really families. While she didn't quite know what she wanted, she knew what she didn't want. She didn't want to live a charade. She didn't want a marriage of convenience where you were together but alone.

Kalila tried to shake off the feeling of dread that had enveloped her and got into bed. As she snuggled under the covers with her book, her phone chimed. Kalila buried her face in the book. Peeking over the top of the pages, she glared with one eyebrow raised at her cell phone.

Just ignore it. It's probably not him anyway. For several minutes, she tried to focus her attention on the book, but it was no use.

"Aghh," she said in frustration while setting her book face down on the covers. She swiveled her legs off the bed, stepped over to the dresser, and grabbed her phone. Flipping it open, Kalila saw she had a new text message. After hesitating for a moment, she opened the text.

"I . . . am . . . a . . . S . . . L . . . O . . . W . . . reader. A.H.A," it said.

Kalila tried in vain to stifle her smile. "Evidently slow at texting too," she said wryly. Now, however, she faced her own conundrum. What to text back? She returned to her bed, propped up her pillow, and crafted a response. Kalila put her thumbs to work.

"RU still reading the paper?" she texted back. She set the phone down in her lap and picked up her book. After a page or two, she was pleasantly surprised to hear her phone chime again. She picked it up.

"No, I finally finished the comics," A.H.A. had replied.

Kalila smiled and responded. "LOL, UR slow Mr. A.H.A.," Kalila typed. All of a sudden, she wasn't interested in the book anymore.

"Call me Al-Faruq. Mr. A.H.A just sounds weird," he answered.

"Ok, Al-Faruq. What does the AH stand for?" Kalila asked.

"Abdul Hafiz. What does K stand for?"

"Kalila."

"That's a pretty name," he responded. Kalila scrunched up her nose at the text.

"Really!?"

"You don't like it?"

"It's ok I guess. People tend to mispronounce it."

"How?"

Kalila had to think for a moment. "They put the i in the wrong place."

"iKalla!?!"

"LOL! No . . . Kailla or Kallia," Kalila answered.

"Such is life," Al-Faruq responded.

"U mean SIL."

"Huh?"

"You don't text much do you?"

"Not really," he responded after a long pause.

"They're abbreviations. U = you. SIL = such is life," Kalila instructed.

"RU sure? Maybe SIL = six iguanas laughed."

"UR CRZ."

"I'll work on it. How old are you? Ooops! HORU?"

"IM20."

147

"I'm probably TOFU."

"TOFU," Kalila read over a couple of times with a slight frown. "Oh, I get it," she said. "That'd be TO4U, but I like TOFU. HORU?"

"You like TOFU. Maybe IM2 young."

"That's not what I meant. HORU?" she asked again.

"IM26," he replied.

"That is old! ;)," she replied.

"Old or TO4U old?"

"That depends. RYS?" She held her breath and clicked send.

"RYS? Are yaks silly?"

"No, are you single?" Kalila asked again.

"Yes, but wouldn't that be RUS?" he responded.

Kalila smiled, but was still feeling a little uncertain. "What DU do?" she asked.

"? Lots of things."

"DU have a job?" Kalila asked with some hesitation.

"Yes," was his reply. Kalila stared at his answer somewhat perplexed that he didn't go into more detail.

"OK. What DU do?" Kalila asked. This time his answer did not come back as quickly as before. Kalila was about to text him back when he responded.

"Law enforcement," he answered.

"Didn't mean 2 pry," Kalila texted back.

"That's OK. What DU do?" he asked.

"IM studying 2B a teacher."

"Cool. My mom was a teacher."

"She retire?" Kalila asked. Once again, there was a long pause before she received his reply.

"She died when I was young."

"Sorry! :(Foot in mouth," she replied.

"YDK."

"?"

"You didn't know."

"THANX 4 the chat Al-Faruq," Kalila texted, suddenly feeling a little tired. "It's L8. I better go."

"OK. Good night."

"CULA," Kalila replied.

"?"

"See you later alligator," she told him.

"??"

"It's a silly English saying. It means araki," Kalila explained.

"Oh, CULA," he replied.

Kalila couldn't resist and texted, "In a while crocodile."

"U mean IAWC," he replied.

"IAWC :)" she concluded. "In a while crocodile," Kalila said quietly to herself. She smiled and returned the phone to her dresser. As she flopped back on the bed, Kalila stared wistfully at the ceiling. "That was fun," she said. "Pointless, but fun." Slowly, she rolled over and turned off her bedside lamp.

Chapter 27: Party Time

While Siraj wasn't sure how his friends were faring with their tasks, he couldn't have been happier. Siraj's primary responsibility entailed documenting monarchy excess. All things considered, he was having a blast. Armed with new video equipment, he'd been shadowing some of the monarchy's more colorful characters. Utilizing old American campaign advertisements as a guide, Siraj was immersed in developing his own attack ads.

Tonight, he was at the Regency Intercontinental Hotel in Bahrain preparing for the New Year's Eve party. Surprisingly, the Christian new year elicited quite the celebration, and parties were everywhere. According to his sources, Prince Amir Bahir was scheduled to attend an exclusive party at the Regency. With help from Professor Ratib's contacts, Siraj would infiltrate the party as a member of the wait staff and set up hidden cameras prior to the celebration.

Anxiously, Siraj surveyed the ballroom. With only four cameras, Siraj couldn't cover everything. *Where will I have the best chance of obtaining useful footage?* Slowly, he traversed across the brightly polished floors. The huge ballroom was decked out with every manner of New Year's Eve decoration. Meticulously, Siraj poked and prodded every float and decoration.

Ultimately, Siraj decided to focus on the head table where Prince Bahir and his entourage would be seated. The dance floor represented another prime target. While all four cameras could be activated remotely, Siraj was concerned about how effective the remote controls would be.

Will they work when the ballroom is jam-packed with party-goers, smoke, and lighting effects? When I activate the cameras, I'll have to be close, but where can I hide them?

Standing in front of the head table, Siraj eyed a decorative archway that led to the dance floor. He grabbed a stepladder and stationed the first camera amongst the archway's glittering stars. After studying his handiwork, he scanned the ballroom once again.

On the other side of the head table, Siraj spied a large float that was decorated with thousands of brightly colored flower petals. Six-foot high letters spelled out "Happy New Year." They were surrounded by cardboard images of exploding fireworks. He positioned the second video camera atop the float.

To monitor the dance floor, the capital Y of a large "PARTY!" sign hid one camera, while the other was perched above the stage on one of the lighting racks. Finally, if all else failed, Siraj had a small digital camera in his pocket as a backup.

While Prince Bahir's security team would conduct a sweep of the ballroom prior to the night's festivities, Siraj had received assurances the cameras would not be disturbed. Nonetheless, he was still nervous. He'd only get one shot at this, and his mind was a jumble of worries.

As Siraj completed his final equipment checks, his biggest concern was the lighting. How would it affect the video quality? If he couldn't clearly recognize Prince Bahir, the footage wouldn't be useful. While the cameras had low-light settings, the party pyrotechnics could render that feature worthless, and he needed to capture the prince in the act.

Apparently, the prince's entourage had ordered 120 bottles of champagne, ten for the head table, ten for the prince's suite, and the remaining one hundred were to be distributed throughout the ballroom. In addition, Siraj's contacts had alerted him to be ready for a midnight-blonde surprise. Having followed the prince's movements around Saudi Arabia for the last few months, Siraj had seen him with several different Western women. They made only token attempts to follow Islamic dress codes. He was certain that Prince Bahir and his crew were ready to let loose in the less restrictive confines of Bahrain.

Although he'd have to spend much of the night waiting tables, Siraj was looking forward to an eventful evening. From what he'd seen, Professor Ratib was absolutely right. Money had corrupted the royal family. Their support of the *mutawa* had more to do with controlling the civilian population than with upholding Islam. The oil money that trickled down to the Saudi citizenry paled in comparison to the lavish riches the royal family indulged in.

His final checks complete, Siraj looked for somewhere to rest. He holed up in a small conference room that was being used as a staging area for the festivities. He found a seat next to a long table that held trays upon trays of decadent deserts. Another table supported warming trays filled with *hors d'oeuvres*. Siraj had never seen so much food in one place.

The ballroom doors opened at ten o'clock in the evening, while the Prince's entourage was scheduled to arrive at eleven-thirty. As he stretched out his legs, Siraj let out a deep sigh and smiled. *I wonder what Prince Bahir's blonde surprise will be wearing. I'm guessing it won't be a habiya.*

"Hey, I thought you were supposed to be working," Jabir chided Siraj when he found him relaxing. A long-time hotel employee, Jabir was Siraj's primary contact. He helped Siraj score the party detail and provided him early access to the ballroom.

"I just finished my final checks," Siraj responded, sitting up straighter. "I thought I'd better take a break while I had a chance."

"Yeah, yeah. Whatever." Jabir said with a smile. Then, he motioned Siraj closer. "Hey Siraj. I've got a surprise for you. We found out that Prince Bahir reserved the entire top floor for an after-party shindig," he said in hushed tones. "We were able to hide a couple of cameras in the master suite. One is pointed at the hot tub, and the other is focused on the king-sized water bed."

"What kind of record time do the cameras have?" Siraj asked, his interest piquing.

"Three or four hours, but don't worry. The cameras have remotes similar to the ones you've installed in the ballroom. I've got a guy who will activate the cameras when he delivers some late-night snacks to the room. I'll get you the cameras before you leave tomorrow morning. It's just a shot in the dark, but maybe we'll get something interesting."

"Ha," Siraj laughed heartily. "Editing tonight's footage should be interesting."

"You think?" Jabir winked. "So, is everything set in the ballroom?"

"Yeah, I'm a little worried about the lighting, but what can I do?" Siraj shrugged.

"We've got spotlights. I could get them to keep one centered on the head table. Prince Bahir likes to be the center of attention, so he won't complain."

"Well, it depends on where the spotlight is. I can't have it shining straight into the camera lens. Both cameras have low-light settings, so I was hoping that would do the trick. Plus, I have some algorithms that can help me lighten up the footage during editing."

"Hmmm. I see what you're saying. Maybe, I can help." Jabir reached in his pocket and pulled out a small diagram of the ballroom. "Okay, here's the head table," he said pointing. "Where are the cameras positioned?"

Siraj showed him the locations.

"Okay! There are eight spotlights. Positioned as follows," Jabir said while placing Xs on the diagram with a pen.

"Are the spots stationary or do they pan back and forth?" Siraj asked.

"Ummm, the ones mounted in the corners automatically sweep back and forth across the ball room. The others are fixed, but I can get a ladder and point them where ever you want," Jabir answered.

"Well, the sweeps can play havoc with the cameras, but given how far away they are from the head table, they shouldn't cause a problem. If you could point two of the stationary ones at the head table and a couple toward the dance floor, that'd be great. I'm betting that's where we'll get the best footage."

"No problem," Jabir answered.

"Thanks," Siraj answered. "All the help you've provided has been great."

"Not a problem. Prince Bahir is a complete asshole. The last time he was here he totally trashed his suite. He's rude. Doesn't tip. He's earned whatever you've got planned for him."

"I'll do my best," Siraj promised.

"All right. I'll get those spots positioned, and then we'll need to start serving the early arrivals."

"No rest for the wicked, eh?"

"Ha, you ain't seen anything yet. Prince Wicked won't arrive until later," Jabir said with a grin.

Siraj looked at his watch. The guests would be arriving soon. Smartly, he stood up, put on his black wait staff jacket, and smoothed out his uniform. He had to look sharp. This was a high profile gig. He checked his reflection in the mirrored conference room doors. *Good to go!*

Upon entering the ballroom, Siraj looked around for Jabir, but didn't see him. A buffet line stocked with mounds of food stretched out in front of him. Members of the hotel security staff were scanning the tickets of the early arrivals. An Arabian gentleman wearing a traditional *thobe* and *ghutra* had just been checked through. On his arm clung a young Caucasian woman who was probably half his age.

"Geez, that guy's my father's age," Siraj said with a grimace.

"You better watch it," Jabir said as he grabbed Siraj's shoulder and pulled him close.

"Huh?"

"You gotta check your attitude. Paint on a smile. It's yes sir, no sir, regardless of how drunk or full of shit they are."

"Okay."

"I'm serious," Jabir emphasized by tightly squeezing Siraj's arm. "To get you in here, I had to vouch for you. You make me look bad and I'll be out of a job. Understand?"

"I understand," Siraj answered, as he broke out in an uncomfortable sweat.

"Go grab a champagne tray and get to work," Jabir ordered. "Let's hustle. The fun and games will have to wait until later."

Siraj grabbed a tray of champagne and bustled out into the ballroom. Upon seeing the gentleman that he'd noticed earlier, Siraj swallowed hard, smiled, and said, "Champagne, sir?"

"Oh, wonderful," the glassy-eyed man said. He grabbed two glasses and motioned Siraj closer.

Siraj held his breath. It was apparent the man had been drinking something significantly stronger than champagne.

"If you could supply us with a bottle of champagne, I'd make it worth your while."

"Of course sir." Quickly, Siraj headed back to the staging area and grabbed a bottle. *Well, we were going to be setting these out pretty soon anyway. Providing him one now shouldn't hurt.*

Nonetheless, he draped a cloth napkin over the bottle before heading back out. After weaving his way through the gathering crowd, Siraj spotted the gentleman. "Your champagne, sir," Siraj said.

"Ohhhh, thank you," the man said. He handed Siraj a sweaty bill. "How about some food? I don't want to fight through the crowd at the buffet table."

"Right away sir," Siraj replied.

"We could use some food and champagne over here too," a gentleman at a nearby table shouted. "Hurry up about it."

"Yes sir," Siraj replied, as he headed for the buffet table. Upon seeing Jabir, he waved him down.

"Hey Jabir. I've got some people that are too lazy to walk over to the buffet table. Can you help me out?"

"Are they tipping?" Jabir asked quizzically.

"Well, the one guy is. I haven't gotten over to the other tables yet."

"All right, what do they want?"

"Food and champagne."

"Okay, I'll grab some champagne and you get the food," Jabir replied.

The rest of the night, Siraj and Jabir kept the party goers' tables stocked. They were the revelers' feet, their maids, and their waiters. Siraj got so busy that he almost forgot about Prince Bahir, but when the prince and his entourage arrived, he took notice.

"Showtime," Siraj said under his breath. Quickly, he walked over to Jabir. "I need to activate the cameras."

"That's cool. I've got it covered."

Cautiously, Siraj worked his way around the ballroom. He had all the camera remotes on a key chain. He sneaked up next to the "New Year" float and pulled out the key chain. For a moment, he froze. Which remote went to which camera? Nervously, he went back through everything in his head. Finally, he remembered.

"Hey, we need some more champagne over here," a reveler yelled.

Siraj nodded and grabbed a tray of champagne. Slowly, he circled the banquet hall, handing out glasses. He kept the remotes hidden underneath the tray. Using the ballroom decorations as cover, Siraj powered up the cameras and hit record. After breathing a sigh of relief, Siraj glanced at the prince's table. "Have fun, Prince Bahir," he whispered. "Your party days are numbered."

Chapter 28: Party Girl

Azzah could barely contain her excitement as her parents dropped her off at Cala's house. For once her *habiya* came in handy as it covered the black silk dress she was wearing. She couldn't believe she'd actually be going to a New Year's Eve party in Bahrain. Walking up to Cala's front door, her eyes darted excitedly. She couldn't wait for her mom to ring the doorbell.

Cala's mom answered the door. While she chatted with Iba, Azzah darted off.

"Have fun, honey," Iba called out.

"Yeah, okay," Azzah answered with a dismissive wave. She quickly headed upstairs. "Cala?" Azzah called. She knocked softly on Cala's bedroom door.

"Come in," Cala answered.

As Azzah entered the room, she was surprised at how dark it was. Then, suddenly the light popped on and Azzah found herself standing face to face with a young man wearing a *thobe* and *ghutra*. "Agghh!" she yelped.

"Ha! I got you good," Cala said. It wasn't a man at all. It was just Cala, dressed as a man.

"What are you doing?" Azzah said angrily. She jabbed Cala in the shoulder.

"Aggh!" Cala teased. "There's a strange man in Cala's room. Help, help."

"Shut up! I swear, you are such a freak. Why are you dressed like that?"

"This is my disguise. Don't worry. I've got one for you too," Cala said pointing to the clothes on her bed.

"Ewww! You can't be serious." Azzah replied. She held the *thobe* up to her chin checking the size.

"Oh, come on. You only have to wear it 'til we cross the border into Bahrain. Then, we can act like normal, Western women."

"Seriously?"

"Seriously, I'm not kidding. In a little over an hour, my cousin's going to pick us up in his limo. Then, it's off to party at the Regency, baby!"

"And we have to dress like guys because?"

"Because, at the border checkpoint, the guards will want to look in the limo. When they see that it's just a bunch of guys, they'll wave us through no problem." Cala lowered her voice. "Come on. It'll be fun."

"You're so crazy," Azzah replied. Smiling mischievously, she removed her *habiya* and donned the *thobe*. "What are we going to do about your parents?"

"They're headed over to my uncle's. As far as they know, we'll be here watching movies. They won't be back until tomorrow."

"Cool!" Azzah replied, staring blankly at the *ghutra*.

Cala snickered. "We're definitely going to need to pull your hair back and lose the eye shadow."

Azzah pouted. "Do you have any idea how long this took?" she asked gesturing at her hair.

"Don't worry. We'll have time before the party to get ourselves back together."

Just then, Cala's mother called from downstairs. "Cala. We're headed out. You two have fun."

"We will," Cala answered loudly. "See you tomorrow."

Cala and Azzah ran over to the window. Peeking through the curtains, they watched Cala's parents drive away. "See, everything's going according to plan," Cala said.

Azzah pulled her long hair back in a ponytail and positioned the *ghutra* on her head. "I look ridiculous. This is never going to work."

"Oh, come on. Why are you being so negative?" Cala chided as she busily removed the makeup and mascara from Azzah's face. Then, she pushed Azzah in front of the mirror.

"Ahgg! I look so blah."

"Well, duh. That's the idea. Don't worry I've got everything we need in here." Cala held up her backpack. Azzah looked inside, it was filled with makeup and shoes.

"Oh yeah, you need to throw your shoes in here too."

158

"What am I going to wear on my feet?" Azzah asked staring down at her brightly colored toenails.

"Tube socks and tennis shoes." Cala snickered. "I'm just kidding. These should cover up those pretty toes." She handed Azzah a pair of closed toe leather sandals.

Azzah put them on and looked at herself in the full-length mirror that hung on Cala's bedroom door. "I look like a clown."

"You look like a guy. Same difference."

The two broke into laughter and headed downstairs. When the limousine arrived about twenty minutes later, the two bounded expectantly out the door. The driver of the lead limo waved and opened the door for them. Loud music and smoke billowed out of the vehicle as a young man stuck his head out the doorway.

"You two ready to party?" Prince Bahir said with a wink as he waved the girls forward. Cala and Azzah climbed in.

Bahir slouched in the rear seat of the limo between his two bodyguards. His black-and-gray-striped silk shirt was visible underneath his partially opened *thobe*. Nonchalantly, he introduced the girls to his friends who lined the couch that slithered the length of the limousine. All the men's eyes were red and glassy. Evidently, the party had started quite a while ago for them.

"Find a seat, ladies. We don't want to be late. Besides, we're starving. Right, guys?" Bahir exclaimed. He exchanged glances with his two bodyguards. The guards nodded, but seemed to pay the prince little attention.

"Crank it up," Bahir yelled to the driver as the limo glided forward. Western dance music filled the interior while music videos played on the flat screen televisions that lined the limo walls. Outside, the bass buzzed as the limousine steamed down the highway toward the King Fahd Causeway. The prince offered the girls some clove cigarettes.

"Give 'em a light," Bahir ordered. His bodyguards complied, leaned forward with their lighters, and lit the girls' cigarettes.

Cala took a long drag and then blew the smoke up at the neon lights that lined the limo's ceiling. Azzah followed her lead, but started coughing midway through her first drag. Everyone laughed, and Azzah looked embarrassed.

"Try again," Cala encouraged. Azzah gave it another try. After holding in the smoke with all her strength, she blew it out slowly to everyone's cheers.

At the border, the prince and his entourage were whisked through. Aside from talking briefly with the limo's driver, the guard didn't even look inside. Azzah turned to look out the window as they sped along the causeway. The moon glinting off the gulf waters gave her a sense of freedom that she'd never experienced before.

"How much longer," she asked Cala loudly over the music's pounding beats.

"Who cares?"

Still dizzy from the cigarettes, Azzah turned back to the window and watched the water stretch out to the horizon.

#

When they reached the Regency, Bahir took his entourage up to the penthouse suite he had secured for the evening's festivities. While the Prince boasted that he needed to ensure the suite was in order, it seemed to Azzah he was simply showing off for his friends. Royalty definitely had its privileges. The suite took up half the top floor.

The tour gave Cala and Azzah the opportunity to slip out of their disguises and prepare for the party.

"Come on," Cala implored with a tug of Azzah's arm. Silently, they slipped into one of the suite's bathrooms and began their transformation.

"I can't believe we're here," Azzah said incredulously as she removed her disguise. "Ahhgg, my hair is a complete disaster."

"Don't worry! I'll have you looking smoking hot again in no time," Cala encouraged her. "I've got our party passes right here," she said brandishing two cards with magnetic strips and lanyards. "Bahir gave them to me when we were getting out of the limo. Once we're ready, we can head downstairs anytime."

Cala unzipped her backpack and dumped the contents on the large marble vanity. Azzah grabbed a brush from the pile and

160

started working it through her hair while Cala plugged in the curling iron. The two worked feverishly to get ready. They didn't want to miss a minute of the party.

Meanwhile, the prince's entourage was entering the ballroom, where his security team led Bahir through the sea of party goers toward the head table. While few within the crowd knew who the prince was, his entrance created the kind of buzz only money can buy. As Bahir and his crew made their way forward, it was announced he had purchased champagne for every table in the ballroom. The crowd let out a rowdy cheer.

Once the head table was seated, the band—an Asian, Prince-tribute band—launched into "Party Like It's 1999." At the ballroom entrance, two young women of Middle Eastern descent were handing their credentials to the security staff. While they were Muslim, their dress suggested anything but. Cala was wearing a one-shoulder, black-lace dress by Valentino while Azzah wore a black silk dress by Yves Saint Laurent. After checking their credentials, the security guards admired the girls from behind as Cala and Azzah entered the ballroom.

"Follow me," Cala urged. Tugging Azzah along, Cala weaved through the crowd to the head table. "I see them," Cala said loudly, pointing at the dance floor. "Over there."

When they reached the head table, a member of Bahir's security team blocked their path. "Hey!" Cala protested loudly. "Get your fat ass out of my way."

Hearing the commotion, Bahir turned. Laughing, he watched Cala scream at the guard. When the guard grabbed Cala by the wrist, Bahir stumbled forward with a drink in his hand.

"Come on, man!" he shouted. "You know better than that. Keeping these two, fine-looking young ladies away from my table. What's wrong with you?"

"She said she was your cousin," the guard replied skeptically, still clutching Cala's wrist tightly.

"She is my cousin, you idiot," the Prince said nastily. Then, he threw his drink in the guard's face. "You take that tone again with me and you'll be working in the stables."

"I'm sorry, Prince Bahir," the guard apologized. Nonetheless, Cala stomped on the guard's foot as she moved past. He said nothing, but his eyes burned angrily.

Bahir whistled as he looked Cala and Azzah over. "I wondered where you two had disappeared to, but I like your new outfits," he said with a Cheshire cat grin.

"We wore them just for you," Cala said.

"Ha, I wish." Then, he leaned closer to Azzah. "You are looking hot, young lady," he said with a wink. "Hey, everyone." the Prince rambled on, "this is Cala and, and . . . "

"Azzah," Azzah interjected.

"They're here to join the party," the Prince yelled, as his entourage let out a drunken cheer. "Here! Have some champagne!" He handed the girls a couple of glasses and sloppily poured some champagne in them.

When midnight approached, Cala and Azzah shouted down the final seconds along with the crowd. "Ten, nine, eight, seven, six, five, four, three, two, one," Azzah screamed. Pyrotechnics erupted and balloons dropped from the ceiling. "Wooo, this is awesome!"

As the band launched into "Delirious," Azzah and Cala ran onto the dance floor kicking balloons into the air as they went. Looking back at the head table, Azzah grimaced. Prince Bahir was kissing a very large-breasted woman who had bright blonde hair and wore a skimpy, gold-sequined dress.

"Who's that?" Azzah asked Cala incredulously.

"Ha! That's Bahir's New Year's present to himself. He likes big boobs."

"Okay?"

"Forget him. Loosen up and have some fun. Have some more champagne," Cala said pointing at the head table. "Get me some more too," she said handing Azzah her empty glass.

Azzah danced over to the table and refilled their glasses. From that point on, the night became a blur. Azzah danced and drank champagne. While she primarily danced with Cala, every now and then, some cute guys would come and dance with them. Azzah liked the way they looked at her. It was nice being the center of attention, as opposed to hiding beneath a tablecloth.

"My feet are killing me. I've got to sit down," Azzah yelled.

Cala nodded, but continued dancing. Azzah sat down at the table, took off her shoes, and rubbed her feet. When she looked back up, she saw Cala dancing with one of Bahir's friends. The band had switched to a slow song, and the two were dancing very close. Azzah looked away, and poured herself some more champagne.

Suddenly, despite all the fun she'd had, Azzah felt down. Watching the champagne bubbles sparkle and fizz in her glass, she realized by tomorrow all the bubbles would be gone, and she'd have to go back to her flat, dull, fizz-less life. She leaned her head tiredly against her hand.

"Hey, don't fall asleep on me," Cala interrupted. "We're headed upstairs to the suite. Let's go." Azzah took another gulp of champagne, slipped on her shoes, and followed Cala.

In the elevator, Cala and her male companion were laughing and giggling, but Azzah didn't quite get the joke. Then a song they all recognized came on, and they danced all the way up to the suite.

Upon entering the suite, Azzah saw a table covered with *hors d'oeuvres*. "Oh, food!" Azzah said brightly as she stepped unsteadily up to the table. She grabbed a crab-stuffed mushroom and popped it into her mouth. "Cala, you've got to try one of these," she said, but Cala and her companion were gone. Azzah shrugged, filled up a plate with food, and slowly toured the suite.

Azzah came upon a pair of French doors with frosted glass. Inside, it was humid and warm, and flowering plants hung from the ceiling. "When you're done snacking, feel free to join us," a female voice called. Azzah looked over and saw Bahir's large-breasted friend sitting in a hot tub along with some other Western women.

"Uh? I didn't bring a swim suit," Azzah answered.

"Oh, that's okay. It's just us girls. You can just go *au naturel*. Come on in. Relax for a while."

Azzah looked at her quizzically, and then over at the male security guard standing motionless at the far side of the room.

"Don't mind him. He's got more important things to worry about than us."

Though skeptical, Azzah walked over to the hot tub. A hot bath did sound nice.

"I'm Celine," the blonde girl introduced herself, "and this is Tammy and Georgia. All the guys are in the theater watching a movie and smoking cigars. Believe me, this is a lot more relaxing."

"That's for damn sure," Tammy said as she closed her eyes and rested her head back on the side of the hot tub.

"The last time I worked one of Bahir's parties it took me a week to get that nasty cigar smell out of my hair," Georgia added.

"You and me both," Tammy concurred.

"Just throw your dress over a chair. You can grab a hotel robe and towel afterward. There's plenty to go around," Celine said motioning toward the stack of robes and towels hanging in the nearby wardrobe.

"All right, you've convinced me," Azzah answered quietly. She walked over to the wardrobe and picked out a long, fluffy, white robe and a towel. After setting them down on one of the tables that encircled the hot tub, she kicked off her shoes and undid the back of her dress. As the neck of the dress fell to her chest, she gathered it in her arms hesitantly.

"Their movie isn't going to last forever," Tammy murmured.

"Oh . . . yeah," Azzah answered. She let her dress fall to her waist and slipped it off her hips revealing her black lace underwear and demi cup bra. Quickly, she sneaked into the hot tub. Still feeling subconscious, she gathered the bubbles around her, embarrassed that the other girls' breasts were so much larger than hers.

"I didn't catch your name," Celine prodded.

"Azzah."

"That's pretty," Celine commented. "Which club do you work at? I haven't seen you around before."

"Oh, I don't work here," Azzah answered without really understanding the question. "I'm here with Cala."

Tammy's eyes popped open. "Bahir's cousin?"

"Yes," Azzah answered. She closed her eyes and leaned her head back.

Now, it was the other girls' turn to feel uncomfortable. They looked at one another, not knowing quite what to say. If they had suggested to Cala she was in their profession, she would have sent them packing. Celine started to apologize, "We didn't mean to imply . . . "

"Huh?" Azzah murmured her eyes closed.

"Uh . . . we've been in here quite a while," Tammy said motioning to the others. "We're going to get out and see what's going on."

"Oh, okay," Azzah answered, sitting up. "Do I need to get out?"

"No, you're fine," Celine said while she dried off and grabbed a robe. "Just don't stay in too long. You don't want to fall asleep in there."

Celine was right. It would be easy to fall asleep in here. A few more minutes won't hurt though.

Azzah let the jets massage her back and legs. Frankly, it was nice just to sit down after dancing for so long. A few minutes later, a young man's voice cut through the hum of the spa. Startled, Azzah sat up. It was Bahir.

"What are you doing in here all by yourself?" he asked from across the room dressed in a hotel robe.

"Umm . . . Your girlfriend Celine said it was a good way to relax," Azzah answered, somewhat embarrassed. "My feet were just killing me."

As she was talking, Bahir whispered something to the guard. The guard exited and Bahir walked over to the spa. "Celine's not really my girlfriend," he said slyly. "She's more of an associate than a girlfriend. I invited her to liven up the party for my friends. They'll be spending more time with her than me."

"Oh," Azzah commented, frowning.

"Would you mind some company?" Bahir asked as he stood next to the spa.

Before she could answer, he took off his robe and threw it on the table next to her clothes. Azzah smirked at the small, bright-blue, Speedo bathing suit Bahir was wearing.

"What? At European beaches, all the guys wear these."

"Well, it's . . . ummm . . . just a bit different," Azzah said, stumbling over the words.

Bahir stepped into the hot tub and let out a loud sigh. "So, did you have a good time tonight?"

"It's been wonderful," Azzah answered.

"The band was really on tonight. The lead singer is a friend of mine. I book them for all my parties."

Azzah nodded, but said nothing.

"You all tired out from dancing?" he asked.

"Not too bad," Azzah answered. "It's nice to sit down though. This Jacuzzi is wonderful."

"I don't know how you girls dance in those shoes," Bahir said. "I'd probably fall on my ass. Yes?"

"Uh . . . probably."

Bahir leaned over the edge and grabbed one of Azzah's shoes. "Plus, I don't think I'd look as good in them as you do."

Azzah laughed as Bahir held her shoe up to his foot. "I'm not sure they're quite the right size."

"What! Are you're saying I have big feet? You don't like my swimsuit, and I have big feet."

"Yes, and hairy legs," Azzah said, smirking.

"Aghhh!" Bahir exclaimed. Slowly, he started to sink beneath the bubbling water. "Saaaave me."

Azzah reached over and pulled him up. "Is that better?" she asked.

"Much better," he said as he put his arm around her waist. "I still can't figure out why you're here all by yourself. I noticed several guys who could hardly take their eyes off you," Bahir said. "Including me."

"You're just saying that to be nice," Azzah said, blushing slightly.

"What do you mean?" Bahir asked as he pulled her closer.

"I'm . . . I'm not as beautiful as those other girls."

166

"No, you're more beautiful," he said as he touched the side of her cheek. "You're not a carnation. You're a beautiful desert flower."

Bahir leaned in and kissed her. Azzah pulled back slightly, then gave in. Deep inside she knew there was no point in continuing, but the beating of her heart drowned out those thoughts. At least for one night, the prince would be hers.

Chapter 29: Who's Who

It was New Year's Day. Agent Jamison strode grumpily along the sidewalk toward his storefront location. Upon reaching his office, he unlocked the retractable metal gate that covered the entrance, pushed it aside, and swung open the door. Although it was barely nine a.m., it had the makings of a bad day. Earlier that morning, he'd finally caught up with Socrates at their fallback site, but Socrates' intel was less than helpful.

Jamison continued to go over it in his mind. "Attack imminent! Oil related targets. I am under almost constant surveillance." He let the front door slam shut and threw his newspaper down on the counter. With his hands on his hips, he stared at the floor.

Attack imminent, eh. Nothing like giving me some specifics, and oil related targets? Really? This is Saudi Arabia for Christ's sake. Nothing like narrowing it down. Where did Rider find this guy?

Exasperated, Jamison wheeled around, locked the front door, and headed to his office. After starting up a new pot of coffee, he turned on his computer. While it was booting up, he worked the dial to his safe.

"I took care of that detective," Jamison said. "Rider's SAID contact said it would be taken care of, but Socrates says he's still under surveillance. Sounds to me like he's afraid of his own shadow."

Jamison yanked out several file folders from the safe and slapped them on top of his desk. "Gimme something," he pleaded as he logged on to his computer. "Finally!" he exclaimed. "I can't believe how long it took to get answers on those RFIs. A facial recognition request usually only takes a day or so," he said while selecting a message from his in-box.

Okay, what have we got? My man with the scar is named Jasim Saqr. He's an Afghan with ties to the Haqqani network. A bomb technician, Jasim's wanted in connection with a hotel bombing in Jalalabad. So what are you doing here in Saudi

Arabia, and why are you knocking on Husam's door? He moved on to the next message.

Husam's unwanted guest. A small-time crook breaking into an apartment, or . . . drum roll please. Aashif Muhanned, the trusted bodyguard of Yaman Utbah. Oh yeah, the Utbah raid. That went down a few weeks before I got here. His brow furrowed, Jamison bent over awkwardly and rummaged through the files.

"Ughh, here it is," he grunted as he struggled to straighten up. Quickly, he skimmed through the file. After about five minutes, Jamison threw it down, open-faced, on top of the other files.

"Goddamn it! Which is it?" he grumbled while flipping the pages back and forth. "A key Al Qaeda player or a two-bit crook? I wish headquarters would make up their mind. Still, would Yaman have this heavy hitter watching over him if he were nothing but a two-bit crook? Doubtful."

Jamison turned his attention back to the e-mail. "Muhanned," he said, his voice barely audible. "He's former Saudi Army, member of the 5th, and he used to work for Zafir. What's that?" After reading a little further, he had his answer. Zafir was a private security firm. The Saudi version of Blackwater. Muhanned left Zafir, and started working for Yaman a couple of years ago.

Jamison looked intently at the files strewn across his desk. He grabbed the one marked Husam and flipped it open. Husam and Yaman Utbah were pretty close at one time. Husam and Muhanned should know one another, but it didn't look like Muhanned's visit to Husam's apartment was a social one. Jamison drummed his fingers on the desk. Then, he got up and poured himself a cup of coffee.

Upon returning to his desk, Agent Jamison stood and sipped his coffee and stared at the files. *Are Jasim and Husam working with Muhanned, or are they competing against him? This Jasim is the wild card. Was Rider tracking anyone else with ties to the Haqqani network?* Jamsion tapped his fingers to his lips. He had read something. It was an Al Qaeda funding report.

He squatted down and flipped through the other files in Rider's old safe. Even in this day and age, he was still working off old scraps of paper. Shuffling through the files, Agent Jamison looked inside one, then another. Finally, he found it.

Agent Jamison pursed his lips and scanned the document. After turning to the second page, he found a list of Saudi organizations that were suspected of funneling money to the Haqqani network. The list contained a prominent local mosque, and in the margin, Agent Rider had penciled in the name, Imam Al-Hashim.

"That's why Rider recruited that young man, Afaz, from the mosque," Jamison said, shaking his head. "Now, why wasn't that detailed in Afaz's file? Goddamn Rider. Geez, I've been here how long, and I'm still just putting the pieces together. For a quiet little outpost, someone sure has turned up the volume."

Jamison grimaced as he stared at the files. *Contact doesn't equal coordination. Nonetheless, I'll have to keep an eye on it. Maybe, I can get BMO1 to plant a couple video cameras outside that mosque.* Jamison glanced up at the clock.

At this time of day, she usually positioned herself outside the *souks*. Jamison rummaged through the safe looking for a couple of the mini-video-capture devices, commonly called MVCs. While some things hadn't changed much over his years as an agent, thankfully some things had. As far as Agent Jamison was concerned, these MVCs were wonderful. Miniature camera lenses that captured video straight to a tiny hard drive, they fit in the palm of your hand.

After sitting back down at his desk, Agent Jamison grabbed two MVCs and put in new batteries. He reviewed his computer files for an image of Imam Al-Hashim's mosque. Upon finding it, he printed out a small copy of the picture, and wrapped it around the MVCs with a rubber band. He needed to use a picture, because according to the file, BMO1 couldn't read, or at least not very well. Nonetheless, whatever she lacked in education, she easily made up for in determination.

"She'll get it done," he mumbled confidently. "I don't know how, but she'll get it done."

Satisfied that he had everything he needed, Agent Jamsion shut down his computer and returned the files to the safe. Once everything was secured, he put the MVCs in his front pocket and headed for the *souks*.

Chapter 30: Reality TV

It was late in the evening on New Year's Day before Siraj finally sat down at his computer to review the footage from the night before. After working at the party until two a.m., Siraj had to help the cleanup crew. Then, he collected his surveillance cameras from the ballroom while Jabir gathered the cameras from Prince Bahir's suite. Siraj didn't get home from the party until almost noon. His father was not amused.

"At least the tips that I got waiting tables helped shut Father up," Siraj said as he uploaded the video from the first camera. "Boy, he really let me have it when I walked in." Memory of their exchange made Siraj chuckle.

#

"Where have you been all night," Siraj's father demanded.

"Working," Siraj answered dully.

"Working? Ha, doing what? Drinking? Playing video games?"

Siraj looked tiredly at the floor wishing he were somewhere else. "Waiting tables at a New Year's Eve party."

"What? I paid Allah knows how much money putting you through college, and you were waiting tables?"

"It pays better than you think," Siraj retorted. "Especially when the people attending the party are the rich Arabian elites you spend so much time kissing up to."

"You got paid?" his father asked skeptically. "But who pays for this house? Who pays for the car you drive? Who pays for the computer you spend all your time staring at?"

Siraj stuck his hand in his pocket, pulled out the wad of cash he'd earned, and slammed it on the table. "Okay, here's a down payment!"

"You made that being a servant," his father scoffed with a disapproving sneer.

"How's that any different than what you do? They paid for the alcohol that I was serving with money that you helped them earn. They paid for the women they were dancing up against with money that you helped them acquire. At least I'm smart enough to see them for what they really are."

"And what's that?" his father asked, his face growing red.

"Privileged hypocrites, just like you."

"Like me! I'll have you know not one drop of alcohol has ever touched these lips."

"You can tell Allah that when he judges you. Explain how you helped them build their obscene wealth. Explain how you helped them dole out scraps to the general population in order to keep it in check. Explain how you looked the other way while your employers raped the holy land for their own benefit and enjoyment. And why did you look the other way? So you could keep your modest civil servant post. Take the money," Siraj insisted as he pushed it across the table. "You've done more to earn it than I have."

#

"He was speechless," Siraj said with a smile. He moved on to the next camera. "Maybe, if I showed him these videos, he'd stop being their lapdog and take a stand." Siraj shook his head in disgust. "What a screwed-up country."

It took Siraj nearly an hour to upload all the video. He had over twelve hours of footage to review. From that, he hoped to come up with a thirty-second spot, a sixty-second spot, and maybe a short feature that ran no more than three or four minutes. "Well, might as well get started," he said with mock enthusiasm.

He opened the first file and hit play. The video was from the head table. After watching for a few minutes, he sped it up to four times normal speed. He hit pause when the champagne was delivered. After reversing it a few frames, he clicked play.

"That's the ticket," Siraj said.

The video showed Prince Bahir opening a champagne bottle and spraying champagne over everyone at his table. One of the prince's female guests got drenched particularly well. It made her already revealing outfit almost see-through. Siraj captured the scene and saved it as "Wet T-Shirt."

Later in the video, he saw one of the prince's male guests rolling what looked to be a joint. Moments afterward, the camera captured Prince Bahir and his guest alternately taking drags off the joint. He saved this scene as "High Times."

"What happens in Bahrain stays in Bahrain. Not this time Prince Bahir."

Siraj continued through the videos one by one, and after three hours he had dozens of scenes to choose from. However, it still lacked bite. While the scenes of the Prince drinking and carousing with Western women were good, many would absolve him because these women were not Muslim. As non-Muslim women, they garnered less respect than their Muslim counterparts. Some viewers would not be surprised that the prince fell victim to these immoral vixens. A few would even canonize him for it.

Still, he had one video left. "I need something with a little more shock value. Ah, the hot tub camera," Siraj said with a smile. He cued the video up. "This should be good." Upon seeing several of the prince's female guests entering the hot tub topless, he decided to play the video at normal speed.

"Oh my," he exclaimed. Siraj hit rewind and watched the three women take off their robes again. Then, he let the video play. "Damn! The bubbles from the hot tub are covering everything worth seeing," Siraj griped. He was about to fast-forward when a fourth woman entered the scene.

This woman was younger than the other three, and although she had on a Western-style dress, she looked to be of Arabian descent. Siraj watched as this new arrival kicked off her shoes and undid the back of her dress. As the neck of the dress fell to her chest, she gathered it in her arms. She had a small birthmark on her neck—it almost looked like a star.

"What are you waiting for?" Siraj asked impatiently. After hesitating for a moment, she let the dress fall to her waist and then slipped it over her hips. Siraj let out a groan at the sight of her black lace underwear and bra. "What? Wait! Don't get in. You're not undressed yet," he said. But his calls went unrewarded as the Arabian girl quickly slipped into the hot tub.

"Oh man, I've got to watch that again." Siraj rewound the video. Although this girl's breasts weren't nearly as big as the other three, she was lithe like a dancer. Plus, her skin wasn't nearly as pale. She had a catlike grace and wasn't as much of a caricature as the other three. "Where did you come from?"

After watching her grand entrance a couple more times, Siraj let the video continue. After a few minutes, the three Western women got up to leave. While he was disappointed to see them go, he took guilty pleasure watching them exit the Jacuzzi. Their naked bodies dripping wet, the three women grabbed towels and dried off, then put on robes and walked out of view.

"Don't go," Siraj pleaded. "Come back." Then an idea struck him. "Even if I don't get anything useful from this video, I could make some cash just by burning it to DVD."

The video continued with the young woman relaxing alone in the Jacuzzi. Siraj watched, entranced by her face. She was beautiful, but seemed out of place. Hesitant, her body language seemed to indicate she didn't quite belong.

"Who are you?" Siraj asked.

Suddenly, the young woman sat up somewhat startled. Self-consciously, she covered her breasts with her arms. "What's going on?" Siraj exclaimed. Then he saw Prince Bahir enter the scene. "No way," Siraj exclaimed as the prince strutted into view of the camera wearing a small, tight swimsuit. "You gotta be kidding me. What's the problem? A little cold in there?" Siraj scoffed.

Siraj watched as the prince laid on the smarmy, self-deprecating charm he'd already shown several times before. When motivated, Prince Bahir could be enchanting. He knew how to make those around him feel important, especially women. Then he could get them to do anything he wanted. However, if they didn't fall for it, the prince quickly turned cold and vindictive.

In this case, there was little chance of that. The young woman was falling for it hook, line, and sinker. It only took a few moments for the prince to break down her defenses. She was smiling and laughing, having forgotten all about the fact she was wearing only underwear. Soon, Prince Bahir had his arms around her.

175

Siraj was filled with jealousy. Why would this prince waste his charms on this young girl? He could have any woman he wanted. Wasn't all that money enough? Wasn't all that power enough? No matter how much the monarchy had, it was never enough.

As he watched Prince Bahir seduce the young woman, Siraj now felt more angry than excited. Though the young woman was now topless, Siraj averted his eyes when the prince stood her up and slid off her wet panties.

However, when Siraj looked back, the young woman was having second thoughts. When the prince pulled her on top of his lap, she shook her head and pushed him away. Despite Bahir's encouragement, she continued to pull back.

When she scrambled out of the Jacuzzi, the prince's smile faded. Abruptly, Bahir grabbed her around the ankles and yanked hard. Her feet slid out from underneath her, and she hit her head on the tile floor. Disoriented, she was defenseless as he climbed on top of her. The prince pressed the girl's arms up above her head with his forearms. He would not be denied, no matter how much the girl struggled. With her head turned awkwardly to the side, she closed her eyes tightly, as if that would somehow help shut him out. Siraj looked away, angry at the prince and ashamed of himself.

Finally, it was over. Siraj looked back in time to see Bahir give her one last thrust before getting off her. Smiling, with a confident sneer the prince talked to her while putting on his robe. Then he strode off screen acting as if nothing happened. The young woman rolled onto her side and sobbed.

Lying on the hard tile, she was naked and alone. Still, the video continued. For almost ten minutes, the girl lay there. Curled up with her hands covering her face, her heaving sobs were the only indication she was still alive. After what seemed like an eternity, she finally sat up. She wiped away her tears and summoned the resolve to get up. Though unsteady, she grabbed a towel, dried off, and began to get dressed.

His eyes red, Siraj minimized the video window and opened his browser. "What was the name of that folk singer Dema used to listen to?"

The images he'd just seen reminded Siraj of a CD that Dema, his college roommate, listened to back then. The CD had a song on it about an honor killing. It questioned why the monarchy turned a blind eye to such things in the name of Islam.

One day, another student overheard Dema playing the music. He'd threatened to turn Dema in for playing the obvious contraband and the two got into a loud argument in the hallway. While the other student insisted that true Islam taught women to be subservient, Dema argued that, according to Islam, women were to be adored and beloved.

"Women are to be put up on a pedestal, not held under foot," Dema said.

"Maybe, if Dema had seen this, he would have joined us in our fight," Siraj said. "He wouldn't have turned to the drugs that took his life. Damn, what's that artist's name?"

He did a generic search on Arab artists and scanned the results. An article caught his attention. The headline read, "Artist Jailed for Heresy." Siraj opened the article and quickly read through it.

"Janan Shadi, that's it," he said in relief. "Think he'd waive copyright for my little movie? Since he's in jail, copyright infringement is probably the least of his worries right now."

After doing a little more digging, Siraj found a copy of Janan's song, called "Safa's Tears." The quality wasn't the best, but he could still make out the lyrics.

How can this be, that the monarchy,
would turn a blind eye, and let the innocent die?
How can they say, that this is the law,
when their own strip it raw? Will this be the last straw?
Islam is the one true religion, not a prison for our mind.
Islam is the one true religion, not rules to keep us in line.

Siraj turned his attention back to the video. The young woman was now fully dressed. She was looking at herself in the mirrored wall that faced the Jacuzzi and was putting on makeup. Upon finishing, she stood in front of the mirror, determined to find her resolve and put the evening's events behind her. Her tears indicated this was easier said than done. Siraj continued listening to the song as he watched.

> Safa's tears fall. Still they fall. Fall on you. Fall on me.
> Safa's tears call. Still they call. Out to you. Out to me.
> Safa's tears weep. Still they weep.
> Weep for you. Weep for me.

After making some slight adjustments to her dress, the young woman wiped her eyes, painted on an aloof expression, and strode out of the camera's view. The video now showed an empty Jacuzzi. Siraj paused the video and turned up the volume to the song.

> How can they say, in this day and age,
> that this is the way, that we should behave?
> How can they be, so devoid of mercy,
> for this young girl, who was lost to this world?
> Islam is the one true religion, not the law of the clowns.
> Islam is the one true religion, not a fist to keep us down.

Siraj went over in his mind how he would put together the video. First, he'd need to tie Bahir in with the monarch's ruling class. He's not just some rogue. He's accepted. He's one of them. He decided to use video he had of Bahir shaking the King's hand after a polo match, and video of the prince attending a state dinner. Janan Shadi's song continued to play.

> How can we stand by, when it's an eye for an eye,
> and let her fall, despite justice's call?
> How can we be still? Is it really Allah's will,
> that none shall thrive, except the chosen hive?
> Islam is the one true religion, not a system of oppression.
> Islam is the one true religion, not a veil to persecution.

Siraj also had images of Prince Bahir as part of the King's entourage when England's prime minister visited. He could contrast those scenes with the ample footage he had of Bahir womanizing, drinking, and so on.

Siraj looked unhappily at the file containing the Jacuzzi footage. While he knew that the young Arabian woman in the footage had suffered enough, he had to use it. The video was stark proof that the monarchy was above the law. Not just man's law but Allah's law as well. As the chorus played for the final time, Siraj thought about how he'd use the video.

Safa's tears fall. Still they fall. Fall on you. Fall on me.
Safa's tears call. Still they call. Out to you. Out to me.
Safa's tears weep. Still they weep.
Weep for you. Weep for me.

"I'll obscure her face and body. Nobody will recognize her." Siraj mumbled, but once again he felt ashamed. "Bahir probably has no idea who she is. I've seen him with dozens of women." Nervously, Siraj tapped his finger on the edge of the keyboard.

"What if I'm wrong? What if she is recognized? It'd be a death sentence for her. Do I sacrifice her to save all the future women that Bahir would rape and abuse? What should I do, Dema?" he said looking heavenward.

"Where's your head," Siraj grumbled angrily. "You have a job to do. Do it. The monarchy is a cancer, an abomination. We need to attack it, no matter the cost. The Imam and Professor Ratib are counting on you."

His resolve restored. Siraj began editing the video. He couldn't let Bahir get away with it. This time the prince would have to answer for his crimes.

Chapter 31: Early Returns

Professor Ratib's heart beat quickly as he entered the mosque. Soon he'd find out, at least to some small extent, how the tactics he'd proposed had worked. When he reached Imam Al-Hashim's office, Professor Ratib peeked around the partially open door. Husam and the Imam were already there. The professor knocked softly on the door to announce his presence.

"Come in," Imam Al-Hashim called.

"I'm not interrupting, am I?" Professor Ratib asked. "I didn't see Afaz."

"He is now serving Allah in a different capacity," the Imam said. "Come, have a seat."

Professor Ratib closed the door, walked across the room, and sat down on the rug with Husam and the Imam. Quietly, the Imam nodded for Husam to pour a cup of tea for the professor.

"How is your family doing?" the Imam asked.

"They are well. Thank you for asking," Professor Ratib responded. "How are you feeling?"

"I am well. Allah has blessed me more than I can comprehend. Have you been watching the news?"

"Y . . . Yes," Professor Ratib replied hesitantly.

"It is very curious all the maintenance problems that these oil tankers are having. Isn't it, Husam?" the Imam asked.

"Yes, very interesting," Husam concurred. "I question whether the reporting is accurate though."

"Why do you say that?" the Imam asked.

"So many tankers come down with maintenance problems all at once. I do not think that the press is telling us the whole story. Then again, maybe they are just a little slow on the uptake. The truth will reveal that Allah has truly blessed us," Husam said with a cruel smirk.

"I read that the price of oil has jumped twenty dollars a barrel, even with these small delays," Professor Ratib offered. "Do you think that the press is underestimating the extent of the problems?"

"Something tells me this is only the tip of the iceberg," Husam replied. "By the way professor, I need to thank you for the contacts you have provided. They have been more helpful than I could have ever imagined."

"You're welcome. Do you need additional assistance?"

"No. We have a good group right now. These projects can be difficult to control when too many people get involved."

"The mosque, as always, is facing financial strains. With greater assets, we could leverage additional resources. Have you been in touch with any of our university supporters?" Imam Al-Hashim asked.

"I have not heard from any of them recently. However, I can seek them out, if Allah wills it," Professor Ratib answered.

"He does indeed," the Imam said. "You cannot build a house without bricks. However, Husam will act as courier for any future donations," the Imam added.

"Is something wrong?" the professor asked nervously.

"An important donor was robbed recently," the Imam said. "Husam will ensure that future donations reach their intended recipient. Husam, are you familiar with the area surrounding the university?"

"Yes, I've worked construction jobs in that area," Husam answered.

"Good, good. I'll give Husam your contact information. He'll be in touch with you later in the week to set something up."

Leisurely, the three men finished their tea. After several minutes, Professor Ratib rose to leave. The Imam walked with him to the door and kissed him on both cheeks. "Blessings and peace be upon you," the Imam offered. Then he returned to his seat and continued his conversation with Husam.

#

The Imam poured himself another cup of tea. "When you complimented the professor on his recruits, were you being honest?" he asked.

"Yes. As I've told you, I was initially concerned about relying so heavily on untrained individuals. However, they've responded very well. That said, success often breeds additional scrutiny. I don't know how they will react to the pressure."

"If fear causes them to become a liability, will you be able to handle it?"

"Jasim and I can keep it under control," Husam answered confidently. "Have you heard from Muhanned recently?"

"Yes, he was here a few days ago."

"And?" Husam asked.

"Do not worry about him. I know where his true allegiance lies. He will not bite the hand that feeds him."

"True, but he does not always act rationally," Husam warned the Imam. "He is a hard man, who often acts without thinking. Yaman never intended for him to be in this position."

"I know," the Imam replied. "But I can no longer let that wolf guard my sheep."

"The wolf sometimes attacks the shepherd too," Husam cautioned.

"My fate is already written," the Imam said. "Don't worry about Muhanned. When the time comes, his presence may prove useful. His lust for Yaman's throne may be both a curse and a blessing. Now, if you'll excuse me, I need to prepare for prayers."

Husam nodded and stood.

Slowly, the Imam rose to his feet. "One more thing," he said, grabbing a backpack that had been sitting on the floor and handing it to Husam. "In the past, you've mentioned that working with our Somali brothers could help broaden our reach. This should help you get started."

Husam unzipped the backpack and glanced inside. It was filled with cash. "Imam Al-Hashim, this is premature," Husam stammered. "I haven't even talked to my Somali contacts. It was just an idea."

"You need to start trusting your own instincts," the Imam responded as he patted Husam on the back. "It's time for you to follow the path that Allah has prepared for you. Blessings and peace be upon you."

As Husam left, Imam Al-Hashim slowly made his way to the bathroom. After taking two pain pills, he headed over to his desk.

The Imam heaved a sigh. His days on this earth were coming to an end. After several doctor's visits, it had been confirmed. His cancer had spread. The only decision to be made was whether or not chemotherapy was truly worth a few extra months of life.

I'd rather spend what little time I have left fighting for something I believe in, than fighting the cancer. It's only a matter of time before Muhanned puts two and two together. In an effort to ramp up these operations, I've been holding back more and more funds from him, but he won't get another dime from me. Ultimately, pressuring me will put the final nail in his own coffin.

Chapter 32: Double Life

Nasim's final semester passed quickly. Now, more than ever, Nasim felt like he was leading a double life. Before Nicole, college was just a means to an end. Despite attending school there for almost four years, he'd always felt like an outsider. Now, all that had changed.

Nathan was gone. His parents had pulled him from school following his second DUI, and he was in rehab somewhere. Thankfully, his parents had paid for his share of the rent for the remainder of school.

With Nathan gone, Nicole had become a fixture in Nasim's life. She dragged him to parties, introduced him to her friends, and enabled Nasim to integrate into campus life to a degree he'd never felt possible. While Nasim had always done his best to hide his Muslim beliefs, he found he didn't need to. In fact, many of Nicole's friends would ask him questions about Islam. He wasn't remotely prepared, not for any of it, so now he found himself seeking guidance from the local imam at a mosque near campus.

Sitting outside the imam's office, Nasim fidgeted nervously. During Nasim's first semester, the imam had helped him refocus his efforts at school when he'd encountered problems, but Nasim had drifted away since then. Whenever the imam had invited him to a mosque function, he'd always come up with some excuse not to go. He was too busy, too tired, and generally not interested.

What will the imam think now, after I've blown him off so many times before? Somewhat embarrassed, Nasim stared blankly at the floor.

"Nasim, it's good to see you. How long has it been?" Imam Sad al-Din asked when he emerged from his office.

"It's been a while," Nasim replied sheepishly.

"Come in," the imam offered. Nasim stood up and followed him into his office. The imam closed the door behind them. "Take a seat Nasim. Now, my secretary said that you wanted to talk. What's troubling you?"

Nasim didn't know quite where to start. "Ummm, well . . . I, ah . . . " he stammered, looking around the imam's office uncomfortably.

The imam laughed and leaned back in his chair. "Take your time, Nasim. I'm in no hurry. Are you going to be continuing on to graduate school?" he asked. Perhaps, the change in subject might make Nasim feel more comfortable.

"Well, yes. Maybe? I've been studying here in the U.S. for almost four years now."

"Yes," Imam Al-Din nodded, "and doing very well from what I hear."

"I'm doing all right," Nasim admitted.

"Everything going well at home?"

"Yes, but . . . "

"But?"

"Well, Palestine and the United States are . . . um . . . well, they're different worlds."

"I assume we're talking about more than geography here?"

"Yes," Nasim continued. "I almost feel like I'm two different people. When I visit home, it's so different. I'm so different. I have many friends there who . . . who hate the United States. They hate Americans, and I've had similar feelings myself from time to time, but lately—"

"But now you have friends in America too, eh, and some of them are probably Christian, Jewish, and atheist. Am I right?"

"Well yes, but . . . but doesn't the Qur'an say to kill the pagans wherever you find them?" Nasim blurted out, while thinking back to one of the verses he learned as a boy. "How is that possible? How can I be both their friend and a Muslim?"

"Nasim," the imam said. "You're taking that particular verse out of context. When you look at the entire verse and take into account the political climate that existed when it was written, you'll see that you are missing part of the story."

"What do you mean?"

"At that time in history, there were many tribal conflicts. Actually, not too much different from modern-day Afghanistan or Libya if you think about it. In any event, that particular verse refers

185

specifically to one of those conflicts. When read in its entirety, you'll see that the verse actually encourages us to be merciful and forgiving when our enemies extend their hands in friendship."

"I see," Nasim said softly.

"Whenever anyone confronts me with the argument that Islam preaches violence," the imam continued. "I always quote to them chapter five, verse thirty-two, of the Qur'an. It states that if anyone slays a person, unless it be for murder or for spreading mischief in the land, it would be as if he slew all people. And if anyone saves a life, it would be as if he saved the life of all mankind."

"But, but what of my brother," Nasim asked, still somewhat confused. "He was killed in a conflict between the Hamas and the Israeli military. How can I be true to his memory?"

The imam thought for a moment, and then responded, "While the verse would certainly seem to provide you some avenue to seek justice, it's certainly not an open invitation for you to retaliate. Who do you think is responsible for your brother's death?"

"The Jews."

"Everyone of Jewish faith?"

"Well, no. I . . . I guess not," he said. Then, after thinking about it for a moment, he said, "Israel."

"The whole nation of Israel? Is there not one innocent person in the entire nation?"

"Yes, there are, but . . . "

"But, it hurts. Your bother is dead and you want to hold someone responsible."

"Yes," Nasim replied, fighting back tears, "but you just don't understand. They knock down our homes to build settlements of their own. They arrest ten Palestinian men for the death of one Israeli."

"I don't understand!" the imam exclaimed as he leaned forward. "My family fled Iraq when I was boy. We didn't all make it! My grandparents and two of my uncles were executed by Saddam loyalists. Don't think for one second that I don't understand! You presume much if you think you are the only one who has suffered loss."

"I . . . I'm sorry."

"Look at me, Nasim. Faith is not always easy. Sometimes, doing the right thing hurts. While revenging your brother's death might fill a temporary void, it would only contribute to the cycle of violence that took your brother's life in the first place. More than likely, you would hurt someone who knew nothing of you brother's death. You would hurt someone who had contributed nothing to your pain, and then what? How are they to react? Where do they turn for justice? More violence?"

Nasim nodded silently and roughly wiped his cheeks with his sleeve. Imam Sad al-Din continued, "Remember chapter four, verse one-thirty-five as well. It tells us not to follow the cravings of our hearts, lest we swerve, and if we distort justice or decline to do justice, verily Allah is well acquainted with all that we do."

"So, what then?" Nasim asked. "My brother is dead, and there is no recourse?"

"Break the cycle," the imam commanded.

"Break the cycle?"

"Yes, break the cycle of violence that took your brother's life. Instead of harboring hatred toward your fellow man—"

"What? Shower them with love," Nasim interrupted sarcastically.

"No, help them see your brother's death through your eyes. Give them a glimpse of the hardships you've faced during your life. Talk about the fighting, the deaths, the checkpoints, and the blackouts, but also be open to their views. We can never hope to open their eyes if we are blind to what our own hatred has wrought."

For a moment, Nasim was silent. Finally, he spoke, "I . . . I understand. Thank you. Thank you for seeing me. I'm sorry."

"Sorry? For what, having questions?"

"No, it's just that you've always been very supportive, but I've generally just tried to go it alone."

"Ah, faith is like the ocean tides. There is a constant ebb and flow, high tide and low. Graduation is just around the corner. Whether you return home or continue your education here in America, keep the friendships you have created close to your heart. Those friendships will do more to help break the cycle of violence that plagues this world than a hundred of my *khutbas*." He paused, then smiled. "Don't tell anyone I said that though."

Nasim smiled gently. "Don't worry. I won't."

"Is that all you wanted to talk about?"

"No, I . . . I mean yes, that's all. I'm probably just stressed out with graduation coming up and everything."

Nasim had to admit he felt better. It was nice to be able to talk freely with someone who understood the pain and did not judge him too harshly for expressing it. Nicole tried. She wanted to understand him, but Nasim was afraid she wouldn't like what she saw. As his discussion with the imam devolved into chitchat, Nasim came to a decision.

Relax and have fun these last few weeks. Screw the Memorial Day attacks. I'm going to graduation and then maybe take off with Nicole for a few weeks. I'll figure out the rest later. I'm tired of the anger. I'm tired of the hate. I'm tired of leading a double life.

"Are your parents coming out for your graduation?" the imam asked.

"No, it's been a tough year for them. Whenever there is violence, even if it's not directly related to Gaza or the West Bank, it is difficult. It's often difficult for them to get into work, and business is slow when security is high."

"I understand." The imam stood up and walked Nasim out. "Buildings rise and fall, but trust between enemies is what's hardest to build."

Chapter 33: Black Moving Object

Agent Jamison parked his white rental car near one of the stone obelisks that lined the parking lot. He grabbed the small notebook he used to jot down prices and patted the outside of his pocket, feeling for the MVCs. Satisfied, he set out to find his contact, BMO1.

Assuming someone hadn't chased her off, she was usually near the entrance to the gold *souks* this time of day. One odd thing about Saudi Arabia, when compared to the other places where he'd been stationed, was how quickly one could go from the 1900s to present day and back, in the space of just a couple of blocks. At times, the modern buildings seemed like nothing more than a facade built up to give the impression that the country was a modern metropolis.

The reality was a bit more mixed. Take a turn down the wrong alley, and you'd be transported back in time. There were plenty of old buildings and history in Europe, but this was different. The glitter of the *souks*, when compared to old, windowless, mud brick buildings that were hidden throughout the city, was more striking than anything he'd encountered before. It made the whole 1%-versus-the-99% business back home seem somewhat ridiculous.

Up ahead, the sunny glow of the jewelry stores beckoned, and there on the corner was BMO1. She was dressed all in black like many of the other women, but the fabric of her *habiya* was rough, more akin to burlap than any modern-day fabric. BMO1 sat cross-legged with a small basket in front of her, selling some small trinkets. The owner of a nearby shop was harassing her.

"Get out of here before I call the *mutawa*. You're scaring away the customers. Nobody wants your worthless trinkets." He tipped over her basket with his foot.

BMO1's hands quickly corralled her trinkets like they were precious gems.

"I said, get!" The shopkeeper slapped BMO1 on the top of her head.

Jamison quickened his pace.

"Excuse me, sir," Jamison said loudly. "I was looking for a necklace for my wife," he lied.

"What?" the shopkeeper looked up.

"I said that I'm looking for a necklace for my wife," Jamison repeated.

"Yes sir, right this way. I've got the best prices in town," the shopkeeper said as he ushered Jamison toward his wares.

"Oh! These are neat," Jamison exclaimed stopping short to look at BMO1's trinkets. A flash of anger crossed the shopkeeper's eyes, but he said nothing. "How much are these?" Agent Jamison asked BMO1.

"One riyal," BMO1 answered.

"Oh, wonderful," Agent Jamison said. "I'll take two," he said as he reached in his pocket for the money and the MVCs. He put everything in BMO1's outstretched hands, which rapidly closed over them. Quickly, she transferred the money and the MVCs into a makeshift purse that was tied to her waist, and Jamison grabbed a couple of trinkets from her basket. He then shifted his attention back to the shopkeeper.

"And now the necklaces," Jamison said brightly. While the shopkeeper recited his spiel, BMO1 gathered her trinkets, rolled up the worn rug she'd been sitting on, and left. Jamison watched her go, confident the cameras would be in place by nightfall.

His energy disappeared as the shopkeeper pushed to make a sale. To maintain his sanity, Jamison cut to the chase. "Is that really the best you can do? What if I take four of the sixteen-inch chains?"

Jamison haggled with the shopkeeper, but his heart wasn't really in it. A few moments later, he succumbed. He didn't want the shopkeeper to feign a heart attack. Although the man's offer was average at best, Jamison paid for the necklaces and headed back to his office.

#

Meanwhile, BMO1 had left the *souks* entirely and was already weaving her way through the back alleys behind the facade. While she would have been reluctant to travel these passages after dark, it wasn't overly dangerous during the daytime. Her safety wasn't a priority in this society, regardless of the time of day. Her full name was Shahidah Laiba, but no one took the time to know it anymore. She was an outcast.

When her husband died several years ago, her brother-in-law was appointed as her *mahram*, or guardian. At forty-eight years of age and with little education, Shahidah's prospects were slim. Her brother-in-law coyly offered to take her on as his second wife, but when she refused, he took custody of her two children and sent her packing. With her inheritance and social insurance, he set her up with a one-bedroom apartment in a rundown complex that often didn't have running water. He kept the rest as an administrative fee. It was all legal under Saudi Arabian guardianship laws, and there was nothing Shahidah could do.

Upon reaching an old overgrown courtyard, Shahidah set down her belongings and inspected the items the agent had given her. There were two small gadgets. They had little eyes on them. Somehow, they helped the man see. Just point them in the right direction and push the button. But where?

Carefully, she unfolded the scrap of paper he'd given her. It was a picture of a local mosque. *Oh dear, that's a long way.*

She looked up at the sun. *I'll have to go right now if I'm going to make it back before dark.* Then, she looked at the money he'd given her. It was more than she'd get begging all week.

Determinedly, Shahidah got up and started planning out the route in her head. In order to complete the trip before nightfall, she'd have to brave some of the more populated areas of the city. While most people tolerated her begging near the edge of the *souks* or outside one of the city's numerous mosques, there were many areas where she was not welcome.

As long as I keep moving, I should be fine.

After zigzagging through the back alleys, Shahidah crossed back into the shopping district. It was already mid-morning and the sidewalks were crowded with shoppers. Shahidah walked steadily with her head down and avoided eye contact. She passed merchants selling gold, silk rugs, and leather goods. One merchant spit on the ground and uttered a derogatory slur as she passed. Shahidah pretended not to notice and kept moving.

Near the end of the shopping district, Shahidah cut down an alley behind a bakery. Sometimes, she could find old baked goods in the dumpster out back. At the end of the alley, she cautiously peered around the corner. The bakery owner had hit her with a broomstick handle the last time he caught her back there. Still, she'd need some food for her journey, and most food vendors overcharged her, in hopes of discouraging her from frequenting their establishments. It was worth the risk.

Shahidah eyed the overflowing dumpster. It was trash day, and the dumpster was full. After surveying her options from afar, she targeted a small white box sticking up from the piles of black trash bags. Once again she checked to make sure the coast was clear, then quietly shuffled over to the dumpster, grabbed the box, and returned to her hiding spot.

"Ah!" she exclaimed in an excited whisper. Inside the box were several slices of bread with a container of hummus. Shahidah ate one piece of bread, wrapped the other pieces in an old newspaper that she picked up off the ground, and slid them into her purse. The container of hummus felt hot, so she left it in the box and set the box down on the ground. Then she continued on her journey.

After leaving the bakery, she walked steadily toward the freeway. While she was unnerved by the speed of the vehicles, the freeway was the quickest way to the mosque. Head down, she walked as far over to the right of the shoulder as she could. For once, she was happy to be practically invisible.

Occasionally, she would scan the narrow, scrubby, strip of land next to her for anything of interest. People threw away all kinds of things. She found a partially full bottle of water that she picked up. Her *habiya* flapped loudly in the wind whenever a large truck would go by. The rush of wind from the semis almost knocked her over, but her black clad form continued down the freeway.

As Shahidah closed in on the exit that would take her to the mosque, a shout from a passing car made her shoulders flinch. A bag of trash flew out of the car and crashed onto the concrete in front of her, bursting into a flurry of trash confetti. Shahidah stepped carefully around the trash and quickened her pace.

"Allah is with those who patiently persevere," she mumbled, though it brought her little comfort. "If I do not receive rewards in this life, they will be waiting for me in the next. Until then, I will persevere. Today, Allah has given me bread to eat, water to drink, and a job to do. I cannot ask for anything more." Shahidah climbed steadily up the exit ramp.

Although the mosque was still several blocks away, Shahidah was relieved to be off the freeway. For one thing, it was significantly cooler. Looking back at the freeway, Shahidah could see the waves of heat rising off the black rubber-streaked concrete. She took a sip of water from the bottle that she had found. It was hot like tea, but it soothed her dry throat. At the next intersection, Shahidah crossed over to the other side of the street where there was more shade. Up ahead, a local shopkeeper was closing up for prayer time.

Shahidah's feet felt heavy and hot. Her pace had slowed significantly, but still she pressed on. She could find shade and rest at the mosque. She'd made good time. If she was lucky, she'd reach the mosque before noonday prayer. Just then, Shahidah heard the call to prayer echoing from the minarets of the now visible mosque.

Is that the first or second adhan?

Shahidah pushed herself to walk faster. Up ahead, she could see people filing into the mosque. Then, just as she was reaching the edge of the parking lot, the doors closed. Breathing heavily, Shahidah weaved between the cars and headed for the courtyard near the mosque entrance. Shahidah breathed a sigh of relief. There was a nice patch of shade near the entryway

"Kneel in prayer," a voice commanded. It was a member of the *mutawa*. "I said kneel!"

Shahidah felt the sting of a switch across her back.

"I'll teach you to be late for prayers," the man growled as the switch whistled through the air once again.

Shahidah fell to her knees and lowered her face to the ground. "Allah forgive me!" she wailed. "Allah please forgive me," she repeated over and over as the switch fell across her back. Tears rolled down her cheeks.

At least I'm in the shade. I made it.

She'd felt the sting of the *mutawa's* switch before. She was used to it, as much as one could be. It was in instances like these that the old, dense fabric of her outdated *habiya* served her well.

His switch would cut through the light silky fabrics that many women wear nowadays. It's another blessing.

"Let that be a lesson to you," the *mutawa* sneered.

"Thank you. I won't ever be late again."

"See that you aren't," he said. The sound of his footsteps faded away.

Shahidah knelt, her back heaving up and down with each breath. The sound of her breathing mixed with the prayers echoing from the minaret loudspeakers. Eyes closed, she let her pain float away with the prayers, higher and higher, around the mosque's minarets, and up to the sky. She thought about the old Arabic saying that a woman has only two exits.

One exit leads from my father's house to my husband's. The other leads from my husband's house to my grave. I'm not ready for the second exit yet.

After composing herself, Shahidah tilted her head and peeked to the side. "He's gone, but for how long?"

Shahidah laid out her rug precisely. Kneeling at one end of the tattered rug, she placed a small tin cup at the other. Then, she bowed her head in prayer. "Allah. Blessings and peace be upon you. Thank you for all the blessings that you have showered down on me today. If you see fit to provide me with any more, I humbly accept."

Shahidah knelt there quietly, head bowed, eyes closed, as prayer time concluded. She heard the mosque doors open and people shuffle out. She heard many voices, but they all blended together into an unintelligible gaggle of sound. When there was a clink in her cup, she answered it by saying, "Blessings and peace be upon you," but no one offered her a blessing in return. With her eyes closed, she felt hidden and safe. She wished that were truly the case.

After several minutes, the voices and footsteps disappeared. In the quiet solitude, she could hear the wind blowing and the muffled sound of traffic in the distance. Shahidah opened her eyes and scanned for a place to put the mechanical eyes. The archway that spanned the entrance would work, but she wasn't sure that she could reach it. She eyed the corner of the arch. She could reach it, but would it be too visible?

Shahidah continued to scan the area. Her eyes traveled from the corner of the archway along the wall of the building. The wall was adorned with little decorative ovals stamped into the wall itself. She wondered if the ovals were deep enough to hide one of the devices. There was only one way to find out.

Shahidah looked over at the parking lot. It was empty. She listened intently for any signs of activity. There were none. As she continued to inspect the area, she reached inside her bag for one of the gadgets, then rose cautiously and crept over to the entrance.

Reaching the entryway, she inspected one of the decorative ovals with her fingers to see how deep it was. She looked at the little eye. *It should fit.* She pushed a small button on the top of the device and a tiny pin light glowed red. Shahidah turned the tiny eye so that it faced out. She reached up and pushed it into the oval that she'd selected.

Shahidah returned to her rug and knelt down. Looking back at the entryway, she examined her handiwork. From that vantage point, even she couldn't tell where it was hidden.

Where should I put the other one? He had me put one of the eyes in a parking garage once. Maybe, he'd like to see the cars.

With the other small camera hidden in her hand, Shahidah rolled up her rug and collected her belongings. Slowly, she stood and started walking. About ten feet from the parking lot, she saw a small electrical box jutting out from the side of the building. A pipe ran from the box up to the roof, but it was not flush against the wall.

Shahidah looked back at the entrance. The coast was clear. Once again, she pushed the small button on the top of the device and made sure that the tiny pin light was glowing. Then she moved up against the wall and wedged the small gadget in between the pipe and the building. Shahidah stepped away from the wall and surveyed the area. Thankfully, she was still alone. After taking a small sip of water, she started the long trek back home.

Chapter 34: First Call

Detective Al-Faruq flopped down tiredly on the couch in his small apartment. He'd spent the entire day interviewing suspects from Professor Ratib's mailing list. Unfortunately, his efforts hadn't resulted in any new leads. Now, as the clock approached eleven p.m., his thoughts turned to Kalila.

He'd texted with Kalila several times over the past couple of weeks, but Al-Faruq still felt apprehensive. In fact, he hadn't texted her in a couple of days. As the chimes on his cell phone alerted him to a new text message, he looked at the phone with a pained expression. Nonetheless, he picked it up, and when he saw that it was Kalila, he couldn't help but smile.

"Salam," Kalila texted.

"Salam iKalla." Al-Faruq replied.

"Ha, ha. What's up?" Kalila asked.

"Not much."

"RUOK?"

"Yeah, why?"

"U been kinda quiet lately," Kalila responded.

"IM sorry," Al-Faruq texted back.

"Sorry about what? What's wrong?"

Al-Faruq took a deep breath and typed, "Would your family be ok if they knew?" He paused, hit send, and then waited.

"About what?" Kalila replied.

"About me." Al-Faruq typed with frustration. Time crawled while Al-Faruq awaited her response. Finally, her reply arrived.

"My mom kinda knows," Kalila texted back.

"And?" his fingers typed.

"Well, she's a mom."

"Meaning?"

"*La a'ref*," Kalila responded. "I don't know."

Al-Faruq stared at his phone unsure what to type next. *What am I supposed to say? I enjoy texting with her, but I don't want her getting into trouble.* Finally, he had an idea. Hurriedly, he punched in a response.

"At work, I've seen women get hurt. RU safe?" he typed. Once again, there was an interminably long pause after he hit send.

"Yes. Can U call me?" Kalila responded.

An expression of surprise crossed Al-Faruq's face as he read her message. "OK," he typed tentatively and hit send.

Ughh, why did you do that? Just call her already.

Quickly, he pulled up her number, but for the first time, he selected "call" instead of "send message."

The phone rang. "Hello?" a female voice answered quietly.

"Kalila? Is that you?" Al-Faruq asked apprehensively.

"Yes, Al-Faruq. It's me," she said, her voice relaxing.

"Oh, uh—" Al-Faruq stammered.

"I thought it would be easier to talk about this than text," Kalila interrupted.

"Yeah, you're probably right. Uh, like I was saying. Since I work in law enforcement, I often encounter people at their worst. You know what I mean?"

"Yes," Kalila answered.

"I . . . I've seen honor killings, or the aftermath, and I just didn't want to get you into any trouble."

"Yeah, I know what you mean," Kalila answered, but then she backtracked. "I . . . I don't literally know what that's like, but it must be difficult."

"Be . . . between being in the army and what I do now, I've just seen a lot of things that I'd rather forget," Al-Faruq continued nervously.

"Well, you . . . you don't have to worry about that with my family. I mean, my parents would be concerned."

"Concerned, yeah. I get that."

"Uh, well maybe concerned isn't exactly the best way to describe it, but they don't know you, so—"

"And I'm not necessarily saying that . . . that it's time they did know me," Al-Faruq interrupted. "I just worry. I run into a lot of crazy people."

"Oh?"

"Not that you're crazy or that your family is," Al-Faruq stammered. "Ughh, maybe texting was easier."

Kalila laughed. "And all this time, I thought you just typed slow. Do you normally delete these wonderful foot-in-mouth moments?"

"Yes. Yes I do," Al-Faruq replied while racking his brain for a way to change the subject. "Is school going well?"

"Yeah, it's going great. I've got two semesters left. Then, I'll have to complete a year of student teaching after that."

"Where would you do that?" Al-Faruq asked.

"Well, there's a school in my neighborhood where I've been volunteering, so I'm hoping I'll be able to complete my student teaching there. Since it's close to home, I could continue to live here with my family."

"That sounds nice," Al-Faruq replied, although he had no idea what that was really like. He hadn't been part of a family since he was eleven years old. "So, what does your Dad do for a living?"

"He works in retail."

"Oh?"

"Yeah, he's a buyer for a local clothing retailer."

"Does he travel a lot?"

"Some, but not as often as when I was little," Kalila replied. "He's in more of a managerial role now."

"Hmmm," Al-Faruq murmured.

"You sound tired. Tough day at work?"

"Oh, I don't know. It was more unproductive than tough."

"A lot of sitting in your car reading the paper?" Kalila asked.

"Well, it just looks like I'm reading. I cut big eye holes in the paper so that I can still see everything that's going on."

"Really?"

"Yeah, like when young women throw notes out their car window."

"Does that happen often?"

"Uh, no, not really," Al-Faruq said, fumbling for words.

"You kind of paused there. Are you sure?"

"Yes, I'm sure. In fact, it's only happened once," Al-Faruq said confidently.

"And what did you do?"

"I tracked that litter bug down."

Kalila laughed. "You did? And what was her sentence?"

"I haven't decided yet. I'm still investigating," Al-Faruq replied.

"Oh, I see." Kalila said. The conversation lulled.

"So," Al-Faruq broke the silence. "Does this mark the end of texting each other, or do we reserve talking on the phone for, uh, special occasions?"

"And what was the special occasion tonight?" Kalila asked.

"I don't know. Does my asking uncomfortable questions count as a special occasion?"

"Hmmm, well it's definitely memorable."

"Memorable, eh. Memorable in a good way?" Al-Faruq asked hopefully.

"In a good way." Kalila said.

"All right, so I'll call you."

"Sure."

"Good night, Kalila," Al-Faruq said with a smile.

"Good night, Al-Faruq."

As he hung up the phone, Al-Faruq felt strangely at ease. For a few moments, his frustrations from work seemed far away, the anxiety that he had felt when he first called Kalila had disappeared, and the hope that their friendship might actually lead somewhere burned bright. Feeling tired but happy, Al-Faruq plugged his cell phone into its charger and headed for bed.

Normally, Al-Faruq would be meticulously planning out the next day while brushing his teeth, but tonight his thoughts seemed jumbled. *Kalila has a really nice voice. I wonder what she looks like.* He tried to recall the look of her eyes the day they first met. He closed his eyes and concentrated, but as he envisioned Kalila's car passing by, he couldn't decide if it was a memory or a dream.

After returning his toothbrush to the coffee cup that sat precariously on the edge of the small sink, Al-Faruq splashed some warm water on his face. He looked at his face in the water-dotted mirror. He needed to get some sleep. Quickly, he dried his face off with the worn hand towel that was draped over the side of the sink and went to bed.

The bed springs creaked as he flopped back on the thin mattress, but for once sleep came quickly. For the first time in a long while, he wasn't fighting a headache. "Maybe I'll call her again this weekend," he mumbled as he drifted off to sleep. "It was a good first call."

Chapter 35: The Realization

In the heart of the *souks*, Tahir stood in front of a *shawarma* stand pacing back and forth in a stilted dance. Across the street, Husam studied him closely while peering over the top of a local newspaper. He'd arrived an hour prior to their meeting to ensure that Tahir was not leading him into some kind of trap. After surveying the area, Husam was confident that no surveillance had been set up. However, he was still waiting to hear from Jasim, who was tailing Tahir.

Husam looked at his watch with a frown. Finally, his cell phone rang. "Hello," he answered.

"Hey, it's Jasim."

"It's about time, what took so long?" Husam said angrily.

"I was checking the rest of the perimeter."

"And?"

"He's got a tail."

"Hmmm, that's not good."

"It's just one guy." Jasim said.

"Still, it complicates things." Husam said. "Where's his tail now?"

"He's on the corner by the rug shop. You going to abort?"

"No, Tahir looks spooked, and I need to find out why. Just mark this guy, and let me know if he makes a move."

"Will do," Jasim said.

"We'll talk more later," Husam concluded.

Husam flipped his phone closed and eyed Tahir warily. *Guess I've made him wait long enough. Might as well go find out how bad he screwed up.* He tossed his paper on the table and headed across the street.

When Tahir saw him, he looked relieved. Husam gave him a forced smile and waved.

"How's it going my friend?" asked Husam. "Let's get something to eat."

"Well, I'm not really—"

"Two *shawarmas*," Husam said to the vendor. After paying for the food, Husam grabbed the *shawarmas* and motioned Tahir to a nearby bench. "Let's sit down. It's been a long time since we've had a chance to talk."

After sitting down, Husam leaned in close to Tahir. "Hold your *shawarma* up in front of your mouth and tell me what's wrong."

Tahir shifted the *shawarma* in his hands and brought it up to his mouth. "My supervisor called in some favors. Now, there's this detective snooping around."

"And?" Husam asked, his mouth half full.

"He knows that the fire wasn't an accident," Tahir said. "He's recommended new security measures. I mean, he's got their attention. They've allowed him to interview practically everyone, myself included. For some reason, he's convinced that even if I'm not involved, I know who is. I had an old college friend who died of a drug overdose, and he brought that up. He said that it wasn't an overdose, that . . . that he'd been killed. I—"

"Calm down," Husam interrupted. "He's just fishing for information. Trying to gauge your reaction. If he had anything on you, you'd already be in jail," Husam reassured him.

"I thought you'd want to know," Tahir said.

"You did the right thing," Husam said. He scratched his chin thoughtfully. "I have an idea that might help. You own two vehicles. Right?"

"Yes, I have a car and a Suburban, but what—"

"Tonight, leave your car outside. Don't park it in the garage."

"Huh?"

"Park your car on the street."

"Why? What are you going to do to my car?"

"Look, it's just a car. If you want this detective off your back, you're going to need to trust me. Are we clear? Where are you going to park your car tonight?"

"On the street, but how—"

"Good!" Husam concluded, ignoring Tahir's apprehension. After slapping Tahir on the back again, Husam stood up. He leaned over and whispered tersely in Tahir's ear. "As long as you do as I say, you've got nothing to worry about. Tonight, park your car on the street."

Husam stepped away. Then, he turned back. "This new friend of yours. What is his name?"

"Detective Al-Faruq," Tahir answered.

Husam nodded and walked away.

#

Mingling in with the crowd, Husam soon disappeared from sight. Fraught with despair, Tahir sat on the bench staring into space. He forced himself to eat his *shawarma*, thinking it would look odd if he didn't. Once he finished, Tahir threw the paper wrapping in a nearby trashcan and headed back to his car.

The reality of his predicament hit him hard. *There's no way out of this now, save arrest or death. Professor Ratib had made it sound so academic, but it wasn't. Regardless of whether we're attacking human- or infrastructure-related targets, it's terrorism. If Husam thinks that I'm a risk, I'm dead.*

Detective Al-Faruq was right. Dema's death wasn't an accident. He was killed because he tried to walk away. How could I be so stupid? Idiot!

When he reached his car, Tahir stopped short. As he stood on the sidewalk staring at his car, a myriad of questions raced through his head.

Why was Husam so late? What had he been doing? Come on! You're being paranoid. If he wanted me dead, he wouldn't have bothered showing up for our meeting at all.

"Tahir!" a voice called.

Startled, Tahir wheeled around to see Detective Al-Faruq step out from the shadows of the alley.

"It's all right, Tahir," the detective said. "He didn't mess with your car, but you've got some dangerous friends."

"What? Detective Al-Faruq? I . . . I didn't recognize you."

"I said that you've got some dangerous friends."

"Uh, I'm not sure I understand what you mean."

"Your lunch partner. He looks like a pretty rough character. What's he want with a college kid like you, anyway?"

Speechless, Tahir just stared at the detective.

"Well, if you ever want to talk about it, give me a call. You still got my number?" Al-Faruq asked.

"Yeah," Tahir nodded.

"I'd hate for you to end up like Dema," Al-Faruq concluded, as he turned back down the alley.

For a moment, Tahir just stared at the spot where the detective had been. Then, shakily, he took out his keys and got into his car. Nervously, Tahir turned the key. As the engine roared to life, he let out a sigh.

The drive home was a blur. Despite his best efforts, Tahir couldn't come up with a single scenario that would result in a positive outcome for him.

Should I run? Where would I go? How would I survive? If I confide in the police, can they protect me? What would happen to the professor and my friends? What am I to Husam? A liability, a fall guy, or both?

Despite his misgivings, Tahir did as he was told. When he arrived at his apartment complex, he parked his vehicle outside. Before heading up to his room, he scanned the car for anything that he couldn't live without. Feeling defeated, he grabbed his CD case off the passenger seat and pulled his proof of insurance from the glove box, then headed up to his apartment. After taking a couple of aspirin, Tahir collapsed, exhausted, on the couch.

Chapter 36: Bearing Fruit

With a cup of coffee in hand, Agent Jamison sat slumped at his desk. Over the past couple of days, the shit had hit the proverbial fan. In the Persian Gulf, explosions had disabled nine oil tankers, and all of them had been dispatched from the Saudi Arabian port of Ras Tanura. The port was now closed, pending the completion of mine sweeping efforts by the Royal Saudi Naval Forces.

Hell, that's right up the road. It happened right under my nose, and what have I got? Nothing.

Jamison rubbed his eyes tiredly. He'd been reviewing surveillance video from the cameras that BMO1 had planted at the local mosque. It was almost midnight, but after the tanker bombings, the RFIs were coming in fast and furious. According to headquarters, a previously undocumented terrorist group called the Islamic Tide had claimed responsibility. Unfortunately for Jamison, he had far more questions than answers.

"I just don't have the staff to keep tabs on all of these guys," Jamison said tiredly. "I'd love to talk to that Jasim character, but aside from showing up on the video surveillance footage of Husam's apartment, I haven't seen him since. He's off the grid—no address, doesn't use credit cards. Hell, even if he was involved in the tanker bombings, he could be out of the country by now."

Agent Jamison took a sip of coffee and tried to refocus on the video. The footage at the mosque was significantly more difficult to review than Husam's apartment. With all the prayer calls, throngs of people came and went daily.

"I should just upload the footage to headquarters and forget about it," he groaned. They had facial recognition software and the processing hardware to zip right through this. Still, he knew that even headquarters didn't have the resources to review every single piece of footage. He needed to prove that reviewing it would be worth their while, so there he sat, eyes glued to the screen.

The first camera showed footage of the parking lot. Agent Jamison played it at eight times normal speed. The cars zipped in and out at a frenzied pace. However, after watching several days of parking lot footage, one car stood out: a black Mercedes.

The vehicle was often there well before prayer time and didn't leave immediately when prayer time concluded. Plus, the car's occupant never got out. The video quality was too poor to identify the occupant, but Agent Jamison was able to decipher the car's license plate number.

"Another one for my NIC contact. He came through for me on the last one," Jamison noted. Surprisingly, he saw Socrates car several times on the footage as well. "Damn, he almost spends as much time at the mosque as he does at the university."

Next, Agent Jamison turned his attention to the camera that was covering the mosque entrance. He wasn't looking forward to it.

"Goddamn rag heads!" he exclaimed. "With everybody wearing *ghutras*, you can hardly see anyone's face. BMO1 didn't get the best angle on these shots. Probably not that many places to put the camera though."

Mobs of worshipers came and went, hundreds upon hundreds of faces. Jamison's eyes flashed back and forth between the video images and his most wanted lists. "This is impossible," he muttered as he got up to refill his coffee.

He came back and hit play. "Come on! Just finish reviewing the footage and then call it a night," he encouraged himself as the images flickered across the screen. The process was slow and mind numbing.

"One service to go," Jamison said. He rubbed his eyes and took a sip of coffee. "Wait a second," he muttered. Jamison stopped the footage. He went back a few frames. "I don't fucking believe it! There he is. Jasim Saqr. Cigarette, scar, and everything."

Jamison zoomed in on the man's face just to be sure. "Sure as hell looks like him. Close enough to garner further inspection from headquarters anyway." He packaged the footage for headquarters. In the message, Jamison noted the time where Jasim Saqr appeared, and he attached a cropped image of the suspect as well. Finally, he hit send.

While the message was being processed, Jamison prepared to leave. After pouring out the remnants of coffee into the bathroom sink, he prepared a new batch, and set the timer. Then he cleaned off his desk. Meticulously, Jamison collected the MVCs, the RFIs, and file folders and put them in the safe. He scanned the top of his desk to see if there was anything else.

"Just the laptop," he said as he watched the progress bar creep along. "Finally," Jamison said tiredly. He logged off the secure program and sent the entry protocols to the background. The screen now looked like your average laptop computer.

After shutting down, he slid the laptop into the safe. Then he closed the door, spun the dial several times, and yanked on the handle. Satisfied that it was indeed locked, he turned to leave.

"Crap!" Agent Jamison exclaimed. He'd forgotten to activate the security cameras. Returning to his desk, he reached underneath and flipped a small toggle switch. It wasn't an alarm. There was really no point. Everything of importance was in the safe, and breaking into it wasn't worth the trouble. Nonetheless, if anyone actually tried, the cameras would catch it.

Irritated at how late it was becoming, Agent Jamison hurried out. He glanced quickly around the outer room to make sure everything was in its proper place. He saw a purse lying on the floor. Evidently, it had fallen off the display shelf. After returning the purse to its shelf, he exited the store.

Jamison stepped outside and looked around tiredly. At first glance the streets seemed empty, but then he saw him. Across the street, a man was leaning against a broken down lamppost. The man lifted a match up to his face and lit a cigarette. Jamison caught a glimpse of a scar on his right cheek.

Hurriedly, Jamison locked the door and slid the metal gate closed. Fumbling for his keys, Jamison glanced back, but the man was gone. Jamison locked the gate's padlock. Warily, he headed for his hotel. It was only a few blocks away. Nonetheless, there were several different routes he could take. Jamison decided to stick to the main streets that were well lit.

Did I really see that, or have I just been staring at those videos for too long? Jasim standing right outside my fucking office? Get real.

The route to his hotel had been committed to memory a long time ago. From the overflowing trashcan on the corner to the feral cats that frequented the dumpsters behind the nearby *shawarma* shop, Jamison knew every detail. He knew when the trash was picked up, and what the sanitation workers looked like. He knew what cars parked along the route and what days certain vehicles were gone. It was all familiar, except for the scar-faced man.

Walking steadily down the sidewalk, Jamison listened intently for any unusual sounds, but he was having trouble processing everything he heard. Upon side stepping a trashcan that had been tipped over, a strange cry set him on edge. Looking back, he quickened his pace.

"Mrroow!"

"Goddammit!" Jamison exclaimed, almost tripping.

It was a small calico cat. He'd seen it several times before. Lately, it had taken up the practice of following at his heels along the block between the market and corner gas station.

"Get out of here! Damn cat."

Jamison wiped his brow with his forearm and looked behind him. His eyes darted back and forth trying to take it all in, but no one was there. His hotel was in sight, but Jamison continued down to the next block. He wanted to double back just to make sure no one was following him.

"Fuck, I'm getting sloppy!" Jamison grumbled as he turned down the alley behind his hotel.

"Screech!"

Jamison jumped back as a trash truck ground to a halt in front of him. The driver brushed his hand against the underside of his chin and barked at Jamison.

"Same to you bud," Jamison countered halfheartedly. As the trash truck rattled forward, Jamison looked back. He saw the wind pushing a plastic grocery bag across the street. Farther down, a cat jumped lithely up on top of a trashcan. Disgusted with himself, Jamison turned down the alley toward his hotel.

When he reached the rear entrance, Jamison pulled out his key card and inserted it in the slot. The light turned green, he removed the card and headed inside. As the door clicked shut, the shadowy outline of a man appeared around the corner at the end of the alley. The faint glow of a cigarette dangled from his lips.

Chapter 37: Lost

The sun perched high in the sky as Professor Ratib walked hurriedly up to the mosque entrance. He was late for his meeting with the Imam. They needed to review Siraj's video productions before submitting them to Al Jazeera. On the surface, all his ideas were working wonderfully. Yet, he was conflicted.

While the Imam is pressuring me to provide more and more input, Husam has become increasingly hostile toward me. The Imam trusts me. Why doesn't Husam?

As the professor entered the mosque, he pushed these thoughts from his mind. His lonely footsteps echoed on the marble floor. Outside the Imam's office, Professor Ratib knocked on the door with his sweaty hand.

"Imam Al-Hashim?"

"Come in, Professor," the Imam answered.

Professor Ratib opened the door and looked in. The Imam and Husam were seated cross-legged on the floor with a laptop open in front of them. Husam nodded seriously as the Imam pointed at the screen.

"We just got started," the Imam said.

The professor walked in and took a seat next to the Imam. He gave Husam a friendly nod, but got no reaction.

"This first video sets the stage," the Imam said. The video focused on the king of Saudi Arabia. It showed the king's yacht, his palace, the limos, and the lavish parties. Next, images of the king visiting with Western dignitaries flashed across the screen.

"They've forced him to appoint women to the Shura Council and want women to run for local office," the Imam said. "This is the first step down the slippery slope toward a Western-based secular democracy. The ruling class idolizes the West. They educate their children in Western schools where these secular tendencies take hold. Just look at how they act."

The Imam selected the next video. It shifted between scenes of prominent young Arabic leaders in their traditional dress and contrasting images of these same young men in Western dress, often with alcoholic beverages in their hands and Western women at their side.

"Allah sees all! The monarchy cannot hide," the voice-over said.

"As you can see, the next generation of leaders will further erode Islam's influence," the Imam commented. "This final video reveals where the path they have chosen ultimately ends."

Suddenly, there was a knock at the door. The Imam pushed the laptop screen closed. "Yes," he said.

A bearded man pushed open the door. The professor recognized him, but he didn't know his name.

"Muhanned!" the Imam said. "Please come in."

"Am I interrupting?" Muhanned asked in a monotone voice. Standing in the doorway, his eyes bore in on the three men.

"Nonsense," the Imam said. "I've got what you're looking for right here." The Imam held up a thick manila envelope. Husam took the envelope from the Imam and walked it over to Muhanned.

Muhanned accepted the package, but he still didn't look happy. Turning it in his hands, his face was twisted in a permanent scowl. "We'll talk later," he said finally.

"I look forward to it," the Imam said.

Then, as abruptly as he'd arrived, Muhanned left. The Imam shook his head and laughed. As a look of concern crossed Husam's face, the Imam queued up the final video. Professor Ratib glanced down at the computer and then back at Husam. Fiercely, Husam's eyes bore in on him. Unnerved, the professor looked away as the video began to play.

The wealth of a nation turned into palaces for a few. The cuts were jarring. They flashed between scenes of palaces versus slums, heretical elites versus pious commoners. After displaying scenes of monarchy-dispensed corporal punishment, the video made its case that the ruling elites were above the law.

Suddenly, a flamboyant young prince became the focal point of the video. Then a young Arabian woman flashed upon the screen. The prince was with her in a hot tub. She tried to escape. He pulled her down. In slow motion, her head bounced off the hard tile floor. Then the prince took what he wanted and left. The rape of a woman. The rape of a nation.

The professor stared in disbelief at the screen. His head felt hot and every muscle in his body was tense. Although the young woman's face had been blurred, she had a small star-shaped birthmark on her neck. It was Azzah!

"The monarchy acts with impunity, but they are not above Allah's law," the Imam preached, but to Professor Ratib he sounded far away.

The professor stared straight ahead. He felt Husam's eyes upon him. He clenched his hands together tightly, lest their shaking reveal everything. Though he felt like throwing up, he swallowed hard, and managed to speak.

"V . . . very powerful," he said.

"Yes," the Imam agreed. "These videos will convey to the public what greed has wrought, and they will yearn for clerical guidance. It's only—"

"I . . . I need to get back to the university," the professor interrupted. It took all his strength to stand.

"I'll walk you out," Husam offered.

"Professor Ratib knows the way," the Imam said. "We still need to discuss that matter concerning our Somali brothers."

Husam acquiesced, and Professor Ratib walked out of the Imam's office without looking back. With every step, his disbelief and fear turned into anger and hate. His mind was in a fog. Before the professor knew it, he was in his car weaving through traffic.

How? Where?

Professor Ratib was filled with rage. His heart pounded. He screamed at the traffic in front of him, and he hit the steering wheel with both hands.

He couldn't remember what he'd said to Imam Al-Hashim, just that he needed to leave. *If he'd known it was my daughter in the video, he'd have spit on me in disgust. How could Azzah disgrace me like this? How did she get there? What was she doing naked in a hot tub with the prince anyway? And what of Iba's hand in this— she raised this viper. Never satisfied. Always wanting more. This is her fault as well.*

213

Angrily, the professor continued to pick his way through traffic. Honking. Yelling. He had to get home. He'd scrapped and clawed to provide for them. For what? The shopping trips, the clothes, the furniture, the constant consumption were signs of their infidelity toward Allah. Idols they placed not only above Allah, but above him as well.

"By Allah, I will see that they are punished," he seethed.

#

Azzah knelt next to the toilet crying. She had thrown up again this morning. With her head in her hands, she rocked back and forth moaning uncontrollably. She hadn't had her period since the New Year's Eve party. Inside she knew, but she didn't want to admit it.

I can't be pregnant. I just can't. Where can I go? Who can I tell?

Fear gripped her tightly.

I'm dead, literally dead. Even if I could explain, what would be the point? No one would listen. They'll think I'm a dirty whore. I'll be stoned or whipped.

A knock on the bathroom door startled her.

"Azzah," her mother called. "Are you all right?"

"I'm . . . I'm fine," Azzah answered. She wiped the tears from her face and stood looking at herself in the mirror. Her eyes were red and puffy. She couldn't let her mother see her like this. Hastily, Azzah put on some makeup.

"You most certainly are not fine," Iba said. She tried turning the doorknob. "You've been hiding in that bathroom all week."

Iba grabbed a pin from her hair and jimmied open the door. She looked at her daughter, eyes red from crying. "What's wrong?"

"Nothing," Azzah answered as she tried to push past.

"You are not leaving this bathroom until you tell me," Iba said.

"Nothing," Azzah whispered tiredly. After retreating, she sank down and sat on the toilet.

"What? Do you think I'm some kind of idiot! I can see that something is wrong. Are you sick? Are you on drugs? Tell me!"

With tears streaming down her face, Azzah shrugged her shoulders and stared at the floor.

"What is it?" Iba asked again, this time less forcefully.

"I think I'm pregnant," Azzah whispered.

"What?" Iba asked coming closer.

"I'm pregnant!" Azzah stated angrily.

Iba's face turned ashen as she sat down unsteadily on the side of the tub. "Are . . . are you sure?"

Once again, Azzah just shrugged her shoulders.

"Your father must never know. We'll figure something out, but your father must never know."

"We'll figure something out!" Azzah yelled. "What's to figure out?"

"Shut up and listen to me. We'll get one of my brothers to take us shopping in Bahrain. There, we'll find a doctor and determine for sure. Then . . . maybe, I can convince your father that we need to visit my sister in Germany. I don't know," Iba said, taking Azzah's hands in hers.

"You mean get an abortion?" Azzah asked unsteadily, not really sure what to think. Her head was spinning. Her mother hated her brothers. They hardly ever spoke, and now she was going to turn to them for help.

"I don't know. Maybe. Who's the father?" Iba asked.

Azzah shrank at the question.

Iba grabbed her daughter by the hand and repeated the question. "Who is the father!?!"

"Cala's cousin," Azzah whispered.

"Cala's cousin?" Iba repeated. Then, her eyes grew wide. "No, not Prince Bahir? You're lying. It cannot be. When?" Iba asked.

"On New Year's Eve, he picked us up in his limousine and took us to this big party in Bahrain," Azzah answered.

Iba slapped Azzah sharply across the face. "Shut up! Just shut up," she said. "Even if it's true, he'd never admit it. It'd be a huge scandal. They'd just find a way to sweep it under the rug, and perhaps you with it. Don't ever mention it again. Not to anyone,"

Iba scolded. "Go get dressed," Iba said, covering her face with her hands.

"I . . . I'm sorry mother," Azzah offered quietly as she passed.

Her mother didn't respond. As Azzah walked back to her room, she heard the sound of the garage door opening.

"What's dad doing home?" Azzah yelped.

"Be quiet and get dressed," Iba snapped.

As her mother rushed downstairs, Azzah ran to her room. Anxiously, she hovered in the doorway and listened.

"Mahmud dear, what are you doing home so early?" Iba asked.

"Where's Azzah?"

"You look upset. Why don't I fix you some tea?"

"Where's Azzah!?!" her father screamed.

Azzah could hear her parents scuffling. Quickly, she slammed her bedroom door and locked it.

"You can't hide from me," her father yelled.

"Stop it! Just stop it!" her mother shrieked. "I won't let you hurt her!"

Azzah hid in her closet hugging her knees tightly.

"She's no longer your concern. You can't stop me!" her father screamed.

There was a loud thump. Azzah listened intently for her mother's voice, but all she heard were the loud stomps of someone coming up the stairs. The doorknob to her room rattled. Azzah closed her eyes tightly.

"Open this door!" her father yelled. He pounded angrily on the door.

Azzah cowered in the closet as her father screamed obscenities at her. It sounded like he was going to break down the door. Thud! Thud!

"You're no longer my daughter. You witch. You whore," he screamed.

Thud! Crack!

"You'll never disgrace me again!"

The next thud sounded different. Clang! Then, it was quiet.

"Azzah?" her mother called. "Azzah! We need to leave. Now!"

Azzah cracked open the door and stared in shock at her father lying on the floor. Iba stood over him. In her hands, she held a large metal *dallah*. Her whole body was shaking.

"Allah will be her judge, not you!" Iba spat, dropping the *dallah* to the floor.

"Come on," Iba urged. "Throw on your *habiya* and some shoes. We need to go!"

Azzah looked around her room frantically.

"Hurry! Just grab something."

Azzah slipped on a pair of shoes and grabbed a *habiya* that was draped over the end of her bed. Cautiously, she stepped over her father who was lying motionless on the floor. "Is . . . is he dead?"

"If I thought he was dead, we could take our time. Now, come on!" Iba prodded.

Quickly, the two headed down the stairs. Iba put on her *habiya*, then rushed to the kitchen and grabbed her purse. When Iba returned, Azzah was standing at the foot of the stairs holding her *habiya* in her arms. Iba jabbed Azzah in the shoulder and glared at her.

As Azzah put on her *habiya*, Iba rifled through her purse looking for her cell phone. "Thank Allah it still has some charge left," she said. "Come on!"

"Where are we going?" Azzah asked.

"We'll walk down to the store. I'll have one of my brothers meet us there. Let's go," Iba said. She opened the front door and stepped out on to the stoop.

Shocked, Azzah stood in the doorway hesitant and confused. "But you hate your brothers," Azzah mumbled.

"Azzah! Come on. We have to go. Now!"

Iba pulled Azzah outside and closed the door. The two walked down the driveway holding hands. As they passed in front of the house, Azzah glanced over, unsure if they would ever return again.

Chapter 38: Complications

Once again, Agent Jamison waited patiently for Socrates at a local café near the university. He was genuinely interested to see what the professor had for him. Headquarters had authorized a bonus in exchange for more actionable information. They wanted names, and they wanted them now. Who was responsible for the tanker bombings? It was time for the professor to put up or shut up.

No one at headquarters was buying the Islamic Tide story. It was nothing but a front and someone else was pulling the strings. Right now, most people had their money on Iran, but they needed evidence. They needed more in order to make the connection.

Jamison took a sip of tea and looked at his watch. *Well, where the hell is he? If he doesn't come through, they're going to cut him loose. I thought I made that point clear.*

Another five minutes passed before Socrates finally appeared with his newspaper in hand.

Better late than never, I guess.

Jamison watched the professor order a cup of tea and take a seat, then scanned the city street for tails. Initially, everything looked clear, but then Jamison saw him.

Goddamn it. What's that detective doing here? I thought I'd gotten that all cleared up. Jamison's eyes twitched from Socrates to the detective and back. *What's that goddamn detective looking at?*

Agent Jamison exhaled slowly and took another sip of tea. He followed the detective's eyes. Socrates had another man following him. At a café on the other side of the street sat a familiar face. Jamison thought for a moment, and finally came up with the name. Muhanned.

That's the same fuck who showed up at Husam's apartment. Was he there the whole time? Plus, is that the black Mercedes that's always parked outside the mosque?

Jamison shifted his focus back to Socrates.

He's going to abort. He really should abort, but then again, I kind of laid down the law. Get us this info or else. What's he going to do?

Socrates sat and sipped his tea. He didn't even glance at the newspaper. To Jamison, he looked distant and preoccupied. As the minutes passed, everyone held their positions. The detective flipped through magazines at the newsstand, Muhanned sat stiffly at a café table across the street, and Socrates and Agent Jamison sipped their tea. Then, per the prescribed protocol, Socrates placed the newspaper on the empty seat next to him and exited the café.

Studiously, Jamison watched the professor leave. Now, it was his turn to make a decision. Rashly, Jamison threw down enough cash to cover his bill and retrieved Socrates' newspaper. As he tucked the newspaper under his arm, Jamison knew he was taking a chance, but it was a chance worth taking.

After exiting the café, Jamison stopped to peruse the wares of a nearby merchant while continuing to mark Muhanned and the detective. After a moment of indecision, the detective left in pursuit of the professor. For his part, Muhanned sat stoically at his table, and it was difficult to get a read on him.

Jamison continued down the street. Slowly, he sauntered from one merchant to the next. The café table where Muhanned had been sitting was now empty. While holding a bracelet up to the light, Jamison scanned the surrounding area. Finally, he spotted him. From the looks of things, Muhanned was pursuing Socrates as well. For a split second, Jamison considered following, but he shook it off.

Protect the information and yourself first. If Muhanned was on to Socrates, he'd have killed him before he made the drop. He's just fishing for information like he was at Husam's apartment.

Convinced that Muhanned was not an immediate threat, Jamison walked back to his office. Still, he doubled back several times and took a more circuitous route than normal. "Better safe than sorry," he told himself.

Upon reaching his storefront flat, Jamison unlocked the gate and hurried inside. He rushed back to his office and spread the newspaper out on his desk. Carefully, he pulled out a blank sheet of paper that was hidden between the folds. He positioned the paper underneath his small desk lamp, switched it on, and then dimmed the main lights. As he returned to his desk, the ink on the paper glowed with two names, Imam Abdul-Mu'izz Al-Hashim and Fakhir Ihsan.

He'd seen the Imam's name many times before, but Fakhir Ihsan? *Where have I seen that name before?*

Jamison got up and turned on the main lights, then returned to his desk and opened the safe. After rifling through the files, he found it. It was a terrorist funding report that his predecessor had put together, and there was Fakhir's name. "Iranian connections," was written in quotes next to the name, and attached to the report was a wedding announcement. Evidently, Fakhir Ihsan had married the daughter of a high-ranking official in the Iranian government.

Suddenly, a buzzer sounded. He had a customer.

"Just a minute," Jamison called.

He swung the safe door shut, spun the dial around a couple of times, and headed toward the front. Glancing through the beaded partition, Jamison froze in his tracks. There stood Muhanned. He looked indifferent as if he were waiting in a long line. Jamison took a deep breath and moved forward.

"Can I help you?" Jamison asked boldly. Side stepping Muhanned, he quickly positioned himself behind the counter and rested his hand on the 9mm handgun hidden beneath.

"Just browsing," Muhanned answered. "You don't seem to have much here."

"I'm primarily an exporter. I connect local merchants with buyers overseas," Jamison said as he studied Muhanned up and down.

"Hmmm," Muhanned grunted. "That must be tough in this day and age."

"Why's that?" Jamison asked while he scanned the outer room for any unwanted packages.

"Some people don't like foreigners. They don't understand our traditions, our way of life."

"Well, as long as I make them money, most merchants are very cordial," Jamison answered as he tightened his hold on the pistol grip.

"Still, you must miss home. It's difficult being somewhere you're not wanted. Sometimes, it can even be dangerous,"

Muhanned commented, his roving eyes settling on Jamison's. "Have a nice day. Sorry to bother you."

With that, Muhanned turned and left. The buzzer sounded as the front door opened and closed. Warily, Jamison watched him leave. He strode to the front door, locked it, and pulled the blinds. He scanned the room again.

One of the leather display purses was slightly askew, and the zipper was partially unzipped. Jamison hurried back to his office. He returned with a small hand-held device that had a flat wand connected to it via a wire. He swiped the tip of the wand back and forth along the exterior and zipper of the purse. Seemingly satisfied with the results, he set the device down on the counter and studied the purse closer. Finally, he removed the purse from the shelf and unzipped it slowly.

After looking inside, he shook his head angrily, zipped the purse back up, and returned it to the shelf. He collected his things and made another trip back to his office. *Things are definitely getting more complicated. It's just a bug, but I gotta handle this carefully.*

Jamsion sat down at his desk and stared blankly at his computer. He hated the thought of having to ask for more resources. In his mind, it was akin to asking for help. Nonetheless, he didn't have much choice. While his cover may have not been fully blown, he was under surveillance and his small cadre of sources was potentially in danger. Given that all the tanker mishaps had happened just down the road, he was surprised they hadn't put more assets in place already.

Working diligently throughout the morning, Jamison constructed his case for additional resources. After detailing his contact with Aashif Muhanned, he once again outlined the results of his video surveillance of the mosque. "A mosque run by Imam Abdul-Mu'izz Al-Hashim and funded by Fakhir Ihsan," he noted. "These two men, who have been identified as persons of interest in previous reporting, were identified as key figures in the recent tanker bombings by Socrates."

As he was finishing up, Jamison looked around his office. Given his encounter with Muhanned, he was conflicted about what his next move should be. At a minimum, he needed to scan and digitize the files in case he had to abandon his office. It would probably be smart to find different lodging as well.

"Aghh!" he groaned. "It's barely noon, and my day's already shot."

Jamison submitted his report, and then delved into digitizing the files. First, he scanned them, then ran the originals through the shredder. It took him most of the afternoon, but at least now it was done. After digitizing the files, he encrypted them and copied them to a flash drive. If he had to disappear, he could mail the flash drive off to headquarters.

"What else have we got?" he mumbled while looking through the remaining contents of the safe.

There were several MVCs, along with a bunch of passports, a handgun, and some extra clips. Jamison piled everything into a dust-covered computer bag along with his laptop. *If I have to move to another location, at least I won't be starting from scratch. I really fucked up today. Led Muhanned right here. I can't believe it. I doubled back several times.*

Jamison picked up the newspaper he'd gotten from Socrates and dumped it in the trashcan. There was an odd noise. Jamison looked down at the trashcan quizzically. Then he bent down and carefully picked out the trash one piece at a time and threw it on the floor. Finally, at the bottom of the can, he saw it. Taped to the back of a small plastic card was a microchip with a tiny, thin wire running from it.

"I'll be damned!" he exclaimed.

Crouching over the trashcan, Agent Jamsion examined the device. The card was nothing special. It had Arabic writing on it and a magnetic strip on the back. It was just an old gift card of some sort. The microchip, on the other hand, looked to be some kind of GPS module.

"The real question, I suppose, is whether or not Socrates knew it was in there," Jamison grumbled. "Could someone have slipped it in there without him noticing?" Curiously, he turned the card back and forth with his fingers.

Agent Jamison picked up the newspaper off the floor. Holding the folded up newspaper in one hand. He used his other hand to slip the card between the folds, then shook the newspaper to see how difficult it was to dislodge the card.

"Hmmm," he grunted after trying it a few times. "More complications. I hate complications."

Chapter 39: Stand

While Kalila hadn't seen the video, she had definitely heard about it. Before the government had shut down access, the internet was rife with stories about Prince Amir Bahir. "Some prince," she said. Kalila remembered one angry blogger who wrote, "They should cut off his head, and not the one that sits upon his shoulders." Other posts were less charitable.

For her part, Kalila wasn't sure how to feel. As she sat at the kitchen table picking at her breakfast, she vacillated from angry, to sad, to embarrassed, and back. Right now, arguing with her father, she was angry.

"We look like fools," she said with disgust, "for following these . . . these charlatans. Saudi Arabia is the keeper of Islam's holy sites, yet because of this scandal, our country is the butt of jokes. Every word that comes out of the government's mouth is nothing short of blasphemy."

Her father hid behind his newspaper.

"Father! Are you listening to me?" she asked insistently. "You need to take me downtown to the protest. We need to stand up and show the government they cannot sweep this under the rug."

"I will do no such thing," her father said.

"What if that so-called prince had raped me? Would you be so quick to turn a blind eye? Am I so worthless to you?"

Her father's newspaper came crashing down. "Kalila, please try to understand. This protest is dangerous. I don't want you getting hurt."

"I am a woman in Saudi Arabia. Life is dangerous. I have no rights!"

"That's not true," her father protested. "I've always treated you and your mother with love and respect."

"I know you do, but what happens when I walk outside these doors? What am I then?"

"You are a beautiful girl who I want to grow up to be a beautiful woman. The government will not sit idly by as these demonstrations occur. They will throw people in jail. Do you want to go to jail?"

"Why would I go to jail when I have done nothing wrong? It's the prince who should be in jail."

"Well, it's not our place to put him there," her father stammered.

"Then, who will stand up for me? If not you, father, then who? If you will not stand up for my rights and mother's rights, then what will you stand up for?"

"So, you want me to go to jail?"

"No!"

"Well, that is what will happen if I go to the protest."

"Not if we stand together as father and daughter. Not if we stand together as one nation."

"We're not going and that's final!"

"Then . . . I'll go by myself," Kalila huffed as she went to the hall closet and grabbed her *habiya*.

"And just how do you plan on getting there?" her father asked.

"I'll walk," Kalila replied. With a determined look, she donned her *habiya* and headed for the front door.

"Talk some sense to her," her father pleaded, looking to his wife for help. But Kalila's mother just rolled her eyes and poured herself another cup of tea.

"Get back here this instant," her father yelled, but his voice was drowned out by the slamming of the front door.

"Have all the women in this house gone insane?" Mr. Mawiyah said as he looked around the kitchen counter for his car keys. "Are you just going to sit there?" he asked his wife.

"I can't go after her. I'm not allowed to drive," she said. "Can't you handle this on your own?"

"Aghh!" Mr. Mawiyah exclaimed, his face turning red. "You two will be the death of me," he said. "Today, I must be patient like the anvil, for I'm obviously not hard enough to be the hammer. Allah give me strength," he said on his way out to the garage.

Once inside his car, Mr. Mawiyah tapped his fingers on the steering wheel while the garage door rose slowly. He backed out and peered down the street for Kalila. He was surprised to see how far she had gotten.

"Maybe, it would be safer if I just let her walk," he said as he watched her black-clad form stride down the sidewalk. "She'd never actually make it down there in time for the demonstration." For a moment, he sat parked in the driveway hoping that Kalila would turn around, but her figure got smaller and smaller.

"Stubborn as a camel," he groused before driving after her.

Slowly, he guided his car down the neighborhood street. He watched her push forward with quick, staccato steps. As Kalila walked, she was punching the buttons on her cell phone at a rapid pace. Finally, Mr. Mawiyah rolled down the car window and called to her.

"Kalila! Please get in the car," he pleaded.

"No!" she answered sharply.

"I . . . I will take you to the demonstration," he said weakly. "Please, just get in the car."

"What?"

"I will take you!" Mr. Mawiyah yelled. "Now, get in the car."

"Do you promise?" she asked without slowing.

"Yes, I promise!" her father yelled out the car window.

Finally, Kalila stopped and got into the car.

#

Anxiously, Al-Faruq stood over his desk. He'd just listened to Chief Hamal address his squadron. Due to the protests, the military had been deployed to all major Saudi cities to instill order. Al-Faruq's squadron would be acting as liaisons between the military and civilian authorities for processing detainees.

Suddenly, Al-Faruq heard his cell phone chime. It was a text from Kalila, but he didn't have time to read it. "Sorry Kalila," he said. Grimacing, he tossed the cell phone in his top drawer, grabbed his riot helmet, and headed out.

As he walked toward the motor pool to meet his team, Al-Faruq checked his side arm. Satisfied that the safety was on, he holstered his weapon. When he reached the motor pool, only one of the unit's prisoner transport buses remained. His squad mates were gathered around it, looking antsy.

"You boys ready?" Al-Faruq asked, trying to sound upbeat.

"What's the holdup?" a young sergeant asked.

"Where's the fire, sergeant? We're supposed to be in place by ten-hundred hours, and we will be. Now, I want your side arms secured with the safeties on."

"What! Why?" another young man complained.

Quick as a flash, Al-Faruq pulled the young man's weapon from its holster and pointed it at his head. "So one of the protesters doesn't grab it and shoot you in the head!"

"They're just rubber bullets," he protested.

"Fired at close range, these things will fracture your skull. Safeties on. Keep them secured. Are we clear?" Al-Faruq asked.

"Yes sir," the young man answered, his face crimson.

"Now listen up. We'll be entering a situation that is filled with emotion and anxiety. Therefore, it is imperative we keep our emotions in check. If we add our emotions to the mix, that's only going to make our jobs more difficult and more dangerous. Our job is simple. Get the detainees onto the bus and transport them back to the detention facility. Your commands need to be short and professional."

"What if they resist?" the young sergeant asked.

"We'll be working in two-man teams. Four of us acting as escorts, two per detainee, and two keeping the bus secure. When escorting a detainee to the bus, be firm but don't try to inflict injury. In many cases, we'll have to carry them. They're not going to walk."

"I'll make them walk," one young man said.

"Really? How are you going to do that? Beat them up? How is that going to encourage them to walk? Oh, and while you're beating on one protester, what do you think the other protesters are going to do? What are they going to do?"

"Uh?"

"You escalate things, and you'll have ten other demonstrators on your back before you know it," Al-Faruq scolded. "What are you going to do then? Pull out your side arm and start shooting? You'll be out of rounds before you know it, probably hitting one of us in the process, and then you'll be at the bottom of a pile getting kicked, hit, and crying for help. Is that what you want?"

"No sir."

"Keep your emotions in check. Be professional! Do you understand?"

"Yes sir," he answered quietly.

"Do you understand?" Al-Faruq demanded loudly.

"Yes sir!" the young man answered firmly.

"Okay. Once we get back to the bus, we'll work together to get the detainees secured. Male detainees in the front. Female detainees in the back. Any questions?"

"No sir," the group responded.

"Now, the military is likely to be using tear gas. Does everyone have their masks?

"Yes sir!"

"All right, let's move out," Al-Faruq ordered.

#

Kalila and her father rode together in tense silence. When they reached the exit for downtown Dhahran, her father finally spoke.

"Keep your *hijab* on," he said.

"Why would I take it off?" Kalila protested. "I'm not demonstrating against Islam."

"Don't give them any reason to . . . "

"You think they need a reason? I'm a woman," Kalila shot back.

"Just be careful," her father pleaded. "Aghh, it's chaos down here. I'll never find a place to park," he grumbled. "I'm going to park at the other end of the shopping district by the fountain."

"Father! You promised."

"We're not leaving. I'm just finding a place to park. Don't worry. You'll have plenty of time to scream your fool head off."

"Aghh!" Kalila exclaimed with a look of disgust in her eyes. She watched every turn that her father made intently.

"I promised to take you, and I'm taking you," he said, weaving his way through the narrow side streets. After a couple of more turns, the streets widened again. Kalila could see the parking lot coming up on the left. There were several police cars parked at the far end of the lot. Mr. Mawiyah let out a heavy sigh.

So far, the crowds milling about the parking lot seemed orderly. No worse than the crowds at the *haj* in Mecca. Suddenly, Kalila saw Inaya, a friend from school. She was walking through the parking lot with her mother and father. Quickly, Kalila rolled down the window.

"Inaya!" Kalila yelled. Inaya stopped and waved. "Inaya, wait."

Kalila turned to her father. "Hey, maybe I can go with them?"

"Hmmmm mmm," her father mumbled. "Okay, but keep your *hijab* on," he reminded her, upon seeing that Inaya's face was uncovered.

"Father!" Kalila exclaimed.

Mr. Mawiyah parked the car and walked with Kalila over to Inaya's family. After exchanging pleasantries, Inaya's parents agreed to look after Kalila. Mr. Mawiyah looked relieved. "I'll be right here," he called over his shoulder. "Don't forget where we're parked."

"I won't," Kalila answered. Then, she turned away and joined Inaya as they hurried to the rally.

The two huddled close together. "Did you see the video?" Inaya asked Kalila in hushed tones.

"No, but I heard about it. Did you see it?"

Inaya nodded. "It was . . . " she paused trying to search for the right words. "Well, it . . . it was just awful," she said with a shudder. "I had my mother watch it. My parents got in a big fight about it, but . . . " Inaya looked up to see if her father was watching them. "Mom won, that's why we're here."

Kalila smiled behind her veil. "My father wasn't too keen on me coming either, but I convinced him."

"How?"

"I told him that if he wouldn't take me, I'd walk down here by myself. I made it three blocks before he picked me up." The girls laughed until Inaya's father shot them a disapproving glance.

When they reached the courtyard, Kalila was amazed at the number of people. The sea of people stretched on for blocks. Here and there, groups gathered together more closely to hear speakers. Closest to them, a woman spoke into a megaphone while standing on one of the benches that surrounded the fountain.

"How long will we stand in silence while half of our nation is chained by ancient, outdated laws? How long will we close our eyes to a tribal mentality that subjugates women in the most base and dehumanizing ways? How long will we hide in the shadows while the ruling elites bask in the rays of wealth and privilege?"

As the woman spoke, Kalila noticed a member of the *mutawa* standing under the awning of a nearby shop. His eyes were steeled on the woman, but he made no move to stop her. Dressed in a black *thobe* and *ghutra*, his form almost disappeared in the shadows. As she watched him, he raised his hand up next to his face.

"What's that in his hand?" Kalila murmured. "Duh, it's a cell phone," she determined. She turned to Inaya and said, "Maybe, we should check out some of the other speakers?"

"What?" Inaya asked. The noise of the crowd was growing.

"Let's check out some of the other speakers," Kalila yelled.

Inaya tugged on her mother's shoulder and pointed over to a man that was standing on a chair outside a popular café. Her mother nodded.

"Let's head over there," Inaya said loudly.

Holding hands so they wouldn't get separated, Kalila and Inaya slowly moved over to the speaker. They found a spot near the café where they could hear him.

"Our king has proclaimed that he will allow women the right to vote in a few years. To what end? All potential candidates must be vetted by the monarchy and the Senior Ulama, all but ensuring that no candidate of substance will ever make it onto the ballot. Their talk of change, their talk of reform rings hollow, does it not?"

"Yeah!" the crowd screamed back.

"Do our elected leaders listen to us?"

"No!"

230

"Do our elected leaders work for us?"

"No!"

"Do our elected leaders care about us?"

"No!"

"And yet we still act like our vote matters. We still act like our voice matters. We still act like our dreams matter, but do they matter? Do we matter? Not to them we don't. They treat us like children, hoping that little treats will mollify our behavior, and scolding us when we speak out against them. Are we children?"

"No!" many of the demonstrators screamed back.

Once again, Kalila's eyes anxiously scanned the surrounding area. *That's funny. The café's practically empty, and the guy behind the counter doesn't look too happy.* Then she realized why.

Sitting stone faced at one of the interior tables was a *mutawa* officer. Like the other *mutawa* member, he too was talking on a cell phone. He didn't look particularly happy either. "Not that the *mutawa* generally look happy," Kalila conceded. Still, it made a cold shiver run down Kalila's spine.

She leaned in close to Inaya and said, "Let's go back and find your parents."

"Okay," Inaya agreed, but this would be easier said than done.

When they turned around, they were greeted by a wall of people. If they thought it was crowded when they first arrived, it was now ten times worse. The street had all but disappeared beneath the crush of demonstrators. Kalila had to stand on her tiptoes to even locate the woman they had been listening to before. The sea of bobbing heads that stretched out in front of her made Kalila's stomach churn.

"Come on," she yelled to Inaya. "We'll have to squeeze through."

Kalila and Inaya inched their way forward, pressing between people, trying to get back to where they had been before. They had gone barely ten feet when by some miracle they bumped into Inaya's parents.

"It's too crowded," Inaya's father yelled. "This is getting dangerous. We need to get out of here."

The girls nodded and followed Inaya's father as he pushed his way through the crowd. However, when they finally reached the fountain, their path was cut off by a line of soldiers. Standing shoulder to shoulder, with their clear plastic shields in front of them, the military police had essentially walled off that end of the street.

"Can we get through?" Inaya's father asked. If the soldier heard him, he gave no indication that he did. "We're just trying to get back to our car," Inaya's father yelled. Still, he received no response. They were trapped.

#

It was only a ten-minute drive to the downtown area. From an overpass, Detective Al-Faruq could see the military forces marshaling. Four Armored Personnel Carriers, known as APCs, were parked barely a block from where the protest was being held. Behind the APCs, a platoon of soldiers in riot gear stood in formation.

"This is nuts," Al-Faruq said, exhaling slowly. He glanced over at the young men on his team. Their eyes grew wide as they caught a glimpse of the throngs of demonstrators that filled the streets below. "Hopefully, you're beginning to understand. If we're not careful, this could get ugly."

"I think we're going to need a bigger bus," the young sergeant commented.

"Our primary objective should be to keep ourselves and the public safe. As long as the protestors disperse, I couldn't care less how many make it onto the bus. Remember, keep your emotions in check. Be professional," Al-Faruq reiterated.

His team remained quiet for the remainder of the drive. As they parked the bus at the edge of the shopping district, the awkward silence was finally interrupted by the squealing of the bus's brakes.

"Pull up over there," Al-Faruq said. He pointed at an alleyway that led to the fountain. "You guys ready?"

"Yes sir!" his team responded.

232

"When you're not helping us with the detainees, you two stay on the bus." The two men nodded. The bus doors swung open and the rest of his team stepped out.

The noise of the demonstrators swirled around them in a loud hum, and they were still over a block away. The protesters rhythmic chants rose to a fevered pitch shaking the surrounding buildings. The air felt hot and close as Al-Faruq and his team navigated down the alley toward the fountain.

"No one is!"

"Above the law!"

"No one is!"

"Above the law!"

The demonstrators' chants echoed off the alley walls. Al-Faruq's heart pounded in his chest as they moved closer to the noise. Subconsciously, he scanned the rooftops for threats. An uncomfortable feeling overtook him, but he and his team pressed on.

When they exited the confines of the alley, the wall of sound stopped them dead in their tracks. Al-Faruq motioned his team forward, and they joined the ranks of riot police separating the throngs of protesters from the city fountain.

Al-Faruq looked at the fountain next to him. Something seemed strange. Then, it hit him. He couldn't hear it. As streams of water hit the pool, the demonstrators' chants rendered them silent. As faint ripples skimmed the water's surface, Al-Faruq couldn't determine whether a breeze or the crowd noise was causing them.

Al-Faruq shook his head and refocused his gaze. The front line, separating the protesters from the fountain, was comprised of soldiers. In tight ranks, they stood shoulder to shoulder. Behind them, the police forces' lines were less defined. The young sergeant on Al-Faruq's team fidgeted nervously with his nightstick. Sweat poured down the young man's face as the sun streamed in through his clear helmet shield.

Anxiously, Al-Faruq repositioned his team. One by one, he grabbed them by the shoulder and pulled them closer. There was no point in trying to bark orders, they wouldn't be able to hear him.

When they start pushing forward with the APCs, we'll be lucky if we don't get trampled. There aren't going to be enough exits to relieve the pressure. Inside, Al-Faruq felt helpless, like he was watching a car accident unfold. Powerless to keep the two vehicles from impacting one another.

What am I doing? Just following orders? At what point is that unacceptable. Will Allah condemn me for my silence? At what point do I stop and say, "This isn't right! This is crazy!"

Before he could come up with an answer, "crazy" erupted in front of him.

#

Cut off from the parking lot and sandwiched between increasingly angry protesters and the military, Kalila was now officially scared. Finally, she understood why her father thought this was a bad idea. While Kalila tried to collect her thoughts, the other demonstrators' chants rang down around her. The woman leading the chants screamed, "No one is!"

"Above the law!" the crowd responded.

"No one is!"

"Above the law!"

Suddenly, four riot policemen pulled the woman down from her perch atop the stone bench. She continued to scream, but after the megaphone was wrenched from her hands, she was only mouthing the words.

Still, the crowd answered her absent call, "Above the law! Above the law!" Over and over, the crowd chanted. The sound was deafening. Kalila couldn't even hear herself think. Then, without warning, a great push came from behind. Everyone in the front was slammed against the line of soldiers and riot police.

"Stop!" Kalila yelled, but she couldn't even hear her own voice. Screams rang out all around her. The line of riot police waved back and forth against the tide of the crowd. In a matter of seconds, Kalila lost sight of Inaya and her parents. Angry men pushed by her and attacked the police line. The force created by the flood of protesters lifted Kalila's feet off the ground.

If I fall, I'm dead. Gritting her teeth she clawed forward hanging on tightly to the shoulders of anyone around her. *I'm not going down. I won't be trampled to death.*

Suddenly the crowd surged forward, knocking the policemen back. Kalila found herself pinched against the edge of the fountain. With her legs pressed tightly against the concrete fountain, she was certain they would break. With all her might, she threw her shoulder into the person next to her. Momentarily, her legs were free, but the subsequent wave of humanity toppled Kalila into the fountain.

Now, a new fear gripped her, the fear of drowning! As she fell into the water, Kalila somehow grabbed a breath, but getting back to the surface was a struggle. Her *habiya*, now soaked, felt like it weighed a ton. Her feet slipped on the fountain's slime-covered bottom as other protesters knocked her over, trying to escape. Every breath was a battle.

Allah! Help me!

Kalila found herself face down again in the water. Walking on her hands and knees, she crept forward. After catching a glimpse of the decorative stonework rising up in front of her, Kalila strained to reach the fountain's center. Although most of her breaths seemed to be filled with more water than air, she made it.

The paper-thin sheet of water emanating from the fountain's centerpiece shielded Kalila from the bedlam. Time seemed to stand still as she clung to the concrete pedestal. She was fighting back tears, but at least she could breathe.

Her eyes searched for an escape route, but people were flying everywhere. *I've gotta move. I can't just sit here. Take a few more breaths, then make a break for the edge. You can do it.*

Behind her, a sharp crackling noise drew her attention. Looking over, she watched as a man fell face first into the fountain. The water around him turned pink, then red. He didn't move. Oblivious, another man clamored over the top of him.

Kalila screamed.

With tears running down her face, Kalila pulled herself up to a standing position and trudged forward. She'd barely taken two steps when she was hit from behind. Once again, she found herself face down in the water. On top of her, something or someone was pushing her against the concrete bottom of the small pool. A kick to her stomach forced most of the air out of her lungs. Kalila closed her eyes in prayer.

#

As smoke bubbled up at the far end of the shopping district, the crowds in front of Al-Faruq rippled into an angry sea. Reflexively, he bent his knees and put up his arms. He prodded the young sergeant next to him to do the same. Still, the push from the demonstrators knocked them back on their heels. They regained their balance and pushed on the backs of the men in front of them. For a moment, their lines held, but then the tidal wave of protesters crashed forward.

The men positioned at the top of the circular fountain were pushed back into the water. Flailing, their plastic shields were pelted by streams of water. Meanwhile, the protesters clawed forward into the fountain. Still, the soldiers at the opposite end of the shopping district continued to press forward.

Al-Faruq's eyes darted back and forth between the fountain and the wall of men in front of him. The soldiers who had fallen back into the water were swinging their nightsticks wildly at the oncoming hoard of protesters. The demonstrators were panicking too, climbing over one another in attempts to escape. One woman, her black *habiya* soaking wet, clung to the centerpiece of the fountain, struggling to catch her breath.

Al-Faruq held his ground, afraid he'd get trampled if he didn't. Next to him, the young sergeant fell to one knee. Al-Faruq grabbed him by the collar and retreated. Bracing himself against a bench, he pulled the young sergeant to his feet as the demonstrators poured through.

Al-Faruq surveyed the chaos around them. The young woman seeking refuge at the center of the fountain was now making her way to the edge. Clenched together, a soldier and a male demonstrator fell on top of her. She disappeared under the water.

Quickly, Al-Faruq threw his legs over the fountain's edge. Above the water's surface, Al-Faruq saw her hand reach out in vain for help. Frantically, he waded forward, pushed the two men aside, and pulled her to the surface.

#

Miraculously, Kalila felt the weight on her back disappear. She started to rise. Coughing and disoriented, Kalila couldn't even stand. Someone, a man, helped her to her feet. With her heartbeat reverberating loudly in her ears, she struggled forward.

"Sergeant! Get over here!" the man screamed. "Take her arm!"

With Kalila's dripping wet arms slung over their shoulders, the two men carried her away. "Where are you taking me?" she asked.

Looking down, Kalila could see her feet tumbling over the uneven stones. She moved from hot, bright sunlight to cool, dark shadows. Kalila tried to look up, but the sea of bobbing heads made her feel sick. Finally, they broke out into the sunlight again. They set her on her feet.

"Can you walk?" the man asked.

Kalila frowned. The voice sounded familiar. Staring, Kalila studied the man intently. It was a police officer. A clear plastic shield covered his face.

"Can you walk?" he repeated.

"Al-Faruq?" she asked pulling her wet veil away from her face.

Al-Faruq's eyes grew wide. "Kalila?"

As Kalila threw her arms around his neck, Al-Faruq stood there in stunned silence, but after a moment, he gently pulled her arms away. "Are you alone?" he asked.

"No, my father's here."

"Do you think you can find him?"

"Yes, I . . . I think so," she answered.

"Then, go home. Get the hell out of here!" Al-Faruq said as he repositioned her veil. "I've got to go."

"Wait!" Kalila replied, but Al-Faruq had already turned away. Quickly, he headed back down the alley dragging the other police officer with him.

Kalila found a light post to lean against while she regained her senses. Logically, she knew that this was the parking lot where her father had dropped her off, but currently it looked more like a war zone. Victims of the melee were everywhere. Sirens wailed, lights flashed, and an acrid smoke hung in the air.

As Kalila watched, two men carried a woman to safety. Blood was streaming down her face. "Help us!" they pleaded, but the injured far outnumbered the quantity of medical personnel.

I can't just stand here. I've got to find my father. Kalila adjusted her sagging wet veil and tried to pick her way across the parking lot. She kept her head down and tried not to make eye contact with any of the riot police or military personnel that were milling about.

"Hey you," someone called from behind, but Kalila pretended not to hear them and quickened her pace.

Upon clearing a row of cars, Kalila saw a woman kneeling next to a man. He was lying motionless on the concrete and had a strange vacant look in his eyes. "Why!" the woman wailed, her hands open to the sky. Shaken, Kalila looked away and scanned the parking lot for her father's car.

Did I go too far? This can't be right. Anxiously, Kalila wheeled around and surveyed her surroundings. She noticed a man standing on the hood of his car.

"Father," she said with relief as she raced forward. "Father," she cried, her voice cracking. "Over here!"

Her father turned around. Upon seeing Kalila, he jumped down off the hood of the car and ran to her. "Kalila! Kalila! You're all right!" he yelled. Excitedly, he gave her a hug. "What happened? You're all wet."

"I'll tell you later. Let's just get out of here," she replied pulling him toward the car.

"I told you this was dangerous," he said looking around nervously. "Where's your friend?"

"I don't know, but we need to get out of here," Kalila insisted. For the first time that day, her father didn't argue with her.

Chapter 40: Taking Flight

While her brother, Ghazi, sat waiting in the car, Iba crept quietly into the house. Although it had only been a few days since she'd fled with Azzah, the house felt strange and foreign. Cautiously, she climbed the stairs. Her eyes shifted uncomfortably. From the looks of things, Mahmud hadn't bothered to clean up anything since the altercation. The pictures that hung along the staircase were still askew. The *dallah* that she'd used to knock him out still lay at the top of the stairs.

Focus! Just get the passports, grab a few clothes, and get out.

In the back of her mind, she knew that Ghazi wouldn't wait long. She'd overheard him talking with Ghasaan, her eldest brother. They were skeptical of her story, and she was lucky that they hadn't called Mahmud for confirmation.

It won't be long before they kick us out on the street.

Iba grabbed a small suitcase from the hall closet and stepped into Azzah's bedroom. The room was in shambles. Azzah's clothes were strewn everywhere, and most of them were ripped and torn.

Has Mahmud gone totally insane?

Iba looked fearfully at the closet. It appeared as if he'd taken a knife and tore through all Azzah's clothes. Her hands shaking, she picked through the mess. Thankfully, Iba found a handful of clothes that appeared to be in one piece. Quickly, she stuffed them in the suitcase and moved on to her own room. Her husband had done the same thing to her clothes.

"That impotent devil," she spat.

When Iba saw what he'd done to Azzah's clothes, she had to fight back tears. But now she could feel her anger welling up inside.

"Damn him to hell. I should have finished him off the other night, and then gone directly to the airport." Angrily she stuffed a few of her own clothes into the bag. "I just hope and pray he didn't think about the passports."

Frustrated, she emptied her jewelry drawer into the suitcase, then ducked into the bathroom and grabbed some essentials. She was going to need more than just the passports. She'd need money too.

Hurriedly, she zipped the suitcase shut and carried it down the stairs. After peeking out the front window to ensure her brother was still there, Iba scurried into the study.

"Which drawer was it?" she mumbled nervously. "That's it," she said reaching for the bottom drawer. "I know it's in here." Frantically, she dove her hands under the mounds of paper and correspondence that Mahmud forbid her to look at. Finally, she found it.

"Ah ha!" she exclaimed as her hand produced a large white envelope. She peaked inside. It was filled with cash. "Yes!" she said triumphantly. "That'll teach him." Quickly, she grabbed a handful of bills and stuffed them into the suitcase. She shoved the rest into her purse.

Next, she looked over at the computer desk. The file drawer next to the computer was sitting open. Iba held her breath.

"No, no, no . . . Please no!" she pleaded.

Kneeling down in front of the file cabinet, her fingers flipped tensely through the file folders. "Oh, thank Allah!" she exclaimed upon finding the passports. Clutching the passports to her breast, she ran to the front door and headed outside.

Her brother eyed her suspiciously. "What took so long?" Ghazi said.

"I didn't want to forget something and make you come all the way back," Iba answered. Slowly, her brother backed out of the driveway.

Once they were a couple of blocks away, Iba put her plan into action. "I talked to Mahmud," she lied.

"He was home?" her brother asked.

"Yes. He suggested this would be a good time for Azzah and me to visit Yasmin."

"Why would you want to visit her?" Ghazi asked.

"She's still a member of the family," Iba said softly.

"Not since she married that Western devil," her brother scolded her. "She's no sister of mine."

"Our parents set up the marriage and approved of the union," Iba protested.

"They weren't supposed to leave Saudi Arabia."

"How's that Yasmin's fault?"

"She knew his plan. She lied to us."

"You don't know that," Iba pleaded.

"Hmpf," Ghazi grunted.

"Well, Ratib has told me to go," Iba said flatly. "What am I supposed to do? Disobey him?"

"Then he should take you to the airport," her brother growled.

"He's busy! Are you going to take us our not?"

Ghazi swore under his breath.

"Turn around. Take me back home," Iba bluffed. "I'll tell him that you can't help, even though you're unemployed, even though your wife had to get a job just to pay the bills."

"Shut up!" Ghazi yelled. Sharply, he slapped her with the back of his hand.

Iba shrunk away, worried she'd pushed him too far.

"I'll take you," he said finally, but the two did not speak the rest of the way home.

When they reached her brother's house, Iba grabbed her things and raced upstairs. She knocked softly on the door to the spare bedroom. "Azzah, it's me. Open up."

"Just a second," Azzah replied.

On the other side of the door, Iba heard something being dragged along the floor. Then, she heard the lock turn. Finally, the door creaked open.

"Did someone try to come in?" Iba asked cautiously upon seeing the trunk.

Azzah nodded.

"Who?" Iba asked.

"Uncle Ghasaan. I heard him cursing when the door wouldn't open. I pushed the trunk up against the door, just in case."

"Good thinking," Iba reassured her. "I think I've figured a way out. I've convinced Ghazi that your father wants us to visit my sister in Germany."

"Germany?" Azzah asked incredulously.

"It's our best hope," Iba replied nervously. "We have to get out of the country. I've got our passports. We'd be visiting family, so that's less likely to raise suspicions. Provided Ghazi doesn't screw things up at the airport, I think we can do this."

"But," Azzah asked anxiously, "when's the last time you talked with your sister? Father forbade you to even say her name."

Iba took Azzah's hands in her own. "The night before she left. Yasmin told me that we'd always be sisters," she said softly. "It didn't matter if we lived in different countries. It didn't matter if we hardly ever spoke. We're sisters and nothing would ever change that," Iba said swallowing hard. "I have her address. Secretly, I've even sent her a few letters over the years. If we can get to her, she won't turn us out. She won't."

Iba let go of Azzah's hands, wiped away the tears that were running down Azzah's face, and then wiped away her own. "Put on your *habiya*," she said. "We need to be able to go at a moment's notice. Ghazi will take us, but we need to be careful. Stay close. Don't speak. Let me do the talking."

Azzah nodded.

"Iba!" Ghazi's loud voice growled from downstairs. "Iba!"

Iba hurried to the door and cracked it open. "Yes," she replied.

"There's a flight leaving for Germany in two hours. You have five minutes to get in the car, or you're walking! I hope you've got enough money. I'll be damned if I'm paying for anything."

"Let's go," Iba urged. "Put on your veil and keep your eyes down. We'll get through this." Quickly, the pair gathered their things and headed downstairs.

When they reached the bottom, Iba saw Ghazi standing by the front door. Ghasaan was sitting at the kitchen table with Ghazi's wife. Even inside the house, they made her wear her veil. After pouring Ghasaan a cup of tea, she sat down motionless with her hands in her lap. Secretly, Iba wished she could take her with them, but it was a pointless thought. Hurriedly, she led Azzah to the door.

"*Ntia zamla koos,*" Ghasaan growled.

Iba squeezed Azzah's hand tightly and pulled her toward the door, following Ghazi out to the car.

"Get in the back," he ordered.

Iba and Azzah did as they were told. Together, the three drove in an uncomfortable silence. While Azzah stared at the floor, Iba kept her eyes peeled to ensure that Ghazi was actually taking them to the airport. She wasn't quite sure what she would do if he didn't, but he wasn't going to surprise her.

Iba felt a sense of relief when the airport came into sight, but she knew they weren't home free yet. *Please Allah,* she pleaded silently. *Please, let us make it onto a plane. Lead us anywhere, anywhere but here.*

All the while, Ghazi did not utter a word. Occasionally, Iba would catch his cold eyes staring at them in the rear view mirror. She wondered what he was thinking, but then again, she probably didn't want to know.

When they arrived at the airport, once again it was time for Iba to hold her breath. The ticket counter was the next hurdle. A portly man sat behind the register. He looked half asleep.

"Give me the money and your passports," Ghazi ordered before approaching the counter.

Iba felt her anger rise, but she swallowed it down. After reaching inside her purse, she handed him a wad of cash and the passports.

"Two tickets to Berlin, Germany," Ghazi said.

"Huh? Oh," the man said sleepily. "What was that again?"

"Two tickets to Berlin," Ghazi said a little louder, gesturing at Iba and Azzah.

"Will they be traveling alone?" the man behind the counter asked skeptically.

"Yeah," Ghazi answered.

"Are you their legal guardian?" the man asked as he looked at the passports.

"I'm her brother."

"Then, I'm sorry, but I can't sell you a ticket."

"Look," Ghazi said impatiently, "my brother-in-law asked me to bring them to the airport. They'll be visiting my eldest sister in Germany."

"Without proof that you're their legal . . . "

"I don't have time for this," Ghazi argued. He pulled out the wad of cash that Iba had given him. "I want these two out of my hair."

The portly man glanced around. It was a relatively slow day, and his supervisor was at lunch. "I'll see if there are any seats available," he said for appearances sake as he counted the money. Then, he looked back at the reservation screen. He paused briefly as if trying to calculate the amount of the bribe in his head. "You'll need to escort them to the gate and stay with them until they board," he mumbled.

"Fine," Ghazi replied. He glared at Iba and Azzah.

"Will they be checking any luggage?"

"Yeah," Ghazi said. Roughly, he threw their suitcase onto the luggage platform.

"Gate C10," the ticket vendor said as he handed over the tickets and passports.

"Let's go," Ghazi snapped. Iba and Azzah followed in strained silence.

As they stood upon a moving walkway, Iba eyed the tickets and passports in Ghazi's hand. "Can I have the passports back?" she inquired.

"Shut up," Ghazi replied. His eyes focused on Iba's purse. "You were always the smart one," he mused as he reached for the bag.

"No! Stop! I need that money for . . . "

"For what?" he asked angrily as he tried to pull the bag forcefully out of her hand. "You want on that plane, then you're going to need to give me a little something," Ghazi demanded.

A man ahead of them on the walkway saw the altercation, but he turned away and said nothing. Ghazi pushed Iba to the ground wrenching the bag from her hand. Then, he rifled through it until he found more money. Satisfied, he threw the bag down at Iba's feet.

Iba picked up the bag, fighting back her tears.

We're so close. Don't ruin it now. The money is nothing. Getting Azzah out of this country is all that matters. If you let your anger get the best of you, he wins.

She took a deep breath, reached for Azzah's hand, and squeezed it reassuringly.

At least Ghazi did his part. He escorted them through security, to the international terminal, and to the gate. He seemed satisfied with the money he'd extracted from them and was basking in his self-imagined power. When the plane began boarding, he finally returned their passports to them. After handing their tickets to the ticket agent, Ghazi turned to leave.

With their boarding passes in hand, Iba looked back pensively. Ghazi strode away without a word and was soon out of sight.

He didn't even look back, and neither will we. Neither will we.

Chapter 41: Road Trip

It was the Friday night before Memorial Day weekend. After carrying their luggage in from the van, Nasim and Nicole trudged into their hotel room, exhausted. They had just visited Yellowstone National Park, and were traveling back to Austin. On the southern outskirts of Cheyenne, reality intervened.

"I'm totally beat," Nicole said as she flopped back on the bed. "We shouldn't have done that hike this morning."

"You're probably right," Nasim agreed. "But we did get some cool pictures."

"Yeah, you're just lucky that buffalo didn't stomp your butt into the ground."

"What?" Nasim protested. "It was half asleep, and aren't buffaloes just glorified cows anyway?"

"They're wild animals, and you were getting way too close," Nicole said while grabbing the remote and flicking on the television. "Is it okay if I watch some news? After four days in the wilderness, I feel totally out of touch."

"Sure, whatever," Nasim said with a shrug.

Nicole scanned through the channels until she found CNN.

"Terror strikes the United States," the commentator said ominously.

"Holy shit!" Nicole exclaimed.

Nasim held his breath.

"Across the U.S., people are on edge as a Maryland electrical plant is damaged in an explosion, and another explosion causes a coal train derail in Kentucky. Are these incidents related? We take you now to Heather Cabot who is reporting to us from Maryland."

Nasim's heart sank into his stomach.

"Thank you, John," Heather said. "I'm standing here, just outside the electrical plant near Elkridge, Maryland, where an explosion has knocked out power to over 100,000 people. While we've gotten no word yet on the official cause of the explosion, the presence of FBI officials suggests this was no accident. There's been no word yet on when power will be restored."

"Wow," Nicole said, her eyes glued to the television.

"Is this incident related to the Kentucky train derailment?" John asked.

"At this point, I'm not sure anyone really knows. Officials have been very tight lipped about the explosion. However, we do have a young man here who was an eyewitness to the explosion. Can I have your name, please?"

"Uh, Charles Mockens," the young man responded, wide-eyed.

"Now Charles, you saw the explosion?"

"Uh, yeah! We was hanging out at the picnic area over thar," he said turning away from the camera and pointing."

"And you saw the explosion?"

"Yeah, it wus uplong that ridge between the plant and the power lines. It was like powshwack! And then thar wus this ball of fire and the power lines snapped, like, crrrack!"

"What happened then?" Heather asked seriously.

"Well, we all freaked out. Like, most of my friends split, cause, well, they wus scared."

"Weren't you scared?"

"No . . . I wus scared too."

"Then, why did you stay?"

"Uh, well I . . . I couldn't find my car keys."

"Thank you, Charles," Heather responded with a pained expression, as the camera panned back to her. "Based on this young man's eyewitness testimony, the explosion happened on the south side of the plant where the transformers connect to the power lines."

While Nicole proceeded to flip back and forth between the various news channels, Nasim felt sick inside. For the last month, he'd done his best to follow the imam's advice. He tried to focus on his new friendships and put his past behind him. He made every effort to cherish his time with Nicole, but in the back of his mind, he knew it wouldn't last. At some point, the other shoe would drop.

"Are you seeing this?" Nicole asked.

"Yeah," Nasim said weakly.

"You feeling okay?" she asked rubbing the back of his hand.

I'm just tired," Nasim lied. He got up from the bed and walked over to the bathroom. "I'm going to get ready for bed. I just need a good night's sleep."

"Yeah," Nicole said as she turned off the television. "We should probably get to bed." She followed Nasim, gave him a hug, and then delved into the suitcases to find some pajamas.

Nasim closed the bathroom door and stared at himself in the mirror. *I was supposed to be part of this. What's going to happen when they find out that I wasn't? Just get some rest. Maybe things will look better in the morning.*

#

Unfortunately, come morning, things were worse. In addition to the Maryland and Kentucky attacks, there were reports across the United States of bombs being detonated at gas stations. According to the news, law enforcement was on high alert due to the attacks. Nasim had no idea how they'd ever make it back to Austin.

Though he tried to dissuade her, Nicole had been glued to the television all morning, gobbling up news on the attacks. For Nasim, all the reporting just gave him a headache.

"Pamphlets found at a gas station attack in Oregon point to environmental terrorists," the news commentator said. "However, an eyewitness from an attack in Nevada indicated that the perpetrators were of Arabian descent. Are these attacks related to the Saudi oil tanker attacks?"

"There is no evidence to support that connection," the government official answered.

"Then, what does the evidence point too?"

"It's too early to say definitively, but rest assured we're utilizing all the resources at our command to bring the guilty parties to justice."

"We really should get on the road," Nasim said. "It's practically checkout time."

"I know. I'm sorry," Nicole answered. "This is so bizarre."

"Yeah. I . . . I'm going to take our bags down to the van. Oh, we still need to get gas."

"Okay, I'm coming." Nicole finally turned off the television, and followed Nasim down. When they reached the parking lot, Nasim and Nicole were in for an unpleasant surprise.

"Oh my God!" Nicole exclaimed.

"You're telling me," Nasim answered as he looked across the street at a nearby gas station. The line of cars for the pumps stretched over a block. "Why don't you get in line for gas while I finish checking out?"

"Okay." Nicole said as Nasim tossed her the keys. "Do you want me to wait for you?"

"Checking out shouldn't take that long. I'll just walk down the street until I find you," Nasim called.

While Nicole drove off to get in line, Nasim followed the sidewalk toward the front desk. It was going to be another hot day. There wasn't a cloud in the sky.

Nasim entered the lobby through the sliding glass doors and was disappointed to see several people waiting in line for the front desk clerk. Nonetheless, he took his spot in line and waited. To his surprise, the line moved quickly, but when it was his turn, the front desk clerk got a strange look on her face.

"Uh, just a moment. I'll be right with you," she said before leaving hurriedly to a back room.

"Okay," Nasim said.

After a few minutes, an older gentleman came out to the front desk. "I'm the manager. May I help you? I'm afraid were all booked up for tonight."

"I'm just checking out," Nasim said, somewhat confused. He slid the room keys forward.

"Oh, of course. Everything fine with the room?"

"Yeah," Nasim replied with a shrug.

"Where are you headed?"

"Back to Austin, Texas. Well, provided we can get gas," Nasim answered, gesturing outside.

"Yeah, it's crazy out there. Well, you're all set. Here's your receipt."

Nasim grabbed the receipt and exited the way he'd come in. As the sliding glass doors closed behind him, he looked back at the front desk. The female front desk clerk had returned and was standing next to the manager. While her manager dialed the phone, she stared straight at Nasim.

Frowning, Nasim turned around. After folding up the hotel receipt and stuffing it in his pocket, he walked down the block in search of Nicole and the van. He'd gone over a block before finally seeing her. Nasim waved and then waited for an opening to cross the street. Just as he was about to cross, a police car pulled up along a nearby cross street.

"Whoop, whoop," the siren rang out as the police car zipped up to where Nasim was crossing. Startled, Nasim stepped back onto the curb. With the squad car lights still flashing, the police officer quickly exited the vehicle.

"Where you headed son?" the officer asked.

"Uh, my girlfriend is in line to get gas," Nasim answered, pointing across the street. "I was just heading over to meet her."

"And which vehicle is yours?"

"The white van," Nasim answered. Thankfully, Nicole had seen him and was smiling and waving in their direction. However, the police officer seemed unmoved.

"Well, if you don't mind, I'm going to need to ask you and your girlfriend a few questions."

"About what?" Nasim asked, his anger rising.

"About where you've been for the past twenty-four hours?"

Nicole started to get out of the van. "What's the problem?" she asked.

"Please, just stay in the van, ma'am," the officer yelled while holding up his hand.

Suddenly, another police car arrived on the scene. It pulled up right in front of Nicole. Evidently, getting gas was going to take longer than Nasim and Nicole had ever imagined.

\#

"What's your name again?"

"Nasim Talib," he answered tiredly. Nasim was now sitting in a small windowless room at the Wyoming State Patrol office. The walls were plain and gray. One wall was adorned with a large nondescript mirror. There was a table with two chairs. Nasim sat in one while his latest inquisitor sat in the other.

"And what brings you to Wyoming?"

"My girlfriend and I were visiting Yellowstone."

"Oh, that's right," the officer said as he flipped slowly through the file folder in front of him.

"Where'd you stay last night?"

"A hotel in Cheyenne."

"What time did you check in?"

"It was around nine o'clock. Is this really necessary? I'm sure that the hotel has all of this information," Nasim pleaded.

"Well, given what's happened, I'm afraid that it is very necessary."

"Yeah, I've seen the news, but the closest attack was like somewhere in Nevada. I've given you all my receipts from the trip. It's fairly obvious where we've been. If there'd been an attack in Yellowstone, I could see your point, but come on!"

"So, you live in Austin, Texas," the officer continued, ignoring Nasim's outburst.

"Yeah," Nasim answered leaning his head on his hands.

"What do you do in Austin?"

"I'm a student at the University of Texas."

"Where are you from originally?"

"Tulkarm, Palestine."

"You mean Israel?"

"Well, I could see how you might think that, but it's part of the West Bank. It's currently governed by the Palestinian Authority. So what? What difference does that make?"

Once again, the officer ignored the question. "What were you doing in Yellowstone?"

"Sightseeing."

"You do that a lot?"

"When I can."

"For example?"

"I went to Disney World once during spring break. I've visited the Grand Canyon. Places like that," Nasim answered. "Where's Nicole? How long are you going to keep asking me the same stupid questions?" As the officer droned on, Nasim wondered how Nicole was holding up.

#

Nicole was probably closer than Nasim could imagine. Barely fifteen feet away, she sat in a room almost identical to his.

"Now, Miss Stacey," the officer said. "You said that you've been dating Nasim for a couple months. Is that right?"

"Yes," Nicole replied. She was sitting back in the chair with her arms folded.

"But, you know him well enough to drive all the way to Yellowstone with him?"

"What? What does that have to do with anything? As I said before, I've known Nasim for years. Okay? We started dating a few months ago. He'd been planning a trip to Yellowstone, and since I'd never been there, I asked if I could tag along. You know? It sounded like fun."

"And was it?"

"Was it what?"

"Did you have a good time in Yellowstone?"

"A heck of a lot more fun than this."

"So, what did you do in Yellowstone?"

"Seriously? We visited Old Faithful, and the upper and lower falls. We spent a day hiking around the Mammoth Hot Springs area. We checked out the visitor centers. We camped out a couple of nights."

"Anything else?"

"I thought it was a vacation. I didn't know there was going to be a test. If you bring me my digital camera, I could walk you through it. We took a lot of pictures."

"And Nasim was with you the entire time?"

"Yeah."

"Even at night?"

"Yes, same hotel room, same tent, one van, we were together the entire trip."

"No way he could have slipped out on his own? Maybe at night?"

"No."

"You're sure?"

"Positive."

Chapter 42: No Choice

It was late Sunday afternoon when Nasim and Nicole finally made it back to Austin. The trip back from Yellowstone had been a nightmare. Even after the Wyoming State Police released them, they encountered checkpoints at the Colorado border and the Oklahoma and Texas borders as well. They drove night and day to get back. Despite taking turns sleeping in the back of the van, they were both worn out.

Nasim was afraid that the whole ordeal had taken its toll on Nicole. As soon as they walked through the door, Nicole flopped immediately onto the couch. After dumping their bags in the bedroom, Nasim came and joined her. She'd been pretty quiet during the last part of the drive. Unsure of what to say, Nasim took her hand and gave it a gentle squeeze.

"I'm sorry," he said finally.

"For what?" Nicole answered sounding annoyed. "You didn't do anything."

"No, but the trip back would have been easier if . . . "

"If what? If you weren't Palestinian?"

"Well . . . "

"If anything, I'm the one who should be apologizing to you. I mean, this is the United States of America and that was blatant profiling. They had no reason to suspect you of anything. They were grabbing at straws."

"Nicole . . . " Nasim answered, trying to search for the right words. "They're just trying to protect everyone. It's not that big a deal. In Palestine, if you live in the West Bank, you have to deal with checkpoints like that all the time."

"How can you stand it?" she asked.

"That's just the way life is."

"Well, it's bullshit!" she griped.

"You're getting too worked up about this," Nasim said gently. "Come on. We're back. Let's order pizza or something. Maybe we can catch a movie."

"What? I can't believe this doesn't bother you."

"Well, I . . . I guess I'm just used to it. I mean it was weird seeing it happen here, but I've seen worse. It's not like there are Israeli tanks rolling through the neighborhood, so I guess I'm cool with it. Frankly, I was amazed we were able to get back at all. When we got pulled in by the state troopers in Wyoming, I figured we'd be stuck in Wyoming until things settled down."

"Well, I'm . . . I'm not used to it," Nicole answered trying to fight back tears. "You shouldn't have to deal with crap like that. We shouldn't . . . "

Nasim pulled her close and put his arm around her. Softly, he kissed her on the forehead. "We had fun in Yellowstone, didn't we? You're just tired, Nicki. How about I go down and get some takeout from that Chinese place you like. You hang out here and rest. Pick out a DVD to watch. I'll only be a few minutes."

"Okay, I guess," Nicole relented.

Nasim got up and headed to the door. Briefly, he stopped to make sure he had enough money. "All right, see you in a few minutes," he called.

"Yeah," she responded quietly.

After closing the apartment door, Nasim leaned his head against it for a moment. *I guess the fairy tale is over. Even now, she doesn't really understand. It's all good, until something goes wrong, and then? Then, they round up the usual subjects.*

As he walked down to the restaurant, Nasim had to remind himself. In actuality, the police had every reason to stop and question him.

The truth is, I am a terrorist. I've been in this country for four years spying on Americans, casing targets, preparing. Preparing for this weekend, and I . . . I simply thought I could walk away, be someone else. But I can't. The Israelis could find my name on some piece of paper in a raid back in Palestine. Then, forward it here to one of the U.S. agencies. There would always be a chance they'd connect the dots. What would I tell Nicole then? Sorry? I'm not who you thought I was. I wanted to be, but I'm just not.

Suddenly Nasim felt very alone. He entered the Chinese restaurant and stood quietly in line waiting to order. A large fish tank decorated the entrance. The brightly colored koi stared at him.

He looked up blankly at the menu above the register, his hunger gone. When it was his turn, he ordered a couple of Nicole's favorites. Then he sat down across from the fish tank and waited for the food.

Twisting and turning, the fish swam back and forth in their small tank. Outwardly, they looked so calm and peaceful. Nasim wondered if they truly were.

Do they realize that they're in a fish bowl, on display, being watched? I'm no more free than they are. I can't go home, and I can't stay here. Unless . . . Unless I do what I was sent here to do, and even then, what would I be going home to? Create violence and destruction here, or be subjected to it there. Are those my only choices? Is that all that life has in store for me? Jail or the grave, it's only a matter of time.

"Excuse me. Hello? Your order's ready," the lady behind the counter said.

"Oh, thanks," Nasim offered, getting up from his seat. He grabbed the food and headed back to the apartment. Nasim's mouth was dry. Although it was pushing seven o'clock, it was still hot out, and the breeze did little to help alleviate the heat.

"I should've gotten something to drink too," he mumbled. "Is there anything other than water at the apartment? Wait, we did have a few sodas left from the trip. I could just throw those in the freezer to cool them off."

As he entered the apartment, Nasim smiled. Nicole was asleep on the couch. She looked so beautiful, so wonderful. He walked past quietly and set the food down on the kitchen table. Then he went over to the computer desk and booted up the computer. While it struggled to life, he saw the sodas peeking out from a bag on the floor.

After putting two cans into the freezer, he returned to the computer and checked e-mail. As the messages appeared in his in-box, one message in particular caught his attention. It was from the Palestinian Education Foundation, and it was marked urgent. *What the hell is that? They hardly ever communicate via e-mail.* Anxiously, he opened the message and began to read.

Dear Nasim,

Congratulations! Your hard work and perseverance were integral to your successful graduation. We were disappointed that you could not join in our celebration over the Memorial Day weekend. Please remember that in order to ensure your scholarship throughout graduate school, you need to complete your PEF volunteer requirements NLT the 5th of July. We know how proud your parents are that you completed your undergraduate work, and how hurt they'd be if you failed to follow through on your post graduate studies. Don't give up now when the finish line is in sight. We're counting on you to fulfill the promise that you displayed when you embarked on your journey to America.

Palestinian Education Foundation

As he read the message, the cold reality slowly set in. *Follow through with the attacks, or else. Come on. You're just reading too much into it. They wouldn't really go after my parents. Would they?*

Suddenly, his phone rang. Nasim picked it up. "Hello?"

"Nasim?"

"Mom?"

"He's there. I got through!"

"Mom! Why are you calling? Is something wrong?"

"No, no. This fine gentleman from the Foundation dropped by. He said we should give you a call. He's letting us use his cell phone."

"Mom, uh, are you okay?" Nasim asked with alarm.

"Yes, yes. Everything is wonderful. Mr. Haidar was just telling us how well you were doing. You've qualified for their graduate scholarship. Congratulations! We're so happy for you."

"Mom, I . . . " Nasim stopped. He could hear someone talking in the background.

"He said that you still need to complete your volunteer requirements."

"Yes, Mom. I know."

"Let me put him on."

"Did you get our e-mail?" the voice asked brightly, but to Nasim, it sounded sickly sweet.

"Yes," Nasim said weakly.

"Then, you know what you have to do. Don't let your parents down. Your mother is so beautiful, so full of life, and such a wonderful hostess. We're all counting on you."

"Nasim?" It was Nasim's father.

"Yes, Dad?"

"I just wanted to say, keep up the good work. We miss you," his father said.

"We love you," his mother added in the background.

"We have to end the call before it gets too expensive for Mr. Haidar," his father said.

"No, wait. I love you too!"

"We love you," Nasim's mother said again. Then, the line disconnected.

For several minutes, Nasim sat there in shock. *I was stupid to think they wouldn't notice, that I could just walk away.*

With a tear rolling down his cheek, he looked over at Nicole sleeping on the couch. He loved her, but he couldn't turn his back on his family. Plus, if the PEF learned about Nicole, then she'd be in danger too. Suddenly, a dreadful feeling enveloped him.

I've got to get out of here. I've got to get away from her. She's in danger.

Hurriedly, Nasim went to the bedroom and retrieved his suitcase. Before leaving the room, he stopped short. He turned back to the dresser and pulled out one of the drawers. Taped to the back of the drawer were three zip lock bags filled with cash. He'd put them there in case of an emergency. He grabbed them and stuffed them in his suitcase.

Thankfully, Nicole was still asleep as he tiptoed out. There's no way he could explain, but he owed her something. Gently, Nasim set down his suitcase. He grabbed a pad of paper from the computer desk and scribbled out a note. After setting the pad down on the coffee table, he grabbed his suitcase and sneaked out of the apartment.

"I'm sorry, Nicole," he mouthed silently as he closed the apartment door.

Nasim ran down the stairs. Halfway down, he stopped. He shook his head angrily trying to blink away the tears. *I've got no choice. There's no way she'd understand, and there's nothing she could do to help. It's better this way. I've got no choice.*

Chapter 43: In Too Deep

Tahir wasn't sure whether the noise of the explosion or the wail of car alarms woke him first. Nonetheless, he awoke that morning at four a.m. with an excruciating sense of dread. He knew he should get up, go see what happened, and express the proper amount of shock. Instead, he just wanted to pull the covers over his head and hide.

Tahir rolled his feet out of bed, sat up, and walked slowly to the window to look out. *I can't believe that crazy fuck blew up my car. I am so screwed. How's this going to help get Detective Al-Faruq off my tail?*

Suddenly, there was a knock on the door. Startled, Tahir flinched. "Ughh," he groaned. "With my luck that's probably him now." Tahir trudged to the door and looked though the peephole. "Oh great!" Tahir whispered sarcastically as he leaned his head against the door. It was Wasif, one of Tahir's neighbors. Another loud knock reverberated through his forehead.

"Just a minute," Tahir pleaded tiredly as he unbolted the door.

"Tahir, did you look out your window?" Wasif asked when Tahir opened the door. "A car bomb went off. I'm sorry man, but I think your car was involved. You better go down and check it out."

"What? Go down there! Are you serious? I figure I'm safer up here. What if another one goes off?"

"You think there might be more?" Wasif asked.

"Heck yeah," Tahir answered, playing on Wasif's fears. "The damn terrorists explode one device to lure the police in, and then BANG! They set off another one."

"I hadn't thought of that," Wasif replied, wide-eyed.

"I'm not going down there until the police have finished checking everything out," Tahir stated flatly. "Go back to sleep," Tahir said as he closed the door in Wasif's face.

From that point on, Tahir tried to rest as best he could. At approximately five-thirty, two police officers came by to take a statement. Tahir was pleasantly surprised that Detective Al-Faruq wasn't one of them. Based on what the officers said, there had been several car bombings that evening. It looked as if the perpetrators were targeting PGORC employees.

I guess Husam really does know what he's doing. He's essentially turned me into a victim as opposed to a suspect. Detective Al-Faruq may still think he knows better, though.

Tahir looked at the clock. *Ughh, no use going back to bed. I might as well have breakfast and head in to work.*

Tahir took his time, ate breakfast, and had some tea. Then he headed out.

In the parking garage, Tahir eyed his Suburban suspiciously. *Come on. If Husam had wanted you dead, he wouldn't have bothered giving you a heads-up about your car.* Nonetheless, Tahir had trouble shaking the thought from his head.

Morning traffic was lighter than usual. However, given what had happened, people probably weren't in a big hurry to jump in their cars and go to work. As he came to a red light, Tahir slowed to a stop. Suddenly, there was a knock on the passenger side window.

"What the!" Tahir exclaimed. He looked over and saw Husam looking at him through the window. Husam motioned for him to unlock the door. Tahir complied. "Like I've got a choice," he mumbled.

Quickly, Husam got in the vehicle. He was carrying a large black backpack, which he set on the seat between them. Tahir eyed it cautiously.

"I have another errand for you," Husam said gruffly, his eyes fixed on the road.

"Umm, okay . . . " Tahir acknowledged.

"Take this backpack in to work. Before you leave, put it in the server room or by the power conduits outside of your boss's office. You know, wherever you think it'll impact operations the most," Husam said. "I'll detonate it remotely, once you've left."

"Won't security be tight, given what's happened?" Tahir asked apprehensively.

Husam shrugged. "Maybe, but they won't give this a second look. Everything's sewn inside," he said while patting the backpack with his hand. "Let me off at the next light," Husam ordered.

Tahir nodded and slowed to a stop.

"Just remember what I told you last night," Husam said as he exited the vehicle. "And don't leave it in your car," he said with a thin smile. Then he slammed the door closed and Tahir continued on his way to work.

"Well, that was a lovely chat," Tahir said. "Don't leave it in the car? Ha! What the fuck is that? Terrorist humor? Don't leave it in the fucking car. I'll try to remember that."

Unhappily, Tahir drove to work. Pulling up to the security gate, he rolled down his window. He was relieved to see a friendly face. "Good morning," he said.

"Morning," Haddad grunted.

"When did you switch to the morning shift?" Tahir asked.

"I didn't," Haddad grumbled. "Due to the bombings, I'm working a double shift. Hardly anybody's showing up for work today."

"Great," Tahir replied as he leaned his head back against the seat.

In his hands, Haddad was holding a long pole with a mirror attached at the end.

"What's that?" Tahir asked.

"We're supposed to check all incoming vehicles for explosives. This helps me look underneath your car," Haddad replied.

"Everything look good?" Tahir asked.

"Yeah, yeah," Haddad replied tiredly as he waved Tahir through.

I guess Husam was right. Haddad didn't even look at the backpack. I don't know if that makes me feel better or worse. Still, if no one's showing up for their shift, today is going to be a complete nightmare.

#

On a city bus, Husam stood stoically as it bounced toward Tahir's office complex. He'd rented out a room above an old grocery store near the PGORC compound. From there, Husam could monitor Tahir and remotely detonate the device.

With help from one of Professor Ratib's contacts, Husam had set up a laptop via which he could track the backpack bomb with incredible accuracy. Combined with the building layout information that Tahir had given him, Husam would be able to determine where within the building the backpack was at all times. In addition, the backpack was bugged so he'd be able to hear what was going on.

The crowded bus swayed back and forth as it moved along the city streets. Husam's eyes scanned the other passengers.

Nothing but a pack of camels. How had Imam Al-Hashim put it? Beasts to ease the monarchy's burden. Without them, the monarchy couldn't exist. Civil servants, merchants, office workers, and such, all under the illusion that the government protects their interests, when in reality, it feeds off them. Are they blind to the corruption? The king is nothing but a modern-day Pharaoh.

Everyone around him twittered about the bombings. Some looked at Husam disapprovingly. His rough hands and sun-carved face made it obvious he was a laborer. *They're probably wondering why I'm riding the bus instead of packing in the back of a pickup truck with the other laborers. If they knew that I was responsible for last night's fireworks, they'd show me more respect.*

With his stop coming up, Husam angled closer to the doors. When they opened, he filed out with the other passengers. Then, he strode purposefully over to the market where he had rented space. Just before reaching the market, he turned down an alley to use the rear entrance. Unfortunately, he ran into the market owner, who was unloading produce.

"Mr. Asad, Mr. Asad!" the shopkeeper said insistently. "Next month's rent is due on Monday."

Husam nodded, but said nothing.

"If you plan on vacating the space, you need to give two weeks' notice," the shopkeeper called.

Husam ignored him and continued on his path. After stepping around the crates of produce, Husam climbed the stairs to the second floor. There were four rooms above the store. The shopkeeper used one as an office and rented out the other three.

Husam walked past the shopkeeper's office and unlocked the door to his rental space. He entered quietly and locked the door behind him. The room was sparsely furnished holding only a foldout table and a couple of metal chairs. A laptop sat open upon the small table. Its power cord stretched to a nearby outlet. Another black backpack sat on one of the chairs while the laptop bag lay on the floor.

Husam sat down at the table and powered up the laptop. Then he connected to a local Wi-Fi hotspot and opened up the tracking program.

"Technology like this certainly levels the playing field," he said, with a crooked smile. With the exception of Israel, he had access to more funding and better technology than most Middle Eastern law enforcement agencies.

Originally, the chip that was sewn into the backpack had been designed for tracking stolen cars. Now, however, it enabled Husam to track the backpack. Husam watched the screen intently. On the digital map in front of him, Husam watched a red dot move along the road and then into a parking lot. Next, it moved over to the building where Tahir worked.

Husam unfolded the office schematic that Tahir had provided him. Tahir worked on the second floor, and his cubicle was located approximately in the middle of the floor. Based on the location of the red dot, that's where Tahir had placed the backpack. The server room was located near the stairwell in the southwest corner of the building, and the power conduits were located in the northwest corner.

Next, Husam pulled out a small receiver from inside his *thobe*. He turned it on and adjusted the earpiece. He turned the frequency knob slightly to get a clear signal.

"Thanks so much for coming in Tahir," a voice said.

"Well, I made it, but my car didn't," Tahir said.

"Seriously!"

"Yeah, my car and a couple others got totaled."

"Are you all right?"

"Sure, I was asleep when it happened."

"Well, that's good. Praise Allah! I think we've all been really lucky."

As the conversation devolved into work-related banter, Husam pulled out a newspaper from the laptop bag and started to read. The morning passed slowly, and the red dot on the computer screen never moved.

#

Tahir was right. Work was complete chaos. Less than half of the staff showed up, and those who did show up were scrambling just to keep things running. After midday prayer, Basim gathered everyone together in the break room.

"I just wanted to thank all of you for coming in today," Basim said. He looked serious. "As you all probably know, terrorists targeted the vehicles of dozens of PGORC employees. Up until now, no fatalities had been reported. However, I just learned that Daaruk Lahar, our IT director, was killed."

Tahir felt claustrophobic. His stomach tightened uncomfortably. *I knew Daaruk. Not very well, but I knew him, and information I provided to Husam led to Daaruk's death.*

Suddenly, Tahir felt sweaty and light headed. Quietly, he exited the room. He walked over to his cubicle, sat down, and put his face in his hands. As Tahir shifted his feet, his foot accidentally bumped into the black backpack. He looked at it nervously.

This was part of Husam's plan from the beginning. With the Director of IT gone, knocking out the server room would definitely impact operations, but can I really go through with it? Do I have a choice? I can't take it with me. As soon as Husam sees me leave, he'll detonate the device. I could throw it in the dumpster like last time, but Husam would know that I chickened out. What then?

Think!" Tahir whispered harshly. *Husam said he'd detonate it at the end of the day. Maybe if I sneak out for lunch, I could stash it someplace.*

Tahir stared blankly at the floor. Suddenly, the answer came to him. He'd call Detective Al-Faruq. His hands shaking, Tahir opened his desk drawer and pawed through the clutter. After finding the detective's number, he dialed the number hesitantly. Each ring seemed like an eternity. Finally, there was an answer.

"Hello? Detective Al-Faruq speaking," the voice said.

Tahir sat frozen unsure what to say. He thought about hanging up.

"Tahir? Is that you?" the detective asked.

"Yeah, it's me," Tahir admitted.

"You see now that you can't trust these people," Detective Al-Faruq scolded.

Once again, Tahir sat in silence.

"Well, don't you?"

"Look, I don't know what to think. I thought that I knew what I was doing, but now . . . " Tahir's voice trailed off. "Can we meet for lunch somewhere?"

"I don't think that would be a good idea," Detective Al-Faruq responded. "Are you at work?"

"Yes," Tahir replied.

"Why don't I come there?" Detective Al-Faruq offered. "Basim's been badgering me for an update. When I'm through with him, you and I can talk."

"Umm . . . " Tahir stammered as he looked down at the backpack. "I guess that would work."

"It's okay. I'm on my way," Detective Al-Faruq reassured him. "I'll be there within the hour."

"See you then," Tahir replied weakly before hanging up.

Tahir looked down at the backpack. *I have to get it out of here. But where? I know! I'll take it out to the car, tell Detective Al-Faruq about it, and he'll get someone to defuse it.*

Regardless, Tahir couldn't leave it sitting there another moment. Quickly, he grabbed the backpack, stood up, and headed out. As he exited the row of cubicles, a voice called to him from behind.

"Tahir! You all right?" Basim Dabir asked. "Where are you going?"

"I . . . I'm headed down to the parking lot," Tahir said nervously as he hid the backpack behind him. "I . . . uh . . . left something in my car."

"Well, I can't have you sneaking out on me," Basim said. "I can't do this without you. The schedule would be in shambles."

"I'll be right back," Tahir replied. "It'll just take a minute."

"I'm going to hold you to that," Basim said with a smile. "One minute."

Tahir exhaled wearily and turned back down the hallway. On his way to the stairwell, he glanced warily at the server room. Suddenly, he heard a strange buzzing sound. It sounded like a cell phone vibrating. Instinctively, Tahir felt for his phone, but it wasn't ringing. Open-mouthed, he looked down at the backpack as it disappeared in a blinding flash of heat and light.

#

Husam set down his cell phone and started packing up his things. The red dot on his laptop display had disappeared. "Signal lost," it said. Husam closed out of the program and shut down the computer.

Suddenly, there was a knock on the door. Husam reached inside the outside pocket of the laptop bag and pulled out a handgun.

"Mr. Asad, are you in there?" the shopkeeper's voice called. He knocked again. "Mr. Asad!"

"Just a minute," Husam replied, trying to hide his annoyance. He reached back inside the pocket and pulled out a silencer. He attached it to his weapon, and walked slowly up to the door. Hiding the gun behind his back, he unlocked the door and opened it.

"Yes?"

"Mr. Asad. We have some unfinished business to discuss," the shopkeeper whined in a pushy tone. "Will you be leasing this space next month or not?"

Before answering, Husam refocused his gaze away from the shopkeeper's eyes to a spot out in the hallway. Annoyed, the

268

shopkeeper turned to look behind him. Husam brandished his weapon and promptly shot the shopkeeper twice in the chest.

"No," Husam answered. He backed away to avoid the falling shopkeeper. Stepping over the twitching body, he glanced out into the hallway. It was empty. Husam grabbed the shopkeeper by the collar, pulled his body into the room, and shut the door. Then he returned to his previous task.

Meticulously, Husam gathered his things. He put the laptop, receiver, and handgun into the laptop bag. He picked up his cell phone and surveyed the rest of the room. There was nothing that wouldn't be destroyed in the explosion. Husam picked up the black backpack and dropped it on top of the shopkeeper's body.

"Sorry Mr. Asad. I can't leave behind any loose ends," he said, nudging the body with his foot.

Husam cracked open the door and checked the hallway. The coast was clear. Quietly, he stepped out, closed the door behind him, and proceeded out the way he'd come in. In the alley, Husam flipped open his cell phone and calmly dialed the number for the remaining backpack. Upon reaching the street, he initiated the call and turned toward the bus stop.

Even though he knew it was coming, the sound of the explosion made him flinch. Looking back, he could see the cloud of smoke, shattered glass, and debris floating through the air. The fruits and vegetables that had been set out in front of the market were crushed under the rubble. The bodies of would-be shoppers lay prone in the street. Expressionless, Husam turned away. He dropped the cell phone in a nearby trashcan and continued down the sidewalk.

Chapter 44: Eyes Open

When Al-Faruq saw the plume of smoke rising in the distance, he knew he was too late. Tahir was dead, and so was his case against the professor. Not wanting to postpone the inevitable, Al-Faruq turned up his police scanner and listened in on the calls. There were reports of explosions both inside the PGORC facilities and outside the main gate as well. He switched it off in disgust.

"Damn it! I was so close, but dead bodies don't make great witnesses."

Anticipating that traffic on his current route was about to grind to a halt, Al-Faruq turned down a side street and zigzagged over to port control. He twisted and turned his vehicle down back alleys and nosed his way in front of frustrated commuters. About two blocks out, he spied a parking space. He'd cover the remaining distance on foot.

When he got closer to the PGORC facilities, Al-Faruq spied a police car blocking the upcoming intersection, its lights flashing. Onlookers were crowded up against it trying to get a glimpse of the carnage. Al-Faruq got out his badge and muscled his way through the herd of spectators. They didn't seem particularly happy to have their reality show interrupted, but Al-Faruq didn't care.

Once he breached the police's makeshift barrier, Al-Faruq could finally get a clear view of the scene. Haphazardly, police and medical vehicles were parked everywhere. The multitude of flashing lights created a strange strobe effect. The officers on the scene were assisting medical personnel with the survivors.

While the main gate to Port Control Headquarters was intact, a nearby market had been demolished. The corrugated metal roofing tiles were bent back like the petals of a flower, and the upper floor opened up crudely toward the sky. Beyond the PGORC facility's main gate, a column of smoke rose to the sky, but Al-Faruq figured that could wait.

"Why blow up the marketplace?" Al-Faruq mumbled.

Al-Faruq's eyes scanned the surrounding area. While most of the civilians present looked shell-shocked, one woman stood out. On the other side of the street, an old woman wearing a dirty black *habiya* was digging through the trash. While Al-Faruq watched, the woman looked up several times as if she were afraid someone would catch her. The way she picked through the contents of the trashcan, it was obvious she was looking for something in particular.

Keeping his eyes on her, Al-Faruq moved forward slowly. The woman's face lit up. She'd found what she was looking for. Diving her arm down into the trashcan as far as it would reach, she grabbed her prize. Then, eyes wide, the woman slipped it into her handbag and scurried down the sidewalk. Al-Faruq plotted a course to intercept her.

"Excuse me ma'am," Al-Faruq said as he came up beside her.

The woman kept her head down and continued walking.

"Ma'am, I'm going to need to ask you a few questions," Al-Faruq said, holding up his badge.

The woman quickened her pace.

Al-Faruq skirted around her and blocked her path.

"Please Ma'am, I need to ask you a few questions," Al-Faruq said.

The woman shrunk from him. "I don't know who did it," she said hurriedly.

"I'm not going to hurt you," Al-Faruq said softly. "I just want to know what you saw."

"I didn't see anything."

"I don't believe that. Why don't I get you something to eat, and we'll start at the beginning," Al-Faruq offered.

The woman nodded. Al-Faruq led her over to a nearby eatery. The proprietor was standing outside staring at the chaos in the street.

"Two *mutabbaq* please, and a couple of Cokes," Al-Faruq said.

"You can't be serious?" the man replied.

Al-Faruq flashed his badge at the man. "If you're not open, then shut your gate and get out of the damn street."

Quickly, the café owner got Al-Faruq the food he had ordered. Al-Faruq motioned the woman over to a table and they sat down.

"Eat," Al-Faruq encouraged her.

Quietly, the woman did as she was told. She dug into the pancake-like bread with her dirty fingers and ripped it apart. Al-Faruq was surprised at how quickly she ate. After eating half of the meal, she took the remaining half and folded it up in a paper napkin.

"You sure that'll keep?" Al-Faruq asked.

"It'll be fine," she murmured.

"What's your name?" Al-Faruq asked.

"Shahidah," she responded.

"Okay, Shahidah. Where were you when the explosion occurred?"

"I was begging on the corner," she replied pointing in the direction of the main gate.

"What drew you to that trashcan near the marketplace?"

"I was hungry."

"It didn't look like you were looking for food to me," Al-Faruq said. He watched Shahidah closely as she shifted back and forth in her seat. She was doing her best to avoid eye contact.

"Why didn't you go into the facility today?" Shahidah asked finally.

"What?" Al-Faruq asked. "And why would I go into the facility?"

"I've seen you go in there before," she stated.

Al-Faruq smiled. There was more to Shahidah than meets the eye. "I'm more interested in what happened at the marketplace."

"Why?"

Al-Faruq smiled and thought for a moment. Then, he said, "It's easy to see why terrorists would attack the oil facility, but why blow up the marketplace?"

"Maybe, they were trying to cover their tracks," Shahidah said.

"Exactly," Al-Faruq responded. "So, I'll ask you again. What drew you to that trashcan?"

"Just before the explosion, I saw a man come out of that alley," Shahidah said nodding toward the street. "He was carrying a phone. After the explosion, he threw his phone in the trashcan. I thought it was odd."

"That is odd," Al-Faruq agreed. "Did you find his phone?" Once again, Shahidah's eyes darted around erratically.

"Yes," Shahidah admitted.

"Why did you fish it out of the trash?" Al-Faruq asked.

"I thought it might be valuable."

"Hmmm, not too valuable I hope," Al-Faruq said, but Shahidah didn't seem to get his joke. "Can I see it?"

Frowning, Shahidah looked inside her worn handbag. After fumbling around for a moment, she pulled out the phone and slid it across the table to Al-Faruq.

Taking it by the edges, Al-Faruq flipped open the phone. The display glowed brightly, but its battery was low. Trying carefully not to touch any of the other buttons, Al-Faruq powered down the phone and closed it. Then he reached inside his *thobe* and got out his wallet.

"Will this do?" he asked, providing Shahidah with a few bills.

Shahidah nodded, but she didn't seem too pleased.

While they finished their Cokes, Al-Faruq took the rest of her statement. He jotted down her description of the man she had seen, and quizzed her on where he could find her if he had more questions. As she departed, Al-Faruq couldn't help but admire her. She was a fighter, that was for sure.

"I'll be in touch," Al-Faruq called as Shahidah shuffled down the sidewalk. "Keep your eyes open," he said under his breath.

Chapter 45: Offshore

Raja hoped that his involvement in operations had ended after setting up the underwater mines. Unfortunately, once again, he found himself on a boat in the Persian Gulf surrounded by dubious company. This time, Jasim had enlisted some of his Somali brethren to assist.

"They're familiar with taking hostages," Jasim pointed out. "However, in this case, we'll be taking offshore drilling rigs hostage as opposed to people."

As luck would have it, Raja's scuba diving expertise was required. Instead of planting mines, this time he'd be placing explosives on offshore drilling rigs. Pay the ransom or we blow up the platforms. Raja wasn't convinced they'd be able to bring down an entire rig, but what did he know?

His Somali counterpart, Samakab, was adamant that the explosives be placed in specific locations to ensure optimal damage. Evidently, he'd spent a considerable amount of time studying the rigs. Samakab could discuss the Deepwater Horizon incident inside and out, and he was positive they could bring the rigs down.

"We take one down, and the others will pay," Samakab said. He seemed certain that their efforts would result in a significant payday. Raja, on the other hand, just wanted to make it back alive.

Once again, the *Amirah* was acting as their base of operations. However, this time they had a ten-foot inflatable ocean runner in tow. The crew consisted of Jasim, Latif, Samakab, Gutaale, and Raja. While Samakab was obviously well educated, Gutaale seemed to be nothing more than a cutthroat criminal. He made Jasim seem friendly, which took some doing.

Fortunately, at least as far as Raja was concerned, he'd be working with Samakab, who spoke Arabic and English in addition to his native Somali dialect. Unfortunately, this was going to be a night dive, and Raja hated diving at night. Before heading out in the ocean runner, Samakab and Raja completed their final walk-through.

"First, you need to place the device twenty feet below the waterline," Samakab instructed. "Once you've secured the device to the platform, you'll need to wind this wire up the leg of the rig above the surface. This wire," he said pointing to the diagram, "acts as an antenna. If it's underwater, we won't be able to send the detonation signal."

"What about the tides?" Raja asked.

"I've taken that into account," Samakab replied. "Based on my calculations, if you plant the device at the proper depth, everything but the antenna will be hidden under the water at low tide."

"Is there an activation sequence?"

"No, but in order to test the signal, I need you to send me a text message after you've put the wire in place."

"Huh?"

"Look," Samakab said as he picked up one of the devices. "It's just a cell phone. I mean, it's been modified to act as a trigger, but it's still basically a cell phone."

Raja looked at the device, which was covered in clear plastic. Samakab was right. It was a cell phone attached via wires to a large wad of explosives. The long strand of wire that stretched out from the top of the pack served as antenna.

"Select menu, contacts, number one, send message, type something, and hit send," Samakab said as he clicked on the plastic-covered buttons of the cell phone.

"I'm going to be twenty feet underwater. I'll have a dive light, but that's a lot easier said than done," Raja grumbled. "Can I try it once above the water?"

"Yeah, sure." Samakab laughed.

Raja pulled on his diving gloves and grabbed the device from Samakab. Seeing that the gloves definitely made it more difficult, Samakab winced. "It doesn't have to be legible, just something to confirm that the device is getting a signal," he said.

"Okay, how's this?" Raja asked, after punching the number-two button three times and hitting send.

After a moment, Samakab's phone beeped. He looked down at his phone. "Cab," he read aloud. "That'll do."

"Should I try the others?" Raja asked.

"Wait until you're underwater. I don't want to run down the batteries. Let's load up. We'll use two per rig." Samakab said as he grabbed one of the packs. Raja grabbed another and followed him topside.

Up on deck, the sun had just set, and the western horizon glowed orange and purple. Gutaale, who was standing watch, grunted at their arrival. Samakab had him pull in the ocean runner. After depositing the explosive devices into the small boat, Raja donned his scuba gear.

"Hurry up," Samakab encouraged him. "This is just stop number one."

Hurriedly, Raja pulled on his wetsuit and loaded his tanks and fins into the boat. Then they set out. The night before, Samakab tagged the rigs with GPS beacons. Now, they could simply follow the signal to each location.

They had moored the *Amirah* about one kilometer from their first target. The rig, which was known as Persian Drill #4, was a jack-up rig positioned in water that was about 300 feet deep. According to Samakab's plan, they would take out two of the rig's three legs.

Their small boat rose and fell with the swells, as the sound of the outboard motor mixed with the sound of the waves hitting the bow. For Raja, time seemed to stand still. He would have been perfectly happy if they never reached their destination. While the spray of the boat's wake helped calm him, it was only temporary.

Upon reaching the rig, Samakab slowed the boat's motor. Its pitch turned from a high whine to a low growl. Anxiously, Raja pulled on his fins and strapped on the tanks.

"Attach this tether to the rig, and then come back for the first pack," Samakab said.

Raja nodded, pulled down his mask, and crawled out of the boat into the dark water. The waves lapped against his mask. The top layer of water was warm from the sun beating down on it all day, but the colder water beneath clawed at his feet. It was difficult to see in the fading light, but the rig's legs were darker than the sky, so Raja swam toward the looming black columns.

Cautiously, Raja sidled over to the rig. He was worried that the swells would push him into it, but somehow he managed. Grabbing onto the metal leg with his free hand, he tried to find a foothold. It was difficult with his fins on. Awkwardly, he hooked the tether around the rig's leg, then followed the line back to the boat. Samakab handed him the first explosives pack, and Raja swam slowly back to the rig.

When he reached the structure, Raja turned on his dive light and climbed down the leg of the structure. Though his heart was pounding, he took slow steady breaths. Once submerged, Raja tipped himself nose down and descended to the necessary depth. The explosives pack tugged at his shoulder.

While securing the explosives to the rig was relatively easy, now came the hard part— extending the antenna up to the surface. Raja hoped that Samakab's calculations were accurate. Gradually, Raja unwound the wire. It was stiff in the cold water. Every three feet or so, he wound it around part of the rig's metal leg. Upon reaching the top, Raja breathed a sigh of relief. He still had about three feet of slack. He extended the rest up the leg, winding it tightly against the cold metal.

One down. One to go. Raja started toward the boat. *Crap! I need to test the link.*

Dejectedly, Raja re-submerged. Upon reaching the device, he grabbed the pack and held it close to his mask. He could hardly see a thing. Deliberately, he punched the plastic covered buttons of the cell phone. After several tries, he was finally successful. Raja breathed a sigh of relief through his regulator and headed back to the surface.

Upon reaching the boat, Raja was greeted less than enthusiastically by Samakab. "What's taking so long?" Samakab demanded, his voice rasping.

Raja spat out his regulator. "The cold water makes the antenna very stiff. I didn't want to break it. Did you get the text message?"

"Yeah, yeah, just get going with the next one," Samakab said as he handed Raja the next pack. Raja did as he was told. It was going to be a long night. He could barely make out the rig's other leg as the sky grew darker.

What's his problem all of a sudden? Raja swam over to the rig's other leg.

While securing the second pack went smoother, Samakab still wasn't satisfied. "Damn it! Pick up the pace! We need to get all the devices placed tonight." After detaching the tether, Raja had barely pulled himself into the boat, when Samakab gunned the motor. They headed back to the *Amirah* in silence.

When they reached the *Amirah*, Raja learned why Samakab had been so impatient. As they stepped on deck, the duo was greeted by Gutaale, along with two armed men that Raja hadn't seen before. Then, Raja saw Latif hog-tied, lying face down on the deck, his face bloodied. The bodies of four men littered the deck. Raja froze. With their guns at the ready, the armed men spoke to Samakab in a language that Raja didn't understand. They looked angry.

"Where have you been? We lost three men before that Jasim fuck was taken out," the gunman said. "You were supposed to be here to help!"

"Planting the explosives took longer than expected," Samakab replied. "Besides, it would have been better if we had waited until morning. All the explosives would have been planted by then."

"Securing the *Amirah* was deemed more important than planting the explosives," the other gunman replied.

"We're still planning on planting the explosives aren't we?" Samakab asked.

"We'll have to if we hope to make up for our losses." The man then looked at Raja. "Will we have any trouble with this one?"

"No, he'll be fine," Samakab answered in his native dialect. Then, he whispered to Raja in Arabic, "Stick with me and everything will be okay." Raja nodded in silent agreement. "Gutaale! Can you get us to the next target?" Samakab asked.

"Take Latif below and clean up the deck," Gutaale instructed his men. Then he left to pilot the *Amirah*. Their eyes still smoldering angrily, Gutaale's men lowered their weapons and did as they were told.

"Let's go," Samakab urged Raja, his voice tired. We need to prepare for the next target." Raja followed, his legs heavy and his

278

stomach tied in knots. Below deck, Samakab readied the explosives for their next target.

"If . . . if there was something we could add to the packs so that they would sink easier, I might be able to arm the targets faster," Raja said, his voice cracking.

"Don't worry about it," Samakab said softly. His mind was obviously elsewhere.

"Latif is a cook. He's no threat," Raja continued, stumbling over the words.

"I know, but there's really nothing I can do," Samakab answered. The two worked silently in preparation for the next target.

After depositing the explosives in the boat, Samakab left to see how far they were from the drop-off point. Raja sat quietly staring at the deck of the *Amirah*. What looked like a small puddle of water turned out to be blood. Raja stared at the small pool as it shimmered in the moonlight. Slowly, his eyes followed the trail of blood from the puddle toward the stack of bodies. Without thinking, Raja picked up a nearby rag and began wiping up the spill. Silently, he wondered who'd be there to cleanup when it was his blood.

Raja looked up with a start. He hadn't heard Samakab return. Without a word, Samakab patted Raja on the back and grabbed the blood stained rag from him and disposed of it in a nearby trashcan. "We'll be at the drop-off point in about twenty minutes," Samakab said, solemnly looking at the bodies. "We should recite the *Salat al-Janazah* for them."

Raja nodded. Samakab motioned for him to stand beside him, raised his hand, and together they began reciting the funeral prayer, "*Allahu akbar!* In the name of Allah, Most Gracious, Most Merciful." The two continued quietly as the *Amirah* glided toward their next target. The wind washed over them carrying their words with it. Their night was just beginning, and how it would end was uncertain. "Peace and blessings of Allah be unto you," they concluded.

At the end of the prayer, Raja turned his attention back to the deck of the *Amirah*. Out of the corner of his eye, he saw Gutaale.

With a sneer, Gutaale laughed at them, threw his AK-47 over his shoulder, and disappeared up the ladder.

"What's the joke?" Raja asked under his breath. Inside, he wasn't sure he wanted to know the answer.

Chapter 46: Wake Up Call

Nicole awoke to the smell of the Chinese takeout. Groggily, she sat up on the couch and stretched. "Nasim?" she called sleepily. "Geez, it's dark. Why didn't you wake me up? What time is it anyway?" She got up, walked over to the kitchen, and looked at the microwave clock. "Ten o'clock! Damn, I was really out."

The takeout was still unopened. Nicole rubbed her eyes. *Nasim must've been waiting for me to wake up, but then decided to crash too. Maybe, I'll surprise him.* Mischievously, she tiptoed over to Nasim's room.

Quietly, Nicole sneaked inside the dark room. She sat gently on the edge of the bed and ran her hand across the blankets feeling for Nasim, but the bed was empty. "Nasim?" she called. Somewhat confused, she got up and turned on the light. Nasim's room was empty.

"That's odd. Where could he be? He wouldn't have gone out to a movie by himself, would he? I wasn't being that much of a bitch. Well, I'm starving. I'm not going to wait until God knows when for him to get back," she grumbled on her way back to the kitchen.

Her mood brightened a bit as she dug into the takeout. "Sesame Chicken and Mongolian Beef, my favorites," she said happily. "Fried rice too! Ha, he knew I'd be pissed about him taking off without me."

She grabbed a plate from the cupboard, filled it up with food, and threw it in the microwave. Impatiently, she opened the microwave door before the time was up. "Eh, good enough," she said as she grabbed her plate and headed over to the couch. "There's got to be something on."

She set her plate down on the table in front of the couch and grabbed the remote. She flipped channels for a while before settling on Myth Busters. "What are they blowing up tonight?" She grabbed her plate and dug in. A notepad, which had been underneath her plate, fell to the floor. "Aghh, goddammit," she exclaimed. Balancing the plate on her lap, she reached down and picked up the notepad.

As she was returning it to the end table, something caught her eye. "Love, Nasim," it concluded. "Huh? He left me a note. That's sweet." She looked at the note closer.

Dear Nicole,

Words cannot describe how much I've enjoyed our time together. You are now and forever will be special to me. You deserve to find a nice guy. I just wish it could have been me, but I'll never be that guy. It was wonderful pretending that I could be, but I'm not. I'd only end up disappointing you. You deserve better.

Love, Nasim

With tears running down her cheeks, Nicole dropped the notepad and put her head in her hands. Her elbows ended up in her food, but she didn't care.

How could this have happened? Was it something I said? Did I get too close? Did he get scared? This doesn't make any sense. In her mind, she ran through the events of the last few days.

Obviously, he blamed himself for all the harassment that we had to deal with at the checkpoints. If we stayed together, there'd always be a chance something like that would happen again, and I melted under the pressure, crying, whining. Plus, why would he want to build something long term in a country that would always be suspicious of him?

Nicole looked down. "Great," she said upon realizing that her elbows were in her plate. "What a frickin' mess."

She grabbed her plate and took it into the kitchen. After setting down her plate on the counter, Nicole grabbed a washcloth to wipe off her elbows. Suddenly, the glow of the computer's screen saver caught her attention.

She walked over to the computer and jiggled the mouse back and forth. When the screen came to life, e-mail was the only program open. A message from the Palestinian Education Foundation was highlighted. Nicole opened it and read through it.

"So, he missed some celebration?" she said with a frown. "Breaking up seems like a bit of an overreaction. Going to Yellowstone was his idea, not mine. Plus, this is a hell of a lot more than a break up. It's more like good-bye, I need to disappear."

"He'll be back," she finally decided. "It was a rough trip. He gets back and sees this message. Once he calms down, he'll be back."

Nicole minimized e-mail and opened up a browser. Absentmindedly, she skimmed the headlines. "I'm so glad I took that nap," she said sarcastically. "It's ten o'clock at night, Nasim's gone God knows where, and I'm wide awake."

Suddenly, one of the headlines caught her eye. "Student Tied to Bombing." Nicole opened the article and began to read.

COLUMBIA, June 1 (Reuters) A University of Maryland student has been arrested in connection with Saturday's attack on the Cosgrove electrical plant in Elkridge, Maryland. The bombing knocked out power to more than 100,000 Maryland residents and caused an estimated $200,000 worth of damage to the plant.

While the student's name is currently being withheld, sources indicate that the student is an Arabian male who was pursuing a degree in mechanical engineering. The junior student was a Middle Eastern Educational Foundation scholarship recipient.

FBI agents arrested the student Sunday morning at his campus apartment, and confiscated several boxes full of bomb-making materials. FBI spokesman Agent Phil Arnold refused to speculate on whether or not the student was involved in planning or supporting the other bombings that occurred across the nation over the holiday weekend.

"While we are working to determine if this weekend's attacks were a coordinated effort, this arrest was made strictly based on evidence gathered in conjunction with the Cosgrove investigation," Agent Arnold stated.

By leveraging power from other plants, electricity has been restored to all of the Maryland residents affected by Saturday's bombing. However, due to decreased capacity, Maryland customers could experience periodic outages until repairs on the Cosgrove plant are completed.

Nicole switched back to Nasim's e-mail and looked closer at the message. Nasim's scholarship was from the Palestinian Educational Foundation. The article indicated that the Maryland student was supported by a similar foundation.

"Come on, it's just a coincidence," she assured herself.

Nonetheless, Nicole kept digging. She opened up a new tab and searched for, "Middle Eastern Educational Foundation."

"Huh," she said with surprise. "There actually is one," she mused. Nicole followed the link. "Wonderful, it's in Arabic. Duh."

She switched to another tab and searched for "Palestinian Educational Foundation." Once again, her search took her to an Arabic language site. Still, she flipped back and forth between the two sites, comparing them. After scrolling down in the PEF site, something caught her eye. It was a picture of a man.

"Wait a second," she said as she switched back to the other tab. "Is that the same guy?" She flipped back and forth several times. The pictures weren't identical, but both sites included a picture of the same man.

Feeling a little uneasy, Nicole scrolled down to the bottom of the PEF website. At the very bottom of the page she saw the word, "*English.*" She clicked on it and was taken to an English version of the site. "All right, where are you?" she said as she scanned the site for the man's picture. Finally, she found it. "Fakhir Ihsan," she read aloud.

She went back to the Middle Eastern Educational Foundation, or MEEF, website, but couldn't find an English version. Flipping back to the PEF website, she looked at the URL.

"It's just the main site with a slash-english after it."

She switched back to the Middle Eastern site and added, "/english" to the URL. An English version appeared. "So, is this the same guy?" she asked herself. After finding the man's picture once again, her hunch was confirmed. She read, "Fakhir Ihsan."

For a moment, Nicole just blankly stared at the computer unsure what to do. First, she printed out the article about the

Maryland student. Then she printed out the main page from the PEF and MEEF websites respectively. Next, she switched back to e-mail and printed out the message from the Palestinian Education Foundation. After printing the documents, Nicole went back to the living room and picked Nasim's note up off the floor. She put everything together and placed it on top of the printer.

When Nicole sat back down at the computer, her hands were shaking. Reluctantly, she looked up the phone number for the local FBI branch office. She was afraid to call, afraid not to call, and generally hoping that it was all just a bad dream.

After spending the entire trip back from Yellowstone defending him, now I'm going to throw him under the bus. Why—because he broke up with me? I mean, that's what it'll look like.

Suddenly, Nicole felt exhausted. "Just sleep on it," she told herself. "You're tired. You're not thinking straight. It'll all work out. Nasim will be back. Tomorrow morning, he'll be back," she told herself. But in the back of her mind, she didn't really believe it. She trudged back to the living room, flopped on the couch, and buried her head in the pillows.

Chapter 47: Escape

As Raja finished winding the antenna up the leg of their final target, he sensed that dawn was approaching.

Screw testing it. I've got to find out where Samakab's allegiances lie. If I go back to the Amirah, I'm a dead man. I stand a better chance getting away from Samakab than those thugs back on the boat. Hell, they overpowered Jasim. I wouldn't stand a chance.

Tiredly, Raja followed the tether back to the ocean runner.

"Did you send a test message?" Samakab asked.

"No," Raja said flatly.

"Look, it's been a rough night. Let's test it and get the hell out of here."

"If I step back on that boat, I'm a dead man," Raja said angrily.

"And if I return without you, I'm a dead man," Samakab countered.

With the sound of his heart drowning out the sound of the waves, Raja swallowed hard and went for it. "Come with me, Samakab. I saw you fill up the tank before we left. We can make it. To . . . together we can make it to land. Then, we'll go to the police, save the rigs, and we'll save ourselves."

"I can't," Samakab said. Shakily, he held up a handgun and pointed it at Raja's head. "My family . . . I . . . I can't fail them."

Holding on to the side of the ocean runner, Raja froze. "I'm sorry," he managed, but Samakab still had the gun trained on him. For a few moments, time stood still. The rolling waves and the rocking boat were the only evidence to the contrary.

"Just go," Samakab said finally. "Go!" he said more forcefully, waving Raja away with the gun.

Cautiously, Raja backed away from the boat. Then, he submerged. He leveled off at about twenty feet down and tried to steady his nerves. He looked at his air gauge.

Okay, how much air do I have left? Damn, only about twenty minutes. I'm going to need to save some in case they come looking for me. But what direction?

Raja looked at his dive compass. The glow was barely visible. Heading west was probably his best bet, but he'd need to adjust for magnetic declination. Frustrated, Raja tried to remember the last time he used his compass. He made his best guess and kicked forward.

I'll stay under for about five minutes. Then I'll surface and hope for the best.

In the back of his mind, Raja wondered if he was doing the right thing. He enumerated all the things that could go wrong. First, he had no idea how far he was from land. He could get hit by a boat, stuck in a current, or die from exposure. Gutaale and his crew could come looking for him. Still, what choice did he have?

These guys are fucking pirates. This is my only chance. If I swim straight, I'll find land.

#

Sitting alone in the ocean runner Samakab reviewed his options. Gutaale would not be pleased. He looked at people as commodities. Raja didn't come from a rich family, but somebody might pay something for him. Plus, if they were able to successfully ransom the oil rigs, they'd need a diver to target new rigs.

Then Samakab had an idea. Gutaale had argued with him before the mission, worried that something would go wrong.

"Well, it looks like something did go wrong," Samakab said.

Hurriedly, Samakab pulled out his cell phone and nervously punched the buttons on his phone to activate the explosives on Rig 8. Then he looked down into the water.

"Come on, work. Please work," he pleaded.

Suddenly, Samakab saw a small, dull glow. The glow quickly grew larger and brighter. As the water bubbled to the surface, he tried to look away, but it was too late. The hot spray of boiling seawater hit him in the face, and the small boat rocked back violently. Samakab hung on desperately convinced it would tip over, but the boat fell back against the waves with a resounding thud.

Drenched by the explosion, Samakab found himself lying on his back at the bottom of the boat. Looking skyward, he could see a small red beacon atop the oil rig. Slowly, the red light began to bend toward the ocean.

The tether!

An alarm echoed across the waves while Samakab frantically searched for his knife. The bottom of the boat was covered ankle deep with water, but somehow his hand brushed against the knife handle. Grabbing it, Samakab cut the tether between the boat and the rig.

He looked at the rig again. Gravity was taking over, and the rig's red beacon was diving for the water. Wildly, Samakab yanked on the starter cord and the outboard motor roared to life.

"Thank Allah," Samakab cried.

Samakab gunned the motor, and the boat lurched forward. Now, if he could only convince Gutaale it was Raja's fault, he'd be home free. Anxiously, Samakab rehearsed what he would say.

When the lights of the *Amirah* came into sight, Samakab kept his speed up until he was practically right on top of the *Amirah*. Then he turned the motor into reverse. With the motor whining, the ocean runner banged into the back of the *Amirah*.

"What the fuck do you think you're doing?" Gutaale yelled at Samakab. "Where's . . . "

"We gotta get out of here right now!" Samakab yelled.

"What? Why?"

"Raja screwed something up and set off the explosives."

"Where is he?"

"He's dead. The oil rig was coming down. You think I'm going to stick around to look for his body?" Samakab replied as he climbed onto the *Amirah*.

"I knew this was a bad idea," Gutaale said.

"Look, we'll be fine as long as we get out of here now! Ditch the ocean runner."

"Fine," Gutaale replied. "Sink it," he ordered his men. They pushed it off. Then, they opened fire on the small craft with their automatic weapons.

"What? Are you nuts!" Samakab exclaimed.

"You're the one who screwed this up. You'll need to answer for that when we get back," Gutaale said. He waved his men over and had them take defensive positions around the deck of the *Amirah*.

Samakab considered engaging Gutaale further, but he decided against it.

So what? He sank the ocean runner. At least I wasn't in it—my plan worked. I should be happy. Raja got what he wanted, a chance to escape. If I hadn't returned, Gutaale would've hunted us both down. I hope Raja makes it, but he better keep his mouth shut. If he ruins our plans, I'll be the one who pays the price.

#

Raja had only been underwater for a couple of minutes, when a hard current sent him tumbling. In fact, it damn near tore his mask off. Instinctively, he dove deeper as visions of a large boat's propeller ripping into his legs danced in his head.

Finally, he stopped. His mask was half full of water, and he was disoriented. Frightened, Raja struggled to clear his mask. He looked up into the blackness, but saw nothing. The cold water pushed tightly against his body.

Whatever it was, it was gone now. Raja checked his compass and continued west. After a few more minutes, he checked his depth gauge. His whole body was shaking. It was too cold for him at this depth. Slowly, he headed for the surface.

Relieved, Raja broke through the surface, removed his respirator, and hungrily breathed in the warm air. He'd escaped, but it was a lonely feeling. The sky was getting brighter, but it was still too dark to see much of anything. There was nothing but him and the waves.

"Damn it," he cursed. "I can hardly see the compass up here. Crap! I'm never going to make it. I'm probably getting pulled Allah knows where by the currents. Even if I find land, these waves will just pound me against the rocks."

Angrily, he spit out a mouthful of seawater. He forced out a sigh and tried to relax.

"Take it easy. Have patience," he encouraged himself. "What's that verse from the Qur'an? Be firm and patient in pain and adversity. Still . . . I could use a little less adversity right now."

Raja tried to convince himself that sunrise was just around the corner. It was dark and he was tired, but things would look better in the morning. Maybe he could latch on to one of these oil rigs. Someone would find him. He could make it.

Raja experimented with different strokes. He tried freestyle, but it was just too difficult with the scuba tanks on his back. Finally, he resorted to swimming breaststroke arms, combined with slow, steady dolphin kicks with his fins.

Breathing heavily, he thought about ditching the tanks. It'd be nice to be able to submerge in an emergency, but was it really worth it? Mentally, he went through the equipment he had with him. What could he get rid of? He could dump his dive belt, but he'd have trouble submerging without it.

He needed to make a decision. *Would the Amirah really risk coming after me?* It was still pretty dark and without a high-powered searchlight, looking for him would be like searching for a needle in a haystack. *Gutaale may be a murderous wretch, but he's not stupid, and coming after me would be stupid.*

After struggling forward a few more strokes, Raja shook his head in disgust. "They're not coming," he decided resolutely. "The elements are a bigger threat than the loss of the tanks are right now. If they find me, I'm dead, with or without the damn tanks."

Having made his decision, Raja slid clumsily out of his tanks and removed his dive belt. Treading water, he attached his dive belt to the tanks. Then he depressed the regulator, and let the air out until the weight of the dive belt was sufficient to pull the tanks down.

"Well, I certainly feel lighter," he said.

He tried swimming freestyle again, but gave up after about twenty strokes. Conserving energy and swimming straight was more important than speed. He looked down at his compass again for a bearing.

Okay, I just need to get in a rhythm. I'll swim fifty strokes, check the compass, and then swim fifty more strokes.

Raja put his plan into action. After fifty strokes, he checked his compass, then began swimming again. Over and over, he completed the cycle. While the accountant in him wanted to keep track of the number of cycles, he forced himself not to think about it. The total number of strokes didn't matter. He'd be done when he was done.

His neck stiff from looking forward, Raja rolled to his back and did some elementary backstroke. To the east, the deep purple sky looked brighter than the blackness he'd been staring at. He could even make out the silhouette of an oil rig in the distance.

Is that the rig where we planted the last device? Well, if it is, at least I know I'm not standing still.

The sun would be up soon. It would be a beautiful sunrise. Seeing it sparkle across the ocean waters would be a once in a lifetime opportunity. He just needed to make it until sunrise. Raja rolled over and swam another fifty strokes.

Once again, Raja rolled to his back. He felt the waves swell beneath him. It felt good to rest. His whole body ached. He was so tired. Looking up at the sky, the light from the stars was growing dim as the sky brightened. His eyes were heavy, but he shook himself awake. It wasn't sunrise yet. He had to keep moving.

He rolled back to his stomach, checked his compass, and started swimming. "One, two, three," he counted with a grimace.

Doubt once again began to enter his mind. Floating on his back felt so wonderful. It wasn't difficult to imagine falling asleep like that, but would he ever wake up? Raja shook the thought from his head and kept counting.

"Thirty-three, thirty-four, thirty-five . . . Remember," he told himself, "If you speak the word it shall own you, and if you don't, you shall own it."

Swimming was doing more than just getting him closer to land. It was keeping him warm. If he stopped, he'd cool off, stiffen up, and . . . Raja shook his head again.

"Sunrise is right . . . it's right around the corner," he said, pausing to check his compass. "One, two, three," he counted out loud spitting the words into the waves. "Two more cycles, and then

I'll look back for the sunrise. It'll be like that time Father took me fishing. Only . . . only warmer."

Raja laughed. He thought back to when he was young boy. His father had dragged him out of bed in the middle of the night, and it was still dark when they reached the pier. Raja was freezing because he had refused to wear a coat and angry because his father had made him carry the poles and tackle box.

Raja remembered.

Why did he wake me up and drag me out here? I don't even like fishing. This is stupid. He never catches anything anyway.

Despite Raja's sullen attitude, his father had Raja set up their chairs, baited the hooks, and cast the lines.

My hands were so cold and raw. I was so tired and cranky.

Then, the two of them sat down, and Raja's father pulled out a thermos of hot tea. Steam swirled up into the air as his father opened the lid.

I was afraid he wouldn't give me any. I'd been such a pain in the ass all morning. I was so ashamed that I was ready to cry. I prayed that he would have mercy on me. I wanted that tea so much.

Without a word, his father produced two Styrofoam cups and poured a cup for each of them.

My hands were shaking as I reached for the cup. I'm lucky I didn't drop it. I wanted to gulp it down, but I waited for him to take the first sip. It felt like forever as I watched him breathing in the steam from the cup before he drank. Then, I took too big of a swallow and burnt my tongue. Ultimately, I held it in my hands to keep them warm.

The sunrise was so beautiful that morning, a mix of purple and red. The colors brightened to oranges and yellows that shone off the waves. We didn't catch any fish, but that was a wonderful day. Will today be as wonderful? Will I ever get to sit down again and have a cup of tea with my father? He was so proud that I finished college. Would he be proud of me now? Proud of how I got caught up in all of this? Allah help me.

Raja swallowed hard. "Forty-eight, forty-nine, fifty," he counted. "Please let the sun be coming up." He rolled to his back and looked eastward.

The sky looked dark red, but the sun was still below the horizon. Raja continued swimming using elementary backstroke to pull himself along. "It won't be long now," he said. "I've made it through the night. The worst is over."

Barely visible, the dark orange edge of the sun peeked over the horizon. At first, it disappeared behind the swell of the waves, but finally it took hold of the sky and climbed higher. The sky above him turned from black, to gray, to blue, and the waves took shape before his eyes. He could now actually see them as opposed to just feel them. When half the sun shone above the horizon, the color changed from orange to yellow, and the light from it radiated outward.

Raja was afraid to turn back over. Afraid he'd see nothing but water and sky.

Come on! You gotta get back to work. Every fifty strokes you do is fifty strokes closer to land, fifty strokes closer to safety, fifty strokes closer to home.

Achingly, he rolled back to his stomach. With the sun at his back, it took a moment for his eyes to get accustomed, but behind the swell he thought he saw something, a reflection in the distance.

He stroked forward harder, forgetting to count. "Yes! Yes! I did it," he exclaimed. Squinting forward, he could see the sunlight reflecting off . . . off of something, a window maybe. Then, as the sun grew higher, he saw them. Land! Trees! A few small buildings!

"What beach is that?" he said. "I know it. Uh . . . Who cares? Just swim. It's right there."

When he reached the shallows, he tried to stand, but the waves knocked him over. Clumsily, he pulled off his fins. The saltwater stung the areas on his feet that were raw from wearing the fins for so long. Clinging to the fins with one hand he tried to stand again, but his legs felt like rubber, and his head was spinning. He toppled over again. Raja dropped the fins and crawled up onto the beach.

He collapsed face first into the hard, wet sand. Even though he was on land, his body still felt the rise and fall of the waves. With the surf still climbing up his legs, he lifted his head forward. *I need to get up to that building. I need shade and water. I can't fall asleep out here. I'll bake.*

It was only a hundred yards away, but it seemed like a thousand as he tripped and stumbled up the beach. "I made it," he said, his voice cracking. "I can't believe I made it. Thank you Allah! I made it. I escaped. I'm alive. Thank you! Thank you!"

Chapter 48: History Lesson

It had been a few months since Nicole had visited her grandfather, but her mother had pleaded with her to stop by. *How had Mom put it? When he doesn't see familiar faces from the present, your grandfather gets stuck in the past.*

As far as Nicole was concerned, living in the past didn't seem like a bad idea. The present was a struggle at the moment. Terrorist attacks at home and abroad had sent gas prices through the roof. In an attempt to stretch the U.S. strategic reserves, gas rationing had been instituted.

With the sun setting behind the trees, Nicole turned into the nursing home parking lot. It was pleasant enough, but looked too much like a hotel for Nicole's tastes. She found an open parking space, and headed for the entrance.

The automatic doors parted to reveal a well-appointed lobby. Nicole always wondered where they got all the antique furniture. Did they buy the stuff, or did they get it as some form of payment from their clientele? Regardless, she always felt awkward sitting on the lobby furniture, afraid of breaking someone's grandmother's favorite chair.

"Hello, welcome to Pineview," the receptionist greeted her. "Are you here to visit one of our residents?"

"Yes, I'm here to see Marshall Stacey."

"And you are?"

"I'm his granddaughter, Nicole Stacey."

The receptionist looked intently at her computer screen. "One moment, Ms. Stacey. I'll get someone to take you to his room. Have a seat," she offered.

"Umm, I'll stand. Thanks," Nicole replied uncomfortably, as the receptionist picked up the phone. After a brief conversation, she turned to Nicole and said, "Joann will escort you. She'll just be a minute."

"Okay," Nicole replied. She began to wander aimlessly around the lobby. She stopped in front of an old poster that had been matted and framed. "Help conserve while they serve," it said at the top, with an image of people carpooling just beneath. Another picture showed a family cleaning out their barn for a scrap metal drive. Then, there was a picture of a homemaker pouring used cooking oil into a container to reuse later. "Together we can make a difference!" ran along the bottom.

Nicole searched the poster for a date. "Copyright 1943," it said.

"You like that poster?" a female voice asked.

"Huh, oh, it's interesting, I guess," Nicole replied.

"I'm Joann," the nurse said offering her hand. "I can take you down to see your grandfather now."

"It's nice to meet you," Nicole said as she shook her hand. Joann led her down a long hallway.

"It's kind of funny that you'd be looking at that particular poster," Joann commented.

"Why's that?" Nicole asked quizzically.

"Well, your grandfather saw a news report about the government's efforts to curb oil and gas usage."

"Yeah," Nicole replied wincing.

"Anyway, it's taken his mind back to World War II and all the rationing efforts."

"Oh," Nicole said with a wry smile.

"He got all upset the other day when I brought him dessert. I guess they rationed sugar back then. He accused me of being in league with the privateers," Joann said. "If it wasn't for that poster in the lobby, I wouldn't have known what the hell he was talking about."

"I'm sorry," Nicole said, but she couldn't help but smile.

"Oh, it's fine. I just thought I'd warn you."

"Where'd that poster come from anyway?" Nicole asked.

"I don't know. It's been there for years. From time to time, families donate stuff to us."

"I guess not that many people still remember rationing," Nicole said.

"Well, your grandfather sure does, so you might not want to mention that you drove here by yourself. Tell him that you took the bus."

Nicole laughed. "I'll keep that in mind."

"Here we are," Joann said. She knocked on the door and eased it open. "Mr. Stacey? Mr. Stacey, your granddaughter is here to see you," she called loudly.

"My granddaughter, eh. Well, don't just stand there. Come on in," her grandfather said from his recliner. The television was tuned to CNN.

"Do you want me to turn that off for you?" Joann asked.

"No, no, quit fussing over me. You're not my granddaughter."

"No, I'm not," Joann replied.

"Then, why are you still here?" he said. "Let the girl come in."

"She's just trying to do her job, Grandpa," Nicole interjected.

"What? She's nothing but a busybody."

Joann turned to leave. "He's all yours. Just give me a buzz when you're ready to leave," she said pointing to the call button by the door.

"Well, get in here and let me take a look at you."

"It's good to see you," Nicole said. She leaned down and gave her grandfather a gentle hug. "Why do you give that poor woman such a hard time?"

"Hard time? Oh, fiddle faddle, what's that woman been telling you?"

"Nothing, Grandpa," Nicole replied.

"What's this I hear about people trying to circumvent government rationing?" her grandfather said pointing at the television.

"Well, people aren't used to it," Nicole said, trying to be diplomatic.

"Then, they'd better get used to it! If they're Americans, it's their patriotic duty. I sure hope that you're not out there hoarding gasoline."

"No, Grandpa."

"Well, you'd better not, if you know what's good for you. They're locking people up. Serves them right, I tell you. When I was a boy, we policed ourselves. If you thought someone was a privateer, you steered clear of him; isolated him. No one needed to call in the military to make sure that we followed the rules. The military's got enough on their hands with them goddamn Arabs."

"Umm . . . "

"Oil and gas is all that's being rationed?" her grandfather asked incredulously.

"That's right, but . . . "

"But what? During World War II, they rationed gasoline, tires, sugar, coffee, meat, and cheese."

"Yes, I know," Nicole tried to interrupt.

"Hell, they even rationed typewriters. Can you imagine not being able to go to the store and buy a typewriter?"

"Well? No, I . . . I can't," Nicole replied.

"Oh, and bicycles too," her grandfather continued. "In my neighborhood, due to the rationing, only a handful of us kids had bicycles, so we had to share. What's wrong with people nowadays?"

"I don't know, Grandpa."

"I remember going to school with my mother to get our ration booklet. Inside each booklet was a bunch of stamps. There were red stamps for meat and cheese. Blue stamps were for items like canned fruits and vegetables."

Nicole nodded with interest.

"We planted a victory garden so that we'd have fresh vegetables in the summer. There was this one time I remember. I knocked over one of our tomato plants when I was roughhousing with some friends. Boy, let me tell you, my father tanned my hide for that. He did!"

"I believe you Grandpa," Nicole answered.

"Now, we've been at war in Iraq, Afghanistan, and . . . and Libya. How many years has it been? We're just now making some sacrifices here at home. No wonder the national debt is a bazillion dollars. Plus, there's these attacks, the oil tankers over in the Persian Gulf. It's crazy I tell you. What the hell are those people over there thinking? I think it's them damn Iranians. What do you think?"

In the back of her mind, she thought of Nasim. Her grandfather would never have understood their relationship, but she just smiled and tried to put it out of her mind. "I don't know Grandpa. It's a tough situation."

"Tough? During World War II, they rationed gasoline, tires, sugar, coffee, meat, cheese, and uh . . . "

"Yeah, you were telling me about your garden."

"That's right. We grew tomatoes, green beans, carrots, beets, and peas. There was this one time I remember. I knocked over a tomato plant when I was roughhousing with some friends. Boy, let me tell you, my father tanned my hide for that."

"Oh . . . "

"And we had scrap metal drives. Anything metal that we didn't use anymore, we set out by the curb. We set out old tools, an old icebox, pots and pans, toys—anything metal. A big truck came by to gather everything up. They took the metal and turned it into bullets, tanks, and plane parts. You name it. Everyone was part of the war effort. Nowadays, I don't think people understand. It took effort! From everyone!"

"I know it did, Grandpa. You did a great job."

"Damn right we did. Being American meant something. Now, hmpf . . . look at this! People fighting over gasoline? Don't they know the purpose of rationing? It's so everyone gets their fair share! Rich, poor, whatever. They should throw these damn fools in jail."

Nicole didn't know what to say. The image on the television said it all. The report showed two people arguing and then coming to blows while waiting in line at a gas station. The scene then shifted to a different gas station where three people were fighting over a gasoline can. When a police officer moved in to break up the fight, the gas can tipped over and spilled on the ground.

"You aren't running into any of these numbskulls, are you?"

"No," Nicole replied, "but it does make you wonder what people are thinking."

"That's the problem. They aren't thinking."

"Don't get too down," Nicole said attempting to cheer up her grandfather. "There are still a lot of good people out there. They just don't put them on the news."

"You don't say."

"My most recent trip to the gas station was rather uneventful. A little expensive maybe, but uneventful," Nicole reassured him.

"Hmmmm, that's good I suppose," her grandfather said. Suddenly, he looked tired.

"Thanks for the history lesson," Nicole offered. She awaited a reply, but her grandfather's eyes were growing heavy. Quietly, Nicole got up, walked to the door, and pushed the call button.

Chapter 49: Home

Exhausted, Raja made it to the buildings that he'd seen from the beach. They turned out to be bathrooms with a small changing area. Luckily for him, they were unlocked. He staggered inside and collapsed on a wooden bench. Sleep came quickly.

When Raja awoke, he had no idea how long he'd been out, but one thing was for sure, it had gotten a lot hotter. As he rose to a sitting position, every muscle in his body ached. His wetsuit felt like sandpaper against his skin.

"Ugghh," he groaned, "I've got to get out of this wetsuit."

Stiffly, Raja reached back to unzip his wetsuit. He looked around as he peeled off the suit. Aside from a few benches, the room was empty. Back by the entrance, there were two toilets and a sink. The concrete floor felt hard, and his still sandy feet felt gritty against it. He walked uncomfortably toward the entrance and looked out.

The sun had risen steadily since he'd crawled up on the beach earlier that morning, but he figured it was no later than ten or eleven o'clock. Nonetheless, the beach was deserted.

Great. What am I going to do now? No shoes, no clothes, nothing. I'm screwed.

Raja went back inside. Upon seeing the sink, he suddenly felt very thirsty. He walked gingerly over and turned on the faucet. The water trickled out slowly, but it was better than nothing. Cupping his hands, he bent forward and drank. Then he rubbed water against his chest and arms trying to clean off as best he could.

Raja walked back to the changing area and looked around. Surprisingly, he saw a crumpled pile of clothes lying on the floor beneath one of the benches. He walked over to inspect it and found an old white *thobe*. Unfortunately, it was stiff and caked with sand.

"Well, it's better than nothing," he said. Raja exhaled tiredly, took the *thobe* over to the sink, and ran it under the water. After working the sand out of it, he stretched the fabric back into something resembling its original form. He laid it out on one of the benches to dry.

"Now, if I could only find something to put on my feet," he said hopefully.

Venturing outside again, he looked up and down the beach. Under normal circumstances, it would have been beautiful, but right now it looked desolate. To his right, about ten feet away, he saw a trash can. Reluctantly, he walked over to it and peered inside.

The can was about half filled. Raja bent over and pushed the top layer of trash aside with his hands.

"I don't believe it!" he exclaimed pulling out a sticky, soda-pop-covered pair of flip-flops. The strap on one of the flip-flops was torn, but at least he had one for his right foot. Now, he just had to find one for his left.

With flip-flops in hand, Raja walked farther down the beach to another trash can. He had to search through three more, but finally found an undamaged flip flop for his left foot. In addition, Raja scrounged some plastic bottles that he could wash out and fill with water. An old, ripped *ghutra* completed his ensemble.

Raja cleaned everything up as best he could and put it on. He had one orange flip-flop and one blue one. The *thobe* hung awkwardly on his body and was too short. "I look like an old beggar," he said, looking at himself in the mirror. "I guess it's better than nothing."

Raja looked longingly at his wetsuit. He hated leaving it behind, but bringing it along wasn't practical. While he was dumpster diving, he'd determined that the beach was only open on the weekends. Assuming he made it back home, he could always come back and get the wetsuit later. With that in mind, he hid it underneath the bench where he'd found the *thobe*. Then he drank some more water from the sink, grabbed his water bottles, and headed out.

It was midday, and hotter than hell. Not exactly the best time of day to be traveling on foot, but there'd be more traffic this time of day. He set out slowly, trying to pace himself. While he'd had plenty to drink, he hadn't had anything to eat, and his stomach kept reminding him of the fact.

Raja tried to rest wherever there was shade, but only for a moment. Then, he pressed on.

"I can't believe I haven't made it to the main road yet," he said after taking a sip of water. "I've got to get there before dark."

After what seemed like an eternity, he finally sighted the highway. Not only that, there seemed to be a fair amount of traffic. Encouraged, Raja quickened his pace, even though his feet were burning and his legs ached. Now, if he could only hitch a ride, in the back of a pickup, anything. He just wanted to sit down.

Luck seemed to be on Raja's side. After reaching the highway, it didn't take long before he'd secured a ride. Plus, he was sitting inside.

"What are you doing out here on foot?" the driver asked. "You're lucky you didn't burn up. It's supposed to be over a hundred today."

"Well, it's a long story," Raja answered. "Thanks for stopping."

"Where are you headed?" the man asked.

"Dhahran, but I'll be happy with however far you can take me."

"Well, I guess today's your lucky day 'cause that's where I'm headed. What's your name?"

"Raja."

"Pleased to meet you, Raja. My name's Dhakiy."

As they sped down the highway to Dhahran, Raja let Dhakiy do most of the talking, and talk he did. Dhakiy was twenty years old and had been driving a delivery van for his father's company since he was fifteen. While Dhakiy met lots of interesting people on the job, he spent most of his time alone on the road. Someday, Dhakiy hoped to get a management job within his father's company, but currently his older brothers held all the management positions.

His father had started their delivery company from scratch. "He started with just one van," Dhakiy said. "My dad purchased the van for just a hundred rials. It barely ran, but he fixed it up himself. Now, we've got twenty vans, and we're making deliveries throughout the Arabian Peninsula."

Eventually, Raja had to say something. He told Dhakiy that he'd had car trouble. After spending the night in his car, he decided to set out on foot. While Raja felt bad lying to him, he couldn't exactly tell Dhakiy the truth. Based on the look Dhakiy gave him, Raja wasn't sure that Dhakiy believed him anyway.

"Did you hear about the oil rig explosion?" Dhakiy asked.

"No," Raja said apprehensively.

"According to the radio, the explosion brought the whole rig down."

For a brief moment, Raja smiled inwardly. *Samakab would be proud. If . . . if he's still alive, that is. I owe him my life.* Raja suddenly felt ashamed.

"What are these terrorists thinking?" Dhakiy railed. "How can we ever hope to rise above the fray through violence? The way to gain the West's respect is through commerce. My father works with all the big delivery companies," he said proudly. "DHL, Fed Ex, you name it. He charges them a hefty surcharge too, but they pay it. That's strength. That's power. What does blowing up an oil rig prove? Nothing. The Americans will park one of their naval ships off shore. They'll blow up the terrorist's family along with whoever is unlucky enough to live next to them. They can take out a whole city block, just like that," he said with a snap of his fingers.

"Yeah, it's crazy," Raja replied as he slunk down in his seat. All at once, his energy seemed to leave him completely.

For the first time during the ride, Dhakiy seemed to run out of things to say. "How about some music?" he offered. He turned on the radio and music filled the cab of the truck with hollow noise as its two passengers sat lost in thought. On the outskirts of Dhahran, Dhakiy finally broke his silence. "Where do you want me to drop you off?" he asked.

"Anywhere is fine," Raja answered. "You've been a real life saver. If it wasn't for you, I'd still be standing back there on the highway."

"I've got several deliveries here in Dhahran," Dhakiy said as he picked up a clipboard off the seat. "Why don't you look at the addresses and see if any of them are close to where you're headed."

Raja picked up the clipboard and scanned over the addresses. "Your third stop is actually pretty close to where I live," he admitted. "Do you need any help?"

"Uh, that's all right," Dhakiy said looking Raja up and down.

Dhakiy went about making his deliveries. Unlike when he'd initially picked Raja up, he seemed self-conscious and uncomfortable with Raja's presence.

"I should have gotten out at the first bus stop that I saw," Raja said. "There's gotta be some way I can thank him."

When Dhakiy left the truck to make one of his deliveries, Raja looked around the cab. "He's got to have a business card or something." Quickly, he glanced in the glove box. "Ah ha! This is just what I was looking for," he exclaimed upon finding a stack of business cards. He grabbed one, folded it up in the palm of his hand, and closed the glove box.

"One more stop and you're home," Dhakiy said upon returning.

"Yeah," Raja said.

"You don't seem too excited," Dhakiy commented.

"It's just been a real long day," Raja answered. "Plus, I still have to figure out how to get my car back," he said. Suddenly, he remembered that his actual car was parked down at the marina where he'd met the *Amirah*. It seemed like a long time ago.

That answer didn't seem to satisfy Dhakiy, but he didn't probe any further. "Here we are," Dhakiy said when they arrived at his next stop.

"Thanks, Dhakiy," Raja said as he got out of the truck.

Dhakiy seemed preoccupied with his delivery. "Good luck," he yelled as he grabbed a package from the back and headed toward a nearby business.

"You too," Raja called back, as he trudged down the street to his apartment complex. Halfway down the block, it dawned on him. His keys were still on the *Amirah*.

How am I going to get in? Ughh, I'll have to track down the apartment manager. No doubt, he'll want to charge me for a new key. Still, it's better than floating in the Persian Gulf with a bullet in my head.

Walking down the street, Raja felt self-conscious. He lived in a relatively affluent, middle-class neighborhood, and everyone was staring at him. A couple of times, passersby made derogatory comments. He couldn't wait to get home and get cleaned up.

Finally, he got to his apartment complex. He punched in his security code and entered the building, then went straight to the apartment manager's office and knocked. When his apartment manager opened the door, at first he didn't recognize Raja.

"What the!" he exclaimed. "How did you get in here?"

"Mr. Iyad, it's me, Raja Ubaydi. I live in apartment 36B."

"What happened to you?" Mr. Iyad asked. To Raja, he seemed more annoyed than concerned.

"It's a long story," Raja replied. "I lost my wallet and keys. If you could help me get into my apartment, I'll get cleaned up and be out of your hair."

Mr. Iyad looked him up and down. "Humpf! Just a minute," he said, then closed the door in Raja's face.

Raja leaned against the wall and exhaled tiredly. "He's probably checking to see if I'm up-to-date on my rent," he said exasperated. "Will this day ever end?"

After rummaging around in his office for several minutes, Mr. Iyad reappeared with a ring of keys. "We'll have to get new locks put on your door," he said. "The bill will be added to your next month's rent."

Raja rolled his eyes but said nothing. When they reached his apartment, Raja briefly wondered if it was safe to enter.

Mr. Iyad put the key in the lock and unlocked the door. The door stuck slightly, then it swung open. Mr. Iyad looked around the apartment suspiciously. He almost seemed disappointed that everything was neat and tidy.

"You still have your spare key? I can't be coming up here to let you in and out all day long."

"Yeah," Raja replied as he stepped through the doorway. "Thanks."

Grumpily, Mr. Iyad turned and huffed off down the hallway. After watching him waddle away, Raja shook his head and closed the door. As he looked around his apartment, Raja still felt lost.

The message indicator on his phone was blinking. Raja walked over and glanced at it.

"A dozen messages? Ughh, it's probably work," he groaned. "Everybody's wondering where the hell I was all day."

Not ready to face the messages, Raja decided to take a shower and put on some clean clothes. He trudged over to the bathroom, turned on the shower, and pulled off his clothes. The sight of the orange and blue flip-flops on his bathroom floor nearly made him laugh.

"Back to the dumpster," he said. It almost seemed sad.

A shower never felt so good. Leaning against the tiled wall, Raja half-wondered if he could sleep standing up. Nonetheless, if the shower felt this good, his bed would feel even better.

Raja finished showering, dried off, and walked into his bedroom with a towel tied around his waist. After grabbing a pair of shorts and T-shirt, he dropped his towel on the floor and slipped on the clothes. He'd never noticed the relative softness of his clothes, but his T-shirt felt cushy compared to the *thobe* he wore all day.

He looked longingly at the bed and then back to the kitchen. "Screw the messages," Raja said. "If they fired me, it can wait until later." At the moment, sleep seemed much more important than his job. Gingerly, he stretched out on his bed. "This sure beats that wooden bench. No matter what happens tomorrow, at least I made it home."

Suddenly, there was a knock on his door.

"You've got to be kidding me," Raja said under his breath. He lay there quietly.

The knock came again. "Raja Ubaydi," a male voice called.

"This can't be happening," Raja said. Inside, he felt like crying. He rolled over and put his feet on the floor.

"Raja? I know you're in there. My name is Detective Al-Faruq. I need to ask you a few questions."

"Just a second," Raja replied, his voice wavering. Resigned to whatever fate had in store, Raja got up and opened the door.

Chapter 50: Is This the End?

As Detective Al-Faruq sat outside the mosque that Professor Ratib frequented, he wondered angrily why he was there. Chief Hamal had told him to back off. Yet, based on his interrogation of Raja Ubaydi, he knew the professor was integral to it all: the fires, the terrorist attacks, everything.

The fingerprints he'd lifted from Shahidah's cell phone discovery belonged to Husam Asad. While his efforts to locate Husam had been fruitless, Al-Faruq was confident the professor would lead him in the right direction. Unfortunately, someone higher up wanted him to drop it.

Dressed as a pauper, Al-Faruq sat cross-legged near the mosque entrance begging for alms. After about ten minutes, the professor drove up in his car.

"Right on time," Al-Faruq whispered.

The professor exited his vehicle and walked right by Al-Faruq without giving him a second glance. A moment later, a black Mercedes drove up and parked right next to professor Ratib's car. A rough looking bearded man exited the vehicle.

Before heading for the mosque, the man lingered next to the professor's car. As Al-Faruq watched, the man knelt down.

What's he doing? Evidently, I'm not the only one following the professor.

After a moment, the man stood up and walked briskly toward the mosque. Al-Faruq eyed him cautiously as he passed. Then, he jotted down the license plate of the Mercedes on a scrap of paper, folded it up, and put it into his collection cup.

While the mosque was relatively deserted, it would start to get busy soon. Evening prayers were less than an hour away. Al-Faruq felt for the GPS tracking device he had planned to attach to the professor's car. He could attach it now, but what had the bearded man done to the professor's car?

Al-Faruq looked back at the entrance. The owner of the black Mercedes had disappeared inside. *Well, I guess it's now or never.*

Al-Faruq hurried to the parking lot. A quick glance at the professor's car told him all he needed to know. The rear tire was flat. Al-Faruq peeked once more toward the mosque. Then, impulsively, he attached the tracking device under the back bumper of the Mercedes.

"I don't know if you'll be taking the professor with you or not," he whispered, "but something tells me you didn't come here for prayer time."

As he moved back to his spot near the entrance, Al-Faruq scanned the area for anything unusual. Suddenly, it felt like he was back on patrol. Seemingly harmless motion caught his eye while his brain worked to process its potential threat. As the wind rustled the palm fronds overhead, Al-Faruq pulled his *ghutra* tight against his face.

He heard the mosque's heavy entrance door opening before he could see it. Out walked the professor, flanked by the man he'd seen earlier. The professor's hands were behind his back.

"Alms for the poor," Al-Faruq said as they passed. The bearded man smacked his outstretched hand and cursed him.

"Muhanned, please," the professor said. "I'm sure we can work something out."

"Keep it moving," Muhanned said. He pushed the professor forward. He had one hand close to the professor's back, and it looked like the professor's hands were tied.

Instinctively, Al-Faruq's hand shrunk beneath his *thobe* and grabbed the grip of his handgun, but he quickly let it go. This wasn't the time or place for a shootout. The professor would most assuredly end up dead, and then he'd be back at square one. He swallowed his anger and watched the two men out of the corner of his eye. When they reached the Mercedes, Muhanned pushed Professor Ratib into the backseat. Muhanned got behind the wheel and started the engine. Then, the Mercedes pulled slowly out of the lot.

Al-Faruq forced himself to wait. He'd tagged the car. Finding them wouldn't be a problem, and he didn't want to tip his hand by rushing. After a few moments, Al-Faruq collected his belongings as another beggar was preparing for the evening prayer rush. Al-Faruq grabbed the coins he'd collected, dropped them in the man's cup, and headed to his car.

Muhanned and the professor rode in silence. Professor Ratib sat uncomfortably staring out the window.

What does this idiot want? Our operations are working. We've got the American dogs on the run, and the corrupt Saudi monarchy has been unveiled. What more could he want? What more do you want, Allah?

"Where are you taking me?" Professor Ratib asked softly.

"You wanted to see Imam Al-Hashim," Muhanned answered. "I'm taking you to see him. Don't worry professor. It's not far."

The professor gazed out the window. They were passing the *souks*, but suddenly the colorful signs faded, and the streets narrowed. The modern buildings gave way to old, mud-brick tenement buildings. The longer they drove, the further back in time they traveled.

After bumping slowly down a narrow one-way street, a clearing appeared. In front of them, Professor Ratib saw a vacant lot. Construction debris cluttered a crumbling concrete foundation. The old building, which had collapsed some time ago, now served as a courtyard amongst the dilapidated structures that surrounded it. In the center of the courtyard stood a single chair.

"Your seat is ready, professor," Muhanned said. He chuckled as he parked the car in front of the courtyard.

"And Imam Al-Hashim?" the professor asked.

Muhanned did not answer. He exited the vehicle and opened the professor's door. Waving his gun, he motioned the professor to the back of the car.

"So, you'd like to see the Imam, eh?" Muhanned asked. He unlocked the trunk and lifted it open. It was lined with trash bags. In the center lay a large, green duffel bag, stained with dark red blotches.

"Open it!" Muhanned ordered.

Professor Ratib reached down. The smell was awful, but he did as he was told and unzipped the duffel bag. Without warning, Muhanned shoved the professor's face downward. Inside the duffel bag, Professor Ratib could see the bloody remains of the Imam.

His torso was naked from the waist up, and there were cuts everywhere. Professor Ratib closed his eyes. His stomach churned.

"I thought you wanted to talk to him," Muhanned said. "Maybe now, you'll talk to me!"

Muhanned pulled Professor Ratib by the arm and set him down roughly in the chair. As Muhanned secured him to the chair with rope, the professor stared blankly at the ground. Like the duffel bag, it too was stained with blood. Professor Ratib looked up weakly at the surrounding buildings. Tattered curtains hung limply in the empty window frames. If anyone lived here, the professor could see no sign of it.

"Perhaps, you would like to tell me what Imam Al-Hashim has done with my money," Muhanned growled, circling the chair. The professor continued to stare blankly off into space. In the distance, he saw an abandoned vehicle sitting on the rock-strewn ground. Its rusty hull had no wheels or windows.

Muhanned brandished a large knife and slit the professor's *thobe* and shirt down the front. He then pulled the fabric back over the professor's shoulders. Kneeling next to the professor, Muhanned spoke softly in his ear.

"Come on, professor. You're an educated man. You saw what happened to the Imam. Don't be a fool."

Bare-chested, the professor breathed heavily as tears streamed down his face. His thoughts spun out of control.

How did it come to this? Is this what I deserve? I worked with the Americans, but I never gave them anything of value. I was cheating them. I was stealing from them. I did it for you Allah, and this is how you repay me? My wife and daughter are gone. The Imam is dead. How could this happen to me? Give me one more chance to repay you. I'll do anything. Anything!

"I'm not a patient man," Muhanned warned him as he dragged the tip of the knife slowly across the professor's chest. Sharply, Muhanned backhanded the professor across the face. "Well?" he screamed. As Muhanned circled, the professor hung his head and sobbed.

#

311

Detective Al-Faruq looked down at the GPS locator. According to the signal, the professor's captor had stopped right in the middle of the old tenement area.

"Damn! I can't drive down there. I'd stick out like a sore thumb." At least he had his beggar disguise, but he'd have to park and cover the last few blocks on foot.

At the edge of the tenements, Al-Faruq parked next to a couple of old, abandoned vehicles. It wasn't ideal, but if he went any farther, he'd be boxed in. He didn't want his only escape option to be reverse.

Al-Faruq reached under his seat and grabbed some extra clips for his handgun. Then he checked the GPS locator again before tossing it on the passenger seat. As he exited the car, Al-Faruq peered down the narrow one-way street apprehensively. This certainly wasn't the smartest thing he'd ever done, but if he didn't get moving his primary lead could go cold, perhaps literally.

Picking his way forward, Al-Faruq scanned both sides of the street. Aside from the occasional homeless person sleeping in the shadows, there was little activity. The local residents, primarily the homeless and day laborers, must have known something was up. While occasionally he'd notice a face peeking out from one of the tenement apartments, it quickly disappeared. Apart from the occasional wail of a baby crying, it was quiet.

After a couple of more blocks, Al-Faruq noticed a clearing up ahead. The shadows created by the old buildings disappeared and bright sunlight strewn in unimpeded. Al-Faruq slid close to the building. Faintly, he heard a man sobbing. As he neared the corner, Al-Faruq crouched down and crept forward. Glancing around the edge, he saw the black Mercedes parked near an empty lot. The *ghutra* of the man who'd taken the professor was barely visible above the car's roof line, but where was the professor?

Al-Faruq surveyed the alley. He needed to get a better vantage point. Quickly, he sidled back along the tenement building until he found an entrance. It had been boarded up, but several of the boards had rotted and fallen away. Cautiously, Al-Faruq ducked through the opening into the dark and dusty building. After his eyes adjusted, Al-Faruq saw a stairway to his left. He headed up the stairs, two steps at a time.

On the second floor, he peered down the hallway. The rooms on that floor appeared to be occupied, so Al-Faruq continued up. The entrance to the third floor was boarded up. Upon grabbing one of the planks, the rotted wood fell away easily. Al-Faruq set it down gingerly and squeezed through the opening he had made. Quietly, he crept into the first room on the left.

Although an old ragged blanket hung loosely over the window's opening, the barren room looked to be deserted. Al-Faruq moved cautiously over to the window and peered out. From this new vantage point, he could see Professor Ratib bound to a chair amidst the rubble of the abandoned lot. The professor was being interrogated.

Grimly, Al-Faruq weighed his options. It would be difficult, if not impossible, to take out the professor's kidnapper from here, but if he did nothing, Professor Ratib was a dead man. Al-Faruq watched the professor's captor circle while menacingly waving a large knife. All of a sudden, a flurry of shots rang out, and Professor Ratib's captor slumped to the ground. Al-Faruq dove for cover, but it was too late. He'd been hit in the leg. Bullets peppered the room while Al-Faruq low crawled for the hallway.

"Sniper! What the fuck! What the hell is going on?"

Al-Faruq grunted angrily as he dragged himself from the room. Bullets shredded the makeshift curtain and ripped through the thin walls. Even the hallway was unsafe.

"What in Allah's name . . . ?" Al-Faruq cried as he scrambled for the stairwell. After crashing headlong through the wooden barricade that covered the doorway, he stumbled down the stairs to the second floor. His left thigh burned painfully.

"You've really done it this time. Fuck! They're coming!"

As he neared the ground floor, Al-Faruq leaned against the wall and inched forward. With his gun at the ready, he looked down the way that he'd come in. The exit looked enticing.

"Okay," he breathed. "Be patient. They may try to come in the same way you did. Whoever is first, you have to put him down."

From his perch on the stairs, Al-Faruq's eyes darted nervously between the second-floor entryway and the outside entrance below. *Am I doing the right thing? There are probably a dozen entrances. Hell, they could just climb through a window! But there couldn't be that many of them. A couple of spotters, a sniper—three or four, max.*

Al-Faruq saw a shadow pass across the entrance. Patiently, he kept his weapon trained on the opening. A *ghutra*-covered figure carrying a rifle leaned in. When Al-Faruq had a torso to shoot at, he fired two shots in quick succession. One shot hit the target in the chest; the other in the neck. The man crumpled forward, knocking down the remaining boards that covered the entrance.

"One down," Al-Faruq whispered, as he retreated back up the staircase. "Time for hide-and-seek."

He looked warily down the second-floor hallway. Worried that there might be squatters hiding out, he continued up to the third floor again. Given the state of his leg, that was easier said than done. Slowly, he pushed himself up the stairs one step at a time.

Halfway up the stairs, he stopped and rested. For a moment, Al-Faruq held his breath and listened. He tried to stay as still as possible, but it was difficult to keep his feet from shifting on the dust-covered stairs. Was there someone up above? Cautiously, Al-Faruq lay down. Using his arms and one good leg, he crawled up the stairs until the third-floor entrance came into view. He stopped and aimed his weapon at the entrance.

It was difficult to hear anything over the beating of his heart, but he needed to be cautious. There was no point in rushing. Then, squinting up the dimly lit stairwell, he saw something. A glint of light shone through a small hole to the left of the doorway, then disappeared.

Al-Faruq waited. The light shone through for a moment and then disappeared again. He'd brought those extra clips, so there was no point conserving ammo. Surgically, he aimed to the left of the doorway where he had seen the light and fired three shots in succession straight into the wall.

An angry scream rose from the floor above. A flurry of bullets hailed through the third-floor doorway, impacting the wall at the top of the stairs. Al-Faruq recoiled, but kept his eyes trained on the doorway. A large man stumbled forward. Al-Faruq let fly two more shots, then retreated, tumbling down toward the second floor.

"Why didn't you listen to Chief Hamal?" Al-Faruq said as he struggled to his feet. "He told you to back off. Next time, listen!"

His head on a swivel, Al-Faruq scanned for threats. Looking down the second-floor hallway, he decided the time for patience had run out. "Anyone in the hallway will be shot dead!" he yelled. Hastily, he changed clips and headed down the hallway.

Staying as low as he could, Al-Faruq limped zigzag down the second-floor hallway. His leg aching, he stopped and rested with his back against the wall. So far, no one was following him, but the other stairwell still seemed far away. He pressed on and finally reached it.

Now what? You've been stumbling like an elephant down the hallway. If anyone's looking for you, they know exactly where you are.

As Al-Faruq caught his breath, he looked down at his blood-soaked *thobe. It probably doesn't matter anyway. Even if I do make it out, I've got several more blocks just to get back to the car, much less a hospital.*

He gritted his teeth and pushed the thoughts from his head. Staying to the left, he fired a cover shot down the stairwell. Leaning against the wall, he started down the stairs. He heard a noise from above. Quickly, he turned and fired a cover shot up.

After taking a couple of deep breaths, Al-Faruq moved. Staggering down the stairs, he kept his back against the wall to hold himself up. Motion above caught his eye. *Bang, bang!* He fired twice and kept moving. At the bottom of the stairwell, he had two choices: out the front and into the street, or out the back into the alleyway.

Al-Faruq crumpled beside the rear exit and looked out. The sunlight was fading. He wanted to rest, just for a minute, but he forced himself out into the alley. First, an old dumpster provided cover, then a dented trash can, and so it continued as he inched back to his car. The enemy was everywhere and nowhere, hiding in every shadow, the cause of every noise, and yet he saw no one.

Finally, with his car in sight, Al-Faruq stopped, exhausted. Something wasn't right, but he couldn't grasp what. Twenty yards from his car, he crouched in agony, uncertain whether he was twenty yards from freedom or certain death.

"Psst!" A noise startled him.

Nearly tipping over, Al-Faruq wheeled around and trained his gun on two women wearing black *habiyas*. As they put their hands up, Al-Faruq blinked at them with a mixture of anger and fear.

"Don't get in your car. Please! It's not safe," one of the women pleaded. "You're hurt. Follow us."

Al-Faruq's eyes darted from the women to the car and back. Then, he lowered his weapon and dropped to his knees.

"Please, we must hurry," the women beckoned. Slowly, they backed away while looking nervously at the rooftops. Al-Faruq struggled to his feet and limped after them. The two women led him through a maze of narrow passageways and back alleys. Al-Faruq struggled to follow, so exhausted he was practically dragging the muzzle of his gun on the ground. At this point, he was unsure if he even had the strength to lift it.

After endless twists and turns, they led him down a small flight of stairs toward an underground cellar. Al-Faruq tried to follow, but tripped and fell headlong down the stairs. Barely conscious, he felt the two women lift him up. They dragged him into a dimly lit room filled with chairs. On the wall hung an old wooden cross, but suddenly it disappeared behind a dark curtain. As they laid him down on the floor, he could hear arguing.

"How could you bring him here?" a woman's voice rasped angrily.

"He's hurt. He would have been killed," the other two replied.

"Then let them kill one another," the angry woman contended.

"But what of the Good Samaritan?" the two women pleaded. "It is more than just a story. Isn't it?"

The angry woman fell silent for a moment. "Yes, yes it's more than just a story," she answered softly. "You were right to bring him here sisters. Forgive me. I . . . I hope it's not too late." The lights dimmed, and Al-Faruq passed out.

With the sound of gunfire echoing in the background, Husam stared at Imam Al-Hashim's decimated body. Glaring angrily over at Muhanned's corpse, he slammed the trunk door shut, stepped over Muhanned and crouched down in front of Professor Ratib. Roughly, Husam lifted the professor's chin with his hand. "Muhanned may be dead, but I'm afraid I've got a few questions of my own."

Teary eyed, Professor Ratib slumped in the chair. "What kind of questions?" he asked, his voice barely audible.

"Who is this businessman you keep meeting with?"

The professor shrugged.

Husam slapped him across the face. "Come on! Wake up! You were dead a long time ago. It's simply a matter of whether or not you can redeem your wretched soul."

"S . . . Steve Jamison."

"And what does Mr. Jamison pay you for."

"Information."

"What kind of information?"

"I never gave them anything of value," the professor insisted.

"Like the Imam's name?" Husam asked, nodding toward the trunk. "Was he that worthless to you?"

"I . . . I had no choice."

Husam smacked the back of his head. "Shut up!" he said menacingly. "No choice? I've got a choice for you. Should I kill you now or make you repent for your unspeakable sins? You'll pay for what you've done!" he screamed. "You'll all pay, every wretched infidel!"

Chapter 51: The Good Samaritans

Sister Mary Catherine Flynn had been working inside Saudi Arabia for almost ten years now. In her mid-fifties, she was a stout woman with graying hair. Nonetheless, her Irish heritage still showed in the flecks of red that sprinkled her hair and cheeks. While she was generally very gregarious, tonight her patience was wearing thin.

As she bent over her patient, Sister Mary yelled for Chandra. "I need more towels!"

"I'm coming," Chandra answered. She soon appeared with a stack in her arms.

"Jahanara, where's that boiling water I asked for?" Sister Mary called. "For goodness sake. Mary, mother of God, where is she? Hold this tight against his leg," she instructed Chandra before leaving to see what was keeping Jahanara. Huffing down the hallway, Sister Mary almost bumped into Jahanara as she exited the kitchen.

"What's the hold up?"

"There was no hot tap water, so it took a long time to boil," Jahanara said.

"Just give it here," Sister Mary replied taking the large pot from her. Quickly, she headed back down the hallway. As she entered the room, Chandra was fidgeting helplessly with the towel.

"What's wrong?"

"He won't stay still," Chandra complained.

"Good Lord! Some days, woman, you're not fit to mind mice at a crossroads. Just give it here," Sister Mary said.

Sister Mary nearly had a heart attack when Chandra and Jahanara came in carrying the wounded man. It brought back painful memories of her youth in Ireland. As she cleaned the man's wound and applied a pressure wrap around his leg, she remembered patching up her brother after a solidarity protest turned violent. At the time, she'd been studying to be a nurse. Though she'd been able to save his life that day, he died in a bombing several months later.

"God rest his soul," she muttered.

After taking her vows, Sister Mary had worked in South America, Africa, and the Philippines. But she'd found a home in Saudi Arabia, helping women that their society had no use for. Widowed, these women were turned out by their families because they were too old to bring any substantive dowry. Since they generally couldn't find meaningful employment, Sister Mary helped these outcasts find purpose in their lives.

With Chandra and Jahanara, that meant dealing with every stray that they led to her door. Though often frustrating, she couldn't be upset with them for long. They had taken to the Gospel with such childlike wonder. She just couldn't stifle it. When she resisted taking in a couple of cats they had adopted, she watched as they smuggled portions of their own meager meals to feed the animals. However, this latest find was another matter altogether.

Sister Mary watched apprehensively as the man slept fitfully on the foldout mattress. The bullet had gone straight through his thigh. While it hadn't hit an artery, he'd still lost a lot of blood and needed to get to a hospital. But getting him there would be complicated.

"If only I could drive," she said. "I could just dump him out in front of the ER," she mused. "I could call Father O'Keefe, but he'd never understand. As it is, he's been pushing me to close this facility, and half the women I care for would be back out on the streets."

Lost in thought, she found herself staring at the pile of the man's belongings. Her eyes kept focusing on the gun. Her first instinct was to throw it out, but that might anger him. On the other hand, he might need it for protection. He was in no condition to run from trouble.

Absentmindedly, she picked up his wallet. Flipping it open, she gasped and dropped it on the floor. He was a member of the SAID. After the recent protests, the SAID had detained several missionaries for inciting the riots. What would this man do upon finding himself here? Now, she was more unsure than ever of what to do. Unsteadily, she reached down and retrieved the wallet.

"Where am I?" he asked weakly.

Sister Mary jumped. She looked warily at the man as he struggled to regain consciousness.

"Where?" he asked.

"You're safe. Just rest."

He leaned forward as if to get up, and then fell back. "Gotta keep moving," he muttered. His eyes rolled back. "Just a little farther. Don't give up," he said before falling silent again.

Perplexed, Sister Mary opened the wallet again and looked for a name. "Detective Abdul-Hafiz Al-Faruq," she read. "Don't die on me," she pleaded tiredly.

Then she saw his cell phone. Grabbing it, she flipped it open and reviewed his contacts. She didn't want to call any of his colleagues, but that was all she was finding. After arrowing down through dozens of contacts, she came across one that seemed promising.

"K," she said quietly, "and whoever it is, they're actually categorized as a friend."

Sister Mary looked over at Detective Al-Faruq and then back at the phone. She had to try something. Finally, she decided to send K a text. Her brow furrowed, she typed in a message.

"Hurt! Car dead. NEED HELP!" she typed. Then she hit send and waited with bated breath.

#

It was eleven p.m. Kalila clicked off the television and tossed the remote onto the coffee table. "Might as well head to bed," she said, more bored than tired. "Nothing's on anyway." With her parents visiting her aunt, she had the house to herself.

"I could drop Al-Faruq a line," she said wistfully, as she lay back on the couch and stared at the ceiling, but then she thought better of it. They had graduated from texting to actual phone calls, but their communications had tapered off of late. While he hadn't said anything, Kalila got the impression he was having a tough time at work. At least, that's what she hoped. On the other hand, maybe he just didn't want to continue investing in their friendship. Right now, she wanted to believe that work had gotten in the way.

320

"Aghh," she growled at herself. "Go to bed. Go read a book. Do something other than mope."

After a couple of minutes, she finally summoned the strength to peel herself off the couch, turn off the lights, and head to bed. Halfway up the stairs, she thought she heard her phone chime. She stopped and listened. Once again, she heard the familiar tone.

"It figures," she said turning back down the stairs. Kalila turned on the living room lights and began searching for her phone. "I thought I left it right here," she said with exasperation while staring at the cluttered coffee table. "There you are!" She flipped open her phone. Al-Faruq had sent her a message.

"Hurt! Car dead. NEED HELP!" she read.

"What!" she exclaimed. "I don't hear from him all week, and he sends me this?"

"Ru serious?!?" she texted back.

"Yes," was all he said in response.

"Y me?" Kalila asked. Confused, she waited anxiously for an answer. Finally, it came.

"Don't know who else to trust."

Kalila stared at the text, her thoughts jumbled. *Wonderful! So, I'm it?* Frowning, she punched in a response. "What can I do?"

"Come get me," he texted.

"What?" Kalila yelled so loud that it echoed throughout the entire house. Angrily, she typed. "Ru insane?!? Do u realize what ur asking me 2 do?"

After a few moments, his response came back. "Don't know where else to turn."

In shock, Kalila stared at the phone, her insides twisted. Over the past couple of weeks, she often wondered what it would be like to meet him, but this? This just didn't add up.

"He can't really expect me to come get him. It's the middle of the night," she said. "What? I'm just supposed to hop in my dad's SUV and drive Allah knows where to get him? I've never even driven a car before. What if I get caught? I'm a woman—a Saudi Arabian woman! I'm not supposed to be driving, much less be alone in a car with a man I'm not married to. Plus, why did he text instead of call?"

Kalila looked at the clock. It was now eleven-fifteen. What if he really was hurt? What if he really was in trouble? She didn't know what to do.

Just then, another text arrived. "Sorry, I'll find another way."

"Another way?" Kalila repeated. "Another way to what? Freak me out? Push me away?" Hastily, she texted, "Where ru?" She buried her face in her hands, unsure if she really wanted him to answer.

After several minutes, his answer arrived. "Do you know the fountain at the end of the shopping district?"

"Seriously?" she said. "You mean the one I almost drowned in? The one where you saved my life?"

Still, knowing where it was and driving there in the middle of the night were two different things. She contemplated not responding, but that would mean the end, and she didn't want it to end. Even though they had no future, even though they had no chance, she didn't want their friendship to end, so she responded. "Yes."

"Can you meet me there at midnight?"

"Yes," Kalila responded, her hands sweating as she typed. She set her phone down and went up to her parents' bedroom. "Are you really going to do this?" she said as she donned her father's *thobe* and *ghutra*.

Despite her nerves, she pushed onward. In the upstairs bathroom, she looked at herself oddly in the mirror. She still looked like a woman wearing a man's clothes. She grabbed a washcloth and washed all the makeup off her face. Though still not satisfied, she didn't have any more time to waste. When she got back downstairs, another message was waiting for her.

"If you don't see me, keep driving."

While she found this message to be somewhat cryptic, it was reassuring nonetheless. "Ok," she answered. Then she grabbed the car keys and headed to the garage.

Nervously, Kalila got in on the driver's side. She grabbed her phone and opened the picture that Al-Faruq had sent her. She stared at the picture, trying to burn his face into her brain.

"Well, it's now or never," she told herself. "You've watched your father do this hundreds of times. The R is reverse. The D is for drive. It's late, so there won't be much traffic."

Kalila took a deep breath, opened the garage door and turned the key. With her foot pressing down on the gas pedal, the engine revved loudly. She took her foot off the gas and put it on the brake. After saying a prayer, Kalila locked the doors and put the Suburban in reverse.

The Suburban lurched back out of the garage and then jolted to a stop. "A little smoother this time," Kalila told herself as she checked the rear view mirror. "Don't stomp on the gas pedal."

"Easy does it," she said quietly. She tried again, then stopped, rocking the SUV back and forth when she hit the brakes. "I guess I need to be a little bit lighter on the brakes, too," she said. With the Suburban now out in the street, she put the SUV in drive and jerked forward.

Thankfully, the residential streets were deserted. Kalila found driving forward was much easier than going backward. When she reached the freeway, her confidence was growing, but she was still reluctant to step on the gas.

"Come on," she scolded herself. "If you drive too slow, you'll attract suspicion." Eventually, she got the Suburban up to speed. "Okay, it's the third exit down. Then, take a left by the bakery. You can do this."

After daring to take one hand off the steering wheel, Kalila turned on the radio. One of her favorite *nasheeds* was playing. She sang along to *Ya Taiba* as she guided the Suburban down the highway.

As she sang, her mind rambled. *There is always hope in faith. I just hope that I'm doing the right thing. Allah help me.*

Kalila saw the exit up ahead. She took her foot off the accelerator and slowed down. Just then, another SUV roared past her, its horn blaring. "Same to you," Kalila yelled, her hands tensely gripping the steering wheel. Nervously, she glanced in the rear view mirror to see if anyone else was behind her. To her relief, no one was.

Unfortunately, the nut who had sped past her was stopped at the intersection up ahead. The driver had his arm out the window and was gesturing wildly. Kalila applied the brakes and stopped several car lengths behind him. However, this only seemed to make the man even more upset. He stuck his head out the window and screamed obscenities at her.

"Please go," Kalila pleaded. "Leave me alone." She checked the doors. Thankfully, they were locked. Teary eyed, she yelled at the SUV in front of her. "Go! If you're in such a hurry, then go."

After what seemed like an eternity, the crazy man finally lurched forward. The screeching tires made Kalila shiver, but at least he was gone. Thankfully, he turned right. All she needed to do was take a left, and follow the road straight to the shopping district.

Slowly, she started forward. After stopping at the intersection, Kalila turned left. Her father's favorite bakery was dark, and its parking lot was empty. The hustle and bustle that usually filled the area was absent, and Kalila had never felt so alone. The fountain was located at the far end of the shopping district. It acted as the centerpiece of a large roundabout. Kalila looked at the clock display on the radio. It read eleven-fifty.

"I should be there right on time," she murmured. "Will Al-Faruq be there?" She wasn't sure whether she wanted him to be or not.

#

Sister Mary looked worriedly at the clock. If they were going to make it to the fountain by midnight, they had to get going. Earnestly, she called for Chandra and Jahanara. "Come and help me get him up."

"Where are we going to take him?" Chandra asked.

"I called one of his friends. We need to be at the fountain by midnight."

"Do you think the bad men have left?" Jahanara asked.

"Yes," Sister Mary answered confidently, though she had her doubts. "If he'd been that important to them, the three of you never would have made it here alive."

"Oh," Jahanara responded, her eyes growing wide.

Sister Mary went over to the detective and shook him by the shoulder. "Detective Al-Faruq! Wake up! We need to go. We need to get you out of here," she said.

"Aghhh," Al-Faruq groaned as he struggled to open his eyes. "Where am I?"

"You're safe, but we need to get you to a hospital," Sister Mary explained. "I called one of your friends. They're coming to pick you up."

"Friend? What friend?" Al-Faruq asked.

"K."

"K?" Al-Faruq repeated quizzically as he tried to sit up.

"I don't know," Sister Mary answered. "The contact list on your cell phone. That's all it said. Just K."

Slowly, the realization hit him. *Kalila? No! How could they have involved her in this?*

Fighting back tears, he swallowed hard and tried to compose himself. "And . . . K agreed to come get me?" he managed.

"Yes," Sister Mary said.

"Where's my handgun?" Al-Faruq asked.

"I've put it someplace safe," Sister Mary replied. "Why do you want it?"

"It might not be safe," Al-Faruq responded. "I'm a police officer. The people I was investigating are dangerous."

"They're long gone by now."

"Please," he said. "In case they're not, we'll all stand a better chance if I have my sidearm. Please." While Sister Mary retrieved his things, Al-Faruq thought about calling for backup, but he hesitated. When push came to shove, he didn't know whom to trust. Despite all the evidence he had on the professor, Chief Hamal kept pressuring him to drop it. Why? Like it or not, Kalila was the only one he could trust.

Finally, Sister Mary handed him a small cloth sack that contained his belongings. Al-Faruq stood up leaning heavily on his good leg. Quickly, he grabbed the bag from her and rummaged through it. He was relieved to see that he still had one more full clip of ammunition. He ejected the existing clip and inserted the new one.

"We've got to get going if we're going to make it," Sister Mary said. "Can you walk?"

Al-Faruq took a couple of tentative steps before his injured leg buckled. He knelt on the floor breathing heavily and cursing his leg.

"Chandra! Jahanara! Help him!" Sister Mary ordered. "We need to go now!"

Chandra and Jahanara ducked under Al-Faruq's arms and helped lift him up. He didn't argue. The three followed Sister Mary out, struggling to keep up with her. As they weaved through the back alleys of the old tenements, Al-Faruq scanned for threats, but it was no use.

Even if I see something, I'd never be able to respond in time. Hopefully, they've decided I'm not worth the effort.

Al-Faruq had to give the women credit, though. If anyone was trying to follow them, they weren't making it easy. In the few minutes that they'd been on the move, they'd made at least a dozen turns. As Sister Mary moved the group efficiently through the maze of old buildings, Al-Faruq had to admit he'd never be able to find his way back to where they started.

After several more twists and turns, Sister Mary finally slowed to a stop. "We're close. Chandra and Jahanara, you stay here with the detective while I see if the coast is clear," she instructed. She then disappeared around the corner.

"Thank you for helping me," Al-Faruq whispered after a few moments of uncomfortable silence.

"Thank you for not shooting us," Jahanara offered quietly.

The three resumed their silence. Al-Faruq shifted uncomfortably. His leg and head were throbbing. His thoughts turned to Kalila. *Would she really come? How could she convince her father to drive out in the middle of the night to pick up some stranger?*

Suddenly, a voice pierced the darkness. "Follow me," Sister Mary said. "Come on. Hurry!"

The rest hadn't done Al-Faruq's leg any good. Now, not only was it stiff and heavy, but it pulsated angrily with every step he took. He was glad to have Chandra and Jahanara's help. He couldn't have made it on his own. As it was, he had broken out in a cold sweat, and he wasn't sure he could make it much farther without throwing up. Luckily, as they turned a corner, the dimly lit fountain came into view, and Sister Mary led them to some benches that encircled a large tree near the roundabout.

Chandra and Jahanara set Detective Al-Faruq down on the bench, and Sister Mary motioned for them to leave. "I can take it from here," she whispered. The two women nodded and disappeared the way they had come.

While it was wonderful to sit down, Al-Faruq was uncomfortable being out in the open. "How long are you going to wait?" he asked warily.

"Your friend should be here any minute," she responded in a low fast voice.

"And if my friend doesn't show up?"

"K will be here," she said. "If not, you can call one of your detective friends. I've done all I can."

"Yes, thank you," Al-Faruq replied weakly as he gripped his handgun tightly. His eyes darted back and forth nervously.

"Look," Sister Mary said. "Here comes a car now."

Chapter 52: The Drive

As Kalila drove through the deserted *souks*, her nerves started getting the best of her. *What if Al-Faruq lost his phone and some stranger picked it up? Even if it was him, what if he turns out to be some kind of wacko? What do you really know about him? Uhg! Why didn't you think of all this before you left the house? A lot of good this does now.*

The shopping district looked a lot less inviting at this time of night. All the stores were closed, encased by metal doors that looked cold and dirty, and the streets were cluttered with trash. Once again, Kalila checked to make sure the Suburban doors were locked. She took a deep breath and exhaled slowly.

"If it doesn't feel right, just keep driving," Kalila murmured, as she looked wide-eyed at the buildings around her. "This is ridiculous. This place is deserted. There's no one here. I should go back home. If Al-Faruq was the kind of man I thought he was, he never would have asked me to come down here."

Tired, angry, and confused, she wanted to leave. With the radio station seemingly stuck on commercials, Kalila turned it off with a punch. She looked outside for any signs of activity.

Her palms sweating, Kalila saw the fountain up ahead. To her shock and amazement, she saw a *habiya*-clad woman helping a man hobble to the curb of the roundabout. Kalila slowed and trained the Suburban's headlights on them. Although the man appeared tired and haggard, it looked like Al-Faruq.

Her hands shaking, Kalila stopped short of the tandem and grabbed her phone. She opened the picture of Al-Faruq and looked closely at it. It really was him. He really was hurt. What now?

Unsteadily, she inched the Suburban forward. Pulling up so that the passenger side door was in front of them, Kalila opened the window. "Al-Faruq, is that you?" she asked, her voice cracking.

Al-Faruq's eyes grew wide. "You came alone? Are you insane?" he blurted out.

"Me! I wouldn't even be here if you hadn't texted me. What did you expect me to do?"

"I . . . I . . . " Al-Faruq stammered.

"It's my fault," Sister Mary interjected. "I'm the one who texted you. I'm sorry. I didn't know. He needed help."

"I'll drive," Al-Faruq said as he turned to go to the driver's side, but his legs buckled. Sister Mary caught him.

"She made it here. God willing she'll be able to get you to a hospital, but we don't have time to debate this," Sister Mary said.

Trembling and light-headed, Al-Faruq didn't argue. Kalila unlocked the doors, and Sister Mary helped Al-Faruq into the vehicle. Wincing, Al-Faruq struggled to get his leg inside.

"Oh, just a second," Kalila stammered as she fumbled with the seat controls. "I can move your seat back." However, her first attempt started the seat forward.

"Aghhh!" Al-Faruq protested.

"Sorry!" Kalila answered. She flipped the control the other way and the seat started back.

Once Al-Faruq was situated, Sister Mary pushed them to get going. "I was able to stem the bleeding, but he's lost a lot of blood. He really needs to get to a hospital," she said, closing the door and backing away from the vehicle.

"Are you ready? Do you have your seat belt on?" Kalila asked insistently.

Al-Faruq cringed. Whether or not he was wearing a seat belt was the least of their problems. Nonetheless, he turned with a grimace and pulled the lap belt across his waist.

Seeing that he was in pain, Kalila offered to help.

"I've got it. Just drive!"

Kalila hit the gas and the Suburban lurched forward. For the moment, the two sat in silence as Kalila navigated back to the freeway. "Do you know where the closest hospital is? Should I go east or west on the freeway?" she asked.

"The hospital will ask too many questions," Al-Faruq answered. "If they see you dump me off on the curb, they'll call the police. You'll be discovered. You'll have to drop me off someplace else."

"But where?"

"I . . . I don't know," he responded. Simply lifting his hand up to his forehead was a struggle. "Go, ah . . . Stop up here at the bakery, and let's figure this out."

Kalila did as he suggested and pulled into the bakery parking lot.

"Are your parents home?" Al-Faruq asked.

"No, they're at my aunt's house," she responded hesitantly.

"I . . . I didn't mean," Al-Faruq stammered. "I just thought . . . Why don't you drive home, and call emergency services from there. You could just say that there's some strange guy sitting on the curb in front of the house. I'm a SAID detective. I'll be fine. Plus, that way I'd know you got home safely."

"Yeah, I guess," she said tiredly. "What if the neighbors notice? What would I say to my parents? I'm pretty sure they'd want to know why the police were outside our house at one o-clock in the morning."

"Well, wouldn't that be easier than trying to explain this," Al-Faruq said, gesturing to the driver's seat?

"Yes, I suppose it would," she replied with a wry smile. "And if you die on the way to my house. What then?"

"I won't die."

"You promise?"

"I promise," Al-Faruq replied with a hint of a smile.

Kalila guided the Suburban out of the parking lot, and soon they were on the freeway. Thankfully, it was empty. Kalila didn't want to have to deal with any more crazy drivers.

As Al-Faruq sat in the passenger seat, he seemed fidgety. He careened his neck looking around.

"Are you doing all right?" Kalila asked with concern.

"Yeah, it's . . . "

"It's what?"

"I just want to make sure that no one's following us."

"Oh," Kalila said. "I haven't seen any other cars since we left the fountain."

"No, neither have I."

"Are you afraid they're still looking for you?" Kalila asked warily.

"Not afraid really," Al-Faruq said. "I don't want to lead them right to your doorstep. I never intended for you to get involved. People like this, they . . . they don't care who they hurt."

Kalila thought quietly for a moment before responding. "As long as people like me are unwilling to take risks, we will always be slaves to extremists who risk everything."

"I'm not worth the risk," Al-Faruq said quietly.

"You are to me."

Kalila and Al-Faruq sat in silence for the remainder of the drive, neither willing to divulge the thoughts flooding through their minds. Neither ready to say what they both were thinking. Al-Faruq looked exhausted, and Kalila had to make a conscious effort not to drive too fast.

The streets were quiet as Kalila pulled into her neighborhood, and the windows of the nearby houses were all dark. Pulling slowly into the driveway, Kalila clicked the remote to open the garage door. Then, she turned to Al-Faruq.

"We're here," she said in a sweet, quiet voice that belied how tired she was. Al-Faruq said nothing. His body was slumped over leaning against the passenger side window. "Al-Faruq?" she said with concern. She shook his shoulder. There was no response.

Quickly, Kalila got out and ran around to the passenger side. When she opened the door, Al-Faruq tumbled out as she tried in vain to catch him. Her *ghutra* fell to the ground as she struggled to get a grip on him. Trembling, she grabbed him underneath the arms and pulled him to the side of the driveway.

"Don't be dead," she cried. "Please wake up. Come on Al-Faruq. Wake up!" she pleaded. Now kneeling, with Al-Faruq propped up against her, she felt for a pulse, but all she could feel was the thundering beat of her own heart. "Get up," she scolded herself. "You've got to call for help. It's not too late. You need to have faith. It's not too late."

After laying him down at the side of the driveway, Kalila quickly ran inside the house. In the kitchen, she hurriedly flipped through the phone book, looking for the emergency numbers. Even when she found them, it took her a couple of tries to dial the number correctly.

"Emergency dispatch," a male voice answered.

"There's . . . there's a man outside. Uh, lying in my driveway. He looks hurt," Kalila stammered.

"Your name, ma'am?"

"Kalila Mawiyah."

"Can your husband come to the phone?" the man asked.

"I'm . . . I'm not married. I'm home alone by myself."

"Is this man threatening you?"

"No! No, he's just lying there. Ummm . . . Look, I was awakened by a noise. Someone knocking on the front door. I came down to look, and it was this man. He said he needed help and flashed a badge at me, but like I said, I'm home alone. I . . . I couldn't let him in. Then he . . . he started walking away, but he collapsed in the driveway," Kalila rattled on excitedly. "Please," she pleaded, "just send someone to check. Anyone! Please!"

"One moment," the man said flatly. Kalila sank to the floor, her eyes red with tears. She tried to wipe them away, but more came streaking down her cheeks. She barely heard the dispatcher return.

"I'll need to verify your address," he said.

Through her tears, she choked out the address. "Please hurry," she said faintly as the call ended. She headed outside to check on Al-Faruq. He looked so pale. "Hold on," she whispered in his ear as she hurriedly looked for his badge. Upon finding it, she laid it face up in his outstretched hand. Then, she kissed him on the cheek, her forehead touching his. After pulling the Suburban into the garage, she rushed back inside to watch from the window.

It took fifteen minutes for a police car to arrive and another ten before the ambulance arrived. Peering between the blinds, she took some comfort from the fact that the ambulance turned its lights and siren on as it left. "If he was dead, they wouldn't have bothered," she told herself. Feeling lost and alone, Kalila threw her father's *thobe* and *ghutra* into the laundry and collapsed, exhausted, on the couch.

Chapter 53: Moving Out

Nicole stared at the haphazard collection of half-filled moving boxes. It was July 3rd, the lease was up, and Nicole was moving out of the apartment she'd been sharing with Nasim. Even though Nasim's and Nathan's names were on the lease, she couldn't bring herself to just desert the place. She'd been renting a storage unit, so she decided to store their stuff there. If she couldn't get in contact with them, then she'd sell everything.

"So this is it?" she said with a shrug. "Is this what life has in store for me? Cleaning up my boyfriends' messes?" She taped up the box she was working on, grabbed a marker, and wrote "Nasim's clothes" on the outside.

With the help of a friend, she'd already transported the beds and other furniture over to her storage unit. All that was left was clothes, books, the computer, and whatever was in the kitchen cupboards. Stepping inside Nasim's room, she did a final walk through to make sure it was empty.

"Oh yeah, don't want to forget that," Nicole said, somewhat disheartened upon seeing a lone box sitting on the closet shelf. Standing on her tiptoes, she reached up and slowly slid the box off the shelf. "What kind of treasure do I have here?" she said sarcastically.

Nicole knelt down and unfolded the cardboard flaps of the nondescript box. "Geez!" she exclaimed. "I remember Nasim having a cell phone, but what's all this crap? There must be at least a dozen cell phone boxes, user manuals, and contracts," she noted as she flipped through everything.

Mixed in with everything else, Nicole found a sheet of notebook paper with a list of phone numbers on it. It was in Nasim's handwriting. *Are these the numbers? But what would he need them for? Oh, that's right—because he's a terrorist.*

While Nicole had filed a report with the FBI concerning Nasim, she'd never heard back from them. Over the past month, she'd resigned herself to the fact that Nasim had simply left. Either he feared commitment, figured that his family would never accept her, or whatever. He wasn't a terrorist, just another stupid guy.

Still, as Nicole looked at the phone numbers, it made her wonder. She closed up the box, but kept the list of phone numbers out. With the list sitting on top, Nicole grabbed the box and took it out to the kitchen, then checked the rest of the rooms to see if she'd missed anything. Satisfied, she grabbed the vacuum and quickly ran over the areas.

Why are you doing this? Who cares whether they get their damn security deposit back?

Angrily, Nicole turned off the vacuum and grumpily took a couple of boxes down to her car. It was late afternoon, and the Texas heat was unbearable. Hot and sweaty, Nicole's energy was flagging. "I should have gotten an earlier start," she grumbled. "It'll practically be nighttime before I'm finished." After slamming the car door shut, she headed back upstairs and started on the kitchen.

It was definitely a college guy's kitchen. Paper plates, plastic cups, you name it. At least, she didn't have to worry about breaking anything. What little food was in the apartment, Nicole dumped into a large trash bag. After emptying out the refrigerator, she started on the cupboards. All in all, it took her about an hour to pack up the kitchen. After setting the boxes marked "kitchen" by the front door, Nicole grabbed the trash and lugged it out to the dumpster.

On her way back, a cheerful voice called out. "Hey Nicole!"

"Heather? I didn't know you lived here," Nicole answered.

"I moved in last weekend. The place I was renting was getting really run down, and the landlord was . . . Well, let's just say he had issues. What are you doing here? Taking summer classes?"

"Uh, yeah. I'm taking a couple of classes."

"So, you live here?" Heather asked.

"No, I'm just helping a couple of friends move out of their apartment," Nicole said frowning.

"Oh, that's nice," Heather said. "Well, if you get bored and want to hang out, I'm right here in 205. It's kind of dead around here during the summer."

"Yeah, I know what you mean. I might have to take you up on that," Nicole replied. "Later, Heather."

"Later gator," Heather said.

Nicole smiled and headed back to the apartment. She transported the two boxes from the kitchen down to her car. "Crap," she said dejectedly. Her car was filling up quickly. "I don't want to make two trips. Ughh," she groaned, "given the price of gas, that'd be an extra ten bucks down the drain." On her way back up the stairs, she ran into Heather again.

"So, where are these friends of yours?" Heather asked. "It looks like you're the one doing all the work."

"It's a long story," Nicole replied.

"You need some help?" Heather asked.

"I've only got a couple of boxes left," Nicole answered.

"Then I timed my offer just right," Heather said. "Let me dump this laundry back in my apartment, and I'll give you a hand."

"Thanks," Nicole said as she sat down on the steps.

"All right," Heather said brightly upon her return. "Where to?"

"It's right this way," Nicole said while leading Heather down the hall. "Here we go. Like I said, there's not much left."

"I can save you a couple of trips," Heather replied as she picked up a box.

"You got a point."

Together, they each took a box down to the car while Heather talked about her summer classes. Nicole had to admit it was nice to have the company. She'd been kind of a recluse since Nasim had left.

"Do your instructors seem engaged?" Nicole asked. "I swear that some of mine are just mailing it in."

"I know what you mean. They want to be on break as much we do."

"As long as I get credit for the class, I guess it shouldn't matter."

"Yeah, but you want to get your money's worth too," Heather said.

The two continued to chitchat as they walked up the stairs. Once inside, Nicole pushed the final two boxes over by the door, and then did one last walk-through. Wandering into the kitchen, Heather noticed a box sitting on the counter.

"Hey Nicole. What about this box?"

"Oh yeah. That needs to go too."

"Ooooo! What's with all the phone numbers?" Heather asked eying the list.

"I'm not sure really. It's my ex-boyfriend's handwriting, but I don't recognize any of the numbers."

"Hmmm, kind of a mystery. Eh?" Heather said slyly, her eyebrow raised. "Have you tried any of the numbers?"

"No," Nicole admitted, "but am I wrong to want to?"

"Heck no!" Heather responded. "I just saw the list, and I'm intrigued."

"You are so bad," Nicole said.

"What? It's probably nothing. Like a list of car mechanics. You're way over thinking this."

"Actually, I think they're cell phone numbers. I found the list inside that box," Nicole nodded. "It's filled with cell phone contracts, manuals, and other crap."

"Hmmm . . . Did he ever give you a cell phone as a gift?" Heather asked.

"No!"

"So, you're secretly upset that he never gave you a cell phone as a gift," Heather joked.

"No, he probably bought them for his family or something. It's not like he was some kind of smooth operator. Just give me the list," Nicole said with an outstretched hand. "You obviously have an overactive imagination."

"I'm not the one holding onto a random list of phone numbers," Heather retorted as she handed Nicole the list.

"Thank you," Nicole said, as she folded up the paper and slid it into her back pocket. She pirouetted back to the front door and grabbed a box. "Can you slide that small box on top?"

"Sure. You know," Heather offered, "when we're done with these boxes, we could head over to Jose's for happy hour. Have a few margaritas? Make a few phone calls?"

"You buying?" Nicole countered.

"For the phone calls or the margaritas?"

"For the margaritas, of course," Nicole responded, as she balanced the boxes on her knee and closed the apartment door.

"My arm could be twisted," Heather said brightly, "but you'd need to promise to try at least one of those phone numbers."

"I'll think about it," Nicole answered.

"Have you been to Jose's before?" Heather asked.

"Yes, I've been to Jose's."

"You know their margaritas are to die for?"

"Yes!"

"Just checking," Heather said. "They've got really good fajitas too."

"Okay, okay!" Nicole relented. "We'll go to Jose's after I dump this stuff off at my storage unit."

"Woo hoo!" Heather cheered.

"It's a pretty short drive," Nicole said, while stuffing in the final box. "You want to come with?"

"You think there's room?"

"Well, you might have to put a box on your lap, but I'm pretty sure you'll fit."

Nicole and Heather squeezed into the car and zoomed off to Nicole's storage unit. As she drove, Nicole turned on the radio.

"Inspection of a U.S.-flagged oil tanker, named *Big Tex*, leads to the discovery of an unexploded IED. The tanker, which had spent several months in the Persian Gulf after encountering mechanical issues, recently docked in Houston. According to government reports, inspection of the IED revealed that the construction methods and materials utilized in the device were consistent with Iranian-made IEDs."

"Geez, isn't there anything on but news?" Heather said.

Nicole flipped through her preset stations. Finally, she reluctantly settled back on the news. "Guess not," Nicole said as the commentator droned on.

"A serial number found on the device's casing indicates it came from a North Korean-manufactured rocket-propelled grenade, commonly known as an RPG, which was shipped to Iran in 2011. In addition, a serial number taken off the device's internal switch was traced back to a Russian electronics shipment purchased by the Iranian government back in 2008."

"On the eve of Independence Day, officials caution everyone to be on guard for anything suspicious," the voice warned. "The Fourth of July symbolizes American strength and power. The Department of Homeland Security urges everyone to remain vigilant."

"I'm getting so sick of this. When's life going to get back to normal? Ughh!" Nicole groaned before hitting scan.

"Music, yeah!" Heather exclaimed.

The two sang along to "Life is a Highway." When the song had finished, the disc jockey came on. "Can you believe that the song we just played was put on the federal government's do-not-play list? Well now, that's not entirely accurate. They don't call it a do-not-play list. How do they put it? The following songs undercut the conservation measures put in place to combat recent terrorist efforts. Well, I say, undercut this muther-beep. Nobody's going to cripple my freedom of speech on the eve of the Fourth of July! So here's a little Sammy Hagar for you. I CAN'T DRIVE FIFTY-FIVE!" he wailed.

"Ha," Nicole chuckled. "We'll have to keep it tuned here. At least for today, we can pretend that everything's normal.

Unfortunately, as they drove past a local gas station, it was painfully evident everything wasn't normal. With the price per gallon now in double digits, gas stations were having trouble posting their prices. There wasn't enough room on the signs. One station simply posted, "Don't Ask."

"Don't tell," Nicole said pointing at the sign.

"At least there's not much traffic," Heather noted.

"That's because no one can afford gas," Nicole said.

A few songs later, Nicole pulled up to the entrance of her storage unit. She punched in her code, and the gate opened. Upon reaching her unit, Nicole slowed to a stop, got out, and unlocked the padlock that secured the sliding metal door. The door noisily rattled open, and Nicole and Heather started emptying the contents of her car.

"Stack the ones marked Nasim here and the ones marked Nathan here," Nicole said.

"What about this one?" Heather asked.

"If it doesn't say, just stick it in the middle," Nicole answered. "That's kind of where I'm at. Stuck in the middle."

"You want to talk about it?" Heather asked.

"I don't know. Nasim was definitely good for me. Good to me for that matter. I just need to make sure that I don't fall for another Nathan type. Too bad I can't simply lock my feelings about them away as easily as I can lock their stuff away."

"Men!" Heather said. "Can't live with them. Can't lock them in a storage unit."

Nicole laughed and pulled the door closed. The drive back from the storage unit was uneventful as Nicole and Heather chitchatted about their summer. Occasionally, they stopped conversing to sing along with the music on the radio. The deejay continued to play "unauthorized" music.

"Given the price of gas, I guess we'd better walk to Jose's," Nicole said when they reached the apartment complex.

"I suppose you're right," Heather conceded. "It's our civic duty. Right?"

"Something like that. I don't know if it's because of the Memorial Day attacks or what, but it doesn't really feel like the Fourth of July to me," Nicole said as she got out of the car. "No fireworks' stands, and the roads are practically empty. It's surreal."

"At least the city is still having fireworks tomorrow night," Heather noted. "A lot of places have canceled them."

"Yeah, it's like, stay home and be vigilant," Nicole said. "As if I wasn't already a mental case before all this happened, now I've got to be on the lookout for terrorists."

"Ha! Well, I think we should go make sure that Jose's is safe from terrorists. Keep your eyes peeled," Heather said peering wide-eyed over the roof of a car.

"There's a Pekinese at the end of the block that I've got my suspicions about," Nicole said. "Nasty little thing."

"Yes, small dogs are very un-American. What's wrong with a nice Labrador? Have you ever seen the dog's owner?"

"Yes," Nicole admitted. "It's this little, white-haired old lady that frankly isn't much more friendly than the dog. She doesn't quite fit the profile."

"Fit the profile!" Heather exclaimed. "I'm shocked. I can't believe you would stoop to profiling. The woman's either suspicious or she's not. Don't let her hair color fool you. It could be dyed. She could be wearing a disguise. You never know. You should definitely call the tip line."

"Yeah, I'll get right on that," Nicole said. She grimaced uncomfortably as thoughts of the report she filed on Nasim popped into her head.

Heather continued to be ridiculous. What did that squirrel have in its mouth, and why did it run away when she ordered it to stop? Are those birds trying to break that electrical wire by weighing it down? Nicole couldn't help but laugh.

"Geez, I hope they're open," Nicole whined as Jose's came into view.

"They should be," Nicole said. "It's just about happy hour."

Nicole and Heather walked through the sparsely filled parking lot and entered the restaurant. "*Buenos dias*," a waitress called. "Two?"

"Yes," Nicole and Heather said in unison. The waitress led them to a booth.

"Can I get you started with anything?"

"Two margaritas," Heather chimed in.

"Geez, what's your hurry?" Nicole asked.

"Ohhhh, you're right," Heather said with wide eyes. "You've got a phone call or two to make first."

"That's not what I meant."

"So, what's the deal with your ex-boyfriend anyway? He just leaves you to empty out his apartment, or is that going to be a surprise?"

"He . . . he just left me a letter and disappeared. Chinese takeout sitting on the kitchen table. It was kind of weird," Nicole answered apprehensively.

"And you haven't heard from him since?"

"Nope," Nicole said, shaking her head.

"How long ago was that?" Heather asked.

"About a month ago."

Heather frowned. "I'm sorry."

"Soooo, the lease on the apartment was up. It just felt wrong leaving everything there."

"If you don't want to call those numbers," Heather said.

"No, I do. It would be nice to have a bit more closure. I'd probably chicken out if I was by myself." Before she had a chance to change her mind, Nicole pulled the list from her back pocket and got out her cell phone.

"Uh, are you sure you don't want some privacy?" Heather asked.

"No, you're fine."

After a moment, Nicole spoke into her phone. "Hi! This is Nicole. If, uh, if this is Nasim, please give me a call back."

"So?" Heather asked.

"It rang a few times and then went to a generic voice mail message," Nicole answered as she set her phone down.

"Well, that was a very calm and measured message," Heather reassured her. "Not that I was listening."

"Thanks," Nicole said with a roll of her eyes. She reached inside her purse and pulled out a pen.

"Here you go," the waitress interrupted, as she set two margaritas down on the table.

"Thanks," Heather said.

"One down, eleven to go," Nicole said as she drew a line through the first number on the list. "Cheers!" she said, holding up her glass.

"Cheers!" Heather echoed.

Chapter 54: July Third

Looking in the bathroom mirror, Nasim barely recognized himself. He'd been on the road for the past month, sleeping in his van, never staying at the same place twice. Crisscrossing the southwestern United States, he'd planted explosive devices here and there as he went. The devices all had cell phone triggers, and Nasim had a ragged sheet of paper in his back pocket that outlined all the numbers. So far, he'd concentrated on small targets, but on the eve of July 4th, it was time to pull out all the stops.

Nasim turned away from the mirror and dried his hands and face with some paper towels. A voice called out to him.

"These checkpoints are something else, aren't they?" a large man wearing leather biking chaps said in a hearty voice.

"Yeah, I guess," Nasim replied.

"It must be tough on you," the man continued. "You're Arab, aren't you?"

"Palestinian," Nasim answered uncomfortably, "but it's something I've dealt with my whole life, so it's not really that big of a deal."

"Your whole life?" the man bellowed.

"My family lived in the West Bank, so we had to deal with Israeli checkpoints on a regular basis," Nasim replied as he edged closer to the exit.

"Well, it's a pain in the ass if you ask me," the man said, as he wiped his hands dry on his T-shirt.

"Yeah," Nasim agreed, breaking into a smile.

In just a couple of strides, the man had caught up to Nasim. "Keep the rubber on the road," the biker said, while slapping Nasim on the back.

"You too," Nasim replied, trudging out to his van. It was eight-thirty at night. The fluorescent lights, which brightened this rundown gas station just outside of Pueblo, Colorado, hummed unevenly. The sun had set, but the air was still hot and dry. Nasim's mind churned nervously as he climbed behind the wheel.

After leaving Nicole, Nasim spent the night alone in his van at a rest stop just outside of Austin, Texas. There, armed with nothing more than a pencil and a spiral notebook, he developed a target list. In his head, he checked off all the equipment he would need. After creating code names for all the targets, he assigned a cell phone to each one. It had been the first of many long nights.

Nasim pulled out the worn list. "Just three more," he said to himself. "Pablo, Spring, and Cici."

Nasim's final three targets included an electrical substation outside of Pueblo, high voltage lines near Colorado Springs, and a Commerce City substation just north of Denver. The forecast for the Fourth of July called for temperatures in the upper 90s. The heat would act as a multiplier, intensifying the effects of the blasts.

"That's provided I get the damn things set up. I've got to be off the roads by one-thirty to avoid the driving curfew," Nasim said anxiously. It was doable, provided there were no surprises.

#

The Pueblo electrical substation was enclosed by a chain-link fence. You'd think it was nothing more than a school playground. Nasim stopped the van in the shadows of a nearby building and turned off the engine. He grabbed a pair of wire cutters from the glove box and got out of the van.

Cautiously, he walked up to the edge of the fence. The one streetlight illuminating the substation was on the corner opposite his position. Starting chest high, he began cutting the fence wires along the edge of the pole. He worked quickly, occasionally glancing up for signs of movement. When he reached the bottom, he pushed the fencing inward. Satisfied, he crept back to the van and opened the side door.

Inside the van, Nasim pulled away a blue tarp to reveal four thirty-gallon plastic drums. Each drum was painted a pale gray and had high-voltage warnings displayed on it. Opposite the warning label, a cell phone was attached to the drum. Wires ran from the phone into a small hole drilled at the top of the drum. Inside was a mixture of fertilizer, gasoline, roofing nails, and three-quarter-inch steel ball bearings. To trigger the explosion, Nasim was utilizing a model rocket launch set he'd modified.

Nasim pulled out a drum dolly and set it on the pavement, then jumped back inside and pushed one of the heavy drums to the edge of the doorway. Breathing heavily, he peeked out and scanned the alley. The coast was clear. He hopped down out of the van and positioned the dolly in front of the van door.

"All right, just guide it down," Nasim said as he hugged the lower-half of the drum with his arms. Slowly, he inched the drum to the edge of the van. He could hear the gasoline sloshing around inside the drum. "Ready, set, go!"

Nasim grimaced as he lowered the drum down to the dolly. It landed harder than he had wanted, and the dolly tipped up and hit him in the shine. "Fuck!" he cursed. With pain still etched on his face, he twisted the drum into place. "I filled these damn things too full," he said angrily.

Hobbling, Nasim grabbed the dolly handle and pulled the drum toward the fence opening. He pushed the fencing in and pulled the drum through. The fencing fell back noisily against the fence pole, but there was nothing he could do about it. There was no turning back now. He had to get the damn thing in place and get the hell out of there.

With sweat pouring down his face, Nasim pulled the dolly over the gravel-covered ground to the concrete pad that supported the main transformer. His lungs burned from the altitude, but this was no time to rest. Struggling, he lifted the dolly over the concrete lip of the pad, then moved the drum into place between the current transformer and the main transformer.

After sliding the drum off the dolly, he rotated it so that the high voltage warning faced outward. Next, Nasim crouched next to the drum. Carefully, he detached the wires leading from the cell phone into the drum.

"With my luck some random text message would set off the whole damn thing," Nasim said as he powered up the cell phone. "Hurry up! Any day now," he whispered. After the cell phone completed its initial cycle, Nasim nervously glanced at the street. A pair of headlights was coming.

"Crap!" Nasim said as he crouched behind the drum. Listening intently, Nasim held his breath. At first, he could barely hear the hum of the car's engine, but as it got closer, he could hear the car's wheels rolling against the pavement. Soon, the sound faded. With one eye, Nasim peered around the edge of the drum.

"Finish up, and get the fuck out of here," he scolded himself.

Nasim faced the cell phone display. The battery was fully charged, and it was getting a good signal. Now, it was time to hook it back up. His hands shaking, it took Nasim a couple of tries to reconnect the wires. He scurried back to the van, closed the sliding door, and jumped into the driver's seat.

"One down, two to go," he said under his breath.

#

Nasim drove anxiously down the highway. Several times, he'd caught himself doing eighty-five miles per hour. Subconsciously, he was rushing. For the first time since he'd set out from Austin, he felt exposed. When the exit for his next target arrived, Nasim let out a sigh of relief as he guided the van down the exit ramp.

Looking down the lonely country road, Nasim gave himself a pep talk. "There's nothing to be afraid of. It's a rural target. Mom and Dad are counting on me. I can't let them down."

With that, Nasim turned east away from the mountains. Soon the pavement turned to gravel. The van's headlights stretched forward, but little seemed to change. The gravel and brush that he'd passed a mile ago was indistinguishable from what he was looking at now. Nasim turned on his high beams.

"Did I miss the turn-off?" he mumbled while looking at the odometer. "Calm down. You've only gone three miles. The turnoff is six miles from the interstate. Be patient!"

Finally, Nasim spotted the turnoff. He turned from one gravel road onto an even narrower one. As the van bounced along the rutted road, he could hear the drums in back sloshing noisily. He slowed his pace and considered dimming the van's lights, but then it'd be impossible to see.

"Don't worry," he told himself as he watched the van's headlights bounce up and down in front of him. "Nobody's out here but you. Get these two drums placed, and then on to Commerce City."

However, in the back of his mind, a question still nagged at him. *What then? I'll go through the call list, set everything off, but what then? I can't stay in the United States. I'd always be looking over my shoulder. At some point, they'll put all the pieces together. But if I return home, I'll be under the PEF's thumb. Anytime they need something, they'll threaten my parents. Disappear? Where would I go?*

With the high voltage power lines in sight, Nasim cleared his mind. Coming to an intersection, he guided the van to the left and followed a new set of ruts along the power lines. He forced himself to drive past the first couple of towers. The likelihood of the device being found would be greater if he set it up right at the intersection. After driving past a couple more, he stopped the van right next to one of the four-legged towers and dimmed the van's lights.

Once again, he slid open the side door, got out the drum dolly, and pushed one of the three remaining drums over to the edge. At least this time the drum didn't crash to the ground. The tower's metal leg was only ten feet away. Slowly, he pulled the drum toward the tower, but one of the dolly's wheels hit a rock and almost tipped over. After kicking the rock out of the way, he dragged the drum into position.

Breathing heavily, Nasim wanted to rest, but there was no time. His legs heavy, he trudged back to the van for the second drum. The more he hurried, the slower time seemed to pass. If he didn't get moving, he'd run the risk of being caught with that final drum at a checkpoint.

It was a struggle, but he finally got the second drum into place. Next, he went to work setting up the trigger, unwinding the lead wires from the drums. In this case, both drums would be tied to the same cell phone trigger.

Once again, he turned the cell phone on before attaching the leads. It was barely getting a signal. He held the cell phone up higher. After a moment or two, it showed two bars. Hastily, Nasim set the phone down, ran back to the van, and grabbed a roll of duct tape. Upon returning, he attached the lead wires to the phone, reached up, and taped the cell phone to the tower's leg. The wires were taut, but it'd have to do.

Shoulders slumping, Nasim hiked back to the van and prepared to leave. After starting the van, he looked at the dashboard clock. It was already eleven o'clock. He was cutting it awful close. With new-found urgency, he threw the van into reverse, turned around, and guided the van forward.

Nearing the access road that lead away from the power lines, the van hit a bump. The final drum banged against the side of the van.

"Damn it! If that drum tips over, I'll never get it cleaned up," Nasim griped. Apprehensively, he glanced in the rear view mirror. Out of the darkness, a bright fireball appeared. Reflexively, Nasim stopped. "What the fuck?"

Breaking out in a cold sweat, Nasim lurched the van forward. The van's wheels kicked up a cloud of dust as the remaining drum slid perilously back and forth. Driving frantically away from the power lines, Nasim didn't know what to think.

Fuck me! What the hell? I don't know what triggered the explosion, but I'm not sticking around to find out!

Chapter 55: Unexpected Trip

Dressed in shorts and a T-shirt, Siraj sat at the kitchen table eating breakfast. Suddenly, there was loud knock on the front door. He ignored it, hoping his Mom would get it. The knock came again. "Crap! Where is she?" Siraj exclaimed, as he plodded to the door. "Mom?"

Siraj opened the door to reveal two men dressed in police uniforms. One was stockily built while the other was tall and thin. They were dressed in dark gray shirts and pants with black berets. "Siraj Raahil?" the thin officer asked.

Siraj's heart sank. "Yes?" he replied.

"Do you know Tahir Rafiq?" the policeman continued.

"Uh? Yes, we attended the university together," Siraj answered. "Is something wrong?"

"There was an accident at his office complex," the officer replied.

"What? What kind of accident?" Siraj replied with concern.

"I'm sorry, but he was killed in an explosion."

"I can't believe it," Siraj said as he leaned his head against the door frame. "He's dead?"

"Yes, I'm afraid so. We've been having trouble contacting his family. We were wondering if you could help answer a couple of questions for us."

"Sure," Siraj said motioning the officers inside.

"Would you mind coming down to the station with us? It'll only take a few minutes."

"Oh! Okay," Siraj nodded. "I'll get dressed."

After getting dressed, Siraj followed the two officers out to their patrol car. As they pulled away from the curb, Siraj stared at the floor, lost in thought. He wasn't really paying attention to where they were going. Before he knew it, they were speeding down the freeway near the outskirts of Dhahran.

"Is it much farther?" Siraj asked, finally noticing how far they'd gone.

"No," the officer driving replied.

They turned off the highway. Up ahead, Siraj saw a large, walled compound that contained several nondescript buildings. It was the Amin detention center. Siraj's stomach tightened, and he began to feel dizzy. "What are we doing here?" Siraj asked with alarm.

"Like we said. We just need to ask you a few questions."

Siraj looked down at his feet. He was afraid that he might throw up right there. You could see the buildings from the highway. He remembered asking his father about them as a child. "It's nothing," his father had responded, but when he grew older, Siraj heard stories about the small compound.

After it had been abandoned by the *Bedouins* decades ago, it had been turned into a detention center. It was a place for foreign laborers awaiting deportation, a place for political dissidents, a place for criminals awaiting sentencing. It was not a place for him.

"I thought you said that Tahir's death was an accident?" Siraj said. The officers did not respond.

As they approached the entry gate, the officer driving honked the horn. The gate guard looked up lazily from his mud brick post and opened the gate. Then he stood up, hoisted his rifle over his shoulder, and walked out to meet the car. After consulting with the driver, he took something from the driver's hand and waved them through. Siraj looked back fearfully as the gate closed behind them.

Siraj sat anxiously as they drove to the rear of the compound and parked next to a small, windowless adobe building. The officer on the passenger side got out and walked around to Siraj's door. He opened it and motioned for Siraj to get out.

Tentatively, Siraj stepped forward. When he was half way out, the officer grabbed him by the neck and pushed him face-first into the dirt. The officer knelt on Siraj's back and roughly applied handcuffs. "We know Tahir's death was no accident," the officer rasped. "It's time to wake up and quit telling lies."

The officers each grabbed one of Siraj's arms and started dragging him toward the building. Siraj tried in vain to get to his feet, but they were pulling him too fast. He couldn't catch his balance. The door to the building was propped open, and Siraj could see a trail of dried blood on the concrete floor as they pulled him inside and set him down on a metal chair. While one officer went to close the door, the other pulled off Siraj's sandals and shackled his legs.

In front of him sat a small, gray metal table. It was empty except for a pen and a fully typed sheet of paper. As Siraj cowered in his chair, the two officers circled. "So, why did you kill Tahir Rafiq?"

"What? I . . . I didn't!"

As soon as the words were out of his mouth, Siraj found himself being hurtled off the chair. "On your knees liar," they yelled. "On your knees!"

Siraj struggled to right himself, but with his hands handcuffed, he couldn't do it. The stocky officer roughly yanked him into a kneeling position. "Let's try this again," the thin one seethed. "Why did you kill Tahir Rafiq?"

"I don't know what you're talking about," Siraj answered.

Whack! Something came down hard against the soles of his feet. Siraj writhed in pain. Out of the corner of his eye he could see the stocky officer dragging a cane pole against the concrete. The officer scraped it menacingly on the floor as he passed in front of Siraj.

"Wha . . . what makes you think I killed Tahir?" Siraj asked desperately.

Whack! The sound of the pole finding its mark once again echoed throughout the room along with Siraj's painful gasps. "We ask the questions here," the stocky one bellowed.

"It's a fair question," the skinny officer said. He bent over and looked into Siraj's face. "Perhaps, our friend just has a bad memory. We found that note of yours at Tahir's apartment."

"What note?" Siraj asked incredulously.

"You and Tahir were very good friends. Lovers?" the stocky officer rasped as he tapped Siraj on the behind with the cane pole. "Which head do you think they'll cut off first?" he asked rhetorically as he moved the pole up alongside Siraj's neck.

"That's bullshit," Siraj retorted, but his response elicited another hit from the cane.

"If I can't have you, no one will," his interrogator wailed sarcastically in an effeminate voice. "You don't remember writing that?"

"No!" Siraj yelled.

Whack!

"Aghh, no. It wasn't like that!"

Whack!

"I didn't do it!"

Whack! The cane snapped down hard across the soles of his feet again and again.

"Stop lying to us!" the thin officer railed. "We know you were in a relationship with Tahir, and when he tried to break it off, you put a bomb in his backpack. It's all right here," he said, waving a piece of paper in front of Siraj's face. "Are you ready to sign your confession?" he yelled, slamming the piece of paper down on the table.

"No!"

Whack!

Exhausted, Siraj toppled over on his side, writhing in pain. With tears streaming down his face, he gritted his teeth and tried to think of anything he could say that would dissuade them. "Mmm . . . my father, he . . . he works for a prominent member of Shura Council."

"Ha, and you think he'll want to help you? His faggot son!"

"Aghhh!" Siraj screamed. "That's a lie! I'm being set up! This is bullshit. I never wrote any note, and I didn't kill Tahir!"

Suddenly, there was a knock on the door. The two officers walked over to the door, opened it, and in stepped another officer. Siraj struggled to see, but from his vantage point it was difficult. Finally, he caught a glimpse of the man. Although he was dressed in the same uniform as Siraj's interrogators, this man was older. He spoke in hushed tones. Siraj couldn't make out what he was saying, but he seemed to be rebuking the young officers.

"Get out!" the older officer ordered loudly. He walked over to Siraj and helped him up into a sitting position. "I can't take these cuffs off," he said softy, "but I can make you more comfortable." This new officer let Siraj reposition his hands in front of him before reapplying the handcuffs. Then he picked up the chair off the floor, and motioned for Siraj to sit down.

"Thank you," Siraj acknowledged.

"I know your father," the officer admitted. "I know in my heart that these allegations against you are false, but . . . "

"But what?" Siraj asked with confusion.

"Those goons aren't lying about the note. They found it in Tahir's apartment after the explosion."

"What explosion? I don't know anything about this," Siraj pleaded.

"Tahir was your friend, right? Did he ever indicate that something was wrong? Was he having financial problems? Who would have done something like this to him?"

Siraj's thoughts turned to Professor Ratib, but the professor would never have done something like this. Then, Siraj thought of the man he'd met at the mosque. The one he gave the Prince Bahir footage to. Siraj looked down at the floor, unsure of what to do or say.

"There is something," the officer prodded. "I can see it in your eyes. Help me, help you."

"I don't know," Siraj stammered.

"Know what?"

"I don't know what to do."

"Tell me what you know, so that I can rip this up," the officer said holding up the confession. "Your fate is not written yet. Your family never needs to know anything about this, but you need to help us find Tahir's killer."

"I don't know for sure, but there was this guy," Siraj admitted reluctantly.

"What was his name?"

"Husam," Siraj answered.

"Do you know his full name?"

"No," Siraj said shaking his head.

"Okay, and how did Tahir come to know this fellow?" the officer asked.

"Uh, well . . . " Siraj hemmed and hawed.

"Hey, wake up!" the officer yelled as he slammed his fist down on the table, but suddenly he backed off. "I'm on your side, but you need to give me something. My superiors will not be satisfied with just a name. You need to tell me the whole story, or they'll send your friends back in here. Is that what you want?"

"No, but it . . . it's complicated," Siraj said.

"The truth is never complicated. What's complicated are the lies you tell yourself. The longer you keep stalling, the less I'll be able to help you."

Siraj swallowed hard. "Okay, okay. Umm . . . Several months ago, our . . . our professor from college came to us, and . . . Well, he said the time had come for us to fight against the corrupt Western influences that had invaded our country. "

"The professor's name?"

"Professor Mahmud Ratib," Siraj answered weakly.

"Go on," his interrogator encouraged.

"He gave each of us an envelope that contained our job, or rather, our mission," Siraj continued uncomfortably.

"And what was Tahir's mission?"

"I don't know. He worked for the Persian Gulf Oil and Refining Company. When I heard about the refinery fire a while back, I kind of wondered, but I didn't know for sure."

"Tahir didn't have the knowledge and expertise to do something like that," the interrogator said.

"No, but . . . but the professor eventually introduced us to people who had those types of skills. I'm pretty sure Husam had military experience.

"Aghh, this is all very interesting, but it still sounds like you're guessing." the interrogator said. "I need facts, not supposition. What was your mission?"

"Well, I'm an amateur cinematographer. I helped put together videos," Siraj said.

"Videos? What kind of videos?"

As he looked at his interrogator, it suddenly dawned on Siraj that nothing had really changed since the previous interrogators had left.

"What videos?" his captor implored.

353

Exhausted, Siraj broke down into tears. Covering his face with his hands, he knew what was coming.

"I'm sorry, Siraj," his interrogator said with fake empathy. "This just doesn't add up."

Suddenly, the metal door burst open. Siraj didn't even need to look. The original interrogators had returned, and they were full of new insults.

"What lies is he telling now?" the skinny officer sneered. "What is he? A terrorist, a faggot, or both?"

"I say both," his companion answered as he pushed Siraj to the floor once again. "On your knees!" he screamed. *Whack!* The sound of the cane contacting the soles of Siraj's feet echoed throughout the room once again. *Whack!*

As Siraj knelt cringing on the floor, the large metal door closed with a resounding thud. *Whack!*

Chapter 56: Final Target

Driving along highway I-25, Nasim was a nervous wreck. Several times he considered turning off the highway and dumping the final drum, but something always changed his mind. He'd see another car, or the area looked too populated, so he pushed on.

"It's going to take time to investigate the outage," he reassured himself, but an exploding headache made it hard to think. Every set of headlights was a potential threat, every noise from the back of the van was a critical problem with the device, and every groan of the engine signaled trouble with the van.

Nasim rolled down the window for some fresh air, but the hot, dry gusts made him feel sick to his stomach. Dejected, he closed the window and turned the air-conditioning on full blast. Nothing seemed to help. His head hurt, and his mind rambled.

How many devices have gone off? I was going to set them off tomorrow, but now, the timing's all wrong. The van's a mess. Will I have time to clean everything up? What if the explosion triggers new checkpoints?

It was becoming too much for Nasim to handle. His head was pounding, and his stomach was churning. The van's headlights seemed dim. Nasim crouched over the steering wheel, as if having his eyes a couple of extra inches closer to the road would make all the difference.

In addition to fighting nausea, Nasim was now having trouble staying awake. He started counting down the mile markers to his exit, but he kept losing track. When the Denver city lights finally came into view, Nasim was filled with a mix of relief and dread. Nasim took a bleary-eyed glance at the time. It wasn't quite midnight.

"I can make it. Everything's going to be fine," he whispered, but even as he said it, he didn't really believe it. His heart ached anxiously. Even if he got the last device planted, what would he do then? Where would he go? He was out of targets and out of ideas. The target list was all he'd been focused on for the past month. Without it he'd be lost.

Time crawled. The first time he'd driven through Denver, Nasim had marveled at Mile High Stadium, at the mountains, and at the city. Everything was bigger than he'd imagined. On this night, however, the city seemed like a dark, never-ending tunnel. The mountains faded into the darkness, and he didn't even notice the stadium when he drove past.

"Almost there!" He was less than ten miles from his exit. More anxious than ever, his heart beat rapidly, he shifted uncomfortably in his seat, and his breathing was shallow and fast. To calm his nerves, Nasim turned on the CD player. But as the music started, he remembered why he'd turned it off in the first place.

"Crap!" Nasim grumbled. "It's that mix Nicole put together for our trip to Yellowstone." Quickly, he turned it off. "Isn't there anything else I can put in?" he said, picking through the clutter on the seat next to him. Frustrated, he gave up. Nasim felt tears welling up in his eyes, but he swallowed hard and fought them off.

It's not the life I was meant to live. It's nobody's fault. Not mine, not Nicole's. What chance does anyone have when they're born into conflict and war? It messes with your head and rips you up inside. Americans just don't know how good they've got it. Just to be born here is a blessing.

The sight of the exit helped him switch off his brain. "This is it," his dry throat rasped.

He'd gone over the route to the target so many times in his head. Right, at the top of the exit, then left at the light, straight for two-and-a-half blocks, and then a right down the alley.

Slowly, he steered the van toward the target. It was just past midnight. If he could finish up in thirty minutes or so, he'd just drive until curfew, pull off, and get some sleep. He'd worry about cleaning up the van in the morning. It would all work out.

Turning down the alley, Nasim misjudged the distance between the van and a nearby trash bin. The sound of the metal scrapping along the side of the van sickened him, but he just kept driving. With the target in sight, he stopped the van in the shadows.

Exiting the van, he stood up too fast and was overcome by nausea. Falling to one knee, he threw up. Shaking, he staggered over to the side door, opened it, and crawled inside, stopping to rest next to the drum.

"I'm never going to get this thing out," he said, feeling defeated. Then he spotted a two-by-four lying on the ground in the alley. "Maybe I can slide it down the board."

It was worth a try. Better than letting it fall to the ground. He was too beat to lift it. Nasim trudged over, picked up the board, and leaned it against the van's running board. He crept inside the van and pushed the drum over to the opening.

"Why is it still so damn hot?" he said, while attempting to catch his breath. He was all out of sweat. Panting listlessly by the doorway, he willed himself on. He could rest later. Grabbing the drum around the middle, he slid it halfway over the edge.

"Just ease it down on the board," he said.

Grunting, Nasim pulled the drum out of the van and lowered it heavily onto the board. The board creaked, and he almost passed out. Nonetheless, with the help of the board he was able to skid the drum down to the ground, then stumbled back to the van to grab the dolly. After sliding the drum onto the dolly, he dragged it unsteadily toward the chain-link fence that enclosed the substation.

"Damn, I forgot the wire cutters," he said, looking longingly back at the van. He started back, but stopped short and felt for the wire cutters in his pocket. "Oh, yeah. There they are."

Starting about four feet up, Nasim cut an opening in the fence. Briefly, he looked at the nearby street, but he was too tired to worry about getting caught. His hands ached as he struggled with the wire cutters. By the time he reached the bottom of the fence, he was using two hands to cut through the wire.

Once the final link was cut, he leaned his weight against the fence to bend it back. The fencing gave way more quickly than he anticipated, and he tumbled to the ground. Unsteadily, with his elbow scraped and bleeding, he crawled back for the drum. As he pulled the dolly through the opening, the fencing caught his pant leg. He pulled free, but the fencing ripped through his pants and cut his calf.

Near tears again, Nasim pulled the dolly forward in spurts to the substation's transformer. Upon reaching it, he turned the dolly upright, and sat on the ground with his back to the drum. He reached over his shoulder for the cell phone trigger, disconnected the wires, and turned on the phone.

He nearly jumped out of this skin when the cell phone rang. His face pale, he looked at the number that was calling. It was Nicole.

"Oh no," he said. "What is she doing?"

The phone continued to ring. Its ring-tone cut through the silence like a car alarm. If for no other reason than to stop the noise, Nasim finally answered it.

"Hello," he answered weakly.

"Nasim?" Nicole asked hesitantly.

"Nicole. Where did you get this number? Why are you calling?"

"The lease on the apartment was up. I found this list of phone numbers when I was moving everything into storage," she answered.

"Oh no. Please tell me you didn't. Have you been calling the numbers on the list?" Nasim asked with tears in his eyes.

"This was the last one," she responded. It sounded like she was crying too. "Nasim, what's wrong? Why did you leave?"

"Get rid of the list! Forget you ever met me," he cried into the phone. "I never wanted to get you into trouble. I never wanted to hurt you. That's why I left."

"Please Nasim, just tell me what's going on. Maybe I can help. Whatever it is, we can work it out."

"Ha," Nasim laughed nervously. "It's too late now. I never meant for you to be involved. I thought that I could escape it, but there's only one way."

"Only one way to what?" Nicole asked. "Calm down."

"I love you. I . . . I really do, but . . . "

"But what?"

"I can't talk right now. I'll call you back in the morning," Nasim lied.

"Nasim wait!" Nicole pleaded.

Abruptly, Nasim ended the call. Feverishly, he worked to reconnect the wires to the cell phone. Glancing around nervously, he saw a utility van pulling up to the substation.

"Stay in the fucking van," Nasim said. "Please, just stay away," he pleaded, but the electrical worker got out of the van and called to him.

"Hey! You're not supposed to be in there," the man yelled.

"Leave me alone!" Nasim shouted with all his remaining strength. "I don't want to hurt you. Get back in the van."

"This is private property," the man said as he opened the entry gate. "You need to get the hell out of there."

"I'm going to blow this place up," Nasim shouted. "It's ready to explode," Nasim warned as he twisted the wires together.

Suddenly, it dawned on the man what was happening. With the entry gate halfway open, he froze. "No! Ho . . . hold on a second," he said. "Y . . . you don't want to do this."

"It's too late for that," Nasim whispered. With tears running down his face, he looked down at the phone as it lit up. Nicole was calling back. Nasim smiled and closed his eyes.

Chapter 57: The Bakery

Grimacing, Al-Faruq limped slowly toward the mosque. His leg was still far from a hundred percent. "Aghhh, I don't know what I'm doing here anyway," he said. "Like I'm really going to find any answers. I haven't attended daily prayers in ages. Who am I kidding?"

It had been a week since Al-Faruq followed Professor Ratib and his captor into the slums. After spending two days laid up in the hospital, he made his official report, but it was too late. By the time he got back to the scene, everything had been cleaned up—no bodies, no blood, no witnesses, no nothing. If he hadn't gotten shot, there'd be no evidence anything happened at all. To top it off, Chief Hamal put Al-Faruq on administrative leave.

"With my luck, I'll be out of a job," Al-Faruq grumbled. Without a job, there was no way he could pursue a lasting relationship with Kalila.

Why couldn't I just leave well enough alone? The Chief told me to drop it, and that's exactly what I should have done. There's no point in being right if no one gives a damn.

Up ahead, Al-Faruq saw a man exiting the mosque. The detective stopped dead in his tracks, as if he'd seen a ghost. It was Professor Ratib. "You've got to be kidding me," Al-Faruq said incredulously. "He's still alive?"

However, as the professor walked closer to him, something seemed strange. While Professor Ratib was a thin man, his build seemed stockier. His *thobe* was tight around his waist, and his posture looked stiff and awkward. Al-Faruq watched the professor closely as he hurried past, but Professor Ratib took little notice. His eyes looked angry and glazed over.

Al-Faruq tried to ignore him. Chief Hamal had given him strict orders. The case was closed, but seeing the professor made the hairs on the back of Al-Faruq's neck stand on end. Something in the professor's eyes reminded Al-Faruq of a suicide bomber he'd encountered during his army days. He'd never forgotten the look on the bomber's face. It was the same strange look Professor Ratib had on his face now, fierce and determined, yet unhinged.

Where are you headed off to in such a hurry? Al-Faruq stopped, pivoted, and watched the professor head to the parking lot. *Allah help me! Orders or no orders, I can't pretend I didn't see anything. If I'm wrong, following him won't hurt anything. If I'm right, a lot of people could get hurt. Dammit, he's getting away!* Wincing, he urged on his injured leg and took off after the professor.

Al-Faruq quickened his pace. The professor had reached his car. Al-Faruq watched intently as Professor Ratib cautiously slid behind the driver's seat and closed the car door. With the professor facing him, Al-Faruq slowed his pace so as not to attract undue attention, but the professor seemed to be looking past Al-Faruq as if he wasn't even there. Al-Faruq fumbled for his keys while trying to keep one eye on Professor Ratib's car. The professor's car inched forward.

"That's it. Nice and slow," Al-Faruq said as he hobbled to his car. After flinging open the car door, Al-Faruq struggled to get his injured leg into his car. The professor's vehicle would soon be out of site. "Damn leg. Aghhh!" Sweating, his leg throbbing, Al-Faruq started the car and zoomed off in pursuit of his quarry. "I see you. Get back here!"

Exiting the mosque parking lot, Al-Faruq was several car lengths behind the professor. Al-Faruq sped up to close the gap. At this point, he was more worried about losing the professor than alerting him to his presence. He glanced in the rear view mirror. There were only a couple of cars behind him, a light-colored pickup and a black sedan.

"I've gotta get closer, or I'll lose him at one of these damn lights," Al-Faruq grumbled. "Stay green, stay green," he pleaded as he pushed the accelerator down to the floor. "Aghh, just a little pink. I've still got him."

Al-Faruq looked down at his police radio wondering if he should call for backup. *Damned if I do, damned if I don't. What if I'm over-reacting? If I call for backup and it turns out to be nothing, the Chief will kick my ass out on the street. But if I'm right? If I'm right, how much is backup going to help? At the press of a button, everything could all go to hell. For that matter, what am I going to do? Gun him down?*

Al-Faruq had closed the distance between his and the professor's cars, and he was now only a few car lengths behind. *Looks like he's heading for the shopping district, but what's his target?*

On the outskirts of the shopping district, the professor's car pulled into a bakery parking lot. Al-Faruq parked across the street and kept his eyes peeled. Looking through the bakery's glass facade, Al-Faruq saw a handful of people standing in line. Outside, a disheveled foreign businessman wearing slacks and a buttoned-down shirt sat reading a paper. There were only a couple of cars. Then, Al-Faruq did a double take.

Isn't that Kalila's father's car? What's he doing here? The car's empty. Damn! He must be inside the bakery.

Weaving between traffic, Al-Faruq limped across the street. Professor Ratib was still sitting in his car. Nearing the bakery, the businessman lowered his paper and looked straight at the professor's car. Al-Faruq watched as the man's eyes switched from the professor to himself and back.

"What the hell?" Al-Faruq mumbled. He watched the man put down his paper and pick up his cell phone. "If you're here to meet the professor, I'm afraid he has a surprise for you."

Al-Faruq pushed toward the bakery entrance. Inside he could see Kalila's father standing in line along with a couple of other bakery patrons. Out the corner of his eye, he saw Professor Ratib's car door open. Al-Faruq quickened his pace and rushed inside.

"Detective Al-Faruq, SAID. You got a backdoor to this place?" he said tersely as he flashed his badge at the man working behind the counter.

"Ah . . . "

"Do you have a backdoor?" Al-Faruq asked again as he looked back at the parking lot. Professor Ratib was walking stiltedly toward the bakery. He was about twenty feet from the entrance.

"Y . . . Yes," the man stammered.

"Lead everyone out the back."

"But I . . . "

"Now!" Al-Faruq yelled as he pulled out his gun and waved it at the baker.

That got everyone's attention, and they quickly moved through the door marked employees only. Hiding his gun behind his back, Al-Faruq turned and trained his eyes on Professor Ratib. Although the professor was looking in Al-Faruq's direction, his facial expression showed no recognition that anything was amiss.

As he slid behind the bakery counter, Al-Faruq quickly looked for the foreign businessman. The man was talking animatedly on his cell phone. Al-Faruq tried to get the man's attention, but his back was turned. Walking stiffly, Professor Ratib entered the bakery. Al-Faruq had run out of time.

"I'll be with you in a minute," Al-Faruq offered, but the professor ignored him and immediately sat down near the window directly opposite the foreign businessman. "I've got to go in the back for a minute," Al-Faruq said a little more loudly, but once again the professor took little notice. The professor's eyes were fixed on the man outside. They were barely three feet apart, separated by a single pane of glass.

Al-Faruq rushed through the bakery's kitchen toward the rear exit. Upon opening the backdoor, Al-Faruq quickly surveyed the nervous group huddled behind the building. Kalila's father wasn't there. "Where's the other gentleman?" he asked angrily. Everyone shrugged their shoulders except the baker, whose eyes darted nervously to the right.

"Get behind that delivery truck over there," Al-Faruq ordered as he went to track down Mr. Mawiyah. "I don't want anyone else leaving."

Al-Faruq moved quickly to the edge of the bakery and peered around the corner. He saw Mr. Mawiyah making his way back to his car. Al-Faruq's adrenaline kicked in, and he ran after Kalila's father, barely noticing his injured leg.

"Mr. Mawiyah, stop!" Al-Faruq called out.

Mr. Mawiyah froze and looked back with a puzzled expression. "How do you know my name?"

"There'll be time to explain all of that later," Al-Faruq insisted. He grabbed Mr. Mawiyah by the elbow and led him back to the rear of the bakery. "Come on, hurry!" Al-Faruq implored.

As they retreated, Al-Faruq looked back at the front of the building. Across the street, parked right in front of his car was a black Mercedes, and standing behind it with a fiendish grin was Husam Asad.

"Run!" Al-Faruq said with alarm. He shoved Mr. Mawiyah toward the back of the bakery and trained his weapon on Husam, but it was too late.

An explosion ripped apart the bakery, knocking Al-Faruq to the ground. Stunned and disoriented, Al-Faruq struggled to regain his senses. The blast knocked the gun from his hand. Crawling on his hands and knees, he frantically searched for his weapon. Finding it, he crouched unsteadily with his gun at the ready.

Wild-eyed, Al-Faruq searched for Husam through the clouds of dust and smoke. The corner of the building where Professor Ratib had been sitting was demolished. The table where the foreigner had been sitting was now lying in a gnarled metal heap in the street.

Through the haze, Al-Faruq saw Husam approaching. Al-Faruq let two shots fly, but he couldn't be sure if they reached their intended target. The more his eyes tried to sift through the mayhem in front of him, the dizzier he became. Coughing and dazed, Al-Faruq slowly crumbled to the ground. As his head fell back, he looked skyward.

"Mr. Mawiyah? Mr. Mawiyah? Are you okay?" he asked weakly. Straining, he turned to look for Kalila's father, but his head felt like it weighed a ton. With his body plastered against the concrete, all he could see was sky. "I'm sorry Kalila. I'm so sorry," he mumbled, as the sound of car alarms mixed with sirens. The sounds faded in and out. It was like his brain was having trouble finding the right radio station.

"There are two more over here," Al-Faruq heard someone say. Then, a face appeared over him. "Hey there bud, can you tell me where it hurts?" the man asked.

"Uh . . . everywhere," Al-Faruq muttered as he tried in vain to sit up.

"Okay, just relax," the paramedic said with a smile. "Can you move your legs?"

"I don't know, you tell me," Al-Faruq answered.

"Good, that's good," the paramedic replied. "This one's in shock. Possible concussion," he yelled.

"Same here," a reply echoed somewhere over Al-Faruq's shoulder.

Al-Faruq summoned all his strength and rolled over to look behind him. About fifteen feet away, he saw Mr. Mawiyah sitting on the ground with a paramedic attending to him. Kalila's father was alive.

"Hey man, just take it easy," the paramedic said. "We're going to take you to the hospital."

"Okay," Al-Faruq said. "Thank you, Allah," he murmured as the paramedics lifted him onto a stretcher. "Thank you." He could only hope that his other prayer would be answered as well.

Chapter 58: Final Drop

Outside a local bakery, Agent Jamison sat reading the paper. To say it had been a hectic couple of weeks was putting it mildly. Although Socrates provided him with the names headquarters had requested, the professor had disappeared ever since. So, while headquarters wanted a few things clarified, Jamison had nothing to give them. He'd just about given up when he received a message from the professor.

Meeting here was his idea. I sure as hell hope he can give me some kind of explanation. Something! Anything!

Jamison's hopes rose as Socrates pulled into the bakery parking lot, but something didn't seem right. Instead of getting out, he just sat there. Agent Jamison scanned the surrounding area. At first, nothing seemed out of the ordinary. Then, he saw him. "Goddamn it," Jamison grumbled. "What the fuck is he doing here? My SAID contact said he'd take care of him. What's this detective's fucking problem?"

The detective was now crossing the street. If he headed for Socrates' car, Jamison wasn't sure what he'd do. Grabbing his cell phone, Jamison looked at Socrates and then back at the detective. While the detective definitely had his eye on Socrates, he was steering clear of his car. Limping noticeably, the detective headed straight inside the bakery.

"Pick up the damn phone," Jamison muttered after dialing the number of his SAID contact.

"Hey, you know who this is?" he growled when his contact finally answered.

"Yes," his contact replied.

"You said that I wouldn't have any more problems with this detective. It's taken care of you said. Yet, I set up a meeting, and guess who shows up?"

"He's on administrative leave. What else do you want me to do?"

"Fire the fucking guy. You told me yourself that he's a nobody. He doesn't have any political connections. So get rid of him!" Jamison railed.

"Geez, the guy just got out of the hospital. Plus, he's a damn good detective. Sure he's a pain in the ass, but I'd rather have him working for me than against me."

As Jamison continued his conversation, Socrates exited his vehicle. If Jamison hadn't been so preoccupied, he would have noticed how pale Socrates looked, he would have noticed that Socrates' *thobe* was strangely tight against his waist, but he didn't. Seeing Socrates walk stiltedly into the bakery only made him angrier. This was all the detective's fault. If this detective would quit harassing his source, everything would be fine.

"Look!" Jamison exclaimed, "Either you get him out of the picture, or I will. This is a critical time. I don't have time for this crap. Do you understand?"

"I understand."

"Do what you're paid to do," Jamison emphasized.

Jamison ended the call and looked around for Socrates. "Where the hell is he?" Jamison turned practically all the way around before spotting him. "What the hell?" he muttered. "He knows better than to sit that close."

Finally, the cold reality hit him. Socrates wasn't following the prescribed protocol. Something was wrong—terribly wrong. Quickly, Agent Jamison scanned the interior of the bakery. Aside from Socrates, the once-crowded bakery was now empty, and Socrates was looking right at him with a cold, sickly stare.

The blast and the impulse to run hit Agent Jamison at the same time. The sensation of flying enveloped him almost as quickly as the flames. The impact of his body against a nearby car extinguished the pain searing through his body. It all took less than a second, and Agent Jamison was dead.

#

Car alarms mixed with the distant wail of sirens. Across the debris-laden parking lot, flames licked the car tires. The explosion had transformed the lot into a junkyard. A bunch of windowless cars sitting motionless, never to run again.

367

It took several minutes for emergency vehicles to arrive and add life to the seemingly lifeless scene. Quickly, the paramedics attended to two men lying on the ground, along the side of the building. As they attended to the wounded men, an unmarked police car arrived on the scene.

From the driver's side, out stepped Chief Hamal. For a moment, he stood still and surveyed the damage with a pained look on his face. Then he sought out the officer who had been first on the scene. After a short conversation with the officer, he walked toward the ambulances that were parked behind what was left of the bakery.

"Hey, I hear you have a SAID detective back here." Chief Hamal said as he flashed his badge at one of the paramedics.

"He's over there," the paramedic said, pointing. "Do you want to hold onto his badge?"

"Sure," Chief Hamal said, grabbing Al-Faruq's badge from the paramedic's outstretched hand. "Mind if I have a quick talk with him?"

"No sir, but we just gave him some pain medication. He might be a little groggy."

"I understand," Chief Hamal replied.

As the paramedic attended to another dazed survivor, Chief Hamal walked over to the nearby ambulance and stepped inside.

"Detective Al-Faruq," Chief Hamal greeted him.

"Chief?"

"You sure have a strange way of spending your leave," Chief Hamal commented.

"Uh, well, I got a little hungry," Al-Faruq replied.

"And you just happened by this bakery, moments before a suicide bomber explodes an IED."

"Something like that," Al-Faruq mumbled.

"Was it anyone we know?" Chief Hamal asked.

"Ummm . . . yeah."

"Well?" the Chief pressed him.

"Professor Ratib," Al-Faruq admitted reluctantly.

Chief Hamal raised his eyebrows. Yet, he didn't seem too surprised. After clearing his throat, he asked, "There was a man outside the bakery who was caught in the blast. Did you recognize him?"

"It was Husam. Did I get him?"

"Who?"

"Husam Asad. Remember, I—"

"Don't worry about it," Chief Hamal interrupted as he patted him on the shoulder. "You saved a lot of innocent civilians."

"Yes sir, but . . . "

"Oh, and one more thing," the Chief said.

"Hmmm? What's that, Chief?" Al-Faruq murmured as the drugs started to take their full effect.

"I'm taking you off administrative leave and placing you on medical leave. You'll be getting full pay while you recuperate."

"Huh?" Al-Faruq asked.

"Never mind. Get better and get back to work," Chief Hamal ordered.

"Yes . . . yes sir," Al-Faruq answered before falling unconscious.

Chief Hamal cracked a smile, shook his head, and exited the ambulance. "Sometimes, things work out all by themselves," he said with relief.

Chief Hamal walked along the side of the bakery. Upon seeing Al-Faruq's service revolver lying on the ground, he stooped to pick it up and continued on toward the front of the bakery. After side stepping some rubble, he looked grimly at the sheet-covered corpse sticking out the back window of a burnt-out car. He walked over and lifted up a corner of the sheet.

"Aghh," Chief Hamal exclaimed in disgust. "The body's too badly burnt. I can't be sure." Then, a thought occurred to him. He reached in his pocket, pulled out his cell phone, and selected a number from his contact list. He heard a faint buzzing sound, but it wasn't near the body.

Cocking his head to one side, he listened intently. The sound led him across the parking lot. Gently, he moved a warped picnic table out of the way where, amongst the debris, he saw the buzzing cell phone.

Chief Hamal ended his call and looked around cautiously to see if anyone was watching him. Seeing that the coast was clear, he bent down, picked up the cell phone, and slipped it into his pocket.

Chapter 59: Fear to Dream

"You idiot!" Husam exclaimed as he limped into his apartment. His bloody hand painted the door as he closed it, and streaks of blood stained the left side of his *thobe*. "Damn cop! Why won't he mind his own fucking business."

Unsteadily, Husam staggered into the kitchen and sat down heavily on the lone kitchen chair. The kitchen consisted of an old rusty refrigerator, a dilapidated gas stove, a few weary cabinets, and a small rectangular Formica table. Along the walls, the edges of the grimy linoleum floor were curling up. Slowly, Husam pulled his *thobe* up above his thigh.

"Ha," Husam laughed derisively. "I get rid of the American spy and get shot by a local cop. Aghh!" he yelled.

Breathing heavily, Husam examined his left leg. The bullet had hit him in the thigh just a few inches above his knee. From there, it had traveled up and across toward the outside of his leg. An angry swollen bump marked where the bullet was now lodged.

"Fuck!" he screamed angrily.

Gritting his teeth, Husam probed the area with his thumbs. The bullet was just beneath the skin's surface, but the tears running down his face proved that getting it out would be no easy task. Lunging forward, he fell to the floor and crawled over to the kitchen cabinet. He flung open the cabinet door and rummaged around inside.

After a moment, Husam pulled out a small black duffel bag. Sitting on the floor, he leaned his back against the cabinet, and set the bag on his lap. It was a first aid kit of sorts, but it was designed for injuries above and beyond your average cuts and scrapes. A veritable treasure trove of pilfered hospital items, it contained several scalpels, a couple of suture kits, iodine wipes, a topical anesthetic called EMLA, pethidine pain medication, surgical gloves, and a variety of bandages.

Husam's hands struggled to free one of the pethidine tablets from its packaging. When he finally succeeded, the pill bounced away from him on the kitchen floor. Cursing, he dove after it, tipping over his first aid kit in the process. As the medical supplies spilled on to the floor, Husam grabbed the pill and put it in his mouth.

After righting himself, Husam uncovered his injured leg and pawed through the pile of medical supplies. Eventually, he found what he needed. His hands shaking, Husam cleaned the area hiding the slug with iodine wipes from the kit. Then he found the topical anesthetic and sprayed it on the spot where he'd make the cut.

Then, he waited. He waited for the drugs to take effect. He waited for his anger to wane. He waited for the pain to subside. Unfortunately, time could only heal so much, and some pain the drugs would never take away.

Absentmindedly, he pulled a scalpel from the duffel bag, extricated it from its packaging, and set it down on the floor next to him. Suddenly, the small dank kitchen seemed larger and brighter. While Husam knew what he had to do, it seemed less important. Groggily, he shook the cobwebs from his head.

After awkwardly pulling on a pair of surgical gloves, Husam grabbed the scalpel and stared down at his leg. He was starting to see double. He needed to hurry. Using his free hand, he probed his leg for the slug. Finding it, he hesitantly guided the scalpel down. When it touched his skin, he felt a strange sensation of pressure. He pushed the scalpel down until he hit the slug.

Blood was seeping out of this newly created wound. Nonetheless, Husam opened the cut wider. When he dug for the slug with the tip of the scalpel blade, a jolt of pain shot through his body. He almost fainted, but somehow he was able to get the slug out. As it rattled upon the kitchen floor, Husam dropped his arms listlessly to his sides.

After a few deep breaths, he searched clumsily through the pile of medical supplies for a suture kit, finally finding it on the third try. Tiredly, he pulled at the hermetically sealed plastic, but the surgical gloves were blood covered and slippery. Exasperated, Husam yanked off the gloves. He tore into the container and removed a fine, curved needle with a long thread attached to it.

"It's now or never," Husam rasped. "Time's against you. Close it up. Then, you can rest."

Laboriously, he went to work. Every little stitch seemed to take an eternity. At times, he almost forgot he was working on his own leg, but if he dug too deep, he was painfully reminded. Finished, he stared blankly at his leg as he tried to remember what was next. Sloppily, he applied bandages to his wounds and rolled to his stomach.

Exhausted, Husam crawled toward his bedroom. Normally, it would have only taken a few steps, but it seemed like a much longer journey. His bed wasn't much. He wasn't sure why it was so important to get there, but he wasn't stopping until he made it. Upon seeing the dusty springs supporting his mattress, he reached up. Initially, his hand missed, but finally it found the mattress.

The bed seemed much higher than normal. It was like climbing a tree as a small child. Husam gathered his strength. Pushing with his good leg, he slithered awkwardly onto the bed. He rolled to his back and stared helplessly at the ceiling. The room was slowly spinning, first one direction then the other. A dull light bulb dangled from the ceiling. Husam's eyes closed.

#

Mr. Mawiyah sat upright in the hospital bed fidgeting with the ties on his gown. In a chair next to him, Abra was sitting with a book in her hand.

"How long do I have to stay here?" Mr. Mawiyah protested.

"Just until they get all the test results back," Abra said.

"I don't need to wait for some stupid test. I feel fine."

"Well, that police officer, Detective Al-Faruq, wasn't so lucky," Abra replied. "He's still in intensive care."

"I . . . I don't want to talk about it," Mr. Mawiyah grumbled. "Where is Kalila anyways?"

"Why don't you watch some TV," Abra said, rolling her eyes.

Grumpily, Mr. Mawiyah grabbed the remote from the bedside table, and turned on the television. It was tuned to Al Jazeera.

"Early this morning, the President of the United States directed American military forces to commence operations against the nation of Iran. American forces will be joined by a coalition of nations including Great Britain, France, Germany, Canada, Saudi Arabia, and Turkey," the reporter said.

A video of the U.S. president came on to the screen. "This great nation will not stand idly by, in the face of foreign-sponsored terror. This great nation will not stand idly by, while tyrannical forces attempt to undercut our freedoms. This great nation will not stand idly by, while cowards send young men to do their evil bidding."

The video image of the American president dissolved and then reappeared. His speech continued. "The Iranian leadership, and the religious clerics that support it, have made a grave miscalculation. In their arrogance, they thought their message of hatred and lies would go unnoticed. They thought their coalition of aggression would go unchallenged. They thought they could act with impunity and without consequence. Well, I'm here to tell you. They thought wrong!"

After another video transition, the clip continued. "These terrorists don't understand the value of heart, loyalty, and commitment. Those values are lost in totalitarian regimes and are instead replaced by suspicion, coercion, and self-preservation. Concepts like duty, honor, and country come from the heart, not via *fatwa*."

"Meanwhile," the reporter continued. "Iranian officials have denied any involvement in the recent attacks."

"The Americans are deluded. Their accusations are totally devoid of any truth or logic," the Iranian representative scoffed. "These supposed attacks were perpetrated by Palestinians, not Iranians. Why don't they declare war on Palestine? Oh that's right, they already have through their Israeli proxies. The great American Satan will strike down any Muslim nation that dares to rise up and demand its sovereign rights to self-governance. We've seen it time and time again in Iraq, Afghanistan, Libya, and Egypt. The unseen American hand longs to hold the strings of power throughout the Middle East."

The television report then shifted to the streets of Tehran as thousands of protesters lined the streets. "Death to America! Cut

374

off Satan's hand! Death to America! Cut off Satan's hand!" the people chanted.

"I hope our government has built an atomic bomb," said one Iranian man who was interviewed. "It's the only way we can protect ourselves from American aggression."

"Aghhh," Mr. Mawiyah said in exasperation as he hit the mute button. "Not another war."

"So it seems," Abra replied.

"I work with Americans all the time," Mr. Mawiyah said shaking his head. "They generally don't strike me as aggressive."

"They don't seem to care much for Islam," Abra noted.

"Like our countrymen are overly fond of Christians or Jews? I told you about my business trip to America, didn't I?"

"You did," Abra admitted.

"One night, I actually attended evening prayers. At a mosque mind you, right there in America itself. There was a sign right out in front of the mosque. They didn't have to hide it or anything."

"But, there had been protests."

"Well, the local imam admitted that they had to deal with protestors from time to time," Mr. Mawiyah conceded. "Still, it's nothing like here. There certainly are no *mutawa*."

"Then, why does their government act like this?" Abra asked. "They wage war against Iraq, Afghanistan, Libya, and now Iran."

"I guess they don't want people blowing themselves up at the local bakery," Mr. Mawiyah said wryly.

Abra sighed heavily. "What are we to do? We're not Americans. They care nothing for our dreams. The American dream is only for them, and we're the ones paying the price."

"I know how you feel, Abra," Mr. Mawiyah said trying to reassure her. "I have to admit their government seems to be the embodiment of all their fears rather than all their dreams."

Chapter 60: The Hospital

"Dead men don't dream," Al-Faruq told himself, but that was little consolation. Back in the hospital again, Al-Faruq struggled to stay positive. He dreamed that Kalila was by his bedside, but when he awoke she was gone, and he found himself alone in a dark, empty hospital room. Half the time, he couldn't tell if it was day or night. "How long have I been in here?" he mumbled groggily. "When can I get out of here?"

"Rest, Al-Faruq. We'll get the doctor," a female voice answered.

The voice sounded familiar. Al-Faruq strained to open his eyes. *Was it just another dream?* His eyes fluttered open, and Al-Faruq looked around sleepily. It was still dark, but he sensed other people in the room.

"Father, can you go get the doctor? He's waking up!" the female voice said.

"Go talk to him," another female voice urged.

"Don't forget to tell him that Chief Hamal stopped by," a male voice said.

Al-Faruq blinked slowly. His eyes were still heavy. Slowly, the young woman's face came into focus. She reached for his hand. "Kalila?" Al-Faruq managed to say.

"I'm here, Al-Faruq," she said, patting his hand.

"Is it really you? Have you been here the whole time?"

"Yes, it's me," she answered, smiling. "I've been here as often as I could."

"How? How did you manage it?" Al-Faruq asked, somewhat confused.

"It's a long story. My mother is friends with the hospital administrator's wife. She was able to pull some strings for us," Kalila said blushing. "My mother implied that we were en—"

Suddenly, the door burst open announcing the arrival of the doctor. Kalila gave Al-Faruq's hand a quick squeeze and stepped away.

"So, our patient is finally awake, eh?" Doctor Jaabir asked, to no one in particular. "How are you feeling?"

"Uh, sleepy," Al-Faruq managed to say as the doctor shone a tiny flashlight in each of his eyes.

"How's your head?"

"Okay, I guess. It just feels really heavy."

"Well, I gather from your medical records that this wasn't your first concussion. Plus, you encountered a pretty big blast, or the shock wave from it. You had a fair amount of brain swelling, so we had you under heavy sedation. It looks like you're starting to come around though. You'll probably be feeling tired for quite a while, but we'll back off on the medication now that the swelling has abated."

"Can we talk to him?" Kalila's father asked as the doctor turned to leave.

"Sure," the doctor answered. "He's going to be in and out, but the conversation will do him good."

"Thank you," Mr. Mawiyah acknowledged. He gave the doctor a hearty handshake and a kiss on each cheek. Then, he turned around and stepped closer toward Al-Faruq's hospital bed. "And thank you for saving my life," he said to Al-Faruq. "I should have listened to you and stayed put."

Kalila's mother pulled at her husband's shoulder. "Talking to you isn't going to help. Let Kalila talk to him. Give them some privacy."

"Leave them alone? Together?" her husband protested as she led him away.

"He was practically in a coma. He just woke up. What do you think he's going to do?" Abra scolded him.

Looking a little embarrassed, Kalila reappeared at Al-Faruq's bedside.

Al-Faruq let out a stifled laugh. "You were saying?" he asked, reaching for her hand.

"When I found out you were hurt in the explosion, I . . . I went hysterical," she admitted teary eyed. "I told my parents everything. I told them that I loved you, that . . . that I had to see you."

"You . . . you love me?" Al-Faruq repeated in disbelief. He tried to reach up and dry her tears, but got tangled up in his IV.

377

"Here, let me help you," Kalila offered. Gently, she untangled Al-Faruq as best she could.

"You love me?" Al-Faruq asked again as he touched her cheek.

"I wouldn't have dressed up like a man, stolen my father's car, and driven downtown for just anyone," she said.

"Borrowed?" Al-Faruq interjected.

"What?"

"Not that I'd recommend telling anyone, but if you ever repeat that story, I'd suggest saying you borrowed your father's car," Al-Faruq counseled her.

"Try telling my father that."

"You saved my life, that should count for something."

"Not as much as you'd think."

"Ha, Allah help us. I love you so much," Al-Faruq said as he pulled her hand up to his lips and kissed it.

"You do?" Kalila asked coyly.

"I . . . I don't text with just anyone," he replied without thinking.

"Well, that's good to know," Kalila replied, trying not to laugh.

"Um, I mean . . . Uh?"

"How about pulling young women out of fountains?"

"Well, that too." Al-Faruq admitted.

Kalila put her finger to his lips. "Shhh, we've saved each other's lives once," she whispered.

"No," Al-Faruq corrected her gently. "You've saved mine twice."

"How do you figure that?" she asked, leaning in closer.

"Just by being here. I . . . I couldn't imagine going on without you."

Softly, their lips met. For a moment, Al-Faruq felt no pain—just love, hope, and relief, all rolled into one.

"Oh," Kalila said suddenly. "I've got a surprise for you."

"What?" Al-Faruq asked.

"Just a minute. I'll go get it," she said. "Don't worry, I'll be right back." Smiling broadly, Kalila exited the room.

Al-Faruq laid back and smiled. He hadn't felt like this in, well, he'd never felt like this. His heart was so excited. He sat up eagerly as the door to his room opened once again, but it was just another doctor.

"Detective Al-Faruq?" the masked doctor asked.

"Yes," Al-Faruq answered. He started to ease back into the pillows, but then stopped short. The doctor pulled down his mask, revealing his identity. Al-Faruq struggled to get up, but his legs felt woozy.

"Don't bother," Husam said, producing a handgun from within the folds of his surgical gown.

Al-Faruq froze.

Slowly, Husam limped forward. "I'm afraid I still owe you for the other day outside the bakery."

"How do you figure that?" Al-Faruq asked while lowering the side railing of his bed.

Husam shook his head dismissively. "You're quite the soldier. Talk about a lucky shot."

"So, I didn't miss?" Al-Faruq asked. Behind Husam, he could see the door to his room open once again. Al-Faruq slid his legs off the bed and struggled to his feet.

"You missed all right, but I won't," Husam said as he pointed his gun at Al-Faruq, but an odd noise made him pull back.

"Doctor Jaabir?" Kalila's voice interrupted nervously. "Did you forget something?"

Husam smiled and pulled his weapon in close to his body. "Visiting hours are over," he said.

As Husam turned and trained his gun on Kalila, Al-Faruq lunged at him, bringing his IV stand down hard across Husam's back.

As they toppled over, Husam squeezed the trigger. A shot rang out! Al-Faruq crumpled on top of him, and Husam's gun went rattling across the floor.

"No!" Al-Faruq yelled as he grappled with Husam.

"You're both fucking dead!" Husam roared.

On the hospital room floor, Al-Faruq and Husam wrestled frantically for the gun, but Husam was too strong. It was only a matter of time. Desperate, with IV tubing dangling from his arm, Al-Faruq twisted the tubing around Husam's neck and pulled with all his strength, but Husam knocked Al-Faruq back awkwardly against the bed frame.

Another shot!

Al-Faruq turned. To his amazement, Husam was lying motionless on the floor as a pool of blood grew around him. Looking up, Al-Faruq saw Kalila standing shakily with Husam's gun in her hands and Al-Faruq's badge at her feet.

"Ch . . . Chief Hamal brought your badge by earlier," she said, wide-eyed.

"Set the gun down!" Al-Faruq ordered. "I shot him. Do you understand me? I shot him."

On his hands and knees, Al-Faruq crawled over to Kalila. He heard footsteps echoing loudly outside in the hallway. Hurtling himself forward, he greedily collected the gun, gripping it tightly in his hands as the door swung open.

"Hospital security. Is everything okay?" the portly security guard asked.

"Al-Faruq!" Kalila screamed.

Al-Faruq wheeled around. Unsteadily, Husam's bloodied arm reached forward with another gun. Al-Faruq fired two shots. This time, they hit the mark.

Chapter 61: The Wedding

Kalila stood next to her father and grandfather as the *nikah* ceremony proceeded. Her henna decorated hands peeked out from the flared cuffs of her long-sleeved wedding gown. Intricate pearl-colored bead-work danced up the arms of the white satin dress, along the shoulders, and down the front. A white sheer veil hid her smiling eyes, while the floor-length dress hid her pink tennis shoes.

His hands shaking, Al-Faruq presented Kalila with a simple gold ring as his *mahr*. He also promised to help her finish her studies and become a teacher, like his mother. Acting as her *walis*, Kalila's father and grandfather signed the marriage contract, while Al-Faruq and Kalila completed their vows.

"*Qabul, qabul, qabul*," Al-Faruq said softly.

"*Qabul, qabul, qabul*," Kalila echoed.

Al-Faruq accepted the pen from Kalila's grandfather and signed the *katb el-kitab*. Kalila took the pen from Al-Faruq and did the same. The two stood side by side while the imam recited the *Fatihah*. With the sun streaming in through the mosque's open archways, tears of joy ran down Kalila's cheeks. After all that had happened over the last few months, it seemed like a dream.

Praise Allah! Blessings and peace be upon Him. I am truly blessed.

Kalila blinked away her tears and stole a glance at Al-Faruq. Evidently, he was relying on his military training to pull him through. Though his eyes were moist, he was practically standing at attention. Kalila stifled a laugh.

After the imam concluded the ceremony with the blessing, Kalila and Al-Faruq were whisked away. With lights on and horns blaring, their procession weaved through the streets. In the wedding party's car, Kalila's mother happily chattered away. Kalila held Al-Faruq's hand tightly while Abra regaled them with stories of her own wedding. Through it all, Al-Faruq nodded politely. Looking out the window expectantly, Kalila couldn't wait to get to the reception.

At the *walima*, Al-Faruq and Kalila took their seats at the dais in the center of the small banquet hall. Al-Faruq looked on, wide-eyed, as all of Kalila's female relatives, friends, and their children filled the room.

"Are you actually related to all of these people?" Al-Faruq asked.

"You mean we, don't you?"

Al-Faruq laughed. "Okay. Are we related to all these people?"

"Most of them," Kalila answered. Smiling, she instructed Al-Faruq on everyone's names. After a while, even she started having trouble.

"Oh, they came!" she exclaimed. Entering the hall she saw Sister Mary Catherine, Chandra, and Jahanara. "Did Shahidah get her invitation?" Kalila asked.

"I made sure everything got to her, but . . . "

"I know. It was a nice thought, though," Kalila said.

As rose-mango *sharbats* were being passed out, a female figure appeared in the doorway. Wearing the new *habiya* Kalila's mother had picked out for her, Shahidah entered the room slowly.

"Kalila. Look!" Al-Faruq said.

"Mother!" Kalila called. Waving, Kalila motioned to her mother. Quickly, Abra walked over and warmly welcomed their new guest. She led Shahidah to a table and handed her a *sharbat*. Once all the guests had been served, everyone raised their glasses and drank to the young couple's health and happiness.

Looking out over all the guests, Kalila beamed. Then, much to her surprise, Al-Faruq stood up and reached out for her hand.

"My mother," Al-Faruq announced to the crowd. "She always told me never to give up hope in Allah's mercy. No matter what hardships you may face, you always have hope in Allah."

Al-Faruq turned and faced Kalila. "Before I ever met you, the hope of you gave me strength. After I met you, the hope of seeing you again brought me through many trials. Now that we are married, the hope I feel in your love makes me yearn for tomorrow. Thank you for seeing the good in me."

Kalila wiped a tear from her cheek. "Thank you for showing it to me."

Al-Faruq turned back toward their guests. "Oh Allah, bestow your mercy on Mohammed!" he said happily.

In response, all the guests echoed his praise. *"Allahumma salli ala Muhammad!"*

About the Author

I graduated from the United States Air Force Academy in 1992. As a member of the Air Force intelligence community, my military service included stops in Saudi Arabia, Bahrain, South Korea, Japan, and Germany. I leveraged my experiences overseas in crafting this novel. Follow me on Twitter at Christian F. Burton@EnergyDepDay.